Crash checked the [...] [...] instrument panel. The touch-sensitive control system included a multipurpose color display that showed flight information, target data, and a moving digital map. On one of two monochrome display panels, the status of the bombs and missiles mounted on the aircraft's eleven weapon stations were visible.

Crash worried about the anti-aircraft missile systems. Normally, if an anti-aircraft weapon powered up, other aircraft would blow its radar away, but the problem was that, with the civilian radar integrated into the anti-air defense, the San Selvans had an extra advantage. They could get away with firing their missiles and moving before Crash could take evasive actions.

Crash tried to focus her forward-looking infrared camera on the target but only saw thick static as the camera strained to see through the smoke.

DEEDLEDEEDLEDEEDLE! The alarm from Crash's AN/APS-109B Radar Homing and Warning Receiver (RHAWS) blared in her helmet. She looked down at the digital map. Several "S" symbols became visible, indicating where San Selvan search radar was detected. Most likely civilian, however, which would prevent the Air Force "Wild Weasel" aircraft from destroying the radar. Crash could only pray. Her AN/ALQ-137 Internal Electronic Countermeasures system was useless against large radar like these.

Another alarm sounded. Several "A" and "3" symbols appeared on the digital map. Crash gasped. The San Selvans were not supposed to have mobile SA-3 missile launchers. . . .

MAJ. JAMES B. WOULFE, USMC
Against All Enemies

LEISURE BOOKS NEW YORK CITY

To Mary Beth

A LEISURE BOOK®

February 2009

Published by

Dorchester Publishing Co., Inc.
200 Madison Avenue
New York, NY 10016

ISBN 10: 0-8439-5140-0
ISBN 13: 978-0-8439-5140-0
E-ISBN: 1-4285-0603-9

The name "Leisure Books" and the stylized "L" with design are
trademarks of Dorchester Publishing Co., Inc.

Printed in the United States of America.

10 9 8 7 6 5 4 3 2 1

Against All Enemies

Prologue

War doesn't decide who is right
Only who is left
—Unit T-shirt for a Marine rifle company

Calcoene Port, San Selva

Dunne sat against the wall in a battle-scarred room of his objective—the building that had sucked so much blood from his Marines. In one night the structure had become both hallowed ground and hellish tomb. Raindrops smacked the exterior walls, reducing most of the pungent odors of battle but none of the memories. Dunne's eyes sat sunken back in his head. The soft whiskers on his young face were now longer than he had let them grow in some time. Normally he would have shaved them. Now he didn't care anymore.

1

Maj. James B. Woulfe, USMC

Staff Sergeant Lee approached and stood over the lieutenant, waiting for a response. Most of the Marines avoided Dunne this morning. Lee couldn't. He took off his gray and black urban-camouflaged helmet and rubbed his head before looking out in the direction where the lieutenant stared. Through a loophole and across the street, in the midst of the rainstorm-drenched neighborhood, a group of children played in the newly formed puddles. It had been some time since the kids had experienced rain, especially enough to create puddles. The rain would help extinguish the fires, but the irony of its presence bordered on cruelty. The downpour had come unexpectedly. Lee wondered if it came as an evil twist of fate.

Two nearby Marines crouched on the floor behind their weapons and peered out of their respective loopholes. Windows and doorways had to be avoided, so the men had painstakingly chipped through the cinder block walls to create the slots for weapons and the observation of fields of fire. Other Marines in ripped and bloody uniforms lay in defensive positions around the interior of the building. They hid behind sandbagged bunkers and hastily positioned furniture, not willing to risk exposure to the street. Those kids were probably some of the ones who did the killing. More shrieks as they played, splashing and dancing in the rain. They were just sanchos like all the rest.

Careful to avoid the open window, Lee dropped to a knee and placed the butt stock of his rifle on the floor. The affixed bayonet—now a permanent sight on the Marines' weapons—sat just above eye level. Looking at the lieutenant's weapon leaning against the wall, Lee noted that Dunne's blade was dull and chipped too. It had been a tough night. He looked back at the lieutenant, seeking eye contact. Dunne continued to stare at the street.

2

"Gotta dip, sir?" asked Lee.

At first there was nothing. Then Dunne shook his head once without uttering a sound.

Lee nodded. The lieutenant's bristled lip stretched beyond its normal position, filled with the deadly carcinogenic-filled tar of smokeless tobacco. Either the whole damn can was sitting in Dunne's lip or he was bullshitting. Maybe he just didn't care enough to answer or pull the damn can out of his pocket. It didn't really matter anyway. It was just something to say.

"Bad shit, sir," said Lee, shaking his head. "It was real bad shit, and you can't blame yourself."

The lieutenant didn't move. Lee kept waiting for him to spit. That was a lot of dip. He had to spit soon. The kids outside laughed louder. The rain started to let up some, but it still produced enough drops to piss everyone off. All of it wasn't even necessary. All of them would still be alive if the damn rain had come two days earlier. That or if the dip-shit weather people would have predicted its coming. Damn rain.

"Scuttlebutt is that the Army is stuck in a bad fight out there," Lee said, trying to find a way to break through to Dunne. Probably not the best thing to say at a time like this, but he couldn't think of anything else. "The first sergeant said Alpha might need to go out and . . ."

A glob of brown tobacco juice smacked into the ground next to the lieutenant.

Progress. Although disgusting, the spit gave Lee promise. ". . . they might go out in amtracs and attempt—"

"I'm not cracking up, Staff Sergeant."

Silence. Then Lee nodded. "I know you're not, sir." He paused, seeking eye contact again and hoping it was true. More were alive than dead because of the

3

lieutenant. "But you're not being yourself either. You need to get back to your old self again. I don't care what they say. This shit isn't over. The Army is learning that fact right now. People like this are going to continue to fight. These sanchos don't know nothing else."

"I'm just really fucking tired. That's all. I'm physically and emotionally drained, but you don't need to worry. I'm good to go."

"Fuck, sir. Why don't you just lie down and get some sleep? We got everything covered for a while."

"I tried, but I can't." Dunne pressed his lips together tightly and locked his stare on Lee's eyes. "Every time I close my eyes I hear O'Brien's screams."

Chapter One

One week before the rain, Jason Barret could see that the *Oklahoma City* was well stocked with food as he walked through the tight passageways of the nuclear-powered submarine. Smashing one hundred and thirty men on a craft the size of a 747 airplane and sending it underwater for months created stringent living conditions. "Hot bunking" was still common, with three sailors sharing two bunks in rotating shifts. When the size of the crew swelled, like when Barret and his SEALs embarked, junior sailors dropped a mattress on the deck of the noisy torpedo room. With the storage space on a submarine also limited, it was often necessary for many items, such as canned foods, to be stored on the deck. Rubber mats covered the cans to reduce the noise produced from walking on

5

them. Taller crew members were more likely to hit their heads on low overhangs when the submarine was well stocked, because extra inches were added to the floor. Things would get better for the tall, however. After several unexpected weeks at sea, the food would go quickly as the crew literally ate themselves into the floor of the submarine.

Barret climbed a ladder and moved forward, precariously balancing as the vessel bounced. The seventy thousand tons of the nuclear-powered attack submarine USS *Oklahoma City* (SSN-723) had traveled at its flank speed for most of the past few days. Its orders remained too vague for the risks that they were taking. A training exercise that Lieutenant Barret and his SEALs had participated in the week prior had been abruptly stopped. The SEALs and the submarine crew had hastily sped away from Belize and the elite British Special Boat Service units they were working with to head in another direction. Now it looked like a short training deployment was to become a long trip from home. Orders like these stung of crisis. The U.S. Navy did not do things like this on a whim, and the *Oklahoma City* existed to meet missions that fit specific criteria.

Barret entered the submarine's control room and looked for the sub's captain, Commander Phil Bradford. Bradford smirked to himself when he saw the always-squared-away SEAL platoon commander. Standing five feet seven, probably weighing one hundred and ninety pounds, Barret was a mean-looking man—or maybe just tough—with short, cropped dark hair, dark eyes, and a build like a professional wrestler.

"Good evening, sir," said Barret as he approached, but the expression on his face was anything but good. He nervously eyeballed the control room. Located in the upper level of a forward compartment, the control room, often called the "heart of the ship," was where the submarine's attack center, sonar section, and navigation experts were located. The submarine's captain sat in the captain's chair located in an elevated position near the periscope. The Chief of the Boat—COB, or the senior enlisted sailor on board—stood behind him talking to young and pimple-faced seamen sitting behind a computer screen and a jungle of switches and dials.

"Are you ready to go?" Bradford ran his hand through his graying, brown hair. His bright blue overalls were neatly pressed, with the gold, embroidered dolphins of the submariner's chest insignia sitting above his left breast pocket. Emblazoned on his right forearm was a traditionally untraditional sight on a submarine captain—a tattoo. But in a generation that reveled in marking skin with ink, it was a more common sight on an officer today than it was in Bradford's father's Navy. The brightly colored chicken and pig squaring off for a wrestling match meant nothing to most people, but it was derived from a superstition that had been in submarine lore since the early days in Pearl Harbor. Chickens and pigs, said Hawaiian legend, would always find something to float on and would never drown.

"Yes, sir. I just wish we had a better idea of what the hell is going on."

"I hear ya." Bradford nodded. "We might learn more during this next comm window."

"I hate operating like this." Lieutenant Barret's voice was dry and cold. It was like a bad curse. A dangerous operation without proper time to prepare was no way to conduct business. He had already learned that lesson the hard way.

Barret had been a SEAL for over fifteen years, but

7

an officer for less than half of that. A decent student and an excellent swimmer, he could easily have gone to college, and a few schools had even recruited him for a partial athletic scholarship to play water polo, but Jason was not interested in any more schooling. He wanted some adventure, and the Navy's SEALs seemed like the answer to his desires. He enlisted when he was still in his senior year of high school.

Barret did well as a SEAL, climbing in rank to petty officer second class before finding himself in his first and only firefight. The mission had been a dangerous and highly secret one: to capture a Yugoslavian war criminal wanted for trial before a United Nations court. The operation was hastily thrown together with pieces of intelligence collected by a number of sources, some whose validity was questionable. Many American and NATO leaders were concerned about civilian casualties, while at the same time insisting that the mission be accomplished. Politicians and generals imposed strict rules of engagement that limited the actions the SEALs could take for self-defense.

The SEALs waited all night outside the former Yugoslavian general's residence. Early the next morning, the general and his bodyguard came out and got into a vehicle. The vehicle was stopped before it could exit the home's driveway, but the SEALs quickly learned that the two men in the vehicle were not surprised. The bodyguard and what turned out to be another bodyguard posing as the general ducked down to the floor of the vehicle. Everything froze at first, and then streams of red tracers poured from the windows as automatic rifle fire pelted the streets.

Swish*Boom!* Swish*Boom!* Rocket-propelled grenades plowed into every piece of cover. Swish*Boom!* The SEALs were dead meat sitting in the open street.

Pinned down with fire coming from all directions,

the lightly armed SEALs stood little chance of surviving. All were wounded during the opening volleys of the fight. In a decision based on desperation, the commander ordered his men to storm a nearby home. Barret refused to move to cover without his best friend, who lay in the street wounded. Barret crawled alone to his buddy. A grenade had impacted next to the SEAL, peppering him along the right side of his body with shrapnel. He bled from his face. Several pieces penetrated his stomach too and he was rolled into a tight ball when Barret got to him. "Fuck, Jason. I didn't hear a goddamn thing."

Barret dragged the wounded SEAL by the belt through the street. Painful screams protested every tug. "Hold on, buddy," he yelled at least a hundred times. Deadly bursts of lead from enemy and friendly weapons danced overhead. Swish*Boom!* The rocket fire continued. A wounded Yugoslav gunman hung precariously out a window, yelling frantically in pleading gasps. The battle raged on around him. Swish*Boom!*

Finally everyone from the platoon was in the building. The SEALs barricaded themselves in the structure and held out until an international relief force could come rescue them. On that fateful day, the SEAL commander's order saved the lives of most of his men, including Barret's, but it also ended the SEAL officer's bright career. By occupying the civilian home he had violated the rules of engagement, and he was second-guessed by most in his chain of command. The officer received an official reprimand in his record that prevented him from being promoted to the next rank.

Barret's personal actions during the mission were noteworthy enough to earn him a Silver Star—the Nation's third highest award for heroism in combat—

and an appointment to the U.S. Naval Academy at Annapolis. After graduating and commissioning as an ensign, Barret spent a short period of time training with SEAL Team Two before joining SEAL Delivery Vehicle Team Two. He had come a long way since first deciding to enlist, but he would never forget that a lack of proper planning and poor intelligence for the Yugoslavian operation had led to the death of several of his closest friends. Now that he was in command he swore his men would never have the same experience.

"I've never seen anything like this." Bradford shook his head. "I can tell that there is a real sense of urgency back home, but no clear directions from higher headquarters."

Barret stood stone-faced and said nothing.

"You going to the chamber now?" asked Bradford, eyeballing the HK P-7 9mm pistol with fitted silencer sitting in the SEAL lieutenant's holster.

"Yes, sir."

"Good luck."

"Thank you, but luck won't have much to do with it."

Bellowing an uneasy laugh, Bradford slapped the SEAL's thick shoulder. Despite the limited information on *why,* Bradford was not surprised with *what* he and his crew had been told to do. Commissioned in 1988, the *Oklahoma City* was among the world's most advanced undersea vessel. Although decades ago the *Oklahoma City* was built to conduct deep, open-ocean antisubmarine warfare, today there was no longer the need for attack submarines like there had been at the height of the Cold War. So the *Oklahoma City* was specially converted to carry Unmanned Underwater Vehicles (UUV) and SEAL Delivery Vehicles (SDV) into the littorals.

The stealth of the submarine had always appealed to the special operations community, because it allowed them to snuggle right up to an enemy without detection. Divers or swimmers could easily be sent ashore or against the hull of an enemy ship to set explosives. Marines and underwater demolition teams first used submarines as launching platforms during World War II and the Korean War. But it wasn't until the creation of the U.S. Navy SEALs—commandos capable of operations at SEa, in Air, and on Land— in the early 1960s that men operating from submarines became commonplace. During the Cuban Bay of Pigs incident in 1961, even before SEAL Team One was officially established, SEALs used submarines to engineer the escape of prominent Cubans from Castro's regime. The commandos slipped from submarines and traveled to land by rubber raft to rendezvous with evacuees who would almost certainly have been jailed or executed if they'd remained in Cuba. It was the first in a number of daring underwater missions. The Vietnam War saw more SEAL and submarine operations, with the highlight being Operation Thunderhead, a 1972 operation from the USS *Grayback* to rescue American prisoners of war.

More recent SEAL and submarine operations were a result of the "new world order." In 1998, SEALs operating from the USS *Tucson* and the USS *Mendel Rivers* conducted a physical reconnaissance of Soviet-built Iranian submarines to investigate propeller modifications that made the old diesel submarines quieter and harder to detect with passive sonar systems. Months later, the two submarines joined other ships in launching precision missiles at terrorist training camps in Afghanistan that had links to the bombings of two American embassies in Africa. Their missions were an excellent demonstration of the dual reconnaissance and strike capability that SEAL and submarine teams provided.

Today, the *Oklahoma City* was a result of the lessons learned during the missions of past decades. Although it was an old trick to send men out the torpedo tubes, the *Oklahoma City* was equipped with a dual dry dock shelter system—two rounded garages welded onto the back of the submarine that each housed a small submarine, or minisub. Each dry dock shelter measured nine feet by thirty-eight feet, and could stand the pressure of depths up to two hundred feet, which was considerably less than the Los Angeles–class's intended maximum depth of nine hundred and fifty feet. With a dry dock shelter, the *Oklahoma City* was now capable of launching not only missiles and torpedoes, but up to twelve commandos to work their dastardly magic. Barret's platoon numbered fourteen enlisteds and two officers, including him, and for Commander Bradford they were a welcomed addition to the submarine's normal crew. To Bradford, the SEALs brought an increase in capability for the USS *Oklahoma City*.

Commander Bradford checked the ballast tanks again to ensure the *Oklahoma City* held a constant depth barely below the surface. Being this shallow and this close to the shore was enough to give any submarine captain a heart attack. The only thing that provided Bradford with some sense of protection was that the sediment discharge of the Amazon River discolored the Atlantic waters for over two hundred square miles, which reduced the chances that the submarine could be spotted by someone on the surface. Mines were detected to the northwest, but, thankfully, this area was left open so the San Selvans could still allow civilian shipping in their waters.

The minisub passed its prelaunch checks, and the dry dock shelter flooded in preparation of the SEALs loading it. Steadying the submarine during the shifts in the weight of the minisub on its back was an essential part of a safe deployment. The *Oklahoma City* had also slowed its speed to prevent a collision with the minisub as it exited the dry dock shelter. For Commander Bradford it was like being a pilot trying to keep an airplane on the edge of stalling.

Six SEALs crammed into one of the dry dock shelter's three compartments. The forward compartment was a hyperbolic chamber to deal with the problems of decompression. The middle chamber, which the six SEALs currently occupied, was used for exiting and entering the submarine. The rear chamber was the hangar for the SEAL delivery vehicle.

How easy operations from submarines had become pleased Barret. The first time he did this he had been crammed into a torpedo tube with his equipment sitting in front of him and his regulator from the scuba gear in his mouth. There was no light, and panic could come easy in the claustrophobic conditions. A loud *whooshing* sound signaled that the worst was coming, as the tubes filled with a violent rush of water, not the gradual flooding as portrayed in the movies. Once the tubes flooded, the torpedo hatches released so the SEALs could exit the submarine. This too was difficult and dangerous. As Barret came to the edge of the opening, he needed to gracefully exit the tube and collect his sinking equipment in one motion before struggling to put it on his body.

But with the dry dock shelter the SEALs now had a much easier and safer exit of the submarine. Once the rear two compartments flooded, and the water pressure equalized with the outside pressure, the SEALs opened the chamber's exit hatch and swam through the water to the rear door of the dry dock's hanger. The men opened the door and wheeled the minisub out on its track to bring the SEAL delivery vehicle and cradle onto the back of the *Oklahoma City*.

Petty Officer Hernandez, the pilot, was the first to enter the minisub, an Mk IX SEAL Delivery Vehicle. He occupied the left front seat as Lieutenant Barret moved to the right so he could navigate. The other four SEALs smashed into the back compartment.

Petty Officer Hernandez started the minisub's electric motor after looking back to see that all were aboard. The U-shaped steering wheel sat chest level, with rollers on each handle for controlling the propellers with his thumbs. He shifted the controls forward, causing the main propeller to accelerate the minisub off the back of the *Oklahoma City*.

MC-130H Combat Talon, Airspace Over the North Atlantic Ocean

The special operations MC-130H Combat Talon aircraft cut through the dark sky close to the disputed San Selvan coastline. The aircraft's four turboprop engines rumbled on the wings, bringing the plane to a cruising speed of three hundred miles an hour. It had taken under four hours for the MC-130H to fly from Hurlbert Field, Florida, home of the Eighth Special Operations Squadron, to this location. In the squadron were some of the best pilots in the U.S. Air Force. The air crews constantly trained with Army and Navy Special Operations Forces, performing clandestine missions in hostile territory.

The MC-130H's loadmaster made hand gestures to the men in back of the aircraft and they rose. The aircraft was capable of carrying over sixty paratroopers, but tonight there was far fewer in the forty-one-foot-long cargo compartment. Twelve of America's best-trained warriors made final checks of their gear and switched from the aircraft's oxygen supply to their own. Flying at fifty thousand feet above the earth's surface, an artificial oxygen source is necessary for survival.

The group moved close together on the aircraft's rear ramp, waddling about because of their heavy, cumbersome loads. As they neared the ramp's edge, lights from small cities below became visible. The aircraft would still be flying in international airspace when the men jumped. Their parachutes would open almost immediately for the high-altitude, high-opening—HAHO—drop.

HAHO was the most advanced method of covert insertion. Unlike its better-known kin HALO (high-altitude, low-opening), HAHO put parachutists on the ground while reducing the danger to aircraft or likelihood of detection. HALO required parachutists to jump from a high altitude and free-fall for tens of thousands of feet before deploying the parachute at the last possible moment. But HALO placed aircraft in danger because they must fly over the drop zone. There was also a loud, telltale *crack* of an opening canopy, providing an opportunity for the enemy to be forewarned of the coming assault. Using HAHO, soldiers could jump from aircraft flying along established commercial routes at forty thousand feet and immediately deploy their chutes. A properly trained and equipped team could fly over thirty miles and land on a building's rooftop. That kind of flying skill would be needed tonight, and this was not a training exercise.

The men made final checks of their gear. None had a biography or history; no war stories to tell you or medals to show off. These were the "quiet professionals"—America's secret warriors. Officially created by the U.S. Army in 1952, Special Forces units were derived from the World War II–era Office of Strategic Services, the predecessor of the Central Intelligence Agency. The new unit trained to infiltrate by land, sea, or air deep into enemy-occupied territory and organize the native populations into resistance groups to conduct guerrilla operations against an enemy country. But there were secondary missions as well: deep-penetration raids, intelligence missions, and counter-insurgency operations.

Today's Special Forces were designed to spend months, maybe even years, deep within hostile territory. They were self-sustaining, requiring them to speak the language of their target area. The Special Forces soldiers also needed to be tough and know how to survive on their own without extensive resupply from the outside world. In recent years they proved they could. Special Forces soldiers performed reconnaissance missions in Yugoslavia and were the first ground troops into Afghanistan. They were involved in capturing war criminals and terrorists across the globe in countries whose names would always remain classified. Tonight the men were to begin a new chapter in the book of American heroes. The MC-130H Combat Talon was twenty-five miles from the drop zone when the soldiers walked off the ramp and disappeared into the darkness.

Chapter Two

United Nations Headquarters, New York

"We'll be starting in just a moment, Mr. Ambassador. I appreciate you meeting with us at such a late hour."

"Sure, my pleasure," said Richard Brock, the U.S. ambassador to the United Nations. "I often watch your show when I'm up after the eleven o'clock news."

Physically strong, intelligent, and blessed with movie-star-like good looks, Brock had become a Washington celebrity. As a young boy he had demonstrated an exceptional ability to thrive in both studies and sports. That ability had continued into adulthood. At Yale he led as student body president and captain of the crew team. At Harvard Law School he edited the law review. During his time attending Oxford, he impressed all by his ability on the debating team and the rugby pitch. Family political ties got him his first work in government as a young member of the Secretary of Defense's advisement committee on the Middle East. Later he moved on to serve in positions with the National Security Council and the State Department, helping negotiate peace in Bosnia. The U.S. president appointed him Special Envoy to Colombia during the height of that country's civil war. Brokering a peace plan, Brock was insistent that any deals include the deployment of American troops as peacekeepers.

Brock was an icon of the educational and cultural elite that dominated public service in the United States, but he had done very little outside of educational institutions and pampered civil service positions. He never once considered joining the military himself, even threatening to disown his children if they chose such a route for their futures. Jobs outside of government—during periods when the "wrong" political party was in office—included a number of seats on the boards of Washington think tanks. Ghostwriters took notes during interviews to write books that he proudly signed as his own. He presented the illusion of having a golden touch, mostly because he quit anything that looked as if it were driving down an embarrassing road to failure.

"Good evening and welcome to this week's episode of *Newsmaker.* The secretary general of the United Nations, Tadashi Yoishi, declared this the month for South America, and a special Security Council delegation led by American Ambassador Richard Brock is just back from a diplomatic mission to the continent. Crises have flared throughout South America in recent months. Tensions in the Colombian civil war have heated up, despite a U.S.-brokered peace agreement and the deployment of more U.N. peacekeepers.

Chilean violence has worsened in recent days. Border clashes between San Selvan rebels and Venezuelan troops erupted during the U.N. visit. More and more of South America's countries slide closer to food disasters after years of unpredictable weather. The steady litany of disaster has caught the world's attention. The U.N. and member nations fret over the failure of peace negotiation efforts in Chile and debate the cost. The *Economist* puts it bluntly, calling South America the hopeless continent. And Ambassador Brock joins us now. Welcome back to the program, sir."

"Thanks, Ray. It's great to be back."

"You were representing the United States on the Security Council, also the chief of mission in this recent trip to South America. Why now?"

"The Security Council has to make some very big decisions in South America. Secretary General Tadashi Yoishi has to decide whether to move forward with the next phase of the peacekeeping observer mission in Colombia. Therefore, the Security Council asked seven of us to go to South America. The other eight members of the Security Council, incidentally, went to Africa at the same time. By the time we got to South America—where things are moving forward, slowly, but they are moving forward—but by the time we got there, the events in Chile were casting a very large shadow over all of our efforts."

"You point out the bad timing of having Chile blow up just as the Security Council mission is trying to put some things in place. Colombia is a much less complicated situation, and the U.N. is having a hard time making headway there. How does that argue well for a new mission in Chile?"

"Well, Ray, the Chilean situation and the Colombian situation are completely different. I'll talk about them one by one. What is happening in Chile is inexcusable. The so-called revolutionaries, which are just a bunch of ragtag, machete-wielding murderers, have broken every deal that they made in the last few years. That has placed the peace process in tatters. Juan Castro, the head of the revolutionary units who has currently disappeared, is a man who has really behaved in a way which I think puts him outside the acceptable limits. He is closely associated with San Selvan terrorist groups, and quite possibly assisted in the chemical attack in Rio. But that has nothing to do with Colombia. The Colombian situation makes progress every day. We have also stopped the fighting that took place between Equator and Peru forces, and put into place a new package to bring demilitarization to that area. Stability in the region is coming. It's slow. It's tough. But I don't think what's happening in Chile affects it."

"What will affect it? And can South American governments create stability without the help from more foreign troops?"

"The second part of your question is categorically *no*. The governments cannot create stability. They do not have the military or political capability. I would say that is especially clear in Chile, and under the peace agreement signed last year, the South American–negotiated peace agreement, which the U.N. is going to help implement, nobody's expecting them to do that. The peace plan is supposed to result in the countries that are now in Colombia pulling their forces back on a phased basis as the U.N. observers come in. But those countries will need to provide forces to other South American countries.

"Peace in this region is important to the world, but even more so to citizens of the United States. We do more business in that region than we do in Europe and Japan combined. Forty-eight percent of our exports go to Central and South America. Venezuela is the leading importer of oil to the United States, providing more oil than any country in the Middle East."

"So how do you create peace there?" Ray Sanchez leaned forward in his chair. "What has to happen first, and then what has to happen subsequently in order to create a space where you can have a peacekeeping mission with some hope of success?"

"There are three key elements, Ray. First, as I said earlier, the South American people cannot do it by themselves. External forces must be included. The second thing is that we must halt the instability caused by San Selvan drug cartels and terrorists. Since declaring independence, the San Selvans are the root of problems in the region. They have direct links to most of the terrorist groups in other South American countries and their damage to the environment is increasing the friction. That leads to the final element: the Global Warming Treaty. We must enforce it. This is not like the Congo or Kosovo or East Timor. The battles in South America are not over ethnic or tribal differences, but instead they are over a fight for resources. Both economic and ecological resources. Peace is only possible if we are willing to help. An interesting point about our South American trip, Ray, is that every country asked for help. For various reasons, every single leader we met with, no matter what their internal differences, is literally begging the outside world, the U.N. or the U.S., to come in and put forces on the ground in order to stabilize the situation."

"And obviously there are different motivations for each of these countries, but certainly, as in the case in Chile," argued Sanchez, "many of these leaders know that the introduction of foreign forces will help keep them in power. I must also say that I think it is ironic that you bring up San Selva. The areas controlled by San Selvan rebels seem to have the *least* amount of internal conflict, including complaints of human rights violations. Why risk additional conflict in the region by trying to pressure San Selva into changing?"

"You know, Ray, I need to start by clarifying our position on the San Selvan situation. We, as most of the world's governments, do not recognize an independent San Selva. When I use the term San Selva I'm talking about a problem, not a place. In addition, throughout all of South America, the area controlled by the San Selvan terrorists causes the most damage to our global community. Their destruction of the environment and export of illegal drugs make them a parasite. I am not in the position to decide if the gains are worth risking war, and all wars are terrible, but some wars are unavoidable. We need to accept that sacrifices might be necessary."

Sanchez paused and replayed in his head what Brock had said: *War?* He asked his next question. "But what sacrifices? And from whom? Is it fair to ask poorer nations to endure the same standards as the wealthy? San Selva makes two very good points that counter your comments. First, they bring up that the majority of health-related problems in their country are from tobacco use, not drug use. And the second point is that both Europe and North America were vast forests before settlement in the nineteenth and early twentieth centuries. In fact, here in the United States we have completely wiped out most of the old-growth forests in the Pacific Northwest. The damage the San Selvans are doing is only a matter of global interest because we've already destroyed all of our forests."

"Ray . . ." Brock paused dramatically. "This is not a new problem that Americans created to burden poor nations. The fact that climate change is a common concern of mankind was asserted in a United Nations' resolution all the way back in 1988, but human history is imbued with examples of cultures being destroyed by abusing the environment. Be sure and remember the Easter Island example."

Brock paused again to let the thought sink in. The Easter Island example had become ingrained in the information banks of Americans' brains as environmental activists pointed to the ancient history for an example of what might lie ahead in mankind's future. "Now I ask you, is the fate of Easter Island's inhabitants a forewarning of mankind's dubious future?"

"Whether or not Easter Island is the direction the world is headed is a question for others much more informed than I to answer, Mr. Ambassador. My concern is that one example like Easter Island doesn't explain why it is important today."

"Those who refuse to learn from history's lessons are doomed to repeat them, right?" Brock smiled and nodded his head. "If we had hours to discuss it I could explain several, like how lead-based pipes destroyed the aristocracy of the Roman Empire by slowly poisoning them, but let me move on to today for the sake of time. The modern global warming fight gained international momentum in the Republic of Maldives, a tiny country located three hundred miles southwest of the tip of India in the northern Indian Ocean and consisting of more than one thousand islands. Maldives is a small, poor nation that wants to halt global warming because only a small rise in sea level will flood most of the country.

"There are plenty of threats here at home too. A new report warns that climate change, deforestation, and overpopulation will make the next ten years a decade of superdisasters. The International Federation of Red Cross and Red Crescent Societies, the world's largest emergency response network, published the report. They said the number of people needing its assistance has increased by more than tenfold over the past six years. Last year's season of natural disasters was the worst on record. Natural disasters created more refugees than wars and conflict. The loss of natural vegetation, particularly forests, has become a major cause of preventable natural disasters around the world. The explosive combination of human-driven climate change and rapidly changing socioeconomic conditions will set off chain reactions of devastation leading to huge problems. The world is at risk of weather-related destruction as never before. The main uncertainty is where and when they will occur.

"In addition, the United Nations–sponsored Intergovernmental Panel on Climate Change confirmed that the average temperature is growing faster than ever. It took twenty thousand years for the temperature to rise seven degrees, but now it is expected to rise at least one degree each century. The reason for the speed of temperature increases is pollution. Not only the pollution caused by automobiles, but also the soot that comes from the burning of wood and coal. Compiling the problem is the fact that the pollution creates health problems in humans and impedes the growth of vegetation by poisoning the plants and soil."

Brock stopped abruptly. Sanchez, surprised by the silence, shifted in his seat. "I'm not suggesting that we just tell anyone, especially the Maldives, *tough luck,*" Sanchez finally replied. "But many critics of your administration's policies say that this stance against global warming is only the result of lobbying by big businesses, especially insurance conglomerates. I have a petition here signed by twenty thousand American scientists that claim the study you mentioned is based on bad science. Actually more economics than science. Big business wants stricter standards because it quashes smaller businesses and discourages new competition. Those scientists making the claims about temperature increases have dedicated their entire lives' works to global warming; they teach classes and write books about the subject. Even the organization that wrote the study relies on donations to pay its employees and fund its operations. What better way to get more money by warning of a decade of 'super disasters'?" Sanchez shook his head. "I don't know. Personally I'll tell you that I am beginning to subscribe to the belief that fluctuations in the energy released by the sun are the real reason we see the average temperature rising, and we have no control over that. So, taking all that into consideration, is it really fair to ask San Selva to bear the burden of saving the world?"

"The better question is whether or not it is fair for the world to suffer because of San Selvan criminals. Research points to the conclusion that global warming may damage not only local areas but the entire global community. In this country the price of cleaner-burning fuels has driven prices up for just about everything. Violent weather destroys more and more property each year. Businesses are threatened and insurance companies are going bankrupt, creating economic recessions across the world. People on one side of the earth are suffering because of changes in global weather patterns caused by people on the other side of the globe. Violent hurricanes ravage the Atlantic. Powerful typhoons destroy the Pacific. Deadly tornadoes rip through the United States. Floods in Africa. Drought cracks in Europe. Farmers in California watch their crops die as lobster boats in New England bring in smaller and smaller catches—all the results of changes in the global climate. There is no time for long-term studies but plenty of questions. How much more warming can we tolerate? For how long? What can be done? Before the Global Warming Treaty was signed there were only these questions. Now we've begun to take action."

"But that's not unique to San Selva," said Sanchez. "Massive environmental concerns have reared up throughout South America as governments attempt to meet the needs of their growing populations. On the borders of Brazil and Bolivia, the huge Pantanal wetlands are being drained to make way for hydroelectric projects, eliminating an entire habitat. Overcrowding in Sao Paulo and Rio, with populations of eighteen million and seven million respectively, has polluted water sources, denuded mountainsides, and spawned outbreaks of disease and unmanageable criminal violence. Why not go after those countries with the same vigor?"

"That's a great question, Ray. First of all, those *are* countries. San Selva is not. The difference is that the countries are cooperating and have implemented long-term plans to resolve the situation. The rain forests occupied by the San Selvan thugs include a large percentage of the world's biological diversity, and the San Selvan population is growing rapidly and nothing is being done. If the Amazon goes, the rest of South America will go with it. I've already explained how this would affect the climate, and I know it's hard to comprehend. Flying over the Amazon it is hard to envision that the solid block of green below is being destroyed at a rate of five *thousand* football fields a day. Mostly from clear-cutting, a process where people cut down or burn huge swaths of forest. Much of this clearing is done to grow the illegal and immoral drugs that poison our children. The sheer immensity of the

Amazon, the largest tropical rain forest in the world and covering an area more than half the size of the Continental United States, means that until recently locals have treated the forest as if its bounty would never end. Soon, it may be too late to save. If we can't find a solution it is very likely that by the year 2050 there'll be very little forest left. The consequences of this are horrid. Enormous decreases in air quality and resulting increases in lung diseases and cancer; the melting of polar ice caps and the submergence of not only the Republic of Maldives, but many more of the earth's inhabited coastlines—among them large parts of New York, San Francisco, Hong Kong, and London. The rain forests play a crucial role in cleansing the earth's air of carbon dioxide, and in turn, controlling the buildup of greenhouse gas. We can not come in after the problem has already happened and spend billions of dollars to try and fix it. It'll be too late. Right now we are trying to come into the region and extinguish the fires that rage out of control in the rain forests, but the rebels threaten to shoot at our fire-fighting aircraft with surface-to-air missiles."

"Mr. Ambassador, San Selva has good reason to fear our becoming involved in their internal issues. We oppose their independence. We supported Brazil during the Rain Forest War despite the atrocities. Because of our sanctions, San Selvans are forced to find solutions to virtually all of the their problems within their own rain forest. Aren't we creating much of the problem?"

"The pressure put on the San Selva by the global community is designed to fix the problems, not contribute to them," answered Brock.

Sanchez waited for Brock to continue but there was only stone-faced silence. Then he asked a question not on his prepared list. "Earlier you brought up the

Global Warming Treaty, Mr. Ambassador, and you even used the word *war*. Countries abide by the terms of the treaty in varying degrees, and in the case of the Global Warming Treaty sanctions have had little affect. The attack helicopter battalion positioned in the region last month has yet to be used. There is now talk of military preparations for additional deployments. Is the U.N. prepared to pass a resolution calling for the use of military force?"

Brock paused before answering. The last thing he wanted was to say something that someone might hold against him as being misleading. He already knew the future. The United States knew a U.N.-sponsored military operation against the San Selva rebels was dead before it was even proposed. As a permanent member of the Security Council, China possessed veto authority. They had recently increased trade in Central and South America. China didn't welcome American military intervention into a region of the world where they were gaining influence. So, the U.S. ambassador had lobbied for a weakly worded resolution that called for member nations to "use the means determined necessary" to put a halt to San Selva destroying the environment. But that was all that the ambassador wanted. The president didn't want to become involved in another United Nations operation. After horrid experiences working with the U.N. in Somalia and Bosnia, the U.S. chose to ally with NATO when Kosovo flared and completely avoided the subject during Enduring Freedom—the operation to destroy terrorism. Now that there was trouble in South America the U.S. preferred to lead an Organization of American States operation rather than become bogged down in the incompetence of the U.N. But with the U.N. resolution, the president had a mandate to move forward with military action. Although potentially controversial, the action fared well during political focus groups, meaning that the president's favorable rating in the polls would likely go up.

"I don't think a resolution for the use of force would be prudent at this point," Brock finally said. "Too many issues exist in both the Security Council and General Assembly, anyway. But I need to be very clear about this, because this is irrefutable: the United States will take all necessary actions to protect its vital national interests. Those people who wish to draw a large Berlin-type wall around themselves are going to learn the hard way that the problems they're trying to seal off seep over to the other side of the wall. The only way to deal with these problems is to tackle them frontally. This is not easy. South America is daunting, but to say that South America is hopeless has a subliminal message I find very disturbing, and an irresponsibility to it that will carry with it the seeds of a much greater problem later. Our great successes of creating peace in Africa should be an example. Don't forget that to come to this point in Africa required military intervention in the Congo. This crisis might require a similar American-led effort. *We* have a moral obligation to do something in South America."

"Mr. Ambassador, I'm going to have to end our discussion here. Thank you. Very good to have you with us tonight."

"Thank you, Ray. It's good to be back."

Chapter Three

MK IX Seal Delivery Vehicle (SDV), Near a San Selvan Port

The long, black sphere cut through the dark water. Its trip from the submarine USS *Oklahoma City* to the port on the river's edge took less than an hour, but it had been one tough hour in the cramped, underwater conditions of the minisub. Tonight's mission was perfect for the SEALs. Now they neared their objective. An air strike could do the job too, but commando missions like this one struck terror into the hearts of men. So Lieutenant Jason Barret and five of his best men had cautiously piloted the eight miles so they could place explosives on several enemy vessels.

Entering the port, Petty Officer Hernandez, the minisub's driver, became even more cautious. The violent currents made driving difficult, and he didn't want his good work to be wasted in the last few meters of the swim. Sediment from the sea bottom mixed with the filth of the water, reducing visibility to almost nothing. Any mistake now meant disaster. A wounded minisub would only put the SEALs in a precarious position—stuck in enemy waters with little supplies and a long swim back to the *Oklahoma City*.

Hernandez stopped the minisub at the base of a pier piling, while Lieutenant Barret tightened swim fins over his booties and locked the AN/PVS-15 submersible night-vision goggles on the frame of his face mask. He exited the minisub. Carefully scanning the general vicinity through the green luminescence of the night-vision device, Barret kicked his legs and finned toward the surface. He wore his rebreather scuba gear, which captured his exhaled breaths and prevented air bubbles from indicating his presence to the enemy above. Gripped in his hand, the small 9mm pistol fitted with a silencer offered his only means of defense.

Slowly bringing his head out of the water, Barret scanned the port. More lights than expected illuminated the area, and he finned toward a shadow to avoid being silhouetted. If he was seen, it would be hard to decide what he looked like, however. The natural outline of the human head twisted into the appearance of a fictional sea monster, with bulging "eyes" from the night-vision goggles and evil-looking "tusks" of the dual-hose breathing apparatus for the rebreather. The pistol sat in his hand chest high and at a forty-five-degree angle below the water. If a threat appeared he would fire the first shot before the barrel protruded from the water. His right arm would instinctively lock out at the elbow, with his left hand meeting the right to stabilize the pistol. The motion allowed enough time to fire five rounds, with most being well-aimed shots, and the movement also propelled him back into the safety of his underwater world. Looking at the features around him, Barret realized that the minisub had stopped short of the intended debarkation point. For a split second he considered staying, but that would require his SEALs to cross more open water than he was willing to risk.

With his free hand, Barret submerged himself again, cautious to avoid letting his legs break the surface before turning downward to return to the minisub. Spotting the dull infrared light that marked the minisub's location, Barret kicked his fins to speed his descent.

Petty Officer Hernandez fixed his eyes on the lieutenant when Barret returned to the minisub. Hernandez watched for the signal to cut the minisub's power. When Barret started to retake his seat, Hernandez knew that something was wrong. The lieutenant grabbed the illuminated board next to his seat and used a grease pencil to mark their position with an X on the sketch of the port. Hernandez saw that they sat several hundred feet short of the planned destination. He grabbed the minisub's controls. Hernandez powered the minisub forward and again moved through the dark waters, thinking to himself, *Not too bad*.

As Hernandez steered the minisub, he began to wish that he was smashed in back with the other four SEALs in the troop compartment. He had a hard time steering. Maneuverability wasn't very good, kind of like driving on ice. The currents from the nearby river continued to create challenges. The fully loaded craft was weighted down with gear and six men, making it slow and heavy. Lieutenant Barret navigated by relying on guidance from the obstacle-avoidance sonar instruments to warn him of underwater objects. The passengers in back were blind and dependent on the driver and navigator to safely move them through the water. The passenger area was cramped, only slightly bigger than the interior of a Volkswagen Bug. The men breathed through regulators attached to hoses connected to the inside of the minisub. Using the minisub's air supply lengthened the time they could spend under the water, but the SEALs also had their own closed-circuit rebreather scuba system available for swimming beyond the minisub.

Hernandez stopped the minisub the second time. Lieutenant Barret carefully slipped from his seat and repeated his swim to the surface. His head remained above water for only a second or two. *This is right.* Returning to the minisub he motioned for the engine's power to be turned off. Then he went to the back compartment to give the other SEALs the signal to debark.

By placing "boots on the ground," or "fins in the water" in this case, military commanders attacked the very root of an enemy's will to fight. Human beings have a natural phobia against interpersonal violence. The threat of it, linked with air strikes and psychological operations, leads to the enemy surrendering without a fight. If successful, this mission would result in more than a few destroyed boats. A simple, unsophisticated investigation would conclude that the destruction was the work of placed explosives, not missiles or torpedoes. The enemy would know that men were right under their very noses to set the charges. *They could have slit my throat or pulled me into the water and held me down until I died.* The underwater commandos were worth their weight in gold.

Those deadly men now prepared to exit the minisub and complete the sabotage mission. The SEALs replaced the mouthpieces from the minisub's air supply with the rebreather systems on their bodies and locked AN/PVS-15 night-vision goggles into place. Exiting the craft was not a free-for-all, but instead a well-rehearsed sequence. Each two-man team swam past Barret before making their way to their designated targets. Their individual equipment list was simple: weapons, explosives, and ammunition. Each wore a dive knife, more a habit than a practical tool for this mission.

Dressed from head to toe in black neoprene wet suits, the SEALs planned to spend several hours in the water. The whole mission profile for a minisub operation like this could range from six to ten hours, making it the toughest mission SEALs performed. Even in the relatively warm water of the North Atlantic Ocean, not wearing the wet suit while submerged would likely cause hypothermia because the SEALs were to be in the water for so long. The time in the water also required them to travel within one atmosphere, or less than thirty feet, of the surface to prevent complications from decompression sickness. This harsh abuse of the men's bodies was merely one reason for them being in top physical condition. The conditions they endured were horrid, but the SEALs were well prepared.

SEALs go through what is considered by many to be the toughest military training in the world at the Naval Special Warfare Command in Coronado, California. It's called "buds," which is short for Basic Underwater Demolitions/SEAL (BUD/S). You could also call it six months of hell. At BUD/S, Navy men (no women are allowed in the SEALs) encounter obstacles designed to develop and test their stamina, leadership, and ability to work as a team. From Coronado the potential SEALs attend basic airborne training before reporting to a SEAL Team or SEAL

Delivery Vehicle (SDV) Team. They participate in three months of SEAL Tactical Training, and also attend Survival Evasion Resistance and Escape (SERE) School to prepare for the misfortune of becoming a prisoner of war. Some receive specialized training like the Military Free Fall Parachutist, the Ranger School, or the Special Operation Combat Medic Course.

SEALs most often work in the ranks of the U.S. Naval Special Warfare Command. It is a small, elite community: less than five thousand active members and one thousand reservists from SEAL Teams, Special Boat Units, and SEAL Delivery Vehicle Teams. Of the active-duty members, nine hundred are officers and four thousand enlisted, with only half being actual SEALs. And only two hundred from the unit are qualified to conduct dry-dock operations with the SEAL Delivery Vehicles, making Barret and his men the elite of the elite of the elite.

Barret counted each man when he passed him. No need to stop any of them and give new instructions. The mission was a go. Hernandez began filming the underwater area with an infrared camera, as each two-man team finished the swim to the boats. The divers' explosives were ready for placement next to the boat's propeller. The explosion would sever the prop and make a hole large enough for the boat to fill with water and sink quickly. The plastic explosives were neutrally buoyant limpet mines backed by a heavy adhesive that made them easy to attach. Detonators came in all shapes, sizes, and methods of initiation: radio-controlled, timed, heat-sensitive, acoustic. For tonight's mission the SEALs used timer devices set for a twenty-hour countdown. Tomorrow night at midnight the charges would automatically detonate to complete the SEALs' mission. Setting them tonight prevented the enemy from scattering the boats for protection. The boats would be destroyed even if moved to different locations. Something that would be especially important if these patrol crafts were to be used in counterattacks against the U.S. Fleet.

Setting the charges progressed quickly. In each two-man team, the one placing the explosives kept his silenced pistol holstered, while the second swam with a silenced MP5 at the ready, thumb resting on a contact pad to turn on the laser aimer. The laser was infrared, which meant only someone wearing night-vision goggles could see it. From putting pressure on the thumb pad the commandos could use the laser aimer to point out the exact place a bullet from the silenced weapon would strike a target. For these men every round counted and every shot was expected to kill someone. They did not have enough ammunition to miss.

San Selvan Airspace

A subtle sound of thunder rumbled through the air as the wind whipped about the canvas wing. It had been over an hour since the men walked off the MC-130H's ramp and immediately pulled their rip cords. The *pop* of the opening canopy met the sharp jerk of a good parachute, signaling to the men that everything was okay. Faint lights hung in the distance, but there was no clear observation of the ocean far below. The twelve commandos flew under the canopies of the specially designed MT-1X parachutes. The custom chutes allowed the men to place their hands at their sides, preventing the loss of functioning in the arms and hands that could be caused by having arms over their heads for the prolonged descent. Having traveled over twenty miles, the men followed each other in a single-file formation.

The lead man navigated with compass and a global positioning system, which was a receiver unit that communicated with satellites orbiting in the earth's atmosphere. The key to good flying was keeping the display on the global-positioning system to read that the operator needed zero degrees to get on course. Shooting for perfection made the task easier in this case. Perfection and keeping as much altitude as possible until directly over the destination, because the commandos could always circle down into the drop zone. They certainly could not take off again if they touched the ground too early.

Nearing the drop zone, all the commandos put on night-vision devices in anticipation of the end of their HAHO insertion. As the ground came into view, the men released the packs from their rigs and carefully brought them down so that the shoulder straps rested on their toes. The packs all contained fragile equipment that wouldn't be able to withstand the jar of colliding with the earth.

The last few seconds of flight took the most skill. Just before landing, the men flared their canopies to slow their speed so they could gently set the packs onto the ground before coming to a standing landing.

Fighting the slight pull of the rectangular chutes in the wind, the men brought their weapons instinctively to the ready: butt stock pulled in to the shoulder, finger on the trigger, torsos twisting as the soldiers scanned with both eyes for targets. A night-vision monocular covered the left eye, while the right strained to use natural sight. The two coupled to provide both depth perception and the ability to see through the dark.

Silently, the twelve split into pairs, with one soldier of each pair collecting the chutes and gear while the other provided security. The navigator made a quick check of the global-positioning system as the patrol leader scanned the area with his M2120 Thermal Imaging device. The M2120 was the size and shape of an old Polaroid camera, and it presented different colors for different heat signatures. The patrol leader could clearly see the heat differential of tree trunks to their colder leaf and soil backgrounds. A few small heat sources bounced around, indicating the presence of some warm-blooded animals, but no sign of any people or vehicles. Within two minutes of landing the commandos loaded up everything and began moving away from the drop zone. The only signs that remained were the footprints from their foreign-made boots.

At first the rate of movement was fast, but once safely away from the drop zone, the patrol slowed to a crawl. This and other patrols of elite soldiers would help give military planners detailed information that was not going to be gained from satellites. The teams were inserted as early as possible and tasked in the field. Waiting too long reduced the effectiveness and survivability of the reconnaissance teams. Lessons learned the hard way during the Gulf War and the battles against terrorists.

After two hours of creeping through the jungle, the point man held his hand up. His palm flat and facing to the front. Each man behind him saw the signal in his night-vision monocular and came to an immediate halt. The point man's hand slowly dropped down to his side, his palm facing downward now. The men again followed the signal, lowering themselves, with most coming to a kneeling position. A few went all the way down until their stomachs touched the dirt. What each man did depended on the terrain around him. What was most important was that each made himself as small a target as possible while still maintaining the ability to observe and fire, if necessary, in his assigned sector.

The patrol leader rose back up from his kneeling position and quietly moved to the point man. He watched for the point man to signal. If the point man sensed danger and wanted the patrol leader to stop, he would hold up a closed fist, signaling for the patrol leader to freeze in place. Each placement of the patrol leader's feet was careful and deliberate: heel touching the ground first; rolling the foot against the dirt; lift off of the toe. Pausing for a few seconds between each step, scanning constantly in search of threats. He felt for sticks or other debris that would produce noise, several times stopping a foot placement because of the potential for it to produce too much noise. With the extra weight on his body, balancing often proved difficult. The men were all armed and equipped the same. Each carried an M4 rifle. A smaller version of the standard-issue M16A2 service rifle, the M4 also fired a 5.56mm bullet, but the M4's maximum range against a point target was only three hundred meters, which was two hundred meters less than the M16A2. It was much shorter than the M16A2, however. Only twenty-four inches to the M16A2's thirty-nine inches. But lengthening each man's weapon to just under thirty inches was an acoustic suppresser, commonly referred to as a silencer. The silencer greatly reduced the weapon's sound, but it did not create a faint whisper. There was still the loud sound of slapping metal as the semiautomatic weapon cocked and chambered the next bullet.

Other weapons—machine guns or grenade launchers—would have increased this patrol's firepower, but would also have increased the men's load of ammunition and weight. On a patrol like this one, you screwed something up if you had to fire your weapon. This patrol was for gathering information and directing air strikes, not fighting. So instead, in an attempt to create something somewhere between GI Joe and Buzz Lightyear, the commandos humped laser designators and sophisticated communication equipment. The communication equipment could send information and imagery across the globe to military commanders who prepared for battle, but the laser designators could send a "smart" bomb or cruise missile from an aircraft or a ship to destroy a target and prevent a battle.

The patrol leader finally reached the point man's position, placing a hand on his shoulder to be sure he knew where the patrol leader was kneeling. The point man looked back slightly, nodding to the patrol leader. The patrol leader saw that the point man pointed the "super ear" to his front. An electronic piece of equipment that enhanced an individual's hearing ability, the super ear was a small dish-shaped object with an earpiece for the operator. If something in front of him made any noise, then the super ear would pick up the sound.

The point man raised his weapon and pressed a thumb pad to turn on the AN/PEQ-2 laser sight. The sight, calibrated to the M4's bullet trajectory, made it an excellent aiming tool when firing, but it could also be used for marking targets. The laser sight sent an infrared beam of light through the trees, and the point man rotated the weapon slowly to make the beam circle the object he was watching.

The patrol leader could see the unnatural-looking lump. He couldn't identify it with his night-vision sight; the same problem that the point man had. Lifting the M2120 thermal sight to his eye, the patrol leader aimed in on the lump. *Cold.* The heat signature was consistent with the ground around it, so whatever it was it did not have a pulse or an energy source. It could, however, be some type of booby trap or pungi pit. The patrol leader handed the point man the thermal sight so he could have a look for himself. After a minute, the point man handed back the thermal sight, nodding as he rose to a standing position. Whatever it was could be moved past, just not too close.

As the point man started moving again, the patrol leader lifted his hand with the palm facing up. The patrol members rose, repeating the signal to make sure everyone saw it. With a swing of his hand over his head in a forward motion, the patrol leader got the patrol moving forward again.

It was eight more hours of creeping through the jungle before the hand went up to again halt the patrol. The patrol leader checked his watch and was relieved that they had reached their first patrol base right on time. The point man made a careful check of the vegetated knoll, being especially watchful for signs of animals that might be hunted by local inhabitants. Water sources were another concern. The men didn't want to be near anything that might attract people.

The patrol leader held his hand out like a telephone receiver and placed it near his ear and mouth, signaling to the patrol to switch on their personal radios. The radios were a great tool but not one that the men were able to use all of the time. Constant use of the personal radios would have increased the need for batteries, thus increasing the amount of weight each man would need to carry. The radio earpiece also reduced the abilities of natural hearing, which reduced the effectiveness of a patrol. But now it was time to enter into a patrol base, so radios were necessary. The sun would be up soon, and the patrol leader wanted to be hidden well before it was light.

He grabbed his radio operator and set up where he wanted the center of the patrol base to be, signaling to the others by circling his hand over his head in a lasso motion. The other patrol members split into five pairs, evenly spacing themselves around the patrol leader like the points on a star. Everyone knew right where he belonged because of the direction the patrol leader faced. This drill had been practiced many times. They could do it in their sleep and often did. Once in position, the men sat quietly and listened.

It took a few minutes before they confirmed that no one followed them. The patrol leader keyed his personal radio twice but said nothing. The double key created a *click-click* sound in each patrol member's earpiece. Three clicks would have indicated that something was wrong. Two for good, okay, or yes; three for bad, wrong, or no. Positive and negative— no need for anything more complicated.

Hearing the *click-click,* the men now knew that they had five minutes to make initial preparation of their positions. One stood guard at each position as the other man unpacked a small camouflage net. Digging holes would have created too much noise, but properly camouflaging the positions would help protect the team. Only needed items were unpacked from the packs, and an area was cleared where each man could lie down.

At the five-minute mark, the patrol leader again keyed his radio twice. The patrol expected this signal, and the men who had been standing watch at each two-man position went to the center of the patrol base. The five men who met at the patrol base knew that they were going out on a quick security patrol of the area. Five was an ideal number of men. If there was a casualty, whether a gunshot or a broken leg, there would be two men to carry the injured man and two to cover the movement. Each knew his job on the patrol and the expected distances and directions they would have to travel. It was all standardized. If a problem appeared and the security patrol couldn't return to the patrol base, or if the men at the patrol base needed to leave quickly, then the two groups would break up and link back up at the last rally point, two miles back in the direction they had come from earlier.

The five-man security patrol exited the patrol base from the same route that the entire patrol had entered from earlier. This kept the number of ways an enemy could follow footprints into the patrol base to one. While the patrol ensured that the area was safe, the men at the base sat quietly, remaining watchful for any sign of the enemy. The patrol keyed a personal radio twice at every checkpoint, and the patrol leader acknowledged the message with a double key in return.

The men could have talked. The radios were set with encryption that made them secure from eavesdropping, but they were not capable of frequency hopping. Frequency-hopping radios operated on a common timing sequence in which the radio constantly switched channel, making it nearly impossible to trace the radio signal. Single-channel radios like the ones that the patrol used could easily be traced with directional scanners available at any electronics store. The men would talk if there was an emergency or a contact with the enemy, but until then it was best to avoid all radio traffic.

The security patrol lasted for less than an hour. They halted for entry as far from the patrol base as they could while still retaining the ability to visually signal. The lead man from the security patrol flashed one infrared beam from his night-vision monocular's infrared light. The patrol base signaled back with two flashes. Three flashes, being negative, would have told the security patrol that something was wrong and they needed to wait. Two for good; three for bad.

The patrol leader counted his five-man security patrol as they reentered the patrol base and each man reoccupied his position on the perimeter. All the men remained alert as the sun rose, and all would remain awake and alert for the first hour of daylight. The patrol leader confirmed that the location was adequate, which was necessary because things always looked different in the light. The patrol's radio operator was almost finished typing the situation report into the palm-top computer before the sun had even been up for two hours.

There was not much to report yet. The patrol was inserted safely and at its first hide site waiting until dark again. Only a few miles were covered in the hours that the men had patrolled. The short distance was mostly the result of their being so careful not to be detected, but it was also because of their heavy loads. There was no need for them to rush if it only meant that they would get caught. Their mission was too important for them to be lost because of careless haste.

Finishing the report, the radio operator handed his palm-top computer to the patrol leader for review. The patrol leader put down his plastic packet of chicken stew and read over the report. Current location. Distance covered. Route covered. No enemy sighted. Some details about the visibility on the ground because of the smoke from the fires. A general analysis of the dirt and vegetation in the area, even a digital photograph attached to the message that showed how things looked on the ground in the thick jungle. Possibly most important of all was a commentary on the quality of the maps they had been issued. The Defense Intelligence Mapping Agency with modern printers and computer equipment produced most military maps. Unfortunately, the information used to produce the maps was often old and inaccurate. During the 1983 invasion of Grenada, for example, U.S. forces had to use tourist maps to plan operations and navigate on the ground. Things were not much better ten years later in Somalia, where most of the maps were the product of a 1923 Italian expedition of the country.

The patrol leader authorized that the message be sent with a nod of his head before returning to his chow. The radio operator connected the palm top to his PSC-7 satcom (satellite communication system) with a cyberdata cable. He keyed the handset of the satcom. The single channel satcom was the primary means for long-range communication, and it provided a secure transmission through a narrow-band signal. The antenna sat on a small tripod eighteen inches off the ground. Its five metal appendages dispersed in a star formation, making the antenna resemble a common office fan. The antenna was aimed in on an exact azimuth and angled so it lined up with the communication satellite.

The radio operator watched the display panel to see if the satcom received a "bounce back" from the satellite. Initially there was none, so the radio operator manipulated the satcom antenna until he received confirmation that it was properly aimed in on the satellite. Switching the satcom to "data," the radio operator sent the entire situation report, digital photograph and all, in one three-second-burst transmission. The signal went twenty thousand miles to a geosynchronous communication satellite that relayed the message back to SOUTHCOM's special operations command center in Florida.

The radio operator waited for confirmation that the message had been received, and he was surprised to see a return message. Scanning quickly through the display on the palm top, the radio operator again nudged the patrol leader and handed him the computer.

The patrol leader's lips moved as he read the message. Things were already changing. The patrol might be in action earlier than originally planned.

Chapter Four

Fort Lewis, Washington

Captain Raymond Summer looked again at the timer on his wristwatch: 19:06. Even at the ripe age of thirty-two he was still in top physical condition. His pace was not as fast as when he was a young lad of nineteen or twenty, but it was considerably better than the vast majority of Americans of his age. He was still young, but after ten years as an Army infantryman, coupled with the fact that the majority of soldiers who worked for him were under twenty years old, Ray Summer often felt very old.

As a company commander in the Army's "Arrowhead" Brigade, the Third Brigade of the Second Infantry Division, Summer needed to be in top physical condition. The Arrowhead nickname was fitting since the brigade was the initial brigade combat team for the United States Army. The nickname was with the brigade decades before the unit took on the responsibility of being one of the firsts in line to deploy to a crisis. Formed in 1918, the brigade first saw combat during heavy fighting in World War I. The unit was later disbanded, only to be reformed in the 1960s for service in Korea. Defending against numerous border incursions by North Korean commandos, the brigade experienced more than its share of firefights, killing and capturing many enemy soldiers without any American deaths. The brigade was again deactivated in 1992, only to be reactivated three years later as an armor cavalry unit. In 2000, it became the Army's first medium-weight brigade—a unit that had traded in the heavy weight of tracks and tanks for Strykers—lightly armored vehicles that traveled on wheels. The name Stryker was fitting; not only did it sound violent and offensive, but it was also the name of two soldiers who received the Medal of Honor for heroism in combat.

Summer and his comrades often bragged that their brigade was on the pointy tip of America's defense spear, ready to deploy anywhere in the world at a moment's notice. Into peacekeeping situations or a show of force to support an ally faced with aggression from a hostile neighbor, the brigade was tasked repeatedly because of its versatility and unique organization. It was designed to be light enough to get to a crisis area while still being lethal enough to be decisive across the spectrum of military operations.

The Arrowhead Brigade combined motorized infantry, engineer, reconnaissance, artillery, and antitank units under one cohesive command. It was organized to deal with the type of contingencies that American forces became involved in after the end of the Cold War. There were three motorized battalions in the brigade with approximately six hundred soldiers apiece.

Each battalion contained three companies of three platoons, a mortar section, and a sniper team. Supporting the battalion was a mortar platoon and sniper squad.

The brigade also had a reconnaissance battalion that had three companies: unmanned aerial vehicle, acoustic sensor, and ground reconnaissance scout. The antitank company was divided into three guided-missile platoons of four vehicles each. The artillery battalion had two batteries with six self-propelled 155mm howitzers and one battery with six 274mm rocket vehicles. The engineer company included three platoons designed to blow breaches in obstacles and minefields, while the equipment platoon had light-armored vehicles that used spades and backhoes for general-purpose engineering. Finally, the medical battalion provided the medical support needed when the brigade took casualties. And the chances of the brigade being sent somewhere that it might take casualties was great.

Being much lighter than the units with seventy-two-ton M1A3 main battle tanks and thirty-three-ton M2A3 Bradley infantry fighting vehicles, the Arrowhead Brigade was easy to deploy to a crisis area. In August 1990, when Saddam Hussein invaded Kuwait, lightly armed airborne troops from the Eighty-second Airborne Division landed in the region within days. But then it took months to land the heavy mechanized forces in Saudi Arabia that were needed for Desert Storm. If Saddam had continued to attack, his tanks would have been a tough match for the airborne troops. Things didn't get much better after the first Gulf War. Much of the airlift that did the work in 1990 was cut out of the U.S. military's budget in the years following the war. Heavy Army units again had a horrible time entering Bosnia in 1994. They were faced with another embarrassing experience trying to get Task Force Hawk to Albania during the 1999 Yugoslav War. So the Army recognized that they faced a dilemma: light forces that were quick but too light and heavy forces that possessed a lot of combat power but couldn't move quickly. The answer was the "medium-weight" brigade. Today, even with the reduction in strategic airlift aircraft, the Third Brigade could deploy in less than four days.

Ray rounded the last turn of his run and leaned into the small hill that separated him from the finish line of the three-mile course. His chest heaved from the stress of his lungs' need of oxygen. The unseasonable humidity made breathing harder, and produced a thick layer of sweat over Summer's body. His gray T-shirt—marked with a black ARMY across the chest— was soaked through, along with the matching gray PT shorts.

Summer sprinted when he saw the finish line. As he covered the last one hundred meters of his run he was surprised to see that the senior enlisted soldier in his company, First Sergeant Christopher Brown, was waiting for him.

"Sir, the men are watching," First Sergeant Brown said sarcastically. His muscular frame stretched the stitches of the camouflage uniform and Brown's dark black face highlighted his bright white teeth, clearly visible in the beaming smile on his face. He always smiled. "They can't see you dying on a short little run like this. What's your time, huh, sir?"

"Go to hell." Summer laughed. Twenty fifty-two isn't too bad a time. A little faster than a seven-minute-mile pace. "Did you just come down here to harass me, First Sergeant?"

"No, sir. The word just came down that our alert level has been raised."

Summer raised an eyebrow. His battalion was part of the Ready Reaction Force, meaning that it was first in line to deploy if something came up. From the brigade there was always a battalion assigned to the Ready Reaction Force with the requirement to be "wheels up" within eighteen hours of notification. The force could deploy directly from the Continental United States to the area of operations. More often, the forces deployed to an intermediate staging base in an allied country to link up with attachments and prepare to conduct operations. An increase in alert level meant that Summer and his company might be going somewhere.

"Is it real or just games?" asked Summer. Drills and exercises that changed the unit's alert level were common.

"Don't know, sir," Brown said with a smile. "But I'm sure you can find out. Here, sir, hide behind my massive lats and I'll get you over to the CP without any of the men seeing you in this condition."

"Those puny little things couldn't even hide my small frame," Summer laughed.

Things were already starting to move forward in the CP.

"Major Martinez," yelled a soldier from the other room. "Another call, sir."

"Hell!" replied Major Jose Martinez. "If it's not brigade or higher tell them I'm in a meeting with myself."

"It's the Brigade Three, sir. Says it's hot."

He grabbed the phone. "Major Martinez speaking."

"Jose, listen, I only have a minute. I'd strongly suggest you call a last-minute meeting and bring all of your key leaders into your CP."

"Did you learn more about this alert, sir?"

"Nothing that can be discussed on an unclass line. Just take my advice on this one. Your boss is coming back soon."

"Roger, sir. Thanks." Hanging up the phone Major Martinez reacted to the sudden sight of Captain Summer standing in the doorway. "Raymond, my good man, reading minds now?"

"Sir?"

"Last-minute meeting. Conference room. I haven't passed the word yet so you have about two minutes to get a shower and change over."

Ray looked down at his sweaty PT gear. "Meeting?" asked Summer. "What's the meeting about?"

"I don't know yet. Just hurry."

Summer rushed back to his office to change over. Ready to head for the showers, he suddenly stopped and thought of something more important. Picking up the phone, he dialed his home number.

"Hi, honey. What are you doing?"

"I just got in."

"I'm going to be late tonight."

"How late?"

"No idea, babe."

"Well . . . why are you going to be late?"

"I don't know that either. I have a last-minute meeting in a few minutes where I'll find out more."

"I thought we were going to go out with Dan and Susan tonight."

"I'm sorry, honey. Go ahead and go without me. I'll catch up with you if I get home in time."

"Can you at least call me later and give me an idea of what's going on?"

"I will if I can. Right now I have to go. Sorry."

After hanging up the phone and estimating that a shower would take too long, Ray began to dress in his camouflage fatigues, or BDU—Battle Dress Uniform—

as the soldiers called it. Still buttoning his blouse, Summer stuck his head into First Sergeant Brown's office. "First Sergeant, give the platoon commanders a call and tell them not to go anywhere until they hear from me."

Without waiting for a response Summer jumped into the hallway and headed for the battalion conference room. The room filled quickly. Company commanders and key staff members all speculated on the reason for their being called together so abruptly. Iran, Sudan, Indonesia; there were plenty of places that the brigade always expected to be sent. Then the battalion commander burst in to tell them to pack up their units. The balloon was going up. The brigade was deploying.

"We're headed to Brazil," the battalion commander said to the shocked crowd. Faced with increased outcry from American civilians and businesses suffering from the severe weather conditions, the president had decided to increase the pressure on San Selva. Ships at sea had changed course and headed for San Selva's shores. It would take some time for the ships to mass off the coast, so it was now up to the Arrowhead Brigade to immediately create a substantial American military presence in South America. Within hours of the meeting's conclusion, the soldiers had a name for their latest contingency: Operation Greenhouse.

Nations in the region were persuaded by American ambassadors to request assistance from the United States. The needs to facilitate stability in the region and protect the global community from environmental and economic disaster were cited as reasons for American military involvement. American forces were going to be organized into a Combined Task Force. The force would include up to twenty thousand U.S. troops and two thousand international troops from a half dozen different countries. The two thousand foreign troops would be mostly military police officers, and their units would be heavily inundated with Green Berets from the Seventh Special Forces Group. There also could be as many as two hundred aircraft from all four of the military services supporting the operation.

Timing was everything at this point. Not only did every hour of burning increase the damage inflicted on the environment, but every day brought with it new potential for the delicate situation to fall apart. Advance forces, like Summer's, needed to move rapidly into position around the San Selva region to intimidate some and reassure others. The U.S. military readied for war—for a very unlikely war to stop global warming.

Summer quickly learned the difference between saying you were ready to be "wheels up" in a transport aircraft in less than eighteen hours and doing it. It was damn hard. There seemed to be an endless list of things that needed to be accomplished. Weapons and equipment must be inspected and packed. Medical checks had to occur to see if there were any new shots or medications that needed to be administered. Soldiers' deployment paperwork was reviewed, with special emphasis on wills. Those who were married made sure their families would be taken care of and those who were single scrambled to store their automobiles in a safe place. Wives and girlfriends began to arrive at the base for a tearful good-bye to their men. No one knew how long they would be gone.

Within twelve hours of notification, Summer led his fourteen light-armored vehicles to nearby McChord Air Base. Once there, the men and vehicles promptly loaded massive C-5B Galaxy transports. Captain Summer's vehicles drove into the cargo doors at both the rear and front of the aircraft, speeding the loading. Each Galaxy was packed with six light-armored vehicles and their sixty-six men. The vehicles fit in the cargo area that was as large as an eight-lane bowling alley, and the soldiers rode in the troop compartment on the second deck of the aircraft. As high as a six-story building and as big as a football field, the Galaxy was the largest aircraft in the U.S. military. So big that it needed four large turbofan engines, each weighing over eight thousand pounds, to climb into the sky. The powerful Galaxy could even carry the M1A3 tank.

Everything went smoothly. The brigade moved quickly. So quickly, in fact, that the State Department could not coordinate things fast enough. Sensitive political issues were involved with using another country's facilities. All loaded up, ready to fly, the lead element of the Arrowhead Brigade sat on the runway and waited for the word to go. They might be ready to take off, but they didn't have a place to land yet.

Chapter Five

"In an act that is being called barbaric by the international community, San Selvan surface-to-air missiles shot down a United Nations' fire-fighting aircraft today. All eight crew members are believed to have perished, and the man-made fires continue to rage. Originally set to clear rain forest for homes and farms in the small country in South America, the out-of-control infernos now send massive clouds of smoke into the atmosphere.

"The smoke from the San Selvan wildfires is contributing to the weather crisis. As the Southwest United States enters another week of record-breaking heat, the movement of a cold front from the north finally brings the possibility of rain. Unfortunately, the cold front also threatens to bring thunderstorms and tornadoes that experts say could be even worse than last year's deadly weather. The weather has destroyed crops and killed livestock, increasing food prices for Americans across the county, many that just recovered from the harsh winter. Stocks are predicted to drop as another insurance company filed for bankruptcy yesterday and many tourism-related businesses reported lower than expected earnings. With another report released today linking global warming to the drastic changes in world weather patterns, the average American is becoming less tolerant of San Selvan violations to the Global Warming Treaty.

"The President is under increased pressure for failing to be more proactive, and some members of Congress are calling for the military to be used to force the officially unrecognized San Selvan government to comply with the treaty. Economic sanctions have had little affect on San Selva, only creating the potential for mass starvation. Polls say fifty-eight percent of Americans support using the military if it will improve environmental conditions, and an anonymous, high-level Pentagon source stated earlier today that a naval expeditionary force may be dispatched to the area early next week."

"Not *again!*" Peter Linsey yelled at the radio. Looking behind him, he immediately regretted his outburst. The children had heard and now sensed his concern at the news report.

"What's wrong, Daddy?" asked Madelyn, the Linseys' oldest. She was five, and her brother, Peter Jr., was just about to turn three.

"Nothing, honey. Daddy didn't like what he heard," he said, turning off the radio. The last thing Peter wanted was another day filled with stress and questions that he couldn't answer. Being married to a Navy fighter pilot was not easy, and Peter's life had become more and more complicated since the birth of the children and his becoming a "house husband."

Peter and Sara had met in college. He was majoring in English and wanted to teach a little and write a lot. She was attending college on a scholarship for the U.S. Navy and wanted to be a fighter pilot. The reversal of traditional goals was a source of humor from the start of their relationship. Shortly after graduation, Sara was commissioned an ensign in the Navy and began flight school in Pensacola, Florida. Peter continued with school, gaining teaching credentials. Just before Sara's completion of flight school the two wed. It was a traditional military wedding, with Sara wearing her dress uniform with sword; Peter wore a tuxedo, however, not a dress.

For the first few years, Sara flew and Peter taught at the schools near wherever they were stationed. But when they found out that Sara was pregnant with Madelyn, a decision had to be made. Both always agreed that one parent should stay home with the children. Now it was time to decide whom. There wasn't much of a decision really. Sara made more money and received better benefits. Besides, thought Peter, he could now dedicate more time to writing. In the end he spent less time writing, especially after Peter Jr. was born two years after Madelyn.

Since Sara often deployed for training or real-world contingencies, Peter frequently became both mother and father. She was currently on the aircraft carrier USS *Ronald Reagan* conducting pre-deployment training at the Navy's bombing range on the island of Vieques, Puerto Rico. The lack of e-mails from Sara was strange and the radio broadcast alluded to a reason. Her ship probably invoked "River City," a code word for an information-protection condition that required all non-classified communication systems to be shut off, which meant that she might be planning for participation in future military action. Nowadays, with the military as busy as it was, there were never enough pilots. The Persian Gulf, former Yugoslavia, Afghanistan, Taiwan Strait—Sara had flown in the major hot spots around the world.

Now a new conflict brewed, and that meant Sara would probably be gone for another unexpected period. Once again, she'd go into harm's way, and the family would worry and wonder when, or if, they would see her again. Peter set the kids in front of the television to watch a video so he could spend an hour or two on the Internet doing what many other military spouses did at that same moment—learn something about a far-off place they had thought little about before the potential arose for their loved ones to die there.

Surfing the Web, Peter soon learned that conflict had consumed South America for decades and the potential for full-scale war had been building for years. Mostly because of American efforts, infant mortality rates decreased as the life expectancy rates increased. Unfortunately, local cultures—largely driven by a history of high infant mortality rates—did not temper their encouragement for women to have many children. Attempts to impose family planning failed miserably because they conflicted with religious beliefs. The birth rate was over four children per woman, and overpopulation in the region was inevitable.

The increase in population crushed the already suffering South American economy. Division between the wealthy and the poor grew, with the number in poverty becoming greater and greater as the rich settled into small, elite groups. Rural areas were not able to support the increase in population, and people migrated to cities in a hopeless search for jobs. The cities offered no relief, serving only as a simmering pot of friction. Those coming from rural areas possessed few technical skills. There were few opportunities; the need for manual labor was low but the numbers looking for work was high, which meant that wages for unskilled laborers were pitiful. Parents sent their children to work in hopes of making enough money to feed the family, but Western countries refused to purchase products made with child labor. Riots and unrest became common in the cities, and the governments' leading elite became more and more brutal in response.

Brutality of the governments turned people to the insurgency groups that had operated in the region for decades. These groups had floundered for years with little support after the fall of communism, but under these new conditions, they had started to gain popularity with the poor. Governments lost more control and directed more violence at their own citizens, creating more insurgents who fought only because they had little else to do. From the suppressed underclass, men and women who had little to no future took guns in hand to murder and to plunder that which they had no other hope of possessing. A warrior class was created. This class did not associate itself with any organized army, nor did it take on the appearance of soldiers. Instead, the warriors wore civilian clothes and relied on banditry to feed their families by stealing from the upper class. Ironically, when they didn't steal, they were paid gunmen hired to protect businesses from theft.

The warriors formed erratic groups of shifting alliances with no stake in civil order. Chaos became profitable for the warrior. Many young boys idolized the warriors from their communities, and they too joined in the anarchy when they became old enough to hold a machete or gun. Violence became their culture.

Expediting the chaos were border disputes and ethnic differences in South America that went all the way back to the times of colonial Europe. Brazil was mostly Caucasian and Roman Catholic, and the official language was Portuguese. Guyana's majority was East Indian, Hindu, and spoke English. The people of French Guinea were Mulatto, Catholic, and spoke French. Suriname's population was a mix of East Indian and Creole, with a religious mix of Hindu and Muslim, and the language was Dutch. Venezuela's majority was Mestizo, Catholic, and spoke Spanish. Ecuador and Peru had similar people, but their conflict over a shared border grew into a long, drawn-out war.

Complicating the situation, the Amazon's Yanomamo Indians began to wage an insurgency to create an independent country. A fiercely independent, warlike people, the Yanomamos were mixed within the borders of these South American countries and had no sustained contact with outsiders before the late 1940s. Sixty years later, their existence was threatened by disease and environmental damage caused by an influx of thousands of gold prospectors into their territory in the late 1980s. Conflict between the wealthy and the poor grew and Brazil came closer and closer to civil war.

The instability that consumed the region provided the Colombian drug cartels with a unique opportunity. The drug cartels always had been organizations that were linked to the people, especially the poor, employing entire villages and contributing money for the creation of schools, hospitals, and other community programs. The drug trade developed from a small cottage industry in the sixties into a multi-billion-dollar enterprise by the year 2000. In just one year, three of the leading coca-leaf-producing nations yielded five hundred tons of pure cocaine. At fifteen thousand dollars for a kilo at one-third purity, the cartels made tens of billions of dollars from cocaine alone. This shadow economy sucked money from legitimate businesses and was not taxed so it threatened fledgling democracies in the region. Drug cartels had their own distribution network and armies of narco-guerrillas, many better armed and equipped than the local military barracks. Drug lords gained power with their vast profits, killing or buying politicians, judges, police, and military officers. Shipment seizures seemed to become bigger and bigger, but the price of cocaine in the United States was not affected. There were so many drugs pouring into the country that supply never seemed to become too low for the demand, even with the demand growing and growing each year. But during Operation Enduring Freedom, because of links between drugs and terrorism, the cartels came under increased pressure from South and Central American governments, as well as the United States. The cartels' ability to operate freely deteriorated as America's war on drugs and terrorism began to become more intense.

To protect their organizations, the drug cartels banded together and organized the warrior class. They formed their warriors into what the U.S. military called a "criminal enterprise army." Criminal enterprise armies had been used before to place thugs in power in places like Africa and the Balkan states. The drug cartels' army grew to be better led, trained, and equipped than the military forces of South American governments. Estimates put their number as high as a hundred thousand gunmen, and they brought in up to one million dollars a day to finance their activities. Throughout the 1990s, only a fraction of the money spent on places like Iraq, Somalia, Haiti, or the former Yugoslavia was spent on battling illegal drug exports to the United States. As politicians and pundits warned of threats from weapons of mass destruction being used by a foreign enemy, drug dealers released a chemical attack on the streets of the United States. Not until the early twenty-first century did the war against drugs finally get the attention it needed. Since so many terrorism networks financed their violence with drug money, fighting drugs became linked to revenge for the September 11 terrorist attacks. Only then was headway made.

With Operation Enduring Freedom, the United States became directly involved in fighting the drug cartels' terrorist army. Millions of dollars poured in for operations intended to destroy drug production and drug transportation systems. U.S. military forces began conducting operations to locate and destroy drug infrastructures. Before, the U.S. military was hampered by being required to work alongside the corrupt law enforcement and military organizations of local countries, but now South American governments were pressured into allowing U.S. forces to operate independently. *You're either with us or against us!*

The war was fought like a war, and the object of raids became the death and destruction of the enemy, not apprehension for criminal prosecution. With the criminal justice systems removed from the equation, the drug cartels were not able to manipulate the situation with bribes and violence directed at judges, prosecutors, and jurors. Under this pressure, the powerful drug lords identified the need for a government that would refuse to deal with the United States. Unable to persuade and bribe any of the governments into opposing the Americans, the cartels decided that they needed a government of their own. Capitalizing on the instability in Brazil's Amazon River region, the drug cartels threw their support behind the Yanomamo insurgency movement and gained control of a large, rural portion the Amazon rain forest, or selvas, and tried to create the country of San Selva. Roughly the same size as the state of Texas, the disputed San Selva region covered seven hundred thousand square miles of South America, and the selection of territory turned out to be ingenious. San Selvan rebels occupied land from Colombia, Venezuela, French Guiana, Suriname, and Guyana, as well as a large portion of Northern Brazil—mostly from Brazil's youngest states of Rorasima and Amapa. Rorasima and Amapa were only territories until 1991, making them prime candidates for breaking away from Brazil. The thousands of miles of rain forest were impossible for the governments to monitor, let alone control.

All the countries that lost land to San Selva had long-standing conflicts and border disputes. Any alliance was precarious. In fact, the countries in the region reacted to each other more than to the San Selvan rebels. As one massed troops and threatened to attack San Selva, another saw it as a threat to their own security and threatened to attack any forces near their borders. More important, any attack into San Selvan–controlled territory was logistically demanding. The area was strategically well positioned, naturally bordered with the Serra de Tumucumaque mountain range to the north and the Amazon River to the south. Brazil launched the largest and most brutal fight. Called the Rain Forest War, the fight dragged on for several bloody years. With the combat destroying its own military, Brazil finally stopped its offensive, but it never admitted defeat.

Other countries tried to take up where Brazil

stopped, but attacks into the new country of San Selva were always repelled with an exceptional level of brutality and savagery. Whenever a foreign army stood on San Selvan ground, San Selvan terrorists attacked civilian targets in the other countries' capitals and major cities. Office buildings were bombed. Tourists kidnapped and dismembered. Snipers shot children on their way to school. It was a new form of warfare, one focused on killing civilians and avoiding military targets, and it worked—San Selvan rebels still controlled most of the Amazon rain forest.

Although internationally unaccepted, the San Selvan government was popular with its new citizens. They offered education, food subsidies, medical benefits, and good jobs to all citizens. New schools and hospitals popped up in every town. The San Selvans even published a schedule for free elections and created a constitution. Ninety-one percent of the San Selvan population voted in the first national election. (That was twice the number of the last American one.) Poor people from neighboring countries continued to execute a mass immigration to San Selva. It seemed for many to be the bright future for South America.

The U.S. government opposed an independent San Selva, but years ago there was little support for intervention from American citizens, especially with the ugly issue of numerous human rights violations conducted by the other countries in the region. In addition, sympathy for the plight of the Yanomamos, driven by Americans' guilt about their own county's history with its Native Americans, played on the nation's conscience. Many also did not differentiate between the independence movements that the American government had supported: Kosovo, East Timor, and Tibet. To most people San Selva appeared to be a new democracy in a region of oppressive dictatorships.

The United States was also unable to gain popular support in the international community. The United Nations, basking in the light of a limited peacekeeping success in Africa, did not want a repeat of the nineties. Budding peacekeeping operations in other South American countries showed promise. The U.N. wasn't willing to assume more risk by jumping right into a mess in the Amazon Basin. Most European countries were standoffish as well, still trying to distance themselves from their colonial histories. Only members of the weak Organization of American States (OAS) were willing to attend summits to discuss what the United States called a "crisis."

Mostly an instrument that the United States used during the Cold War to protect Latin America from the threat of communism, the OAS accomplished little, only presenting the illusion of a unified opposition to San Selva. The only action taken by the OAS was an embargo, but since the country's economy was based on the distribution of illegal drugs, economic sanctions had little effect. In fact, they helped the drug-cartel-backed government by preventing other forms of commerce or industry from having a fair chance to succeed. The San Selvan government gained public support by providing support to those who were suffering because of the sanctions.

Television commercials had been aired in Western countries by "volunteer" organizations that were secretly financed by the drug cartels. These commercials showed hungry, homeless children suffering from the economic sanctions. Although very little money was raised with these commercials, they planted the propaganda seed.

Today only a handful of rogue governments recognized San Selva's sovereignty. Its economy, although based on illegal drugs and under economic sanctions, was the strongest in South America, and it grew stronger and stronger every day, increasing the power and political clout that San Selva's government could wield. However, as the drug lords became richer and richer, they kept the majority of the populace satisfied by ensuring a standard of living that at least guarantees more than enough food for everyone. So much food, in fact, that farmers were better off growing products for the drug cartels.

But even with the money from the drug industry, most of the San Selvan people continued to live by primitive standards. Farmers grew cocoa and poppies, which they sold at nearby public markets. The markets flourished and local economies bloomed, creating many urban centers that provided jobs at drug-production factories. Most people defined happiness as a piece of land to call their own, so they set fire to rain forests every spring to clear land for more houses and cities. The burning was a wasteful practice because much of the land became denuded and unproductive for farming, forcing farmers to clear even more rain forest. This deforestation was a technique that had been used for generations, with over 25,000 square miles of Amazon rain forest per year destroyed during the worst period. Countless animals and plants, many valuable to medicine, vanished even before they were identified. Without vegetation, the hillsides were susceptible to mud slides and other erosion, destroying many communities and creating the need to deforest more rain forests.

Seasonal rains normally extinguished the fires set each year in San Selva, but this year's drought led to the fires growing out of control. That was bad. The rain forest destruction altered the earth's climate because the burning released pollutants into the environment and destroyed trees that helped control the level of carbon dioxide in the atmosphere. San Selva's burning was a threat to neighboring countries' very existence. Residents of Sao Paulo, Santiago, and Bogota were breathing some of the world's dirtiest air. Hurricanes smashed into Central and South American countries, growing more and more violent each year. Border clashes between nations were brutal and tensions in the region rose daily.

The South American situation was different from anything seen before. With global warming affecting the everyday life of the average American, the war drums began beating. Annual burning of rain forest was usually a mere nuisance, a ninth-page story in the newspaper, but this year the fires raged out of control and the huge plumes of smoke were visible even from southern states. The news media sensationalized the story, driven by news directors' personal beliefs about the horrors of global warming and a lack of real news stories. The American public was barraged with information about how global warming hurt economic opportunities. Americans wanted something done to curb global warming, but they balked at suggestions that they trade in their gas-guzzling sport utility vehicles for more environmentally friendly automobiles.

Americans instead became outraged as the economy continued to suffer from weather-related disasters. Politicians were bombarded with e-mails and phone calls from angry constituents calling for action. As the average American saw his or her standard of living degrade, global warming suddenly became a hot political issue. Ecological stability and economic prosperity became linked in the minds of Americans. Most wanted the Global Warming Treaty enforced, although few understood what the treaty said.

The Global Warming Treaty defined limits on the acceptable amount of pollution countries could disperse into the atmosphere, but it set standards for all countries, failing to take into account that most past damage had been caused by the wealthiest nations. The treaty also failed to provide alternatives to poor countries that still relied heavily on wood as fuel. At first, some of the poorer nations refused to sign the treaty, only to be pressured into signing through economic sanctions and an end of aid and support from the United Nations, United States, Britain, and other powerful nations. Now almost all had signed but they adhered to the treaty in varying degrees of compliance.

Peter could see the storm sitting on the horizon. He'd become cynical over the years. The worldwide recession had created public support for military action against San Selva. With the American people and the world's countries concerned about increasingly violent weather patterns, the U.S. government had an opportunity. Both global warming and the illegal drug trade could be ebbed by attacking San Selva.

Chapter Six

Columbus, Georgia

It was the perfect plan. The two Rangers entered the main terminal of the Columbus Airport and beamed with pride. This wasn't their first trip to the airport. Both had flown in here when they were young Army recruits headed to basic training. Six months later they had returned to the airport as U.S. Army Rangers—the premier light infantrymen in the U.S. Army. Now they were two of America's hardest warriors, specially trained and tempered in a grueling Ranger School course at nearby Fort Benning, Georgia. Graduates of the course filled the ranks of the Seventy-fifth Ranger Regiment. The regiment was made up of two thousand men divided into three battalions: First Battalion at Hunter Army Airfield, Georgia; Second Battalion at Fort Lewis, Washington; and the Third

Battalion at Fort Benning, Georgia. Each battalion numbered just under six hundred men, with no women allowed in the units because of their likelihood of being quickly employed in combat. A typical Ranger mission might involve seizing airfields for follow-on use by more conventional forces or conducting raids on key targets of strategic importance.

The Rangers' new tan berets (they wore black berets for decades before the Army made it standard issue for all soldiers) were respected throughout the world, and most of the men in the battalion wore the coveted Ranger tab earned during the fifty-six-day Ranger School. Expertly trained in small-unit operations in mountain, swamp, and forest environments while experiencing sleep and food deprivation, Rangers were one of the country's oldest units. They first formed in 1758 under the name "Robert Rogers Rangers," and the colonial force performed risky raids deep within British-controlled territory. They'd taken the cliffs that dominated the beaches of Normandy on D day and perfected the art of long-range patrols in Vietnam. Rangers held the perimeter of Desert Two, a not well known helicopter landing zone in the hills of Iran that was to be used in the 1979 attempt to rescue American hostages. They battled in the streets of Mogadishu during the most intense firefight the U.S. military had been in in over twenty-five years. And they were some of the first infantry forces on the ground in Afghanistan during Operation Enduring Freedom.

"Should we check on his flight?" asked Scott Deforeno. Called "Def" by his buddies, he was twenty-two years old and already had had three years in the Army.

"Hell no!" answered Mario Jackson, looking quicky for an indication of where to find the nearest bar. "Why waste valuable drinking time? We have three hours until his flight comes in, anyway. Info probably isn't even posted yet. We'll check later."

"It's this way." Def turned and walked in the direction of the airport watering hole.

Def's first trip to this airport had started in a fast food restaurant in Trenton, New Jersey. A stocky kid who exaggerated a *ya'no* accent to near perfection, he was barely out of high school with no intention of going to college and looking for adventure when he walked into the recruiting office.

"What do you want to do?" asked the Army recruiter.

"The toughest thing you can find for me."

The recruiter smiled.

At first, Deforeno was terrified that the Army would learn that he had been medicated for attention deficient hyperactivity disorder (ADHD) as an adolescent, and then he worried about problems he might have when he stopped taking his meds. He'd bounced from doses of one drug to another throughout his youth. The different drug combinations were an attempt to change Def's behavior, but nothing seemed to work. What was surprising was that when he stopped taking the medication and began basic training he felt better than he had in years. All of the physical training and mental stimulation calmed him. And as long as he studied hard and never let the fact that he had "learning disorders" prevent him from believing that he could learn, Deforeno had no difficulty in mastering the academic requirements of his training.

Now, as a Ranger, Deforeno occasionally regretted his cocky comment to the Army recruiter, because the recruiter had definitely found the toughest thing for

Deforeno. Baking in the hot southern sun or freezing in the northern snow—life as a Ranger was tough. Deforeno hated the exercises to Korea the most. He'd already been on two. Sitting in a cramped Air Force jet for the fifteen-hour flight to parachute into Korea and conduct forty-eight hours of constant operations. He couldn't imagine anything tougher.

The noise of the airport faded as the two men entered the confines of the bar. A sports game ran on televisions behind the bar and in corners of the room. Several men in suits with loosened ties sipped on drinks and blankly stared at the television screens, but that was not what Scott and Mario really hoped for.

"Where are all the stewardesses?" asked Def. He sat down on a bar stool and motioned for the bartender.

"It's still early. Don't worry." Mario took the seat next to Def and nervously drummed his hands on the bar. "Trust me."

Def could only shake his head and laugh.

"What can I get for you?" asked the bartender.

"Two beers," said Mario. "One Bud and one Sam Adams."

"Y'all got your IDs with you?"

"Yeah." The two soldiers painfully produced their military identification cards. It never failed. They always got carded in a bar. The bartender picked both of the green plastic cards up from the bar and closely looked at the pictures.

"Do you have driver's licenses too?" asked the bartender, lifting an eyebrow. The two men were obviously soldiers and they looked damn young—too young to be of drinking age.

Mario and Def dropped two more plastic cards on

73

the bar and coldly stared at the bartender as he reviewed them. He didn't look much older than they did, they thought. Just fatter and with more hair.

"Bud and Sam Adams coming up." The bartender dropped the four identification cards on the bar and grabbed two chilled glasses, which he quickly filled with draft beer.

"I told you they wouldn't be hanging out in here," teased Def.

"I told you, man, it's still early."

As the bartender placed the beers in front of the Rangers, a voice behind them said, "Let me get that."

Def turned to look at the man who stood behind him. Fiftyish and dressed in a conservative blue suit, the man, Def noted, still had his tie tightly knotted. There was no slacking off like the other businessmen in the bar.

"You don't have to do that, sir," said Mario.

"Yes, I do." The man smiled and dropped a twenty on the bar.

Turning to face the man, Mario stood and offered his hand. "Thanks, sir."

"Hooaah," answered the man, still smiling as he shook Mario's hand. "John Stevens, Ranger class of ninety-one."

"Hooaah, sir. I'm Specialist Mario Jackson. This is Specialist Scott Deforeno," motioning to Def.

"Def, sir. My buddies call me Def." Scott shook the man's hand. Firm grip and a look of strength in his eyes. Def could tell that the man still had plenty of Ranger pride pumping through his veins. "I'm sorry that Mario here insists on drinking that expensive New England stuff. I've been trying to turn him on to the beauty of macro beers." Def lifted his glass. "But he's too much of a beer snob." He took a large gulp from his glass.

"Price is no problem, guys. Just quit calling me sir. My buddies call me John." He gave Def a playful wink. "And I would rather not hear what year you two graduated from Ranger School. It'll just make me feel damn old."

"Who were you with?" asked Mario.

"Company B, Third Battalion."

"You got to be shitting me." Def laughed. "Mario and I are both machine gunners in Bravo Company."

"Is that a fact? Wow." John's eyes drifted down to the bar. He stared for a long moment, then said: "Yeah, I was with them ninety-one to ninety-four."

Def's and Mario's faces lost their smiles. Def decided to break the silence: "Were you with them in Somalia?"

"Yes." John nodded while looking down at the bar. He lifted his head and locked eyes with Def for a moment. Then John looked back down at the bar and drank a gulp from his glass. "You know, I rarely ever fly through this airport. I can't believe I bump into two machine gunners from my old unit here like this. Wild."

"Yes, sir," said Mario, "and I think we should be buying you the beer."

"Not until that twenty is gone. Then you'll get your chance. Headed out somewhere?"

"Here? Now?"

"Yeah."

"No, sir. We're here to pick up a buddy coming in off leave. The battalion canceled all leave and raised the alert level. We gotta be ready to deploy to San Selva fast," said Mario. He didn't know that the Arrowhead Brigade was already loaded in aircraft, but he'd heard rumors that the staffs from the Third Battalion, Seventy-fifth Ranger Regiment and five battalions from the Eighty-second Airborne Division planned for a possible invasion of San Selva.

"San Selva?" asked John, trying to remember where it was located. "They might be sending you to San Selva?" He placed his empty glass on the bar and signaled to the bartender that he wanted another round. "Why the hell would we send anyone to San Selva?"

"I don't know. Something about global warming. It just looks like that's what is going to happen," answered Def. "Our friend's leave is canceled so he's coming back early."

"Yeah, but we're making the best of it." Mario's smile was so wide that it seemed his teeth were about to fall out of his mouth. "We come to pick up our buddy a few hours early so we can get smashed and make our buddy drive us back."

"But part of the plan was to pick up *stewardesses* here in the bar," joked Def.

"*Stewardesses?*" John bellowed a laugh that rippled from deep in his belly. "The last place you're going to find a stewardess is in an airport bar, men."

Mario shrugged his shoulders and laughed at himself. "Well, it was almost the perfect plan."

Over the next few hours the three men traded stories, with the conversation deteriorating into the all so common "one better" taking over. As one finished a tale, another man added a similar story intended to be slightly better than the last. Sort of like the fables that fishermen told of the big one they caught, the Rangers tried to outdo one another with humorous anecdotes. The conversation and the laughs became louder and louder, as the subject of the conversation bounced around like a playground ball.

Def and Mario silently noted to themselves that John deliberately avoided talking about his time in Somalia. The two younger Rangers didn't push for information, but they knew the story well. On October

3, 1993, members of Company B, Third Ranger Battalion loaded onto helicopters at the Mogadishu Airport and lifted into the sky on a mission to capture Somali warlords. It was supposed to take an hour, but the soldiers were ambushed and pinned down during a brutal night of fighting in the hostile city. They became locked in a desperate struggle of kill or be killed. The next day eighteen Americans were dead and almost one hundred wounded; over five hundred Somalis were killed with at least one thousand injured. The Somali warriors were not just adults and teenagers, but also young children and women who joined in the savage attack against the besieged Rangers. It had been a night of hell.

"Boy, is my wife going to be pissed when I get off that plane." John looked at his watch and shook his head, smiling as he said, "Oh well." He stood and offered his hand. "Mario, Def, it was good to meet you. Good luck to you both."

"Thanks, John."

They all shook hands and John collected up his jacket and bag. Just before he exited the bar he stopped and turned around and walked back to the table. After a long pause he spoke. "I'm going to say a prayer that you don't go to San Selva," he said in a painfully serious tone. "But if you do . . . if you do you're going to be scared shitless the first few minutes after the shooting starts. Then you're going to get mad that anyone would have the balls to shoot at you. Whatever happens next depends on the people you're with. Be careful, because whatever happens stays with you forever." He smiled awkwardly, turned, and exited the bar.

Mario and Def finished their beers in silence. Both felt the affects of the alcohol. They rushed to the AR-RIVALS screen and then to the security checkpoint in front of their friend's gate, getting there just before he stepped off the plane. All three of them immediately recognized that they had a problem. Everyone was drunk. No one could drive back to the base.

"Coffee?" asked Mario sheepishly.

"So much for your perfect plan," gibed Def.

Belem, Brazil

Captain Ray Summer stepped from the large aft door of the huge C-5B transport plane and squinted painfully. It had taken over twenty-four hours for the brigade to receive their execute order so the C-5B's twenty-eight tires could start to roll down the long runway in Washington.

Summer focused his vision on the gray of the city's skyline, surprised by the lack of visible vegetation. He had expected a jungle but not an urban jungle like this. Smog sat over the buildings, and the loud commotion from traffic in the nearby streets mixed with the hum of the airport. He could envision the merchants, scamsters, and ladies of the night who always seemed to collect outside the gates of military installations. Ray already had an uneasy feeling about the layout. *Opsec—operational security—is going to be a challenge.* Civilians from the nearby towns and villages already protested outside the main gate to show solidarity with San Selva. The noise was menacing, and Summer worried if he and his soldiers were safe from terrorists in this location.

Reaching into his load-bearing vest, Summer grabbed his aviator-style sunglasses. The sun was extremely bright down here and the malaria medication magnified its effects. Back in Washington the weather was unseasonably hot, but nothing like the near ninety degrees and high humidity Ray experienced here in

Brazil. *Is it always this hot or is this global warming at its best? And the damn humidity.* But it was global warming. Warmer air meant more water in the air, and that disrupted the earth's hydrologic cycle—the continual cycle of water from the ocean to the atmosphere to the land and, after several delays, back to the ocean again. Nearly every enterprise undertaken by humans on the surface of the earth modified the hydrologic cycle in some way. Over the centuries vast amounts of land were converted from forest to fields and pasture. Some savannas were produced when the original forest was cleared for farming. Overgrazing changed many landscapes from steppes to deserts. The introduction of nonnative grasses and plants caused more damage, with many areas finding forests that burned down never to be replaced by anything other than the nonnative, more dominate vegetation.

By cutting forests, plowing land, draining swamps, building reservoirs, and creating urban complexes people greatly altered the exchange of moisture between land and atmosphere. Desalinizing salt water to create additional fresh water also affected the cycle, as did digging deeper wells to tap aquifers in which water had entered into almost permanent storage. These changes modified the precipitation phase of the hydrologic cycle, making weather more extreme and less predictable.

Now Summer felt the consequences of those changes, an added frustration after the trip to Brazil had been a long game of hurry up and wait for him and his soldiers. The word on when they would be cleared to leave kept changing. Finally, the agreement was worked out with the Brazilian government and now Summer and his soldiers walked on South American soil. He and the several hundred soldiers getting off the C-5s were the first from the Arrowhead Brigade to fly into Belem. The city was planted on the northeastern coast of Brazil, less than two hundred miles from the border with San Selva. Its airport was the closest one to the border that could handle the huge C-5s.

Ray's battalion and another from the brigade would stay in Belem, while the third battalion moved by road to the city of Gurapa on the San Selva and Brazil border. In Gurapa the battalion would threaten the San Selvan border, and also provide security at an expeditionary airfield for helicopters and turboprop C-130s capable of landing on the small dirt runway.

The Arrowhead Brigade made up the bulk of the Army forces that would be forward deployed for Operation Greenhouse. The border areas of Colombia, Venezuela, Guyana, Suriname, and French Guiana did not have the infrastructure needed for the introduction of a large military force. The rough mountain roads also made travel dangerous and costly. Logistical support would be nearly impossible, and a broken-down vehicle could block a narrow mountain road for hours. Even more restricting, the mountain roads passed over hundreds of bridges that might not support the weight of the Army vehicles.

Although tired from the trip, Summer's body buzzed with excitement. In a strange twist of fate and timing, this deployment was a first for Ray. Not only a first trip to South America, but also the first time he'd been deployed for a real-world contingency. While most of the military jumped from hot spot to hot spot, Summer somehow sat in the United States. He normally would have chalked up his experience, or lack of experience, to bad timing, but there was a tradition that he was living up to. A bit of a family joke, the Summer family seemed to sit out every war or military operation. The tradition had began back with his grandfather, who was too young to join the service during World War II, but was seriously hurt in an auto accident and ineligible for service during Korea. Ray's dad spent two years on Okinawa during the height of the Vietnam War, but never stepped foot in Vietnam or saw a day of combat. Ray's uncle experienced a similar fate when he missed the Gulf War because he was stationed at Fort Jackson serving as a company officer at Army boot camp.

In Ray Summer's case, he spent his days as a lieutenant with the Sixth Infantry Division (Light) at Fort Wainwright, Alaska. He joined his first battalion right after they returned from a deployment to Europe. As a motivated new Ranger School graduate and infantry officer, Summer had a zeal and desire to train his men to survive on the battlefield that was just what the unit needed to regain its combat skills lost during the prolonged peacekeeping operation. He did so well, in fact, that when one of the other battalions failed a readiness inspection, Ray was one of the first selected to move to the faltering battalion and help bring things back up to par. Being selected for the transfer was flattering, but it also prevented him from deploying on the next peacekeeping operation with his original battalion. Ray stayed at Fort Wainwright and watched his former battalion mount out for the trip overseas.

Now Ray worried that he was going to miss another operation. With elements of the brigade moving closer to the border, Ray could see his unit being used as rear area security around the Belem Airfield, which was not where he wanted to be. But he and the other officers would still do everything they could to ensure their soldiers were ready in case the order to attack came. Every free moment in the coming days and weeks would be dedicated to preparing for the move into San Selva. The Arrowhead Brigade had proved that they were ready to move. Now Summer hoped they would need to prove that they were ready to fight too.

Chapter Seven

USS Ronald Reagan, *North Atlantic Ocean*

"The situation back home is not looking good. There is serious concern that the economy might collapse. Time lines are being moved up. An Army brigade and Air Force special operations groups are moving into air bases along the disputed Brazilian and San Selvan border. The political situations in Colombia and Venezuela are too tense for those countries to allow us to station forces on their soil. The amphibs with the Marines are on the way, but they'll stay far away from the San Selvan coast until the mines and antiship missiles are cleared out. Countermine ships and the shallow-water mine teams are going to be busy in the coming days. Special operation forces are already operating along the coast and within San Selva's interior, but you won't hear much about their actions until all the books come out in a few years."

Navy Lieutenant Commander Sara "Crash" Linsey's ass already ached. She hadn't even strapped herself into her F/A-18E Super Hornet yet, and she'd already been sitting on her butt for far too long. It helped that the officer presenting the brief was charismatic and intelligent, but paying attention to the preflight brief became more and more difficult. Not helping matters, she worried about her family back home. Unable to e-mail Peter, she wrote and mailed a letter explaining what she could, which was not much, but it could take weeks for the letter to reach them. Everything might be done by then, especially with the rate this operation accelerated. Sara had never seen anything like this operation, but that seemed to be a common comment from everyone.

Linsey's journey to this point in her career had been long in the making. She had been selected for an NROTC scholarship during her final year in high school. Sara did well during college and always dreamed of one day becoming a fighter pilot. There were some problems at first in flight school at Pensacola, Florida, but she was determined to succeed. Hard work and long hours of studying allowed her to overcome her initial problems, and now, despite what her call sign might insinuate, she was considered to be one of the best F/A-18E pilots in her unit. Sara's call sign was not the most sought after for a military pilot, but it was not a result of her flying ability. The call sign "Crash" was the result of a cyber-accident, a time in flight school when Sara had crashed the computer server by trying to send a digital picture via e-mail.

The USS *Ronald Reagan*'s ready room overflowed with men and women dressed in flight suits. Every seat in the room was filled, with many standing along the walls and some even forced to stand in the passageway and listen through the open door. Commissioned in 2004 to replace the USS *Constellation* (CV-64), the *Reagan* was the Navy's newest aircraft carrier. It carried cutting-edge naval and weapons technology, but the CVN-76's power was in her aircraft. The aircraft carrier and its embarked carrier wing possessed more air combat ability than most countries, with ten F-14 Tomcats, thirty-four F/A-18E Super Hornets, four EA-6B Prowlers, four E2-C Hawkeyes, eight S-3B Vikings, and six SH-60 helicopters.

The F-14 was designed to attack and destroy enemy aircraft threatening the carrier battle group, but because of enemies like San Selva that had little to no air force, Tomcat pilots also learned to perform strike missions. F-14 Tomcats first demonstrated this capability in 1995 during Operation Deliberate Force in Bosnia, where they delivered smart bombs against targets that other aircraft designated with a laser. The Hawkeyes provided early warning and air control with their large radar disks atop the fuselage. The EA-6Bs provided electronic attack by jamming enemy radar and radio signals. The S-3B Vikings performed a number of tasks, such as aerial refueling.

The backbone of the USS *Ronald Reagan*'s combat power was in the two squadrons, one Marine and the other Navy, that flew the F/A-18E Super Hornet. Sara loved flying them. She was pleased when she learned at flight school that she would be flying an attack/fighter aircraft. It meant that she could roll in on bombing runs and also engage in dogfighting. Twenty-five percent larger than the older F/A-18s, the "E" version was a single seat maritime attack aircraft. The F/A-18F was a two-seat version, with the rear seat being filled by not a pilot but a weapons-system officer. The "wizzo," as he or she was called, had the task of coordinating strikes. There were no F/A-18Fs on the *Reagan* yet, but soon they would replace all of the aging F-14 Tomcats.

Escorting the *Reagan* were the cruiser *Anzio*, the destroyers *The Sullivans* and *Radford*, and the submarines *Hartford* and *Springfield*. They provided additional strike capability to the naval force because they could fire sophisticated missiles at targets hundreds of miles away. The fast combat support ship *Arctic* was along to keep the carrier battle group stocked with fuel, food, and other supplies.

"It's hard to say that San Selva even has a military," continued the intelligence officer. He turned to face the image projected on the screen. "What they do have is a nation where everyone owns a weapon. Most only have a pistol or two, but assault rifles are prevalent. Being a gunman is a profession in San Selva. Bandits and pirates travel in dilapidated trucks and boats to steal all that they can. There is no infrastructure or chain of command for us to destroy. The gunmen operate as groups of five to twelve men, all related by blood or having come from the same neighborhood. Occasionally groups work together under the control of a more influential and an often older leader, someone like an uncle or a father/father-in-law who is trusted by the others.

"Those with money hire these groups to create their own small armies to guard estates and businesses. Foreign investors learned the hard way that part of the cost of operating in the San Selva region is to pay for hired guns. Vehicles with machine guns mounted on them have been outlawed, with only the police allowed to possess them, but I don't know if I'd bet a paycheck on that. There's no telling what is left in the hands of the average civilian after the war for independence from Brazil.

"The city of Manaus was completely destroyed during the Rain Forest War." On the map, a red dot from a laser pointer slowly made circles on the map to point out the city's location. "Seven hundred and fifty miles down the Amazon River from the Atlantic Ocean and seven hundred and fifty miles from the Colombian border, Manaus is dead center of San Selva's southern border with Brazil. Brazilian soldiers first entered Manaus to quell the movement to cede from greater Brazil. Most of the buildings were destroyed or severely damaged during the months of fighting. In the largest offensive, four thousand detonations per hour from bombs, mortars, and artillery shells were counted impacting the city. Fuel-air explosives were used extensively, too. Tens of thousands were killed and hundreds of thousands displaced. There was little progress made by either side. The Brazilian military was depleted, both emotionally and physically. It had been bloody, *bloody* warfare. It was horrible. Ambushes hit from the sewers, ground level, and rooftops. The San Selvans used RPGs (rocket-propelled grenades) so much that they pretty much became the national weapon. They fired them at everything that moved. Snipers were also used effectively. Wounded soldiers were hung in the windows of rebel-held buildings, requiring the Brazilian soldiers to shoot at their buddies if they wanted to get to the rebels. Much of the rebels' equipment was stuff captured from the Brazilian army, so episodes of friendly fire casualties were frequent. Desertions from the Brazilian army were out of control. There were even some reports of soldiers selling their officers to the rebels. Although the Brazilians *controlled*, if you can even call it that, Manaus, they couldn't mount any productive offensive into the

Amazon rain forest. Then the San Selvans started their terrorist strikes in Brasilia, Rio de Janeiro, and other major cities. They blew up school buses, sniped at people on the way to work, and attacked a subway terminal with nerve gas. That was the nail in the coffin. Neighboring countries got involved for short periods of time when they realized that San Selva was taking some of their land too, but the results were the same as before.

"San Selva's Armed Forces grew from a rebel organization and it has never stepped far from its terrorist origin. General Moreno commands the police, army, navy, and air force. The distinction between police and military is a fine one, which is posing a difficult political problem. But don't kid yourself; the distinction is purely political, because the police are soldiers more than anything else. Within their cities they will have, depending on the city's size, one to several forts as they call them. Each fort contains jails, courts, and police headquarters. There are eight thousand police officers across the country, all trained and armed with a variety of small arms, mostly old M16s and a few AK-47s. Light machine guns and RPGs are also stored in each fort's armory. The army, navy, and air force only number about one thousand each. The army is made up of commando-type terrorists who rarely wear uniforms. They normally operate outside the borders of San Selva. They're the ones who've been blamed for conducting the bombings and shootings of civilians during past battles between San Selva and her neighbors. The navy has only a few small patrol-type boats and several antiship-missile systems, mostly the truck-mounted, Swedish-built RBS-15— max range of just over one hundred miles. The air force operates a few helicopters and small fixed-wing planes. The helicopters are normally located at the police forts in major cities, but they've been hidden throughout the country during the past few days. Most of the aircraft will be destroyed pretty easily, so the real threat from the air force is their very portable surface-to-air missiles. The San Selvans has hundreds of these things. Most are the older SA-7s and SA-14s, but they do have some of the more advanced SA-18s. All can be easily carried and operated by just one gunman. There are also a few French-built Roland II antiaircraft missile vehicles that were captured during the war for independence with Brazil. They give the San Selvans a medium-altitude antiaircraft capability.

"General Moreno is a former Colombian military officer with close ties to the drug lords. He's more loyal to the cartels than the San Selvan president. The president knows this, of course, and that dictates many of his actions and decisions. It's a very precarious relationship. General Moreno was trained in the United States twice through our active engagement programs with the Colombians. He trained for a year with the Marines at Quantico as a young officer, graduating from both the Basic School and Infantry Officer Course. Later in his career he attended the Army's School of the Americas, or . . . what are we calling it now?"

"Institute for Progressive Military Education Training," answered one of the U.S. Army officers who was from the Naval Expeditionary Force's staff.

"Okay, whatever. New name but same school that Panama's Manuel Noriega and Roberto d'Ambiusson, the El Salvadorian death squad leader, graduated from. It's the same one Martin Sheen is arrested in front of every year or two. Moreno being a graduate does not help us out at all. First because the media is going to rip us apart for that, but also because he knows much about us. Moreno is familiar with both

89

Marine Corps and Army doctrine. He's already doing things that will reduce the effectiveness of our bombs and missiles, not to mention the mines being placed along the coast and the antiaircraft defenses. Probably worst of all, this is the guy Americans are already putting on wanted posters. Pundits are stating that all we need to do is take this one bad guy out and the rest of the pieces will fall into place. I beg to differ. I'm not a betting man. No one ever calls me Mr. Vegas, but I'll wager that getting Moreno will do nothing for us. Any handshaking or treaty we have with the San Selvan president means nothing. He has only nominal control over the country.

"Overall the situation is scary. Many believe that air power will bring San Selva to their knees, but I think we're in for a rude awakening. I don't believe we'll find many worthwhile targets. Uniforms have been abandoned and the police forts are empty, with the police operating out of civilian homes. Avoiding urban areas is impossible, because anything of operational value is in or near a city. Ninety percent of the population lives within one hundred miles of the ocean. The urban sprawl runs the length of the coastline, with many of the civilians desalinizing their own sea water for cooking and drinking.

"Our first strike will occur with Tomahawk missiles launched from our ships in the Atlantic. Their targets are headquarters facilities, airfields, radar installations, and communication hubs. The San Selvans have learned well from our past adversaries' failures. They're making it hard for our analysts to identify worthy targets. Everything is spread out to the maximum extent possible. The situation on the ground is completely decentralized.

"Once the Tomahawks kick open the door, the stealth fighters and bombers will quickly be in to attack more difficult targets in urban areas, especially in Manaus and Macapa. Nobody wants a repeat of the Chinese embassy incident from the ninety-nine Yugoslav War, so we're sending planes instead of missiles. You know how it is; it's easier to blame you guys for a mistake than an intel weenie back in Washington."

"What about intel weenies here on the ship?" joked one pilot from the seats. The atmosphere in the room was tense but filled with bravado. In the past a dark haze of cigarette smoke might have hung over the ready room, but not anymore. Things had changed. There was little darkness—neither from cigarette smoke nor from attitude. The men and women flying tonight's missions knew they would be risking their lives, but the technological superiority of the U.S. military meant that it was unlikely that anyone would be shot down.

"That excludes intel weenies here on the ship," said the briefer, laughing. "If you hit the wrong target our butts will probably be in a sling too. They just need someone far from Washington to blame.

"Now, of course, the Air Force will have several Wild Weasel aircraft ready to hit any anti-airradar systems that light up during the Tomahawk attacks, but our own EA-6Bs will be in the air providing offensive electronic warfare attack and antiradar support. Most of your targets are along the borders with Brazil, Guyana, Surinam, and French Guiana. We'll be hitting our targets right after the stealth strike. All of you should know your primary and alternate targets by now, and if you compare them with each other you'll see a mix of military facilities and bridges. The party line concerning the bridges is that we are preventing San Selva from being able to cross into a neighboring country and conduct a ground attack, but don't kid yourselves, warriors. This coalition of South American countries is very tense. Border disputes have gone on for years, and they are not going to go away just because they have a common enemy in San Selva. There is serious concern that some of these countries could go to war with each other if things don't calm down soon. We're just as concerned with our OAS allies as we are with the San Selvans. We're destroying many of the bridges to prevent them from being able to easily enter into San Selva and seize land or commit atrocities. And if anyone cares to quote me on that you can plan on me calling you a liar, because I'm denying I ever said it."

A harsh reality for Linsey and her comrades: part of their mission was to keep the United States' "allies" from entering the war. As an experienced and knowledgeable warrior, Linsey knew that the modern world was complicated. It was important to the operation's credibility that regional nations were involved, but those nations could also discredit the operation. The United States fought under rules of engagements that dictated what level of force was acceptable in different situations. Most other nations did not use rules of engagement. And if they did, they were rarely as stringent as those of the United States were. For Linsey, this was nothing new. It was business as usual.

Sara was now an experienced Navy fighter pilot and this would not be her first combat flight. She flew missions over Yugoslavia to enforce the no-fly zone, Afghanistan during Operation Enduring Freedom, and Iraq during the second Gulf War. But that didn't negate the fact that she would be dropping bombs on real targets as people on the ground shot back at her. That was an experience no person in his or her right mind would ever get used to.

Worst of all, many of the pilots around her were not as well trained as their predecessors from conflicts past. As air combat tactics and gear had become more complex, opportunities to train rescinded. The term "training in combat" became the norm. For example, Sara only had experience with satellite-guided munitions during operations over Yugoslavia and Iraq, and the younger pilots flying with her tonight were about to have their first experience.

Being the senior officer in her flight, Sara would lead three lieutenants in their dangerous mission. Sara was getting close to being promoted to commander, and she also had more experience than the pilots she would be leading. Although well prepared, she was still nervous. She had spent a lot of time the past few days thinking of her family: Peter, the kids, and even her parents. Now they were at home, knowing that she might soon be in combat, but certainly not knowing how soon.

"The actual San Selvan air defense that you'll encounter is unclear," continued the briefer. "Like most of the San Selvan forces, their air defense is an ingenious mix of technological and primitive systems. Old-fashioned antiaircraft guns are everywhere, but the backbone of their air defense system is the shoulder-fired missiles. As I said earlier, the SA-18 Grouse missiles are the most advanced they have, but they may be modified versions. If so, they will have improved range and speed, making them capable of downing advanced aircraft up to fifteen thousand feet in elevation. Hard to electrooptically jam, the SA-18 hones in on its target by following an aircraft's heat source. If one locks on to you, hit countermeasures and chaff in accordance with squadron SOP and accelerate away from the incoming missile. Hitting afterburner will not help you get away, because the heat is going to draw the missile away from the chaff you just fired and into your ass.

"In smaller numbers, probably no more than half a dozen, are the Roland anti-air-missile vehicles. These weapons give San Selva a medium-altitude air defense weapon. Mounted on a light tank chassis, the Roland's dual missile launcher hits targets up to twenty thousand feet elevation. The weapons were initially captured from the Brazilian military during San Selva's fight for independence. They were originally designed to detect targets by radar, but the San Selvans have also modified them. We believe they can now make target identification with infrared sensors. This increases the survivability of the weapon system and its three-man crew. The Roland sees the target aircraft's heat, and then the crew turns on the radar for less than a minute so the missiles can be aimed at the target and then launched. With the missile's guidance system locked in on the target, the Roland's crew can shut off the radar and quickly move before a HARM (High-Speed Anti-Radiation Missile) fired from our Wild Weasels can impact.

"A couple of the Rolands have been detected by Special Forces teams on the ground, and they will be destroyed in the opening stages of this operation, but several are still unaccounted for. The San Selvans demonstrated exceptional camouflage and deception ability this week. They have effectively hidden weapons systems while offering dummy systems for satellites to find.

"Intelligence experts have concluded, or *guessed,* that the unaccounted-for Rolands are hidden by camouflage netting and under the jungle's canopy."

The briefer used a computer-generated picture to describe what a Roland site might be like. "The vehicle is well hidden under thick vegetation, but we can expect many large branches to be cut away so the missiles will have a relatively clear flight path to exit

94

the jungle's canopy and come fly toward yours—your aircraft's canopy, that is.

"The Roland systems are shut down, preventing our sensors from detecting a heat signature or electronic impulses. If they turn them on we'll kill them, and they know that. I doubt we'll see many of the Rolands light up their radar systems unless they are ready to fire. Instead, the San Selvans will make initial contact with civilian radar systems. We've asked to hit the civilian radar, but Washington has already said no. The civilian radar are essential for running the civilian airports, and many are even being protected by civilian *volunteers* who say they are using themselves as human shields. Its a tough political issue, and I doubt we're going to see authorization to destroy the civilian radar until some of our aircraft have been shot down."

The room stirred with side discussions concerning the limitations on targeting the civilian radar. Such rules were common in recent wars and battles, but that didn't mean the pilots became accepting of them. By integrating their air-defense system with the civilian radar, the San Selvans created a coordinated, multilayer defense that posed a touchy political problem. If American forces destroyed radar at civilian airports and airfields, they would likely face international scrutiny.

Destroying power plants to cut off power sources was another option, but it was an option that brought with it many consequences too. What would the loss of power do to the San Selvan public, and what would that do to the American and international opinion? Bottom line was that, at least for the near future, San Selva's civilian radar systems and power plants were off-limits to attack, which increased the effectiveness of the Rolands. Sara worried about them. She suspected antiaircraft guns and a few shoulder-launched missiles would defend her target, but she hoped they would not be valuable enough for the Rolands. Accomplishing her mission was going to be hard enough. Reports indicated that the smoke from San Selva's fires would interfere with laser designators, making it impossible for pilots to drop their smart bombs from high altitudes.

The smoke also obscured satellite images, making it more difficult to gain precise locations of targets for satellite-guided bombs. The situation developing looked like it would require low-altitude bomb runs, which made the pilots more vulnerable to antiaircraft fire. Of course, the bombs could have been dropped dumb—without a laser or satellite guidance—from high altitudes. It was the way in which most bombs during the world's wars had been dropped, but dropping dumb increased the possibility for the bomb to miss its target and strike a civilian structure. Too much collateral damage was not acceptable to the American people. Expectations that only those in uniform get hurt during war had tempered America's use of military power, and also increased the threat to members of the American Military. Insistence that bombs hit the antiaircraft missile site next to the hospital without any harm coming to the hospital meant that pilots had to fly lower and slower to ensure that they hit their target. That only increased the likelihood that an American plane would be shot down. Maybe the target wouldn't be attacked at all because of the threat to civilians. And the enemy knew this, which was why they put the antiaircraft missile next to the hospital in the first place.

"Okay, okay . . . at ease, people," said the briefer. "Let me finish this before y'all start your commentaries for tomorrow's newspapers. The Roland has a three-man crew that we expect has been augmented a few infantry soldiers for local security, so there is not a lot of activity to detect. They are probably linked to the outside world only by cellular phone, which will be hard to identify because of the large number of cellular phones used by civilians. By the time this area started to develop, it was easier and cheaper to install cellular systems than landlines, so the country has fewer of the traditional phones. By conducting a normal conversation that contains a few code words—words that are common in everyday speech but hold a special meaning for the Roland crew—the San Selvans will communicate with the anti-air-missile site without drawing attention to the conversation. In that conversation a person near the civilian radar will tell the Roland crew that one of you is in their airspace. The Rolands will try to acquire you with an infrared targeting system; they'll then turn on the radar and fire a missile or two before we can react. It'll be a tough act to counter, and before you ask, the answer is *no!* We cannot knock out the cellular phone network. At least not yet."

USS Oklahoma City, *North Atlantic Ocean*

Barret's and Hernandez's minisub cut through the brown water. Behind it followed another minisub commanded by Barret's assistant platoon commander, Lieutenant Junior Grade Markwell. This mission for the SEAL platoon didn't involve contact with an enemy. Today the team would conduct reconnaissance of the minefields along the San Selvan coast. The pace of doing back-to-back missions was painful, which was made even worse by a hard deadline that the SEALs had to return to the sub by. It was going to be a busy day for everyone on the USS *Oklahoma City*.

One SDV commanded by Lieutenant (jg) Markwell would go to one area of the minefield while Barret's and Hernadez's minisub went to another area. The minefield posed an ominous obstacle for the coming Navy and Marine Corps force. Minefields could begin as far out as the six-hundred-foot depth line, and antiship and anti-landing-craft mines could block the route to the shore. Antihelicopter mines might be mixed in to destroy low, slow-flying helicopters trying to clear the antiship mines. Coastal artillery and antiship weapon systems could also cover these minefields. Once within range of the weapon systems, ships would be extremely vulnerable because they would not be able to freely maneuver to escape incoming missiles or rockets.

Getting to the beach was only part of the problem, however; mines and obstacles in the surf and on the landing beach were harder to detect and clear. Modern mines were becoming more and more sophisticated and deadly, and they were now able to discriminate between different vessels to specifically pick a target. The most dangerous mines, or the proverbial "brick wall" for an amphibious assault, were those mines in shallow water (less than forty feet) and in the surf zone, where mines could be both tethered and buried in the sea floor. Identifying and avoiding the minefields wasn't always the best answer, because the enemy might have placed the minefield hoping for that result. The shore defenses could also be so well prepared that there were no gaps in the minefield leading to a suitable landing beach.

These facts made amphibious warfare potentially costly and very bloody. As one commander said during the 1991 war with Iraq: "World War One–era mines delivered by boats built with the same designs as the time of Christ can stop the most technologically advanced navy too far from the beach to matter." It was a hard lesson learned by the Navy Marine Corps team in the Persian Gulf. In one hour on February 18, 1991, the USS *Tripoli* (LPH-10) and USS *Princeton* (CG-59) were disabled by sea mines. The *Tripoli*, carrying almost three thousand Marines and sailors, was able to stay on station with a twenty-foot hole in her bow, but the Aegis cruiser *Princeton* almost sank and had to limp back to port.

San Selva's hastily created minefields already worried military planners. Areas near the mouth of the Amazon River and San Selvan ports were clear of the deadly obstacles, but the San Selvan navy blocked landing beaches needed for an amphibious assault. Clearing mines was always difficult, especially since it was so hard to clearly map the layout of the minefield. Satellites could be used to locate the minefields, but they revealed little detailed information. To dissect the layout of the minefield, sensors needed to be placed in positions to assess the minefield from a number of angles.

Barret's and Markwell's groups of SEALs assisted in that effort. Skirting the edges of the minefield in their minisub, the men would exit the craft to place hydrographic reconnaissance sensors in precise locations. Later today, after the SEALs would have been recovered aboard the *Oklahoma City*, an Unmanned Underwater Vehicle (UUV) would swim directly into the minefield. The UUV's reconnaissance ability was new to the U.S. Navy. The Advanced Research Projects Agency created them for the National Underwater Reconnaissance Office—NURO, which was a top-secret Navy-CIA organization created for underwater spying.

For several decades, submarines were used for reconnaissance and espionage missions, more commonly known as "Ivy Bell" operations during the Cold War. Submarines tapped underwater telephone lines, allowing American spies to listen in on conversations of Soviet, Libyan, and Chinese leaders for years. But now the submarines were capable of even more. Born in 1993, the unmanned underwater vehicle program allowed the *Oklahoma City* to send its "fish" into waters too dangerous even for the SEALs. The UUV could be launched and recovered from the submarine's torpedo tubes, and they used an AN/AQS-14 sonar system to scan the water for mines.

Computers would analyze the data collected by the satellites, SEAL-placed sensors, and UUV. The computers would then provide a clearer picture of the density and makeup of the minefield. Knowing more about the minefield would enable mine countermeasure ships to conduct an "in stride" breach of the obstacle to speed the landing of Marines if it became necessary; however, there was still a complex task of clearing those shallow-water mines that loomed over the force. To counter the noisy and chaotic environment encountered in the surf zone, another secret unit prepared for their mission later tonight. Code named "Nimo," the unit was centered on several three-hundred-and-fifty-pound dolphins—*friggin' Flipper on steroids!*

The U.S. Navy Marine Mammal Program began in 1959 at Marineland of the Pacific with a Navy scientist and a Pacific white-sided dolphin named Notty, and the marine mammals first operated in a combat environment during the Vietnam War. From the capabilities demonstrated in the first decade of the Navy's Marine Mammal Program, three marine mammals were enlisted in the naval service. Dolphins were used because of their exceptional biological sonar that is unmatched by hardware sonar in detecting objects in the water and on the ocean bottom. Sea lions have very sensitive underwater directional hearing and low-light-level vision. White beluga whales can dive as deep as one thousand feet to listen for sounds that an electronic device is incapable of detecting. All of these marine mammal species assist the Navy in the detection of enemy divers, swimmers, mines, and weapons.

The marine mammals were priceless tools for Operation Greenhouse. After the first Gulf War it was recognized that more needed to be done to counter mines. In the mid-1990s, the Navy and Marine Corps created a detachment made up of about one-third Navy Special Warfare sailors, one-third Marines, and one-third explosive ordinance disposal experts. The men mixed with the marine mammals in units called systems. There were five different types of systems. The Mk4 was a dolphin mine-searching system that detected and marked locations of mines moored off the ocean bottom. Mk5s were sea lion mine-recovery systems that located pinged mines. Dolphin swimmer- and diver-detection systems capable of detecting and marking the location of an intruder made up the Mk6 group. An Mk7 system was a beluga that detected and marked the location of objects deep on the ocean bottom. Finally, the Mk8 was a dolphin shallow-water mine-detection team that found mines in the noisy and hard-to-operate shallow water and surf area.

Chapter Eight

Somewhere in San Selva

The sun was still up far off in the western sky, but it had already started to get dark in the jungle. Soldiers began to pack up their gear and prepare for the coming challenges. The patrol leader stretched his arms over his head. There was something about sitting around all day that fatigued the body. Many of the men stretched and rubbed their arms and legs.

The radio operator packed up the small solar panel that he had for recharging the patrol's radio batteries. With the solar panel the patrol did not need to carry as many extra batteries, but it had taken all day to recharge the one battery that had already been drained. Being in the thick jungle as he was, there was no location where the radio operator could lay the solar panel in the direct sunlight. It still sucked in ultraviolet rays, just not as efficiently.

Just before dark the patrol leader gave the signal for radios to be turned on. He then waited until it had been dark for several minutes before he gave two *clicks* over the radio to signal that it was time to start moving. The point man rose and the cover man followed. They had had all day to check and recheck maps, and now every contour line the patrol would cross in the long trek was tattooed to the men's brains. The patrol leader and his radio operator went next. In the middle of the formation walked the "pack mules" that carried the heaviest gear. The soldiers tasked with protecting the flanks came next, and finally the rear security man and his cover man stood to bring up the rear.

The patrol moved awkwardly through the dark jungle. After spending the entire day moving as little as possible, the soldiers' bodies now ached. At least this would be the only time that the patrol would lie sedentary for an entire day. The patrol had a long night ahead of them, but tomorrow they might be able to draw some blood.

Jacksonville, North Carolina

Elizabeth Dunne walked through the garage door into her kitchen. Her actions had become nearly the same every day. Newman, a long haired black mutt, got a quick pet and a "hi, boy." Linus and Leisel, two overweight cats, also received a quick "hello" as Elizabeth rushed down the hallway to the spare bedroom she and her husband, Bert, used as a den. She sat down at the desk, turned on the computer, used the remote control to turn on the television, and picked up the phone to check her voice mail in a flurry of hands and fingers. As the computer ran through its start-up she called the phone-messaging center on the telephone. While she pressed buttons on the phone to review the telephone messages, she flicked the remote control, changing the television station from one news channel to the next.

This ritual of rushing home to check news, e-mail, and phone messages provided her only link to Bert. Unfortunately, the most desired link took the longest. By the time the computer finished its start-up she had reviewed the phone messages and hung up the phone, making the line clear for her to log on to the Internet to check e-mail. Bert, a Marine Corps lieutenant embarked on the amphibious assault ship USS *Beirut*, e-mailed every day. Since the messages came from the ship at sea, some days there were none and others there were many. The ship's e-mail servers used satellites to send the messages. It was not as efficient as communicating via e-mail with two computers attached to a direct phone line, however. There was often a delay, and sometimes messages simply disappeared into cyberspace.

"Good evening." The television anchorman's hands sat folded on the desk. His dark gray suit and tie had been carefully selected to match the occasion. Grim faced and speaking with a dramatically serious tone, the anchorman continued. "As negotiations between San Selva and the United Nations continue to falter, the U.S. military readies for war. Air Force aircraft at stateside bases have been viewed going through pre-flight checks and being fueled and it is becoming obvious that military action may begin as early as tonight."

The camera angle changed and the anchorman paused to turn slightly in his seat. Behind him a mock newsroom busied with people acting as if they were talking on the phone while others rushed in and out of the camera's view. Above the left shoulder of the anchorman, a brightly colored picture flashed the words: CRISIS IN SAN SELVA. The image was carefully designed by the news show's art department and then paraded in front of several focus groups who helped modify the image until it seemed to appeal the largest group of people.

"Military action will likely begin with the destruction of antiair-weapon systems by Tomahawk cruise missiles fired from U.S. Navy ships positioned in the North Atlantic and North Pacific Oceans. Following close behind the cruise missiles, aircraft launched from the aircraft carrier USS *Ronald Reagan* and land-based sorties from the Continental United States and airstrips in the region. This operation will be the first time that attack helicopters will participate in the first night of strikes. The aircraft will probably attack San Selvan headquarters and communication cells. . . ."

The log on to the Internet finally finished and Elizabeth turned her attention to her e-mail program. *Yes!* she thought. New mail. She'd been worried that Bert might be diverted to South America. He was five months into a standard six-month deployment, and Elizabeth wanted him home safe and on time. Hopefully the e-mail would tell her want she wanted to hear. But the mail was not what she expected. Instead of messages from Bert, she had a message from an unfamiliar address. A note from "Child Care."

Elizabeth opened the e-mail. She read the short note, but it didn't say anything that made sense. There was one digital picture as an attachment. Elizabeth clicked on the picture icon, only to be immediately disgusted by a picture of almost naked children suffering. In bright, clear color sat four children, all with burns across much of their bodies. Blood pooled on the ground in their vicinity and a charred countryside sat in the background. It looked like hell. Two of the children were lifeless. All seemed to have wounds that looked like a mangled mush of meat and blood. One child looked catatonic, only staring at the camera. The worst child held the most life in her broken little body. She was obviously burned over most of her body, with what remained of her clothing stuck to her skin, and her mouth was opened painfully in a cry. Across the top of the picture it said THE UNITED STATES MILITARY AT WORK IN SAN SELVA.

Elizabeth tried to close the file with tears streaming down her cheeks. Who was Child Care and why would they send such ghastly pictures to her? They were horrid! The file automatically switched the image of a map from one of the many people-search Internet sites. *A map to Elizabeth Dunne's house.* WE'RE COMING TO SEE YOU rolled across the screen. The computer then went crazy as the virus embedded in the e-mail burrowed itself into the computer's files and started forwarding the Child Care virus to everyone in Elizabeth's address file. The virus worked with blinding speed. Before she could rip the phone cord from the wall the message had been sent to over one hundred people.

Elizabeth frantically collected the dog and two cats and threw them into the car that she had just parked minutes before. She grabbed no change of clothes or personal belongings. The television and computer were still on when she hit the button for the automatic garage-door opener. She did not know where she was going. She just had to get out of the house.

* * *

The information about Elizabeth and Bert Dunne had been easy for the San Selvans to find. They knew that the USS *Beirut* might head to San Selva. It was not difficult to figure out. The U.S. Marine Corps Web page provided information about what units were embarked on the ship. A search of Web pages from periodicals like the *Marine Corps Times* and *Navy Times* for stories about those units offered quotes from Marines and sailors onboard—including a quote from Second Lieutenant Bert Dunne in an article about a training exercise. Learning that Dunne's unit was based at Camp Lejeune, North Carolina, the San Selvans did a quick search on the Internet for phone numbers, home addresses, and e-mail addresses for "Bert Dunne" in the cities surrounding the base, yielding a short list of people to whom the San Selvans sent e-mails.

Elizabeth was one of the first to receive it. The Child Care e-mail virus was headed to thousands of Americans across the country. Soldiers, sailors, airmen, and Marines' families would receive them. But tonight was only the first wave of psychological attacks. Tomorrow the phone calls would start.

U.S. Embassy, Manila, Republic of the Philippines

Another thunderstorm lit up the night sky, as Marine Sergeant Walter Malone gazed through the bulletproof glass at the lack of activity on the street. Few people would be out on a night like this. It was the kind of night that encouraged sleep and required a good cup of coffee to stay awake. Malone scanned the television screens that provided observation of the outside area, sipping occasionally from his warm mug of coffee.

Malone thought of embassy duty as good duty but

not as exciting as being in the operational forces. He completed one rather than the normal two deployments before applying for duty with the Marine Security Guard Battalion. A "float" with Third Battalion, First Marines to the Persian Gulf, he served as a mortar man during the six months on ship. Hurting to fill crucial billets, the Security Guard Battalion had quickly accepted Malone's request even though he was still rather new to the Corps. It used to be that a Marine needed over four years of service to be eligible for promotion to sergeant or to serve in an embassy, but with the pace of things nowadays, more junior military members were expected to do more and more. It was too hard to keep experienced people in the service.

Malone took another sip from his coffee mug and scanned the television screens again. It was hard to stay alert when nothing ever seemed to happen. Night after night Malone stared at television screens during his watch. Things that were out of the ordinary quickly gained his attention, like the flash that appeared on the television screen that monitored the front gate area. He thought about what it might be when a *whish* and a trail of smoke brought his head to face the bulletproof glass. The explosion of the rocket-propelled grenade shocked Malone into a surreal experience of confusion and pain. The force of the grenade slamming into the security post flipped Malone backward from his chair as a large shard of glass separated his left hand from the rest of his body.

Without thinking, Malone instinctively reached for the lock-down button on his console with his right hand. He needed to lift steel plates in front of the embassy gates and sound an alarm that warned other occupants. Failure to do so would leave the building vulnerable if a truck bomb was coming next. A volley of rocket-propelled grenades slammed into the embassy's security post and killed Malone as his arm hung in the air. He never knew whether or not his hand reached the button.

Similar attacks created explosions across the world: the Bank of America building in Hong Kong, a fast food restaurant in India, a USAID office in Africa, cafés in Europe that were popular with Americans. The attacks were small, but the effects would be huge. Sergeant Malone would be the only casualty in uniform. Government and military facilities had too much security. Civilian targets were easier to hit and civilian casualties would make for better headlines.

USS The Sullivans, *North Atlantic Ocean*

Seaman First Class Shauna Stout wiped the sweat from her brow yet again. Moisture collected on the edges of her blue denim uniform. The room temperature inside the ship's fire-control center hovered at a comfortable seventy degrees, but nervousness about the mission caused Stout's perspiration. Her shoulder-length black hair stuck to the back of her neck and face, itching and making the experience more frustrating than it normally was. As did the Navy chief occasionally leaning over her shoulder to check progress. Shauna didn't want to screw up her task. Her job was an important step in the ship's Tomahawk missile hitting its target. The USS *The Sullivans* (DDG-68), was a guided-missile AEGIS destroyer— the most capable and survivable surface combatant. It would fire the opening volley in Operation Greenhouse, but it and its crew might be in for more than they bargained for from the war.

Chapter Nine

F-117A Nighthawk, Venezuelan Airspace

Air Force Major Ken "Wig" Davelle of the Forty-ninth Fighter Wing continued to focus on the director's lights attached to the tanker's belly. The UP-DOWN elevation marker and the IN-OUT boom extension marker were both illuminated right in the center of the display, indicating that Wig's stealth fighter was properly positioned to plug with the KC-10 Extender and take on fuel.

A modified jumbo jet, the KC-10 provided fuel to attack aircraft like Wig's stealth fighter. The "tanker war" was not as glamorous as the bomber or fighter plane war, but it was almost as important. This one KC-10 would refuel dozens of strike aircraft tonight, and with its universal fuel nozzle, the Extender was capable of refueling all types of helicopters and fixed-wing aircraft in the American military. It created options for military planners. Wig had flown his F-117A two thousand miles from a New Mexican Air Force base to meet with the KC-10 so he could go on to drop bombs on San Selva. Without the tanker support, the F-117A would need to be forward-deployed to a base in South America, which would have created the need to also forward-deploy a maintenance team, as well as a security force to protect the aircraft and its crew and support personnel.

Inching forward, Wig kept all of his attention on the director's lights. It was instinctive for a pilot to turn his attention toward the fuel nozzle—to eyeball the insertion of the long black refueling probe into the nozzle. But that was the director's job. Somewhere in the KC-10 sat the director, a senior master sergeant who probably had more time in the Air Force than Wig and his F-117A combined. After a slight scrape of the probe on the nozzle's basket came the welcome sound of *ch-clunk!* The lights on the director's panel changed, indicating that Wig's jet was now locked in place and ready to take on fuel, and then, when fully fueled, to cross the border and strike his target in San Selva.

Wig was an extra attachment to the Eighth Expeditionary Aerospace Force, which was now the Air Force component of Combined Task Force San Selva. The Expeditionary Aerospace Force was the Air Force's answer to the demanding operational tempo of the twenty-first century. It was made up of one hundred and fifty fighters, bombers, tankers, radar, and electronic warfare aircraft. Specially designed to be lean and lethal, the Force was capable of quickly deploying to a crisis area to operate in environments ranging from military operations other than war to major-theater war.

111

Flying in a section of two F-117As, Wig had not communicated with his wingman. They would maintain radio silence until they dropped their bombs to reduce the likelihood that the San Selvans would detect them. The Nighthawk was practically invisible to radar systems, and the radio used a frequency-hopping capability that made it impossible to track without a broad-band directional scanner, something the San Selvans did not have, but keeping communications to a minimum was just the way to do a bombing mission. An old-fashioned procedure at work in the most advanced fighter the world had ever seen.

The unique design of the single-seat F-117A Nighthawk, known as the "Frisbee" or "Goblin," provided exceptional combat capabilities. The stealth fighter was designed for missions into highly defended target areas by using a material on its outer skin that absorbed radar energy. It was built by Lockheed Martin after the development of advanced stealth technology and a test aircraft, Have Blue, was created in 1975. The first F-117A was delivered in 1982, and it first saw combat action in 1989 during Operation Just Cause in Panama. The stealth fighter attacked the most heavily fortified targets during wars with Yugoslavia and Afghanistan, being the only jet allowed to strike targets inside Belgrade and Kabul's city limits. It could employ a variety of weapons and was equipped with sophisticated navigation and attack systems integrated into a state-of-the-art digital avionics suite.

Before taking off for tonight's flight, Wig transferred the mission data to an electronic data module that downloaded into the onboard computers. The F-117A's computers then took the mission information and integrated it with navigation and flight controls to provide a fully automated flight management system. The system was so advanced that the pilot could hand flight controls over to the mission program after takeoff. Wig then resumed control of the aircraft for refueling and the delivery of weapons.

Wig didn't want to admit that he felt cocky, but he did. He needed to. It went along with being an Air Force fighter pilot, especially one flying a stealth fighter. Wig had been on these missions before. He knew the San Selvans were going to get pounded. There was little chance of his being shot down, and even if it happen, or if the aircraft went down for mechanical reasons, Wig knew that the Combat Search and Rescue (CSAR) teams would come and get him. Tonight's "fight" hardly seemed fair.

USS Ronald Reagan, *North Atlantic Ocean*

Three hundred miles off the coast of San Selva, the aircraft carrier turned into the wind to commence flight operations. Escort ships altered their course too so they could continue to protect the precious carrier.

Navy Lieutenant Commander Sara "Crash" Linsey made a second, final check of her personal equipment. It was too late for her to do anything if she discovered something missing, but it helped her pass the short period of time. Another F/A-18E roared, engines spewing heat out the rear of the aircraft as the ship's catapult threw it from the flight deck.

Crash adjusted her oxygen mask and gave her nomex gloves a good tug. Her hands sweated because of the natural nervousness accompanying an act that could so quickly kill someone. The thrill and fear of taking off from a carrier, a rush topped only by landing: nothing replaced the feeling of landing forty thousand pounds of screaming metal onto a flight deck that seemed to be a speck in the ocean. Sara looked over her gauges. Next she checked the connection hose from her flight suit to the aircraft. Resembling a girdle, the olive-drab G-suit she was wearing had several bladders that could fill with air and prevent blood from pooling in extremities during flight. Normal earth gravity equals one g-force, but a wild roller coaster can score as high as three on the g-force scale. Jet fighter flying creates even more g-forces. Women are capable of enduring more g-force than men, but at five-gs man or woman is in jeopardy of unconsciousness. Blood will not get to the brain in adequate amounts without help from the g-suit.

On her head was a custom-fitted flight helmet. Its bright white, reflective surfaces hidden by a camouflage cover so she'd have better chance at survival if she had to eject. Crash's 9-mm pistol was strapped into a shoulder holster, with one magazine loaded in the weapon and a spare in her right-leg pocket with an evasion map. There was also a blood chit in the pocket. A blood chit was a note written in eleven languages promising that the U.S. government would provide a cash reward to anyone who helped a downed American pilot. Survival gear—like a raft, water, and food—was located in the F/A-18E's ejection seat. Over the g-suit was a vest that held more survival gear and a brand-new global-positioning radio. The new radio had been issued to her just before she departed the ready room. It was larger than her old radio, so the pocket strap didn't fit over it properly, which presented Crash with something else to worry about.

Finally it was her turn. Moving to the port bow catapult, one of the *Reagan*'s four catapults, Crash carefully followed the hand and arm signals of the flight deck crew. The men and women on the flight deck wore a myriad of different colored shirts. Yellows were the traffic cops. Greens hooked the aircraft to the catapult. Reds were always nearby in case there was a fire or an ammunition problem. Purple people—the "grapes"—pumped fuel. Brown was the one who strapped Sara into her seat and conducted final preparation. Blues brought aircraft up from the hangar deck to the flight deck via the elevator. And the white-shirted ones hovered about constantly checking over safety procedures of everyone else involved in the flight operations. Many of the sailors on the deck tonight were not yet twenty-one years old—not even trusted to legally drink a beer in the country they risked their lives to defend. But Crash's life and her F/A-18E were at the mercy of these young Americans. She had total trust in them.

With the slack removed from the launching mechanism, Crash's jet was ready: wings locked and flaps and slats set. A yellow-shirted member of the deck crew signaled the catapult officer ten feet farther up the flight deck. Engines were running on full afterburner. Hydraulics okay. Crash saluted the catapult officer with her right hand. Then she positioned it behind the aircraft's stick. She pushed her head into the seat's headrest.

The catapult officer lunged forward, touching the flight deck with his right hand. The shooter pressed a button and Sara was on her way. Valves opened to admit steam to the catapult, which released the holdback to force the piston forward and throw the three-hundred-foot-long catapult along the flight deck. The force accelerated the F/A-18E from zero to one hundred and fifty knots in two seconds, bringing the bow of the *Reagan* rushing toward her. Suddenly the hard flight deck of the *Reagan* disappeared, leaving only the dark water of the North Atlantic below the F/A-18E.

Accelerating and climbing away from the ship, Sara glanced quickly at the vertical display indicator, altimeter, and airspeed. She reached eighty feet and kept going up. Two hundred knots and increasing. No warning lights. Everything looked good. Still accelerating, Crash quickly checked her speed . . . three fifty . . . three-seventy-five . . . four hundred—altitude continuing to climb.

USS Oklahoma City, *Atlantic Ocean*

"Diving officer, make your depth eight zero feet," ordered Commander Bradford. "Fire control, how's it coming?"

"Firing solution entered, sir," answered the fire direction officer. Each of the missiles was now powered up, and the mission plans and flight data were downloaded and accepted.

"Ready tubes one through four," ordered the captain.

"Aye, sir," said the fire direction officer, then turning to a subordinate sitting at the command and control system. "Firing point procedures, ready tubes one through four."

The *Oklahoma City*'s vertical launch system held eight Tomahawk missiles. The submarine was capable of carrying all four of the Tomahawk versions: the TASM tactical antiship missile; the TLAM-N tactical land-attack missile, nuclear; the TLAM-C tactical land-attack, conventional; and the TLAM-D tactical land-attack missile, conventional but with bomblets. The missiles were loaded en route from Belize to San Selva when the *Oklahoma City* rendezvoused with a submarine tender that loaded the submarine with a full combat load of munitions. But the submarine currently carried only TLAM C and D variants, because there was no threat from San Selvan ships and there was no chance that a nuclear missile would be needed.

Firing missiles so close to land could let the San Selvans know where the submarine was off the coast of their country, but there were not enough ships available to launch the Tomahawks. Much of the U.S. Navy was already deployed to conflict-prone regions like the Persian Gulf, the Red Sea, and the Straits of Malacca. Those that were not already deployed were recovering from recent deployments, and even if the ships could have been prepared to participate in Operation Greenhouse, there really weren't the sailors available to crew the entire fleet.

"Tubes one through four ready, Captain."

"Very well, *fire*."

The fire-direction officer turned the LAUNCH key and pressed the FIRE button. On the outer hull of the *Oklahoma City*, a hydraulic hatch on the first vertical launch tube noisily opened. An explosive charge detonated and the first Tomahawk broke through the thin rubber membrane over the missile's canister. The missile rocketed through the ocean toward the sky. As it broached the water's surface under the power of the booster rocket, it made a violent turn that sent the missile from a vertical climb to a horizontal trajectory. The expended booster rocket fell away, and the missile increased speed to five hundred knots.

Three more explosions followed the first. With the final missile out of the vertical launcher and on its way to its target in San Selva, the tube filled with water to compensate for the weight of the missing missile before the exterior hatch closed. The launch of the four missiles took just under five minutes.

As the missiles rocketed away, Commander Bradford couldn't help but feel that they were being wasted. Even worse, there weren't many of these missiles available. The targets he'd been given for the missiles hardly seemed suitable for the expensive Tomahawks. He was mostly shooting at empty buildings. But there was not much more that could be targeted, because an enemy like the San Selvans did not have many targets large enough to be effectively attacked by missiles and bombs. Bradford worried that it would take a lot of ground troops to produce real results.

Chapter Ten

USS The Sullivans, *North Atlantic Ocean*

Seaman First Class Shauna Stout watched anxiously over the shoulder of Petty Officer Third Class Jimenez. The rows of sailors jerked their heads back and forth in hopes of gaining a view of the small television screen, unintentionally blocking the view of the sailors behind them. Shauna and her peers had grown up seeing videos from warhead cameras. Tonight they watched the show live, but Shauna was one of the more junior-ranked sailors fighting for a good vantage point, so she was stuck behind many of the others.

"Oh!" yelled a voice near the front.

"What happened?" shrieked Shauna.

Maj. James B. Woulfe, USMC

F-117A Nighthawk, San Selvan Airspace

Wig leveled off from his descent at five thousand feet. He had little fear that antiaircraft fire would hit his stealth fighter. The San Selvans had not yet detected the strike force. They had not begun to wildly fire their antiaircraft cannons. Attempting this stunt in an hour would be a much more difficult endeavor.

Deliberately unstable aerodynamically in order to have a high degree of maneuverability, the F-117A Nighthawk's onboard computers executed hundreds of small electrohydraulic adjustments each second to keep the aircraft flying smooth. In his heads-up display, Wig checked the altitude shown in the right-hand corner. Direction heading was at the bottom and the airspeed was portrayed in the left-hand corner. Everything looked okay. Now he just needed to find the target.

USS The Sullivans, North Atlantic Ocean

Seaman First Class Shauna Stout laughed and gave a friendly shove to the sailor next to her. "Well, what am I supposed to think when he yells like that? I thought the missile had hit its target."

"You can bet that all of us will *cheer* when the missile hits, Stout," said Petty Officer Jimenez.

"Okay, here comes the lights of the city now," said a voice to the front. The days of blacking out cities and countries to counter air strikes were long over. The Yugoslavs and Taliban learned early on in their wars with the United States that aircraft and smart bombs didn't use such things as navigation aids. Computerized mapping systems and position-guiding satellites now ensured that missiles like the Tomahawk hit their targets. The missile used radar to "read" the terrain, comparing it to the stored reference map. If the missile got lost, it was capable of making a course correction to get back on track and find its target.

Once it neared the target, which could be as far as six hundred miles away from the ship, the Tomahawk was nearly unstoppable. Its small size—eighteen feet long with a wingspan of just under nine feet—and speed nearing six hundred miles an hour made it difficult to shoot down. And it never missed when programmed properly. An onboard digital scene-matching correlation system compared a stored image with the actual target image to confirm the target before destroying it. Hitting the wrong target, like in the case of the Chinese embassy in Belgrade, was due to incorrect programming.

Stout made a snap decision to leave the fire control center and go to the mess deck. It was a choice rooted in adolescent impulsiveness and a lifetime of expecting immediate gratification. The missile's camera image was being shown over the ship's internal television system. The big-screen televisions on the mess deck would provide her with the view she wanted. Technically, leaving her station during general quarters constituted a failure to properly perform her duties, but she wanted to see this for herself. *They won't miss me,* she thought, turning to sneak to the hatch.

Exiting the fire-control center and heading aft, Stout made her way down a starboard ladder well to a passageway that led her to another ladder well and then the mess deck. The ship swayed violently. One motion—back and forth or to and fro—was part of being on ship. But the combination of both motions made walking through the dark passageways more tedious. There were neither windows nor colorful pictures. Everything other than the dull gray paint had a purpose, whether it was the wires and pipes overhead or the pressurized doors between the passageways.

Every time Stout lifted a handle to loosen the tight braces holding the pressure doors shut she violated the ship's Zebra condition. Zebra was set during general quarters to prevent flooding from spreading through the ship. The strong doors would hold the water in a compartment and prevent it from pouring into another, thus reducing the chance that the ship could sink.

Stout just reached the bottom step of the ladder well when she heard the explosion of yelling and cheering. "Did you see that?" yelled a voice. "What a shot!" Stout turned the corner to peer into the mess deck only to see a few 'high fives' that confirmed that she'd missed it. Then she turned and ran back up the ladder well. Since she missed the missile's impact, she might as well get back to her station before the jubilance subsided and her petty officer noticed she was missing. The celebration would give her a minute to sneak back into the fire-control center. The ship was filled with elation. None of the sailors thought about the reality of the situation: they had just killed dozens of fellow human beings.

-117A Nighthawk, San Selvan Airspace

Wig first saw his target in the large video monitor in the center of the stealth fighter's console. The monitor originally displayed the image from the forward-looking infrared camera, and then from the downward-looking infrared camera that was joined with the laser designator. By properly aligning a series of shapes, Wig aimed the laser. Once locked on, the laser designator was fixed onto its target by a stabilizing system.

Only with the laser fixed on-target did Wig open the bomb-bay doors. There were no racks of bombs and missiles hanging off the sleek jet, because they would have increased the radar signature of the aircraft. A ninety-degree angle of incidence provided a huge echo, but a sixty-degree angle, like most of the angles on the F-117A, scattered radar energy and sent a much smaller echo. So ordnance for the Nighthawk was stored in internal bays. Opening the bomb-bay doors created sharp features to the jet's outline, thus increasing the "blip" that radar would portray. This was the point when Wig and his aircraft were most vulnerable—with the stealth capability of the F-117A reduced and Wig on his final run into the target.

Before this point the threat to Wig came mostly from the heat that his stealth fighter produced. While radar was still the primary sensor for detecting aircraft, infrared sensors were being used more and more. To decrease the F-117A's infrared signature, the aircraft's engine was a non-afterburning turbofan engine. Exhaust was dispelled from special nozzles that flattened out the fume so it dissipated and rapidly mixed with ambient air.

The laser-seeking device on the nose of the bomb identified the spot of laser energy reflected from the target and told Wig with a message in the lower left-hand corner of the heads-up display.

Carrying a payload of two 1,000-pound Guided Bomb Unit-27 (GBU-27) laser-guided bombs, Wig was attacking an air-defense operation center so that other aircraft could attack targets in San Selva without being vulnerable to an integrated air-defense system. The GBU-27 was a newer-model bomb designed especially for F-117 stealth fighters. It used a penetrating warhead against hard targets and hit over ninety percent of its targets during the Yugoslav and

Afghan wars. It was designed specifically for the stealth fighter's advanced target-acquisition and designator system, and it used a modified Paveway II guidance-control unit, which provided "terminal trajectory shaping" for optimum impact angle against various target structures. For example, it hit an aircraft shelter with a vertical impact, but made a horizontal approach to a bridge support.

Nonstealth aircraft during tonight's initial strikes would use weapons that allowed for more "standoff" distance between the pilot and the target. For attacks on area targets, AGM-154 Joint Standoff Weapons would be used. Guided by an onboard global-positioning system that communicated with satellites, the AGM-154 could be released from the aircraft and fly forty miles to drop its submunitions on the target. The AGM-130, on the other hand, used a television camera in its nose, so it could be dropped eight miles from the target and fly to hit a precise spot. A few of the aircraft flew with AGM-88 missiles, which were high-speed antiradiation missiles—HARMs. Called "Wild Weasel" missions, Air Force jets armed with antiradar missiles intentionally flew low and within missile range to entice the San Selvans into exposing their missile radar. Together, the aircraft and missiles being launched tonight by members of all four military services would create a layered attack intended to cripple San Selva's defenses in the opening minutes.

Flying just low enough to be below the massive plumes of smoke, Wig released the first bomb. The Paveway II tail assembly's folding wings deployed and began adjusting continuously to place the missile on track to the target. The "smart" bomb gained speed during the descent, closing quickly on its target. Wig checked the digital timer on his heads-up display. *It should be hitting just about now—perfect!* He locked on again with the laser, confirmed the bomb was reading, and dropped his last bomb, holding the laser designator on-target until impact. He then pulled back on the stick to bring his aircraft up through the smoke to its cruising altitude.

Wig's wingman came up from behind him, having made his own drops seconds after Wig. "Nighthawk Four Two, this is Nighthawk Four One," said Wig, breaking the radio silence for the first time.

"Roger, Four One, gottcha."

"BDA?" asked Wig, short for battle damage assessment. The bombing was recorded on the aircraft's internally mounted video system, but Wig had not seen the drops of his wingman.

"Four bombs. Four hits. Target destroyed."

"Roger, target destroyed. It's *Miller time*, Nighthawk Four One, out."

F/A-18E Super Hornet, San Selvan Airspace

Crash checked the F/A-18E's illuminated forward instrument panel. The touch-sensitive control system included a multipurpose color display that showed flight information, target data, and a moving digital map. On one of two monochrome display panels, the status of the bombs and missiles mounted on the aircraft's eleven weapon stations were visible.

Crash worried about the antiaircraft missile systems. Normally, if an antiaircraft weapon powered up, other aircraft would blow its radar away, but the problem was that, with the civilian radar integrated into the antiair defense, the San Selvans had an extra advantage. They could get away with firing their missiles and moving before Crash could take evasive actions. With the ingenious way the San Selvans would fire the SA-18s or Rolands, Sara could expect to hear the loud *deedledeedledeedledeedle* alarm erupt in her helmet earphones at the same time that the F/A-18E's MISSILE WARNING and MISSILE ALERT lights came to life. There would be little time to react.

Radar is a double-edged sword. The electronic signals it sends out might be detected—detected at a greater distance than it sees—by an enemy and used to locate American aircraft. Each type of radar has its own signature too, which means that radar from an F/A-18E would identify the aircraft as being an F/A-18E. To remain hidden as long as possible, Sara was linked by a secure radio-burst transmission link to an E-3 Airborne Warning and Control System (AWACS) aircraft somewhere overhead. The AWACS was a valuable tool, because it stayed far away and used its powerful radar to find targets that it relayed to the hidden fighters and bombers. It was a modified Boeing 707/320 commercial airframe with a huge rotating radar dome on the top of the aircraft. The E-3 Sentry could fly for more than eight hours without refueling, and its range and on-station time could be increased with in-flight refueling.

The thirty-foot-diameter radar dish on the airplane's back permitted surveillance from the earth's surface up into the stratosphere for a range of more than two hundred miles. The radar combined with an identification friend-or-foe subsystem that looked down to detect, identify, and track enemy and friendly low-flying aircraft by eliminating ground clutter returns that confused other radar systems. The radar interfaced with computer systems that could gather and present broad and detailed battlefield information. Data were collected as events occurred. In support of air-to-ground operations the E-3 provided direct information needed for interdiction, reconnaissance, airlift, and close-air support for friendly ground forces. It also provided information for commanders of air operations to gain and maintain control of the air battle. As an air-defense system, E-3s could detect, identify, and track airborne enemy forces far from the borders of friendly countries to direct fighter-interceptor aircraft to these enemy targets. The information also could be sent to major command and control centers in rear areas or aboard ships. In a time of crisis, this data could even be forwarded directly to the president if necessary.

Crash tried to focus her forward-looking infrared camera on the target but only saw thick static as the camera strained to see through the smoke. She reentered the coordinates of the target into the camera, and the camera automatically pointed at where the target should be, but there was still nothing.

Deedledeedledeedle! The alarm from Crash's AN/APS-109B Radar Homing and Warning Receiver (RHAWS) blared in her helmet. She looked down at her digital map. Several "S" symbols became visible, indicating where San Selvan search radar was detected. Most likely civilian, however, which would prevent the Air Force "Wild Weasel" aircraft from destroying the radar. Crash could only pray. Her AN/ALQ-137 Internal Electronic Countermeasures system was useless against large radar like these. At least she was high enough to be just out of missile range.

Another alarm sounded. Several "A" and "3" symbols appeared on the digital map. Crash gasped. The San Selvans were not supposed to have mobile SA-3 missile launchers. Then the symbols began to disappear from the video screen. The Wild Weasel's HARM missiles zeroing in on their electronic signal destroyed some of the missile sites. The HARMs flew along an invisible string to impact the source of radar energy, but many of the antiaircraft missiles had probably turned off their radar systems after firing their missiles so they could move before incoming American weapons.

"Viper Three Two, this is Viper Three One, over," said Crash over the aircraft's radio. She hated to use the radio, but Crash needed to communicate with her pilots because the mission was not going as planned. Flying this high prevented the pilots from seeing their targets, but reducing altitude increased the risk from surface-to-air missile attacks.

"Roger, Three One," answered Sara's wingman.

"Negative target acquisition." Sara knew the answer to her question but asked anyway. "Are you having any luck? Over."

"Negative. I can't see through the smoke. We're too high."

"Three Three and Three Four, do you copy?"

"Three Three is negative."

"Three Four, same, same."

"Roger," said Crash into the microphone. "We'll give it one pass from the opposite direction. If we still can't acquire the target we'll have to hit the tanker and I'll contact the ship." She didn't say it, but they all knew that if they couldn't see the target on the next run, then they were going to need to go in at a lower altitude after refueling.

Chapter Eleven

Belem, Brazil

"Captain. Sir, are you awake?"

"What? Yeah, First Sergeant Brown, is that you?"

"Yes, sir. Sorry to wake you. Thought you'd like to know it started."

"You mean we're moving out already?"

"No, sir. We started bombing. Some of the comm guys hooked a satellite antenna up to get CNN. We've been watching it in the mess tent."

Summer sat upright, pushing away the light poncho liner that he used as a blanket. "Is it still on in the mess tent?"

"Yes, sir. I'm headed back there now."

"Save me a seat. I'll be there in a few."

Ray rubbed his eyes and focused on the activity of the airfield a few hundred meters away. Lumps of sleeping men lay around him. He picked up his jungle boots and shook them out before putting it on. The shaking is habit, a way of ensuring that no critters had crawled into the boots. Since he had been sleeping in his uniform, Summer was soon fully dressed and walking to the mess tent. Soldiers standing in the entryway blocked the glow of the tent's lights. The mess tent was packed with men and women who had their attention focused on a nineteen-inch television set. He didn't see First Sergeant Brown, but Summer found a place to stand at the edge of the tent where he could see most of the television screen. The image looked similar to ones he'd seen many times before: the view through a night-vision lens on a video camera. The greenish tint of the night vision obstructed clear view of the picture, but it was good enough to see what was happening. In the upper right-hand corner of the screen was the word LIVE, and the words at the bottom of the screen said BILL CAMPBELL, MACAPA, SAN SELVA.

Bright flashes of antiaircraft fire shot into the San Selvan night, the soft *blump blump blump* of distant weapons faintly drifting from the television's speaker. The unaimed fire had little chance of bringing down an aircraft or a missile, but it would, however, come down on the city, creating more damage and destruction.

The camera focused on a slower-moving bright flash. "Here comes another of those cruise missiles," said an unseen commentator. The missile streaked across the sky and disappeared behind a high-rise building, but a flash of light indicated that it had impacted against some target. "We've seen several of those hit in that same area now. I know that the San Selvan Parliament building is located in that direction."

"Lisa Hunt might be able to tell us more," said another voice. "She is out at Brinwhich Air Force Base. Lisa, what can you tell us?" A clear image of a female reporter appeared, but a smaller picture of the live view from Macapa remained in the lower left-hand corner of the screen.

"Tony, jet aircraft continue to take off from the airfield behind me." The picture focused on two Air Force F-22 Raptors streaking down the runway.

Bastards, thought Summer, as the group in the mess tent groaned. The reporters knew damn well that the San Selvans were just as capable of seeing the news report as anyone else. It wouldn't take a rocket scientist to calculate how long it would take for the jets to be crossing the border into San Selvan airspace. The news report put the American pilots' lives in danger.

"Earlier tonight, I counted sixteen jets take off, but I've only seen fifteen come back."

And now the enemy has accurate counts! Thanks to the American media. Not to mention that all the parents with a child in the Air Force were worried sick that the missing aircraft carried their son or daughter.

"Bill," asked Tony, "are there any reports of aircraft being shot down?"

"No, not that I've heard yet, Tony. But I can't rule out that some may have been shot down. There's been a lot of antiaircraft fire."

"Lisa, what is the Air Force saying about the missing aircraft?"

"The Air Force refuses to talk numbers, only stating that the operation is going well and that they will have more information at a news briefing in the morning."

"Well, fortunately, retired Air Force General Stew Brodrick is here in studio with us. General, why is the

Air Force so slow to respond about the missing aircraft? Why wait until tomorrow?"

Summer didn't know whom to hate more at that moment: the commentator sensationalizing the story to keep viewers tuned in or the retired general who was sucking up money at the expense of American fighting men and women. The Air Force was not slow to respond. The reporter may have simply miscounted, and there may not have been a jet missing at all. Even if there was, the only *slow response* was in the minds of the media because the military didn't want to waste time answering questions for the reporters' stories.

"Not surprising, Tony," said the general, dressed smartly in a fashionable business suit. If it weren't for the small colorful pin on his left lapel, there would be nothing military about the man other than the caption at the bottom of the screen that mentioned his former rank in the Air Force. The pin that the general wore symbolized the Distinguished Flying Cross that he was awarded during one of his many nights risking life and limb fighting for his country. On that night he too would have been disgusted by any retired officer playing news commentator, but tonight the general justified his action by reasoning, *It's about time someone who knows what is going on got on the air.* However, the general didn't know what was going on—he was guessing—and the television network didn't really care anyway. He was there because it gave their reports credibility. "The Air Force will notify the families of those involved before making any official comment about any pilots who have been killed, injured, or captured tonight."

"So would you expect more information to be released sometime tomorrow then, General?"

Released? More information *released,* as if the military were holding it from the news media in a malicious act to disrupt ratings.

"Yes, I think tomorrow we'll know how things went tonight."

"And what would you say about the operation thus far, General?"

"It's been standard air dominance thus far, Tony. The cruise missiles have been sent in to destroy *hard* targets—hard in the sense that they pose a greater threat to American aircraft because they are well defended, like communication nodes, radar installations, and headquarters facilities. The missiles were followed by stealth fighters; now we see conventional aircraft from air bases in the Continental United States and off the USS *Ronald Reagan*."

"Nothing taking off from air bases in the region?"

"Negative." The general shook his head; then he corrected himself. "At least no fixed-wing aircraft. The Army has had an aviation attack squadron in Brazil for several weeks now, and my friends inside the military tell me that they will be used tonight, which is a change from the way things have been done in the past. Normally there are several weeks, if not months, of bombing before attack helicopters join a fight. Their joining this early is yet one more example of how urgent this situation is. But only Army and attack Air Force Special Operations helicopters will operate from the advance bases. It's safer that way, because a lot of security troops are needed to forward-base attack aircraft like that."

"Concerning the American aircraft that is possibly down over San Selva, at least missing at this point, what air defense capability do the San Selva forces have?"

"Rather primitive by American standards. We can expect that for most bombing missions our aircraft will drop from an altitude of ten thousand feet or greater. For the most part, the San Selvans rely on old SA-14 manpacks, which are portable missiles with a maximum range of seven kilometers. They hone in on the exhaust fumes of aircraft, but can be defeated pretty easily with most of our aircraft's countermeasures."

"And what about their air force? Will that pose any threat?"

"No, probably not. The San Selvans have a few fixed-wing and rotary aircraft, but I'm sure that those have already been destroyed in the opening stages of tonight's missions."

"You said we'd be dropping bombs at least as high as ten thousand feet, General. How effective can we expect our pilots to be?" It was a loaded question. One that the reporter used to move the discussion to a new topic. The commentator had been prompted by a voice in the earpiece, telling him to make sure the conversation didn't get too technical and dry. *You gotta watch these old military guys.*

"Very effective, Tony." The general leaned forward in his seat to rest his elbows on the tabletop in front of him. With his hands he made gentle, well-rehearsed gestures to highlight his points while presenting a calm demeanor. Thinking the whole time, *God, I love this!* "With most of our aircraft capable of self-designating with laser technology, all of the bombs dropped tonight are *smart* bombs, with some even being *brilliant,* meaning that they are capable of self-correcting if they become lost."

"But the pilots need to see the target to designate with the . . . the . . . laser, right, General? So how will the smoke from the burning rain forests interfere with tonight's mission."

"There is the potential for a substantial loss in effectiveness of aircraft-delivered munitions if the smoke blocks visibility. I had that same problem myself during the ninety-nine Yugoslav War." The general gestured at his lapel pin that represented the Distinguished Flying Cross medal by lightly tapping it with his right hand. "Except in Yugoslavia it was clouds that blocked our vision. Clouds are very difficult because our infrared sights cannot see through all of the moisture. The sights are designed to see through smoke on the battlefield, but the thickness of the smoke over San Selva will obscure many targets. Many of the Tomahawk cruise missiles in the U.S. military's inventory are upgraded to be satellite directed, so they are able to strike a target in just about any conditions, but those are small in number and very expensive. These missiles have been used a lot the past few decades. There aren't that many left, and we *cannot* build them quickly."

"Hmmm, interesting. And I would assume that the reduction in visibility increases the likelihood of collateral damage." *Time to shift gears.* "Correspondent Bill Campbell is live in Macapa, San Selva, at great risk to his own life, I might add. Bill, how are things there?"

"Other than the occasional bomb or burst of anti-aircraft fire, Tony, things are quieter here than they were an hour ago."

"Well, Lisa Hunt is reporting that planes continue to take off, so there is probably more on the way. From what you've seen and heard, are there any reports of damage to civilian facilities?"

"Unfortunately, yes. Yes, there are." The green tint zoomed in on the reporter's fuzzy face. Macapa, San Selva, appeared again at the bottom of the screen. "San Selvan authorities are reporting that one of the first missiles missed its target and hit a children's hospital in the downtown area. The reports are unconfirmed at this time, but I expect that if true, the San Selvans will take us to view the destruction tomorrow."

"Sad. Very sad if it's true. Please be careful, Bill. You're risking your life to report this important story. Keep your head down. Okay, buddy? Lisa, is the Air Force commenting on the alleged bombing of the hospital?"

"No, Tony, there has been no word on that. I do have an update on that missing jet, however. The confusion has been cleared up. The command here is reporting that all aircraft from the first waves of the attack have returned here safely, but, unfortunately, I have seen many jets return still with bombs attached to their wings, probably unable to drop them because of the smoke that blankets much of the country. But again, they are now saying that all the pilots from the initial strikes are back safe. So that's very good news."

Bitch! Captain Summer was livid. There never was a missing aircraft. Some reporter probably counted wrong in the first place. The dramatically well rehearsed *that's very good news* infuriated him even more. Acting as though she gave a damn about the men and women flying when her reporting put their lives in greater danger and scared the hell out of loved ones at home. Giving a physical location where the operation was being conducted. Providing detailed information about the number of aircraft taking off, even photographing them so that a trained eye could see the type and number of bombs each plane was carrying. Telling the San Selvans that many planes were unable to drop their bombs. And the other idiot, Bill, who Tony said was "risking his life" so he could help spread San Selvan propaganda. The retired general—one of the military's own—added legitimacy to everything the media said. Worst of all, the information he provided might aid the enemy in shooting down an American aircraft.

The reporting was not intentionally designed to assist the San Selvans, but news shows had become more show than news. Journalism had been replaced by media; making money required a presentation that was entertaining to the viewer, creating stories that exploited situations so they could improve ratings and sell commercial time. Action news, helicopter reporting, and live satellite feeds all contributed to the information nightmare that upset Summer. Even worse, some major networks now operated their own "spy" satellites. Capable of taking detailed pictures from hundreds of miles above the earth's surface when placed in proper orbit over a crisis site, these satellites enabled the news agencies to give detailed and immediate information. Just a few years ago the general public only saw these pictures when the Pentagon released them from secret files. Now everyone saw them on a daily basis. Soon the American public would be captivated by satellite photographs from news satellites, as would the San Selvan forces, very likely learning more from the media about the damage in their own country than they would from internal communications.

Chapter Twelve

*RAH-66 Comanche, Airspace Over Macapa,
San Selva*

The night grew blacker by the minute as the two helicopters zipped down the dark street, dangerously
close to the ground. They were on a hunt. Small and
sleek, with U.S. ARMY stamped on the fuselage, the
aircraft flew close to the buildings bordering the
street. The forty-foot rotor blades came to within
inches of the structures, threatening to come close
enough to strike them.

As the lead bird popped upward in a right-hand
turn, the pilot and the gunner gained a quick view of
the surrounding city before bouncing over the buildings and dipping down to make a run through an ad-
jacent street. The canyons of three- and four-story
buildings made for good flying. In his heads-up dis-

play, the pilot used infrared images and overlaid symbols to navigate the helicopter. This nape-of-the-earth flying was dangerous in an urban environment, even more so at night.

The aircraft was the newest generation of helicopter, a Boeing-Sikorsky Reconnaissance Attack Helicopter (RAH) 66, better known as the Comanche. It was the first helicopter developed specifically for the dual role of both attack and reconnaissance. Several years before, there would have been two helicopters needed for a mission like this: an OH-58 Kiowa light-observation helicopter and an AH-1 Cobra attack helicopter. The faster and electronically sophisticated Kiowa would search out the enemy so that the slower but better protected and armed Cobra could destroy it. Now the Comanche was capable of completing both missions. It was advanced enough to scout and tough enough to kill.

As the Comanches drew close to a four-story parking garage, a San Selvan heavy machine gun opened fire on the fast-moving helicopters. The lead helicopter began evasive maneuvering, the pilot powering the RAH-66's engines to push the bird in a climb of eight hundred feet per second to avoid the tracers. The pilot twisted the throttle grip on the collection control and eased the stick to one side. Driving the helicopter away from the San Selvan weapon, he accelerated the Comanche to one hundred and seventy-five knots. None of the antiaircraft rounds impacted the helicopter.

"Comanche One Six, this is Comanche Five Zero, over," the pilot of the lead aircraft said over the radio. A major was at the controls of the lead bird, while a warrant officer sat in the front seat, or gunner's seat, of the two-seat helicopter. All the men and women from the helicopter task force were tanned a golden brown color after sitting in Brazil for the past month enduring an endless parade of rumors on when they would cross the border but never really believing that this night might become a reality.

"Comanche Five Zero, go, over," said Chief Warrant Officer Mike Myers, pilot of the second RAH-66. He and his copilot, Chief Warrant Officer Ken Simms, were rare breeds. They were warrant officer pilots. Both were carefully selected from the enlisted ranks and placed through a barrage of comprehensive tests before being selected to wear the strange-looking bars of a warrant officer. Similar in appearance to a first or second lieutenant's rank insignia, the warrant officer bar had the additional markings of red squares to represent what level warrant officer the individual was.

"Quick turnaround on them," said the major. "I'm setting to the north. You hammerhead from the west. Time to target: four-five."

"Roger." Myers was impressed that the major recovered so quickly from the brush with death to give detailed instructions on how he wanted the target to be attacked. The major would suppress the enemy with 20mm cannon and rocket fire from the north, while Myers maneuvered to attack the parking garage from the west. The attack would begin in forty-five seconds.

Pound for pound, the Comanche was the most heavily armed helicopter in the history of warfare. A three-barrel, 20mm Gatling gun sat in the nose turret. Retractable doors for internal weapon mounts carried antiarmor Hellfire missiles, 2.75-inch laser-guided rockets, and air-to-air missiles. The internal weapon mounts reduced radar signature, but additional weapon mounts could be utilized to carry more ordnance outside the aircraft.

The major's Comanche began its attack from the north as Myers moved to the western flank. Myers kept the helicopter below the tops of the buildings, out of sight of the enemy in the parking garage. The "flying tank" doctrine the Comanches used played on two key aspects of combat: maneuverability and firepower. The heavily armed attack helicopters could quickly move around an urban battlefield. True, they were vulnerable to fire, but their ability to move in so many directions made them more survivable than a ground vehicle that was forced to use roads. Flying this low and fast reduced the enemy's ability to fire well-aimed shots at them because it only gave the San Selvan rebels a few seconds to engage the helicopters. Surface-to-air missile were easily defeated by the ALQ-144—nicknamed "disco ball" because of its shape—that confused incoming missiles by radiating electronic impulses so strongly it knocked out the missile's sensitive seeker head. But "dumb" rocket-propelled grenades fired at close range were not vulnerable to electronic countermeasures. They posed the greatest threat to the low-flying Comanches, and the key to avoid being shot down in this environment was to keep moving.

Looking for potential targets, Myers scanned in all directions. As he moved his head, the cannon hanging below the aircraft mirrored his movements and pointed wherever he looked. Myers stopped the Comanche so it hovered above one of the buildings. The Comanche expressed the telltale "whooping" that helicopters' rotor noise usually produced as a whisper. Its noise was reduced by use of a five-bladed rotor and an internal fantail that eliminated interaction between main rotor and tail rotor wakes. This advanced rotor design also permitted operation at low speed, allowing the Comanche to sneak closer to a target than an

Apache without being detected by an acoustical sensor.

Since the San Selvan vehicle's gun crew had their attention directed at the other Comanche, they did not see the shark attacking from the periphery. The AN/AVS-7 infrared sighting system identified the heat signature produced by vehicles and people and presented an image that allowed the pilots to see through the darkness and thin smoke. The image was portrayed in the heads-up display, which also showed critical flight information from aircraft sensors in visual imagery. The system allowed continuous situational awareness by the pilot while reducing the pilot's need to look down at the flight instrument panel. Simms and Myers clearly saw the enemy's disposition. Not only could they see the armored vehicle dug into the building, but they could also see individual San Selvan rebels moving into firing positions around the parking garage.

Simms illuminated the enemy vehicle with his laser designator and fired a volley of precision rockets from a distance of seven hundred meters. The laser seekers positioned on the cone of each rocket guided the rockets along an invisible string of energy. They impacted exactly where Simms held the crosshairs of the laser designator. The rockets vaporized the gun vehicle, causing a fireball that blew through the third floor of the parking garage. A burst of high-explosive 20mm cannon rounds added insult to injury. Simms redirected his fire at the second floor of the parking garage. The garage was torn to shreds and there was no sign of life when Myers ducked the Comanche back below the building.

Myers turned and accelerated down the street. Banking in a steep turn, he made an error during his victory-induced zeal. As he came around the corner of a building moving too fast and flying too low, the rotor blades of the helicopter struck against an electrical pole on the side of the street. Flames erupted from the engines and a horrid tearing sound filled the air as the rotor assembly ripped off from the aircraft. With the rotors torn off, the helicopter rocketed through the air out of control, slamming to the ground and skidding down the street. Dust and smoke filled the street. Sparks flew from the fuselage as it bounced down the street's pavement with Myers and Simms trapped inside and screaming. There was little fire but more noise than anyone would expect from such a crash. After three hundred meters, the helicopter hit a building and broke through the wall, finally stopping inside the structure. Then there was total silence.

After recovering from the initial shock of the crash, Myers pulled himself out of the Comanche's cockpit. His head throbbed with pain from smashing against the side window. He stripped his broken night-vision goggles off of his head and moved up to the gunner's seat. Simms was unconscious and still strapped in, and Myers immediately began trying to free him from the wreckage. Myers looked around his destroyed Comanche. He could see that the helicopter had come to a stop inside a building, but it took a few seconds before he realized it was some kind of store.

Myers finally pried Simms from the gunner's seat. Simms bled profusely, but Myers couldn't detect the source of the blood. He searched Simms and found that something had created a deep cut high on Simms's right leg. Myers ripped Simms's flight suit open and took out his small flashlight. Holding it in his mouth so the light illuminated the wound, Myers could just make out the image of the artery that was severed and spurting massive amounts of blood. Then he reached into Simms's leg and stopped the bleeding by physically squeezing the artery in his left hand. Fortunately, there was no fire from the aircraft or the impact into the building.

A commotion outside the building caught Myers's attention. With his right hand, Myers removed his pistol from its holster. *Damn sanchos,* he thought but was quickly reminding himself that he was not supposed to use that word. It was the latest contemptuous epithet to describe an enemy, and it flowed off his tongue easier than he thought it would. Mike didn't have a racist bone in his body, but a lot of things happen when human beings lock in a battle of life and death. Most of those things are ugly. First comes an attempt to turn the enemy into an object or a thing, not a person with a family back home. Then comes anger at the bastard on the other side of the lines who tries to kill you and your buddies. Sometimes hate jumps on for the ride too. In a few years the word sancho would be considered a racial slur, but right now it was just easier than saying "San Selvan." Myers shuddered at the thought of what might come next. The sanchos were savages. He knew that. They would not capture him and send him to a prisoner-of-war camp. Best-case scenario was that they would rip him apart right there where he and Simms lay; worst-case they would cart the two Americans off to be slowly tortured to death. Neither scenario was appealing to Myers, so he put his pistol down where he could quickly grab it and took out his survival radio.

"Any station, any station, this is Comanche One Six, over."

"Psycho, this is Boogie," said the major in the other Comanche, using personal call signs.

"Boogie, I'm alive. I'm *alive!*"

"Roger. You're *alive!* Good to hear, Psycho. Can you give me a location?"

"Negative. We crashed into a building. Ken is hurt bad."

"Roger. Hang in there, Mike. I'll find someone to come pull you out."

MH-60G Pave Hawk, Brazilian Airspace

"Did you hear that back there?" asked United States Air Force Major Mark Gunwitz, wondering if his crew had heard the E-3 sentry's radio transmission.

"Negative," said Sergeant Riggs, Gunwitz's right-door gunner for the MH-60G Pave Hawk helicopter. The crew in the back of the helicopter could clearly hear the internal communications from the pilots and other flight crew, but transmissions from outside aircraft were often too faint to hear clearly. "Transmission was muffled."

"Army bird is down inside Macapa," said Gunwitz. "The AWACS has comm with the wingman. We're going in to have a look-see." His thick, meaty hands manipulated the stick and collective to aim the helicopter toward the location where the Army helicopter went down.

Gunwitz was a veteran special operations pilot. At six feet six, his large frame looked better suited for a football field than crammed into a cockpit. In fact Gunwitz had been one heck of a nose guard in high school, but not good enough to find a college that would take him on an athletic scholarship. He could easily have walked onto his college's Double-A team, but instead he decided to play rugby for the school. The practices were more fun, because they focused on tackling, and a beer bash hosted by the home team was part of the rugby match ritual. But at this point in his life, thirty-five years old with a dozen of them in the Air Force, Gunwitz had to cut down on the beer drinking. His large frame seemed to carry more and more fat as he grew older, regardless of how hard he worked out to prevent it.

Gunwitz was just "unplugging" his helicopter from the tanker when he heard the call requesting help for Comanche One Six. With the helicopter's internal and external fuel tanks all full, Gunwitz's MH-60G was now capable of covering four hundred miles before needing to refuel again. Unfortunately, the second helicopter in the flight, an older but better-armed MH-60L Black Hawk, was still taking on fuel. The combat search-and-rescue flight worked as a two-bird team, with the better-armed MH-60L serving as the firepower for the mission. With its dual-weapon pylons on both side of the fuselage, the MH-60L could use cannons, rockets, and missiles to augment its door guns. The situation for the Army pilots sounded too bad to risk waiting for the escort aircraft. Reports indicated a crowd had begun forming near the crash site. Gunwitz had immediately decided that he could not waste time waiting for his wingman. He needed to go in alone.

"We're going to cross the border to make a run in," Gunwitz said into his microphone. After switching radio frequencies, he spoke into his microphone again, but this time he reported his intentions to the E-3 AWACS. In this role, assisting a search-and-rescue effort, the E-3 acted as the quarterback on a football field. The E-3 crew called the plays and coordinated the details necessary for the proper aircraft to become involved in the search while the unnecessary ones got out of the way. There was no time for confusion at a time like this. A captured American pilot was valuable whether the aircraft fell from the sky because of antiaircraft fire or mechanical problems. It provided a political bargaining chip for the San Selvan government. So American planners had placed the Air Force special operations helicopters in the air to react to an unfortunate situation like this one. Now it came time for the rescue team to earn their paychecks.

Comanche Crash Site, Macapa, San Selva

Myers could hear people in the street outside. It was dark, and he could see little more than shadows. The noises grew closer and Myers could hear muffled voices. He aimed the pistol at the hole and wished he had his night-vision goggles. *What will the civilians do? Is there any chance that they might be friendly to Americans?* The answer to Myers's question came in a flurry of activity, with people rushing through the hole and into the shadows of the rubble. "Who's there?" yelled Myers. "Halt or I'll shoot."

Suddenly someone jumped on top of him, and others began kicking and hitting his body. They came from nowhere. Too shocked to fight back, he rolled into the fetal position for protection instead. He saw nothing and could not understand anything that the angry mob shouted. Someone grabbed his foot and started to drag him to the hole. Bright flashes of light filled his eyes as fists and feet pounded his head. He felt himself bounce over Simms's body. Myers reached for Simms with his left hand as he realized his pistol was still in his right. A rush of air hit him and the roar of the mob grew louder as Myers was pulled into the street. He pulled the pistol's trigger but nothing happen. He tried again—*nothing!* Realizing he still had the safety engaged on the weapon, Myers froze for a second, not remembering what to do. Then his head cleared. Flipping the selector switch of the M9 to FIRE with his thumb, Myers pulled the trigger again. The blast startled him. The barrel of the

147

pistol had been just inches from his head. His ears rang from the sound, but the crowd scattered.

Unable to see from both the blinding flash and the beating, Myers scampered back into the hole to Simms. After what seemed like a marathon crawl, he finally reached Simms and frantically searched for the wound again. Feeling the artery between the index finger and thumb of his left hand, Myers resumed his grip on Simms's life. With the right hand he tightly gripped the pistol, which seemed at the moment to be equivalent to his life.

Chapter Thirteen

MH-60G Pave Hawk, Brazilian Airspace

Major Mark Gunwitz was flying the MH-60G Pave Hawk at its top speed. There was never time to waste when a pilot was down in enemy territory, and the quicker they got there the better the chances that the airmen would get lucky and fly into an environment that allowed for a quick pickup of the pilot. But if the situation was hostile, everyone needed to be ready. Even more important now because Gunwitz and his crew had crossed the border without the firepower of the MH-060L Black Hawk.

Coming from the Air Force's Sixteenth Special Operations Wing home stationed at Hurlburt Field, Florida, Gunwitz's crew was one part of an elite Air Force team from the Fifty-fifth Special Operations Squadron, which specialized in using MH-60s for combat search and rescue (CSAR). Although the Sixteenth Special Operations Wing was not formed until 1990, the history of air commandos dated back to World War II, when specially trained pilots dropped spies over Nazi-held Europe. A year after the modern-day unit was formed, its helicopters led the opening assault on Iraqi radar installations in the first Gulf War.

The entire special ops Wing comprised ninety aircraft and seven thousand people split into nine unique squadrons. The Sixth Special Operations Squadron provided advisers to foreign countries' air forces to improve performance and coordination with U.S. forces. The Eighth and Fifteenth Special Operations Squadrons flew MC-130E and MC-130H transports, respectively. Their sophisticated aircraft supported unconventional warfare missions that required clandestine infiltration and exfiltration for special operation forces in hostile territory like the insertion of the Special Forces teams last night. The Ninth Special Operations Squadron flew MC-130P tankers for refueling other special operations aircraft. The Fourth and Sixteenth Special Operations Squadrons flew the AC-130U and AC-130H gunships, which provided fire support to troops on the ground. Armed with 105mm howitzers, Gatling guns, and advanced targeting systems, the AC-130s were the best friend of a lightly armed special ops warrior on the ground. Finally, the Twentieth Special Operations Squadron, like Gunwitz's unit, specialized in combat search and rescue, but they flew the larger CV-22. One of their CV-22s circled off to the west in a holding area. The CV-22 was a special operation version of the Marine Corps' MV-22 Ospery. It was the aircraft expected to penetrate strong air defenses during war to rescue American pilots that were deep behind enemy lines. The hybrid half helicopter, half turboprop plane CV-22 was capable of traveling farther than the old MH-53J Pave Low that it replaced and it was one of the most technologically advanced helicopters in the world. Unfortunately, the CV-22 was a much larger aircraft than the MH-60. It couldn't fit into tight landing zones and spaces. It would be called in if things got too tough for Gunwitz and his team, because packed in the belly of the CV-22 was a platoon of Rangers from the Joint Special Operations Command, ready to fast-rope down and provide additional firepower to a rescue.

As the word that an American pilot was down in San Selva spread throughout the Combined Task Force, different units prepared rescue forces. The SEAL platoon on the USS *Ronald Reagan* rushed across the flight deck to load a spinning helicopter. Rangers in the CV-22 passed notes to each other to communicate despite the loud sound from the aircraft's engines. A reinforced platoon of Marines on the USS *Beirut* were called from their berthing spaces to the hangar deck. If things became too hot for the Air Force CSAR mission, the fourteen SEALs, thirty Rangers, or forty-eight Marines could be called on to come in and help.

In Gunwitz's crew, everyone made second checks of their equipment. Captain Nushi, Gunwitz's copilot, checked the all-weather radar and the avionics suite. The helicopter was equipped with the latest technology: forward-looking infrared, digital map generator, terrain-avoidance and terrain-following multimode radar, radar- and missile-warning systems, and infrared jammers. In back, the two-door gunners checked their M134 miniguns. The miniguns were equipped with AIM-1, an infrared laser that provided a beam of light invisible to the naked eye. Night-vision goggles needed to be used to see it. The laser beam was effective for aiming at ranges up to two miles and was bore-sighted to miniguns, allowing the door gunners to use the two-hundred-rounds-per-second weapon with uncanny precision.

Next to the door gunners were two pararescue jumpers. Staff Sergeant Randy Collins was teamed with Technical Sergeant Gordon Harris, a longtime friend. The two had first met during their initial training to become pararescue jumpers, commonly called PJs. Numbering only three hundred, the PJs were some of the U.S. military's most elite troops. Specially groomed in a grueling eighteen-month training course, PJs trained to battle through hell to rescue fellow Americans. They were trained to jump from the safety of an aircraft into rough seas, thick jungle, frozen glaciers, or desolate desert. There was no place a PJ could not go to make a rescue.

PJ candidates were handpicked from the finest airmen the Air Force had to offer, but ninety percent of them did not make it through the first two months of the course. Most fell victim to "water harassment," where instructors deliberately tried to drown the PJ candidates. The survivors moved on to four weeks of Special Forces Combat Diver course, followed by three weeks of Basic Army Airborne School, then four weeks of Army Free-Fall Training, and finally six months of pararescue training to learn combat medical skills. The maroon beret worn by these men symbolized the blood sacrificed by PJs and their devotion to duty by aiding others in distress. PJs lived up to their motto: "That others may live!"

The primary purpose of the PJ was to save lives. Their history began in August of 1943, when twenty-one persons bailed out of a disabled C-46 over an uncharted jungle near the China-Burma border. So remote was the crash site that the only means of getting help to the survivors was by paradrop. Lieutenant Colonel Don Fleckinger and two corpsmen volunteered for the assignment. This paradrop of medical corpsmen was the seed from which the concept of pararescue was born. For a month these men, aided by natives, cared for the injured until the party was brought to safety. News commentator Eric Severeid was one of the men to survive this ordeal. He later wrote of the men who risked their lives to save his: "Gallant is a precious word; they deserve it."

From this event the need for a highly trained rescue force was discovered and the PJ was brought into being. Rescues since then had occurred in virtually every corner of the world. Since that first rescue, many service members and civilians have had firsthand experience that when trouble struck, PJs were ready to come to their aid. Nearly one thousand pilots were rescued during the Korean War and more than three thousand were saved in Vietnam. PJs were among the first U.S. combatants to parachute into Panama during the 1989 invasion. In Somalia PJs operated in a search-and-rescue role on Army helicopters, inserting into a firefight on one occasion to administer lifesaving medical treatment and extract injured personnel from further danger. PJs made daring rescues of pilots forced to bail out behind enemy lines over Iraq, Yugoslavia, and Afghanistan. Tonight Collins and Harris intended on adding San Selva to the list.

Staff Sergeant Randy Collins and Technical Sergeant Gordon Harris checked their gear and prepared to exit the aircraft and search the ground to save the downed pilots. But to save life in combat it is often necessary to take life, and the two PJs were armed with M4 carbines. A full thirty-round magazine was in each M4, and their assault vests held six more magazines for a total of two hundred rounds. Harris's M4 had an M203 grenade launcher attached to the bottom of the rifle's barrel, and he was carrying twenty-four 40mm grenades of various types. The PJs' backup weapons, 9mm Berreta pistols, were hooked on their belts and each carried smoke grenades to mark for air strikes. Packs were filled with survival gear and medical supplies, and a small radio was attached to the bulletproof vest they wore over their torso. The small hockey-style helmet held their night-vision goggles and radio earpiece. Bottom line: the PJs were ready.

Comanche Crash Site, Macapa, San Selva

Unable to use his left hand because he needed to keep it gripped on Simms's wound, Myers carefully set his pistol down and wiped his face, only to realize that blood soaked his hand. He wanted so badly to run, to make it out of the city where he could hide in the jungle. He felt for Simms's pulse. His copilot barely held on to life. No running for Myers—at least not now. Not while Simms was still alive. He picked up his radio again. "Any station, any station, this is Comanche One Six, over."

*MH-60G Pave Hawk, San Selvan Airspace,
Nearing Macapa*

"That's on the guard freq," said Gunwitz. "We got him!"

"Roger, Comanche," said Nushi. "This is Pave Hawk One Zero."

Gunwitz pushed the MH-60G's two General Electric 1,843-horsepower turboshaft engines toward their maximum speed. The automatic flight-control system helped to stabilize the aircraft during what otherwise could have been a rough flight. Still flying alone over San Selva, Gunwitz felt naked. The slower

MH-60L was just now crossing the border. It would be several minutes before they caught up.

"Pave Hawk! Thank God. I'm down in the city. Not sure where. I crashed into a building. My copilot is hurt bad but alive."

"Gottcha, Comanche. We're a minute or two out. Activate your beacon and hang tight. We're coming for you."

"You gotta hurry. I don't know how much longer my copilot is going to last. He's hurt real bad."

"On the way," responded Gunwitz. "Get ready back there," he said to the PJs. "They have one hurt bad."

"He sounds like he's stressed to the breaking point," said Nushi.

"Well, wouldn't you be?" said Gunwitz.

"I just hope he can hang in there."

"You better send a request for help to the CV-22. I think this might get worse before it gets better." *What are the chances that an urban rescue could be successful?*

Gunwitz and his crew saw the affects of a fight well before they found the downed helicopter. Three Army Comanches circled the crash site. The mean-looking attack helicopters angrily buzzed around the rooftops. They fired their weapons a lot, probably more than necessary, thought Gunwitz, but they did have two buddies stuck down on the ground somewhere. Bravely facing off against the occasional rocket-propelled grenade or burst of machine gun fire, the Army pilots could not see the Comanche or any wreckage in the confusion below. The crowd of people provided the best indication that the pilots were alive somewhere, but if Gunwitz and his team didn't get them out of there soon, the men on the ground would be at the mercy of the angry San Selvan mob.

As Gunwitz began circling the crash site, the Army helicopters pushed farther out to establish a perimeter. They reported seeing several trucks full of gunmen approaching. The trucks were only a few miles from the crowd of civilians. In hopes of delaying the gunmen from joining the melee, the Comanches attacked, while the Air Force Pave Hawk began to search for the downed pilots.

"Can anyone see anything?" Gunwitz asked his crew.

"A lot of damn people," said Riggs, the right-hand door gunner. "Something down there is getting their attention."

Comanche Crash Site, Macapa, San Selva

Myers placed the pistol on his own thigh and felt again for a pulse on Simms's neck. He wanted to escape but he could not leave Simms. For a second he hoped he would not find a pulse. Then he would be able to run away. But Myers seemed to find a pulse everywhere, most likely because of the hard pumping of his own heart. Convinced that Simms was alive, Myers again spoke into the survival radio.

MH-60G Pave Hawk, San Selvan Airspace, Nearing Macapa

"Pave Hawk! Pave Hawk! People are everywhere," the downed pilot screamed into the radio. "Help me."

"Somebody tell me something," snapped Gunwitz. He repeatedly circled the crowd with his helicopter, doing everything he could to let his crew see the ground below without crashing the helicopter into a building. "Where the hell is he?"

"We're taking small-arms fire on my side," said Lee, the left-hand door gunner. "But whoever is shooting is intermixed with the crowd of civilians. Can I shoot?"

"No! Not if you can't do it without shooting the civilians," said Gunwitz. He could hear explosions from the direction of the RAH-66s fighting enemy vehicles.

"I think I see them," said Collins.

"Where?"

"Nine o'clock. There's a hole in the building," said Collins. The PJ used his night-vision device to search the ground. "The bird must in there. You see it?"

"Yeah," said Riggs. "That might be it."

"Any sight of the pilots?" asked Gunwitz.

"Negative."

Gunwitz made another rotation around the crash site but couldn't find a place to set the helicopter down on the ground. He couldn't decide what to do. The Comanches reported even more vehicles moving into the area. Even worse, many more civilians began taking to the street and moving toward the crash site.

"RPG!" yelled Lee to warn the others that he saw someone below holding a rocket-propelled grenade. "RPG!"

"Fire!" said Gunwitz. There was no time to waste. Rocket-propelled grenades are antitank weapons, but they are deadly when fired at low-flying helicopters. Volleys of rocket-propelled grenades were used very effectively against American helicopters during combat in Somalia and Afghanistan. The cheap weapons easily brought down even the most sophisticated aircraft.

Lee used the laser sight to aim his M134 minigun and then pulled the trigger—*wwiiizzz!* The minigun spat a stream of lead. Hundreds of 7.62mm bullets ripped through the gunman, exiting his body and ricocheting off the ground and into the crowd of civilians. Sparks sprouted up on the street below. Several of the civilians near the impact of the minigun dropped to the ground. Most probably fell in fear, but some were undoubtedly wounded. The burst from the minigun raised the ante, and more gunfire began to be directed at the Pave Hawk. The door gunners carefully returned fire. Riggs and Lee tried to identify gunmen, but it was too difficult in the chaos below. Every time they fired the miniguns the gunners knew that they were hitting civilians, but they had no choice. If they didn't shoot back, then they would be blown out of the sky. And they couldn't just leave the pilots at the mercy of the mob.

"RPG!" yelled someone in back.

Wwiiizzz!

"Holy shit!" screamed Nushi.

The force from the rocket-propelled grenade impacted right below the troop compartment. The helicopter rocked forward and the tail section lifted up so the pilot and the copilot looked straight down at the ground. Smoke seeped into the cabin as warning lights flashed in the cockpit.

"Hold on!" yelled Gunwitz. "We're going down."

Comanche Crash Site, Macapa, San Selva

A man boldly stepped around the corner. Myers never heard what the man screamed because his brain focused all of its attention on the sense that provided the best chances for survival—sight. The San Selvan man's eyes glowed with rage and the veins protruded from his neck and head to create an inhuman appearance that was magnified into a devilish figure by the little illumination trickling in from the street.

Myers's peripheral vision narrowed to center on the machete the man swung over his head. Myers instinctively lifted his pistol and aimed in on the man, repeating the same actions he had performed hundreds of times before during training: aligning the front sight post in the rear sight with the fuzzy target that was only a few feet away. The episode progressed in slow motion. He pulled the trigger and never heard the pistol's blast, but he plainly saw the flash of the weapon's discharge. The San Selvan man's face became visible with the flash, and Myers thought he actually saw the 9mm projectile pierce the gunman's thin, white cotton shirt. A small mark appeared on the gunman's left pectoral. Then a burst of blood and meat flew in the air behind the gunman. One large glob of blood hung in the air for a second before spinning down toward the ground, flattening to the size of a quarter as it fell. Myers followed the blood glob in its fall until it hit the dirty ground.

The blood splash disappeared as the San Selvan body dropped on top of it, head hitting last and striking the ground with a gruesome *thud*. It seemed like the first thing Myers had heard in hours. His first reaction to the bullet striking the man's chest was exhilaration—the same exhilaration that he had experienced when he scored a point during childhood basketball games—but that was quickly replaced by anger. Shooting the San Selvan was not like the movies. The man's body convulsed violently as inhuman sounds projected from his mouth and the smoldering wound in his back. Myers could see a growing wet spot appear on the man's crotch. Then came a faint smell of blood, which was soon replaced by a strong smell of shit, indicating to Myers that the man had defecated in his trousers.

"Why did you do that?" Myers screamed at the man's convulsing body. Now watching the body respond violently to the inevitable death that awaited it, Myers was consumed with guilt that his first response to killing another human being was so gleeful. He

questioned if he was going to be able to kill again. Then he kicked at the body. *"Stupid fucking sancho! Couldn't you see I had a gun? Didn't you know I'd shoot?"*

Chapter Fourteen

MH-60G Pave Hawk, San Selvan Airspace Over Macapa

"Help!" screamed the pilot on the ground. "For Christ's sake, get us out of here!"

Bullets ripped through the tail section of the helicopter, sending the aircraft into another violent spin. Gunwitz pulled back on the stick to regain control of the helicopter. He was barely able to keep it in the air after the rocket-propelled grenade. They would not survive a second hit. In back, Lee and Riggs whiteknuckled their miniguns. Collins and Harris lay flat on the floor hanging on to the base of the seats. Sensing that the helicopter was about to depart the area and leave the pilot on the ground, Collins yelled into his microphone, "Sir, put us on the ground."

"There's no way we'll make it to the damn ground,"

said Captain Nushi. "There's nothing but city down there."

"A roof!" yelled Harris. "Put us on a roof then; we can't just leave those guys."

"Sir, you gotta put us down."

"Shut the hell up back there," said Gunwitz.

"We can't leave him, sir," said Collins.

"We're not!" said Gunwitz, and the helicopter, now shaking and sputtering from the damage it received in the firefight, turned and headed back in the direction of the Comanche crash site. Collins turned to Harris and gave him a thumbs-up—they were going in!

The MH-60L Black Hawk, Gunwitz's wingman, radioed that he was now in the area and could link up with the Pave Hawk quickly. Nushi announced their position; Gunwitz hoped the Black Hawk would arrive in time to cover the insert. It was a deadly machine. Called DAP (Direct Action Penetrator), the MH-60L armaments included several 30mm chain guns, racks of missiles and rocket pods, and a 40mm grenade launcher.

Gunwitz brought the Pave Hawk in as close as he could to the crash site without flying over it. After all of the battle damage the helicopter sustained, it would not be able to remain in the air if it took many more hits. The door gunners fired the miniguns in short but deadly bursts at targets invisible to the pilots flying the bird. With each pull of the miniguns' triggers, chunks of cement and wood ripped from the buildings below. Sporadic gunfire entered the sky around the helicopter, but the miniguns gave the enemy little opportunity to fire well-aimed shots, and the helicopter made good progress. The MH-60L arrived just in time and added to the destruction. Gunwitz hovered the helicopter over the tallest building. They were within five hundred meters of the pilots and barely out of the mob's sight. For a second, Gunwitz considered pulling away and telling the PJs that they couldn't go into the hell below, but Gunwitz knew that the PJs would never have agreed. They probably would have made a fatal jump from the helicopter before they would agree to leave the Army pilots in harm's way.

There was no need for orders, because as soon as the helicopter came over the building's roof, Collins and Harris jumped. Both PJs rolled as they hit the hard roof, rising with weapons raised and ready to fire at any targets that appeared. Collins darted to the stairway door. Harris quickly removed two 40mm M203 rounds from his vest: one high explosive and one tear gas. Harris loaded the tear gas round into his M203 and fired down into the stairwell.

The use of tear gas without authorization violated the rules of engagement that existed for Operation Greenhouse. Created by politicians, bureaucrats, and lawyers, the ROE set the playing rules for the operation. The gas was not to be used without the approval of some high-ranking commander, but there was confusion over who could actually approve its use. Besides, Collins and Harris didn't care. The thought of court-martial for violating the ROE was the last thing the two PJs worried about at this moment. *What fool thought that ROE cards matter in a situation like this one?*

"Let me go first," said Collins. "I want to be able to cover you if you need to reload that thing," jerking his head at the M203.

"Roger," said Harris as he slammed the high-explosive round into the M203's breach.

The tear gas began billowing in the stairwell, but the two PJs moved down the stairs into the noxious cloud. The gas was painful but not deadly. Anyone in the stairwell would be panicked, and Harris and Collins were willing to withstand the discomfort if it meant they could get to the ground floor safety.

The M4s led their way, with butt stocks pulled tightly into the pockets of the PJs' shoulders as the barrels pointed out at the unknown. They bounded down the stairs, clearing floor after floor in a matter of seconds. Doors to apartments opened but quickly shut when the occupants sensed the presence of the tear gas. Sounds of people yelling and fumbling with windows consumed the building, but no one entered the stairwell. In the flash of an eye, Collins and Harris dashed to the ground floor and got ready to exit into the street.

"I know this is a stupid question, but which way do we go?" asked Collins.

"I think it's a damn good question," said Harris, chuckling, as he checked the compass attached to his watchband. "We're on the south side of the building now. I think we need to go left, turn left at the building's corner, and then right at the next street."

Collins took a deep breath and bolted from the door, his M4 still leading the way. Harris came right behind him, with his weapon scanning to their rear, both high and low. Speed was their security at this point. Anyone who saw them would probably be so shocked that they would initially panic. The two PJs needed to keep moving before the enemy realized that Americans were on the ground trying to rescue the pilots.

Comanche Crash Site, Macapa, San Selva

Myers snapped out of his daze when the San Selvan's body stopped moving. Someone was shooting outside and he began firing a round out the hole at the crowd every few seconds. Then suddenly the slide for his pistol locked to the rear, signaling that the weapon was out of ammunition.

"Oh, damn," screamed Myers. "Hang on, buddy," he said to Simms's lifeless body. Myers released the empty magazine with his right thumb and removed his left hand from Simms's wound so he could reload the pistol. "I'll only be a second, Ken." Myers pulled at his magazine pouch and removed a full magazine. His hands were slick with blood and he fumbled his grip on the magazine. "Oh, damn! Goddamn!" The magazine *clanked* as it hit the floor.

Myers looked at the magazine, the opening of the hole out to the street, and Simms's gushing wound at what seemed like the same moment. Everything happened at once. He just couldn't get the pistol loaded fast enough. Either another threat would appear around the corner or Simms would lose more blood in the time that he wasted. The sounds of gunfire raged out in the street. Finally, the magazine seated in the pistol, Myers released the weapon's slide to chamber a round. Myers's left hand moved back to Simms's leg and he tried to pinch the artery again. The artery kept slipping from between his fingers. The growing pool of Simms's blood began to saturate Myers's flight suit.

Streets of Macapa, San Selva

A San Selvan in a second-story window fired in the direction of the Army pilots' crash site. Harris aimed his grenade launcher and pulled the trigger. The flash from the M203 drew gunfire from down the street, and Collins dropped to one knee and launched a stream of red-hot tracers into a group of people. Harris's high-explosive round entered into the window and exploded, silencing the gunman. He quickly reloaded another grenade and fired his M4 at a figure that poked around a corner. Collins began firing at everything that moved. At this point in the fight anyone who was in the area was there for no good reason. Any "noncombatants" had had enough time to run away, he reasoned.

The two PJs had come in behind the mob harassing the Army pilots. The first bursts of the PJs' weapons cut down several of the San Selvans, and Collins and Harris quickly closed the distance to the pilots' position, the PJs bounding over dead and wounded San Selvans as they ran down the street.

Harris fired back in the direction the PJs had come from when Collins broke around the corner of a building and headed for the hole.

MH-60G Pave Hawk, San Selvan Airspace Over Macapa

"Papa Hotel, Papa Hotel; cease fire. I say again, *cease your fire!*" said the pilot of the CV-22 that had just arrived. "You're hitting civilians."

Gunwitz clenched his teeth. *What the hell is this guy trying to do? Get everyone killed?* Gunwitz didn't want to kill civilians and he knew his gunners tried to fire well-aimed shots at identified enemy threats, but not firing to avoid hitting civilians only meant that the enemy would have free rein on the ground. And the enemy would also be able to fire on helicopters in the air with impunity, making it very likely that a helicopter would soon be shot down. Right now the situation was bad, but another crash site would make this a catastrophe.

"What should we do, sir?" asked Riggs. He and Lee heard the radio transmission and now sat with their weapons at the ready but quiet.

"Hotel Juliet, Papa Hotel," said Gunwitz. "We have

four of our guys down there. Are you trying to get them killed?" Gunwitz could see the infrared lights on top of each PJ's helmet, clearly indicating where they were on the ground.

"Put your mouth in check. You're committing a massacre down there. You will not fire unless I give you authority to do so."

"Hotel Juliet, Papa Hotel," said Gunwitz. "There are San Selvan gunmen in the street. I need to fire or they will get right on top of our guys."

"Negative, *negative, negative!* Goddamn it, Major. If you fire you're going to hit dozens of civilians."

"They're hiding behind the fucking civilians. And the civilians are free to leave but they know they are providing protection for the gunmen. Those people are participating. They are *combatants.*"

"Papa Hotel, you are relieved. Your copilot is to take control and vector your aircraft to a holding pattern at least five miles from this situation."

"Well, that's not going to happen," sneered Nushi over the helicopter's internal communication system.

Comanche Crash Site, Macapa, San Selva

Myers instinctively fired his pistol at the figure that appeared around the building's corner. He fired two rounds before he realized that his latest target did not look right.

Streets of Macapa, San Selva

"Aaahhhh!" Collins screamed as he fell to a knee and buckled from the pain of Myers's bullet impacting his body.

"Americans!" shouted Harris. "Hold your fire! We're Americans!" He waved his hand in the hole before turning to fire on more San Selvans down the

street. Collins was on his knees. Myers's first shot had missed, but the second round hit Collins in the torso below his right armpit. The bulletproof vest that Collins wore had prevented the bullet from penetrating his body, but the force of the impact broke several ribs.

"God! I'm sorry," said Myers. "I'm so sorry." Myers wanted to crawl to the PJ but he couldn't release his grip on Simms's wound.

Harris grabbed Collins's load-bearing vest and dragged him through the hole and out of the street. As Harris turned to return to the hole, he slipped on the blood-slick ground. His cheek hit the ground and his lips were struck with a salty taste from the blood covering the ground. Harris rolled through the blood pool to the hole and fired more rounds into the mob. Collins flopped on the ground in pain and tried to catch his breath so he could talk.

"Come on! Snap out of it!" yelled Harris. He rotated his stance so he could watch both to the left and right of the hole. "I need your help!" He fired a few rounds in each direction.

Collins still couldn't talk, but he swung his left arm over his head in acknowledgment. He struggled to his feet and moved toward the pilots, stumbling and falling once along the way. Collins fought to remain conscious, knowing that the beginning signs of shock were starting to overtake his body. "I'm . . . okay," he gasped.

"Check them out for me," said Harris, gesturing in the direction of the pilots. Harris began to rethink his joy of being dropped on the rooftop for this rescue mission. Now he was cornered, severely outnumbered, and the three men with him were all hurt. In addition, ammunition would begin to run low quickly. Urban warfare like this required a lot of ammunition.

Each of the PJs was almost done with his second magazine, meaning each had less than one hundred and fifty rounds remaining.

Collins crawled across the broken glass and debris to get to the two pilots. Although it was only a movement of twenty feet, Collins had to stop and rest. He squeezed his eyes tight and tried to fight the coming unconsciousness that he sensed. Now was not the time to succumb to the pain. "How are you doing, sir?" choked Collins as he got to Myers's location. His voice wasn't the booming sound of confidence that he hoped for, wanting to proudly say, *We're here to get you out, sir.* But every breath brought pain, and talking hurt like hell.

"I'm fine, but my copilot is bleeding to death," said Myers. "Can we get him out of here?"

"Yes, sir. We'll get you both out of here." Collins could see that Simms was in horrible condition. Collins placed his middle and index fingers on Simms's neck. He could not find a pulse. He looked down at the puddle of blood that now covered the width of the room. "Sir, I think your friend is dead."

Myers's brain spun inside his head as he listened and replayed what the PJ just said: *Dead.* In the moment of a millisecond, Myers thought about how alive Simms had been earlier in the day. They had been joking with each other before the preflight check of the Comanche. *And maybe he's been dead for a while. I could have gotten away from here. Why the hell am I thinking about that?*

"Where are you hit, sir?" Collins said to Myers. "Sir! Can you get up?" he yelled, trying to be heard over Harris's firing while cringing at the pain his yelling created.

"What?" Myers's head weakly swung in the direction of the PJ and then down at his own legs to see his uniform soaked with Simms's blood. "No."

"You can't get up?"

"No . . . I mean I'm not hit. I can get up." Images of Simms's smiling face raced through Myers's brain. Why did he live but Simms died? He could have done more to save his friend's life. Was it when he took his hand off Simms's wound to reload the pistol? Was that what killed him? *I shouldn't have been worrying about protecting myself. If I had surrendered, then maybe Simms would have received medical attention and would be alive right now. It's all my fault,* thought Myers. He had even prayed that he would not find a pulse on Simms. *Why am I so selfish?*

Harris fired a burst from his M4 at targets down the street. "I see more gunmen coming," he yelled. The presence of the armed Americans sent much of the mob fleeing for cover, but the coming gunmen would be much bolder than the unarmed civilians. "We need to move. The helicopter won't be able to pick us up here. We need a flat roof we can get up on top of." He could hear the helicopters circling overhead. *Why the hell aren't they firing?* He fired another burst at a man with a rifle who tried to cross the street. The man crumpled under the impact of Harris's bullets. *Yeah!*

Collins helped Myers to his feet and then tried to lift Simms but buckled in pain. It was an impossible task. With his broken ribs, Collins would never be able to lift the weight, let alone carry it. Myers tried to help, but he too was injured and unable to be much help. A horrid thought hit Collins. They might need to leave Simms's body if they wanted to live.

Chapter Fifteen

The White House, Washington, D.C.

There was an awkward look on the president's face when the red light illuminated, but then he realized that the camera was on and he began speaking. "My fellow Americans." He nodded his head and paused again, this time deliberately. *Remember not to smile,* he reminded himself. *It's not that kind of speech.* "Tonight our armed forces join with our allies from the Organization of American States in military operations against San Selvan terrorists. We have acted with resolve for several reasons. We act to protect millions of innocent people across the globe from a mounting environmental crisis. We act to prevent a wider war—to diffuse a powder keg at the heart of South America that has exploded several times with catastrophic results. And we act to stand united with

171

our allies for peace. By acting now we are upholding our values, protecting our environmental interests, and advancing the cause of a united global community.

"I want to speak to you about the tragedy taking place in Brazil's rain forests and why it matters to America that we work with our allies to end it. Last year our diplomacy, backed by the threat of force from our OAS alliance, stopped the annual burning for a while. Now the rebels are burning the rain forests again and the fires have grown out of control. We are all threatened by these hostile acts. The soot produced by these fires contributes to our global-warming problems and worsens the violent weather patterns we have experienced for years. Tens of thousands have been killed. Millions are out of work. Economic tragedy invades our own borders. Stopping this horror is a moral imperative.

"All around the area occupied by the San Selvan terrorists there are other small countries struggling with their own economic and political challenges—countries that could be overwhelmed by more weather-related problems. All the ingredients for a major war are there: ancient grievances, struggling democracies, and in the center of it all an illegitimate, rogue government who has done nothing since its declaration of independence but start new wars and pour gasoline on the flames of ethnic and religious division.

"Over the past few months we have done everything we possibly could to solve this problem peacefully. Ambassador Brock worked tirelessly for a negotiated agreement. San Selva has refused to agree. Last week I sent Ambassador Brock to South America to make it clear again, on behalf of the United States and our OAS allies, that they must honor the terms of the United Nation's Global Warming Treaty and stop this raping of the environment or face military action. Not only did they refuse, they attacked an unarmed United Nations fire-fighting aircraft and killed the entire crew.

"Today, we and our OAS allies agree to do what we said we would do, what we must do to ensure peace. Our mission is clear: to demonstrate the seriousness of the Global Warming Treaty's purpose so that the San Selvan leaders understand the importance of reversing course. To deter an even bloodier offensive in South America and, if necessary, to seriously damage the San Selvan military's capacity to attack its neighbors. In short, if San Selva will not stop burning the world's rain forests, we will come in and forcibly make them stop.

"Now, I want to be clear with you, there are risks in this military action—risks to our pilots and the people on the ground. San Selva's guerrillalike air defense is strong. Its navy has already mined much of the Brazilian coastline and threatened international waters. Its army of criminals and terrorists could try to begin assaults on other South American countries. We must deliver a forceful response.

"Hopefully these terrorists will realize their present course is self-destructive and morally unacceptable. If they decide to accept the terms of the Global Warming Treaty and agree to help to implement it with a fire-fighting force, then we will halt our campaign.

"Do our interests in South America justify the dangers to our armed forces? I've thought long and hard about that question and reflected on my own service in our country's guard and reserve forces. I am convinced that the dangers of acting are far outweighed by the dangers of not acting—dangers to the global weather patterns and to our national interests. If our allies and we were to allow this burning to continue

173

with no response, San Selva would read our hesitation as a license to continue. There would be more fires, more deadly storms, thousands of casualties, tens of thousands more refugees, more victims crying out for revenge.

"Right now our firmness is the only hope the people of the world have to be able to live without having to fear for their own lives. We must also remember that this is a conflict with no national boundaries. The damage the San Selvan's evil fires inflict on the environment is a danger to our entire global community. Let a fire burn here in this area and the flames of destruction will spread. Every second that the fires continue to burn makes things worse and does irreversible damage. Eventually, key U.S. allies could be drawn into a wider conflict, a war we would be forced to confront later—only at far greater risk and greater cost.

"I have a responsibility as president to deal with problems such as this before they do permanent harm to our national interests. America has a responsibility to stand with our allies when they are trying to save innocent lives and preserve the environment, freedom, and stability in South America. That is what we are doing. That is why we have acted now. Because we care about saving innocent lives; because we have an interest in avoiding an even crueler and costlier war; and because our children need and deserve a healthy environment."

Atlanta, Gerogia

"Our thoughts and prayers must be with the men and women of our armed forces who are undertaking this mission for the sake of our values and our children's future. May God bless them and may God bless America."

Bob Montgomery turned down the radio and was hit by a blast of hot air as he rolled down the car's driver-side window. It had to be hotter than hell outside. *Blame what you want on the poor San Selvans, Mr. President, I know the truth.* Infrared images of Atlanta from space showed it as a hot spot. This heat island effect caused more problems than pollution. Bubbles of hot air brought irregular weather patterns. The urban sprawl engulfing the Atlanta region contributed greatly to the temperature changes. Heat meant more evaporation, which led to increased moisture in the air and more and more unpredictable weather patterns. All while people ignored methods that could lead to heat reduction, thought Montgomery. Most of the United States might blame poor nations like San Selva, but he blamed those within the United States because they chose to do stuff that increased temperature. Stuff like building obscenely huge, energy-sucking houses. Simple changes could make a huge a difference. White roofs were cooler than dark roofs because light colors reflected heat while dark absorbed it. White roofs could be seventy degrees cooler than traditional, dark roofs, but Americans thought the white roofs looked ugly and few buildings were built with them.

Montgomery saw what he wanted and slowed the vehicle. A man cautiously walked to the car window, looking to his left and right as he entered the street. "What do you want, man?"

"A little rock."

"Forty."

"*Forty?* Are you kidding?" Montgomery wiped the sweat from his forehead.

"War in South America, dude. The price has gone up."

"You've gotta be shitting me!"

175

"Hey, you want it or not?"

"Yeah, yeah, I'll take it," answered Montgomery. The price increase for crack cocaine was ridiculous. Hopefully this silliness would end soon, and the price of drugs would get back down to a reasonable price. As a college student, he didn't have a lot of extra spending money. He didn't need to pay more for his crack because the military was trying to justify their obscene budget by spending more money on some war.

Pulling away from the curb after making his purchase, Montgomery turned the radio volume back up.

"Critics of Operation Greenhouse are calling for congressional hearings concerning the legality of military action, while supporters are saying that the opponents are putting American soldiers at risk to advance their political opposition of the president. Both sides have agreed that the way in which the operation has begun does not make sense. Many, including Senator Kidd, are calling for the immediate use of U.S. ground troops. Too many legitimate targets are going untouched, and in a country where it is practically against the law not to own a gun, destroying the San Selvan government may only open the door into an ugly quagmire. San Selvan civilians are prepared to conduct terrorist acts against any ground forces. Many are warning that ground troops mean many American casualties."

"Just don't start talking about starting a draft and we'll be okay," Montgomery said aloud. He didn't want to waste his life. The military was for people who couldn't make it in life. All those losers, who couldn't be like him and get into college to make something of their lives.

Chapter Sixteen

MH-60G Pave Hawk, San Selvan Airspace Over Macapa

"We need help down here." Harris's radio transmission hung in the earphones of the helicopter air crew's, almost echoing for all to hear again and again. The situation below was bad and getting worse. If Gunwitz didn't quickly get the PJs and pilots out of the hell below, then they would all probably be captured or killed. In addition, fire from the sanchos grew in intensity and accuracy. He should never have put the PJs on the ground. The bravado that surrounded the legends of military service also killed many people.

Muzzle flashes became visible from the street and the Comanche's crash site, indicating that an intense firefight raged between the San Selvans and the PJs. Something had to be done quickly.

"Bravo Hotel, this is Papa Hotel," Gunwitz said, calling his wingman in the better-armed helicopter.

"Roger," said the pilot of the MH-60L. "I'm with you."

Gunwitz was relieved. He didn't even need to ask the MH-60L if they were willing to follow him in his assault of the gunmen below, even though the MH-60L crew had heard the earlier radio conversations between the CV-22 and Gunwitz.

RAH-66 Comanche Crash Site, Macapa, San Selva

"RPG!" screamed Harris. Swish*Boom*. He ducked down behind the wall just before the rocket-propelled grenade slammed into the side of the building. His ears rang from the explosion, and he spat a mouthful of dirt before returning to his firing position.

Inserting a high-explosive round into the M203, Harris slammed the breach closed and fired the weapon around the corner. The familiar *whooop* sound from the round being thrown from the weapon was reassuring to Harris's ears, and he fired rifle rounds from the M4 before the explosion from the 40-mm grenade shook the street. Harris opened the breach and inserted another grenade, blasting out another stream of rifle rounds before he fired the M203 again.

A man stepped forward and threw a Molotov cocktail at the Americans. Harris fired at him but missed. He aimed his shots as best he could before firing again. Every round had to count. There wasn't enough ammunition to let any go to waste. People ran everywhere. Most threw things at the Americans, but more and more shot weapons. Harris did everything he could to hold back the San Selvans. Finally the helicopters swooped down and sent the sanchos running for cover. *Where the fuck have they been?* "We've got to get the hell out here. We can't stay. They're going to blow us apart with RPGs soon."

"Let's go, sir," Collins said to Myers. "Grab your buddy. We've got to move."

"Hurry up!" screamed Harris.

Collins tried again to lift the dead pilot but couldn't with the pain from his ribs. "Gordo!" he yelled. "I just can't carry this guy."

"Can you cover us? Because there are a lot of them."

"I think so." Collins moved to replace Harris. His ribs killed him, but this wasn't the time to be weak. He moved to the hole and immediately began firing his M4. Dust and debris from the San Selvans' rifle fire kicked up around him and a horde of people pressed forward. Collins fired again and was amazed by the mob. They showed no fear, continuing to come after the Americans even though some were being shot. It had to be pure hate that drove the San Selvans. There was no other explanation. More rocks and rifle rounds pelted the area around the hole.

"We're ready!" yelled Harris. He held the dead pilot's upper torso, and the other pilot struggled to carry the legs.

"There's too damn many of them," shouted Collins. "I've got to push them back first."

Harris put the pilot down for a second and fired another high-explosive round from the M203, but this time he aimed directly at the crowd. Both PJs fired now. Collins threw a hand grenade before reloading his weapon and continuing to fire. Harris reloaded the M203 and fired another round. And another. And another. Bodies crumpled as the fragments from the grenades spewed into the mob. Hot shrapnel sliced through legs and torsos. The tide began to turn as the

San Selvans moved back from the destructive effects of the grenade launcher.

"Let's go!" yelled Harris, grabbing at the dead pilot under the arms again.

The three men struggled out of the hole and into the street. The mob lunged forward when they saw the Americans, but then Collins fired in all directions. Some people fell and most moved back. An angry few stood their ground, refusing to yield ground to the invaders. Collins shot one stubborn woman in the head before he realized she was unarmed. He didn't know how to feel. He had to do something to keep the momentum going and she stood in the way. The group of Americans moved quickly down the street to the corner. They had to get to a roof.

MH-60G Pave Hawk, San Selvan Airspace Over Macapa

"They're all over us," yelled one of the PJs. Gunwitz couldn't decipher which one. "Where the hell are you guys?"

"Hang on, hang on," said Gunwitz. "We're coming. Can you make it to a roof?"

"I don't know. We're oscar mike now." His talking was rushed. "I'm hit." To Gunwitz it sounded like the PJ was running. "Gordo is trying to carry the dead one." Loud noises could be heard over the PJ's microphone. "The live guy isn't much help."

"Dead?" *Good God! One of the pilots is dead?* "Are you sure he's dead?"

"Hell, yes!"

"Leave the body if you have to. Just get the hell out of there—now!"

"Gordo's hit! Gordo just got hit!"

"Mark your position. I'm coming in now," Gunwitz said to Collins. "Riggs, Harris; they've got one dead, the other three are wounded down there. Once they mark their position, we're going to blast the hell out of everything else."

"Roger."

"Bravo Hotel, PJs are going to mark. We need to blow a perimeter for them."

"Why don't you move aside, Witz?" answered the other helicopter. "Let me get in there with my rockets first."

"Good idea. Come up and take the lead."

"RPG!" *Wwiiizzz!* The door gunner blasted away with the minigun at gunmen on the rooftops. Clouds of dust and dirt spat up around the gunmen. *Wwiiizzz! Wwiiizzz!*

Streets of Macapa, San Selva

"I've thrown IR smoke. Can you see it?" asked Collins. The cloud forming from the soda-can-sized smoke grenade would normally have been very difficult for the helicopter crew to spot in the darkness, even with their goggles, but the infrared affect of the IR smoke made it shine brightly through the night-vision device.

"We got it, get your heads *down!*"

"In here!" Collins pushed Myers and dragged Harris into a narrow alleyway, leaving Simms's lifeless body in the street. "Watch out," yelled Collins to Myers. "Get your fucking head down!" The buildings exploded as bullets and rockets ripped a protective circle around the three men. Simms's body lay nearby but far enough away that it too was hit by the firing.

Collins used the firestorm as an opportunity to check Harris's wound. "Where the fuck are you hit?" At first he couldn't hear Harris's screams over the sounds of the aerial bombardment.

"In here. Oh, fuck. It hurts." Harris held his right side with both hands. Collins reached in and felt the hole. Harris screamed again as Collins's fingers slid along the slick opening. A rocket exploded again and sparks from the miniguns striking the street lit up the alley.

"We need to get Kenny," said Myers.

"What's that, sir?" Collins looked up. He had almost forgotten all about Myers.

"We need to go get Kenny." He pointed out into the street.

"We aren't going anywhere but out of here, sir. I'm sorry about your friend, but he's dead now."

"No, no, no. Go get him. You go get him right now. It's your job."

Collins ignored Myers as he removed Harris's body armor so he could see the wound. The bullet had entered Harris's body through a seam in the armor plates. It created a minor entrance wound along the right side of Harris's torso, but when the round reached the other side of his body and tried to exit it hit the front plate of the body armor and ricocheted back into his body. The second trip through the body ripped right through Harris's midsection, creating horrible damage. The gurgling of the entry hole indicated the lung had been hit. Collins put the plastic battle-dressing cover over the wound and pushed hard. He then covered the plastic with the battle dressing and tightly tied the bandage in place to seal the sucking chest wound.

"Oh, *shit!*" cried Harris when Collins began to roll him onto the side of the wound.

"You gotta lie on it or you'll drown in your own blood."

Harris screamed in a piercing girlie pitch. Swish-*Boom*. Another RPG but fired away from the alley.

Gunman must have been aiming at a helicopter. More explosions as the birds responded. They wouldn't be able to keep it up forever.

"Why the fuck are you just going to leave him there?" yelled Myers.

Harris groaned, too exhausted to scream again.

"Shut the fuck up. I'm going to goddamn leave your ass here if you don't stop whining. You go get him."

Myers didn't move. The pilot was not seriously wounded, but he demonstrated little ability to fight effectively. He now stared blankly into space and babbled. Fewer rounds rained down from the helicopters. Checking his ammunition load, Collins was horrified to find that he had two magazines and a few high-explosive rounds for the grenade launcher. He found only one magazine in Harris's gear. *Shit!*

MH-60G Pave Hawk, San Selvan Airspace Over Macapa

"Keep it coming!" yelled Collins over the radio. "We're low on ammo."

"Keep it up back there," Gunwitz said to the door gunners. Then hitting the microphone switch to talk to the PJ on the ground, he said, "How's Gordo?"

"He's bad, sir. He's hit real bad and is out of it. The pilot is catatonic."

"Can you get out of there to a roof?"

"There's no way I can move Gordo."

"Randy, you may need to leave him. Can you and the pilot get to a roof?"

"Affirmative, sir . . . I mean *no* . . . I'm not leaving Gordo. I need the Rangers from the CV-22."

"Watch out!" yelled Nushi. The CV-22 came dangerously close to the Pave Hawk helicopter. Zigzagging left and right, the other Air Force helicopter attempted to block Gunwitz's line of fire.

"Papa Hotel, Cease fire! Cease fire! Cease fire!"

"Hotel Juliet! Roll to net ID one one eight and listen to my guys on the ground. One of the pilots is dead. One of my men is down hard. The other two are wounded and fighting for their lives. *For Christ's sake,* if you're not going to help, then at least stay out of my way."

"Holy shit!" yelled Riggs. "Did they just shoot at us?"

"I need fire support!" Collins screamed over the radio. *"Why the fuck did you stop shooting?"*

Streets of Macapa, San Selva

"Fire! Fire! Fire!" screamed Collins into the radio handset. "Sir!" he yelled at Myers. "You gotta help me." Gunfire came from all directions. Myers fired back. "For Christ's sake, *fire!"* he yelled into the radio again. People closed in, shouting angrily and throwing anything they could pick up. There was a roar of noise. The mob's hostility hung in the air with the smoke from the Americans' weapons.

Myers looked at him blankly. "That guy smelled so bad after I shot him. I wonder if he was still alive when he shit himself."

Collins grabbed Harris and started to move him. Harris screamed each time that Collins pulled. A San Selvan threw a firebomb that brightly lit the area, catching the Americans illuminated and in the open. Something hit Collins in the arm. Sanchos surrounded them. They were everywhere. Collins pulled again but because of his wounds he couldn't move Harris. He fired more rounds from the M4 and M203.

"Just leave me here," moaned Harris. "Take the pilot and go to the roof."

"Shut up." Collins brought the M4 up again and fired a deadly burst. He scanned for more targets, firing as they appeared until there was the horrible *clunk!* sound from the weapon as the bolt for the M4 remained locked back in the chamber. The ammunition magazine was empty. Knowing it was his last M4 magazine, Collins instinctively drew his 9mm pistol from the holster. He only had one magazine for the pistol. That meant that Collins only had fifteen rounds left. He frantically checked his and Harris's gear for another magazine. With a maximum range of fifty meters, the pistol did not provide the fire support needed. He found an M67 fragmentation grenade but no ammunition magazines.

"Sir, where is your pistol?" Collins asked Myers. "What the hell did you do with your pistol?"

"Please go," moaned Harris.

Collins keyed his radio. "Witz, I *fucking* need help, sir. I'm almost out of ammo down here."

MH-60G Pave Hawk, San Selvan Airspace Over Macapa

Gunwitz clenched his jaw tight before keying the microphone on the air-to-air frequency. "Hotel Juliet, did you copy that?" asked Gunwitz. "Can you hear them?"

"Negative, Papa Hotel. We're unable to come up on that net ID. Our timing or crypto must be different than yours. Can your PJs roll to our freq?"

"*Whhaattt?*" cried Gunwitz. "No! They're out of goddamn ammo. I can't have them waste time switching freqs. I need you to put your Rangers on the ground." He'd already requested, begged really, that the Ranger Reaction Force or Marine TRAP (Tactical Recovery of Aircraft and Personnel) Force be deployed to rescue the PJs and the Army pilot, but no decision had been made by higher headquarters yet.

"I can't do that without permission."

"You little *bitch!*" cursed Gunwitz, then switching to the PJs frequency Hotel Juliet. "Hang on, Randy. I'm coming in for you." Switching back to the CV-22's frequency, "*move!* I'm going in and I'll blow you out of the fucking sky if you get in my way!"

If Collins couldn't, or really wouldn't, move to a roof, then Gunwitz needed to go to him. The street next to the alley might be just wide enough for the Pave Hawk's rotor blades to fit, but Gunwitz would not know for sure until he tried.

"I don't think we're going to fit, sir," said Riggs.

"We gotta try," answered Nushi. "Talk us in."

People ran everywhere. *Wwiiizzz! Wwiiizzz!* One of the miniguns spat a stream of fire into the street below. Gunwitz couldn't see what door gunners fired at.

"There's people on my side," said Lee.

The MH-60L circled overhead and fired a deadly ring of rockets and bullets around the descending helicopter. Too bad the Comanches had already departed the area after running out of ammunition and fuel. Their firepower would be helpful right now.

"Come right," said Riggs.

"No, no!" said Lee. "There's no room over here."

"How much room do I have, Riggs?"

"None, sir. It's going to be a damn tight fit."

Out of the corner of his eye, Nushi caught Gunwitz's attention. The copilot held his pistol in one hand, obviously thinking that he was about to become an active participant in some real close combat.

Wwiiizzz! Wwiiizzz! The miniguns spat tracers in a laser-beam-like stream of light, and the acrid smell of burning gunpowder hung inside the helicopter. Fifty feet from the ground and dropping fast, the door gunners fired at any San Selvan who was not in a dead sprint to get out of the area. The mob divided like the biblical Red Sea, and Lee could see the huddle of Americans in an alley between two buildings. One, who must be Collins, fired down the alley and at least two bodies sat near him. The men seemed close enough to spit on but too far to save as the flash of a rocket-propelled grenade being fired from farther down the street snapped Lee's attention to another direction. "Jesus Christ!" he yelled, firing his minigun at the incoming high-explosive warhead. "RPG! RPG!" A stream of smoke followed the warhead in toward the helicopter.

Gunwitz didn't see the projectile until after it screamed under his aircraft and slammed into the building on the left side of the MH-60G Pave Hawk. The MH-60L Black Hawk still circled overhead. At least the CV-22 stayed out of the way for the time being.

There was a sharp *pop pop pop* and *clank* of metal as San Selvan bullets impacted against the fuselage of Gunwitz's bird. Swish*Boom*. Just as Gunwitz brought it within twenty feet of the ground, a violent impact shuddered through the aircraft as a rocket-propelled grenade hit the helicopter. It was as if a truck had plowed into the side of the Pave Hawk.

Gunwitz wrestled for control as the helicopter wildly swung closer to a building. He increased power to speed the rotors' RPM, fighting the entire time to keep control of the wounded bird. His thoughts were fuzzy. He focused on the sight of a building coming toward his windshield. As if in answer to a prayer, the building magically dropped below and out of sight.

The sounds of alarms screeched over the roar of the engines, but no other crew members said anything. *Why aren't the others helping?* Gunwitz thought, as he looked down at the compass and turned the nose of the bird due south. *How far is the Brazil border?*

There was still pitch control. Maybe he could make it back. Then he remembered the PJs on the ground and he shook his head to try and remember how long it had been since he'd spoken with them.

Another building became visible in the windshield, but it didn't move closer to the helicopter. Gunwitz focused on a strange object that suddenly appeared in front of him. The controls to the helicopter did not respond to his manipulations of the stick and pitch, and he realized that the object in the windshield was a crack. The shrieks and alarms grew louder, no longer competing with the sound of the engines. The MH-60G was on the ground.

Streets of Macapa, San Selva

Back two blocks away, Collins anxiously waited for the San Selvan gunmen to get closer. He could see them in his night-vision monocular. They were getting smarter, he thought, not rushing up to be shot. Now they tried to sneak in.

As two drew within five meters, Collins sprang from his hiding place and fired his pistol. The two San Selvans dropped after three shots from the 9mm, and Collins jumped on top of them and thrust his combat knife into their bodies repeatedly. He couldn't afford to fire more shots than absolutely necessary. He hunted men now, and every one he killed provided the opportunity for him to obtain weapons and ammunition from their lifeless bodies.

Convinced that he'd killed or seriously wounded the two San Selvans, Collins leaped forward to attack any gunmen that followed. The alley was dark and confusing. People began to appear in the windows above him. He couldn't stay in this location much longer. After a second or two, he returned to the two bodies and searched them. *Jackpot!* Three 5.56mm magazines on the men.

Suddenly red tracers ripped through the alley. The fire flew around, erratic and unaimed, but ricochets bounced everywhere. A bullet fragment pierced Collins's quadriceps, sending him tumbling to the hard ground. Collins reached for the hand grenade he'd taken earlier from Harris's gear. Pulling the pin with his left hand and flicking the safety clip away with his right hand, he released his grip on the grenade's spoon. The spoon flipped off and the hammer snapped down on the primer to arm the grenade. Now came the guessing game. "Milking" a grenade was dangerous. The fuse was suppose to be set for three to five seconds, but as was often the case with munitions produced by assembly lines of human workers, an unknown number of the grenades did not "meet standard." Was this a grenade that traveled down the assembly line on the day before a holiday weekend, when workers were not focused on the task before them? If the grenade fell below standard, it might blow up in Collins's hand. If it exceeded standard, the San Selvans might have time to pick it up and throw it back at Collins before it exploded. Randy quickly lost track of time as he stared at the baseball-sized object, practically panicking when he finally threw it down the alley.

Boom! The blast shook loose debris and created a huge plume of smoke and dirt. Thousands of fragments from the grenade's body had penetrated the skin of several San Selvans, creating a new pile of bloody bodies that squirmed violently. Screams from the newly wounded San Selvans tore through the air. Collins did not fire, because he did not want to waste more ammunition on them. Before going to search the new kills, he recovered his M4 and loaded a 5.56mm magazine in it. Then he took out his bayonet and connected it to the end of the M4. The nine-inch knifelike bayonet was a primitive weapon, with its origins connected to the days before gunpowder, when men fought with the blades of pikes and swords. The faint *click* of the bayonet connecting to the lug on the rifle brought home the realization to Collins that he might soon be completely out of ammunition. When he stabbed the San Selvans earlier it was to conserve ammunition. Now Collins might need to cut and stab to stay alive.

MH-60G Pave Hawk Crash Site, Macapa, San Selva

Gunwitz turned his head to look at his copilot. Nushi leaned forward lifelessly in his seat. Gunwitz couldn't turn his head far enough to see the two door gunners in back and he could not sense any indication of movement either.

With a deep sigh, Gunwitz removed his nomex gloves and held them in his hands calmly. He pressed his lips together. *Well, what now?* He looked out the side window. *How far did I fly before crashing?* No sign of the PJs and Army pilots. He began flipping switches on the helicopter's control panel, just like any other postflight, when the CV-22 came to a hover overhead and created a storm on the ground. Two fast ropes dropped from the huge aircraft and a steady stream of Rangers slid down to the ground in front of Gunwitz. Within fifteen seconds thirty heavily armed Rangers were on the ground.

"Are you okay, sir?" yelled a Ranger who suddenly appeared next to Gunwitz. It was a lieutenant who looked far too young enough to command a rescue force. "Sir, are you okay?"

Gunwitz weakly nodded his head, turning again to look at Nushi.

"Doc!"

Rangers fanned out around the crash site. The CV-22 and MH-60L circled overhead and fired occasionally. As Gunwitz was removed from the aircraft, a Ranger climbed into the cockpit and began to zero the classified radios. He then placed explosives at specific points on the helicopter's control panel.

"Hurry up!" screamed an unseen man outside of the helicopter. "We've got to move quick!"

The four airmen were removed from the helicopter wreckage and strapped to collapsible backboards. One medic worked on each man. Gunwitz could tell that everyone was alive, although in varying degree of consciousness. Riggs's left arm was ripped off and the Rangers were having a tough time extracting the severed limb from the wreckage. Their hands shone from the slick blood as they pulled and hacked to free the arm.

Gunwitz was worried the two door gunners' backs might be broken. They didn't have shock-absorbing seats like the pilots. He kept trying to ask about the PJs and Army pilots, but the Ranger medics kept telling him to be quiet and save his strength.

Streets of Macapa, San Selva

Collins fired a flurry of rifle rounds at the San Selvan gunmen. They kept getting closer. Another magazine run dry, he reached for a full 5.56mm magazine as two gunmen suddenly appeared on his right flank and rushed his position. Collins rose and stumbled at the gunmen. Flustered by Collins's reaction, the gunmen fired wildly. Miraculously none of the bullets hit Collins as he closed the ten feet in half a heartbeat. He

191

thrust the metal butt stock of the M4 upward against the first San Selvan's head, which snapped backward as the force of the blow split his head open.

Collins then brought the bayoneted weapon around to strike the other gunman in the chest. The gunman screamed and grabbed at the rifle. Kicking the gunman's feet out from under him, Collins tried to stomp the man to death with his boot, but the pain from the wound in Collins's quadriceps sent him tumbling down. He landed on top of the gunman. The M4 became lost in the tangle of limbs and debris. Now completely unarmed because he couldn't remove his rifle from the mess, Collins ripped off his helmet and began to beat the two gunmen to death. He felt the skull of one man collapse under the force of a third or forth blow, and then he turned his efforts toward smashing in the head of the second sancho. Finally, with the two new bodies gushing blood from open head wounds, Collins fumbled around the carnage in search of a weapon. More San Selvans were coming and he couldn't kill all of them with his helmet. He retrieved his M4 and reloaded the rifle with his last ammunition magazine.

The fight continued, but future killing came harder for Collins. The San Selvans demonstrated what they'd learned from their failures. That, or better-trained troops had joined the fight. The sanchos no longer attempted tactically inept frontal attacks. Now the gunmen attacked from two locations or more. Obviously coordinated attacks: one group would fire so another could move closer to the Americans. And the technique was working. Although Collins was stacking up San Selvan bodies around the perimeter, he couldn't hold out forever. *Where the hell is that rescue force?*

Crawling to Harris, Collins whispered, "Gordo? Gordo, are you okay?"

"Yeah."

"Okay, sit tight. They'll come for us soon. They won't just leave us here." Collins took Harris's pistol and crawled to Myers. "Sir, here, take this pistol. I want you to go to the rooftop of this building. Don't make my life a waste. *Earn this, sir!* Go to the roof so the helo can pick you up."

"Just give me another minute or two. I'm too tired to move right now. Do you know what time it is?"

MH-60G Pave Hawk Crash Site, Macapa, San Selva

An old man stepped from behind a building and Rangers fired on him from three different directions, dismembering the San Selvan in a plume of red vapor.

"Sir, how many were on board?" It was the young Ranger lieutenant again.

"Four of us," said Gunwitz. "Are the PJs here too?"

"No, sir. There's so many RPGs in the air over there that it is a miracle you got as close to the ground as you did. We roped in immediately so the sanchos couldn't get to you, but if we don't get the hell out of here now we never will. We gotta extract now."

"No!" gasped Gunwitz. "No, we can't leave without them."

"Right now you need to tell me if there is anything special in the helicopter that I need to remove or destroy. *Sir!* Did you hear me?"

Streets of Macapa, San Selva

"Go, Randy," whispered Harris.

It was so quiet now. Something had happened. No helicopters above.

"Don't worry. They'll be here soon."

MH-60G Pave Hawk Crash Site, Macapa, San Selva

Two men grabbed each wounded airman and carried him on his backboard across the street and to a building. Major Gunwitz couldn't help but think that the Rangers were doing it wrong. The new training standard, the one created to compensate for the number of women now in the Armed Forces, required four soldiers to carry one stretcher. But the Rangers were not into minimum standards. They were hardened warriors, most of whom were firing carefully aimed shots from their rifles. Guided by the infrared aiming devices on their weapons, the Rangers blew San Selvans apart with every pull of a trigger. No wild firing. No long burst on full auto. Only the sighting of a target, the placement of the laser pointer, a pull of the trigger, and another head was vaporized. It was just so easy.

Gunwitz must have lost consciousness for a moment, because the next thing he knew he was on the roof of a building. A whine from the aircraft stung Gunwitz's ears. He lifted his head as he was carried feet first over the rear ramp of the Ospery. The faint lights from the cockpit illuminated the large cargo area, and the Rangers piled into the partially landed, partially hovering CV-22. The MH-60L ferociously circled.

"My PJs?" Gunwitz said weakly.

"What, sir?" yelled a medic, moving his head closer to Gunwitz's mouth.

Gunwitz lifted his head. "Did you get my PJs?"

"Sir, I can't hear you. Just be still now. Be still."

But he never heard the last few words. The last thing Gunwitz remembered before falling back into the blackness of his brain was the CV-22 pilot looking back from his cockpit seat and shaking his head disapprovingly at Gunwitz.

Streets of Macapa, San Selva

Collins sat with his back against a wall and wished there were enough light for him to see the picture. He squeezed it in his hand, considering whether or not he should turn on a flashlight for a quick peek. What harm could it do? He was fucked anyway, and the risk was worth seeing the faces of his family one last time.

"How you doing, sir?" Collins asked Myers. The pilot wouldn't run to the roof as Collins requested, and Collins still refused to leave Harris. *Hopefully help is coming soon,* he lied to himself.

"Have you seen Chief Warrant Officer Simms?" responded Myers.

"Yes, yes, I have." Collins laughed. "He's that ripped-apart body over there," he said, motioning to the lifeless body that lay several meters away. Collins checked Harris's neck again for a pulse. He was still alive.

Before Collins removed his flashlight for that last look at the picture of his family, chips from the concrete wall above rained down on him as the San Selvans began firing again. And then rocket-propelled grenades began to impact from all directions.

Chapter Seventeen

F/A-18E Super Hornet, Nearing San Selvan Airspace

Streaking through the air just below the speed of sound—seven hundred and sixty feet per second—Crash Linsey's jet flew two hundred feet above the treetops. A pair of cylindrical pods under the fuselage of the aircraft held a LANTRIN system that allowed for the amazing flying feat. The AAQ-13 Low Altitude Navigation and Targeting Infrared for Night (LANTRIN) system combined terrain-following radar and forward-looking infrared sensors to generate a video image for the pilot's heads-up display that enabled Crash to fly through total darkness.

The low altitude and high speed put the pilots in a better position to drop their bombs, while protecting them from antiaircraft missiles. Because they moved so fast and so low, it would be harder for the San

196

Selvan air-defense gunners to acquire the jets and fire a missile. The threat now came from unsophisticated antiaircraft guns firing wildly into the night sky. It would take an unlucky twist of fate for an aircraft to be hit badly enough to crash.

In this first night of combat, the San Selvans proved to be a tougher adversary than expected. Intelligence analysts were learning that San Selvan civilians used fires all over the country to disrupt American visual and infrared sensors. The smoke created would also continue to complicate American efforts by preventing laser-aiming devices from seeing their targets. Along with the primitive methods of jamming sophisticated sensors, the San Selvans had also crept across the borders with portable surface-to-air weapons. Several were already fired at aircraft from the Venezuelan, Brazilian, and French Guianan jungles. This development complicated the operation, because now American aircraft needed to bomb an ally country as a defensive measure.

Crash listened to all the traffic on the radios. The radios were used only when they must be, like with the problems Crash and her pilots had experienced a short time before, but the airwaves buzzed with transmissions from aircraft that had already conducted raids. Many pilots reported battle damage as sheer curtains of antiaircraft fire intermixed with surface-to-air missile launches to blanket the sky.

Suddenly Sara experienced the horror for herself. First a flash and streak of light appeared in front of her Super Hornet. Then explosions rocked the air around her. There was no electronic warning or countermeasure for the large-caliber, high-explosive projectiles fired from antiaircraft guns. Crash's only defenses at this point were her eyes and flying skills. She swung the F/A-18E into a sharp turn. Bright tracers cut through the darkness and flung off in all directions. The audible *boopboopboop* warning told her that she needed to climb to avoid crashing into terrain below, forcing Sara to adjust her evasive maneuvers.

Deedledeedledeedle! A flashing "14" symbol appeared on the map's screen and the bright yellow MISSILE WARNING and MISSILE ALERT lights illuminated at the same time. An SA-14 antiaircraft missile headed for Sara's jet. *Smart motherfuckers. Taking advantage of the smoke to use old-fashioned antiaircraft guns and high-tech missiles together.* The AN/ALE-28 automatically deployed chaff and flares—sending white-hot magnesium and bundles of tinsel-like strips of metal to misdirect the incoming missiles. The audio alarm ceased after five seconds, but then started again as another missile flew toward Sara's jet.

She banked hard in a starboard turn, slightly climbing again to get terrain between her and the missile. G-forces rippled through her body and threatened to cause unconsciousness. Her special flight suit inflated with air and prevented all of the blood from being pulled to extremities and away from her brain that needed the blood the most.

She jerked her head around uselessly to try and find the incoming missile. At just under four feet long, it would only be seen after it was too late to react. The MISSILE WARNING light still burned bright and she was careful not to push her Super Hornet into afterburner. She bounced over another ridgeline, with the *boopboopboop* warning her again.

There was a bright flash below her and the MISSILE WARNING light went dark. It had been the longest four seconds of Sara's life, but it wasn't over. More antiaircraft gunfire ripped through the darkness in front of her F/A-18E. This time fire came from San Selvan S-60s or ZU-23s antiaircraft gunfire. The S-60 was towed behind or mounted in a truck and fired 57mm rounds. The ZU-23 had twin 23mm cannons. Both weapons fired armor-piercing, high-explosive bullets at low-flying targets. The San Selvans had held their fire during the Tomahawk and stealth strikes, waiting for the more vulnerable conventional aircraft to join the fight.

There was no way around the ground fire, and altitude would just lead to another missile being on her ass, so Crash pointed the jet into the storm. She increased speed and tipped the jet into sideways flight to reduce the target size for gunners on the ground. Bright tracers shot past her canopy. Small concussions from explosions disturbed the air, but Crash flew right through the hellish scene seemingly without a scratch on her aircraft.

"Whooohooo! Fuck yeah!" She leveled the aircraft.

Crash stripped off her oxygen mask and relived the minute or two of terror. It was a small miracle that she was still in flight. The sky turned dark again as she distanced herself from the antiaircraft defenses. Checking her display panel, she breathed a sigh of relief when she saw that all of her strike team still flew behind her. No one even reported any serious battle damage through the automated systems. Before long they would be over the target and then headed home.

Suddenly the aircraft shuddered. There was a *pop,* causing Crash to think for a second that she had been hit by antiaircraft fire. But the Hornet's missile-warning systems had not activated and there were no tracers. She was just about to make a radio call to her wingman when the F/A-18E made another loud sound and banked hard to the left and down, bringing the aircraft dangerously close to the treetops.

Crash didn't have time to think. Her training took over as she fought to regain control of the aircraft.

She pulled back on the stick and powered the engines in an attempt to climb higher. Barely able to hold altitude, Crash knew that if she didn't fall to the ground, she would probably fly right into it. *Boopboopboop! Boopboopboop!* She needed to gain altitude, but the aircraft would not respond. It was going down. *Boopboopboop!*

Looking at the handle with PULL TO EJECT written on it, she took only a millisecond to make the decision, but it seemed like a year. She tucked her elbows into her side and locked her neck in place. She reached for the ejection handle and pulled it. Adjusted to require forty to fifty pounds of pressure, the handle came up with ease in Crash's hands.

Pyrotechnic charges blew off the fighter's canopy, and then a rocket motor fired the cockpit seat free from the aircraft. Sara heard the jettisoned canopy *pop* away into the darkness. The ejection seat blew clear of the aircraft. A blast of warm air ripped her kneeboard, NVGs, and other poorly attached items off of her body. The force of ten gs stunned Sara. She'd never ejected before because it was too dangerous an event to practice.

The seat was programmed to release its parachute automatically at fourteen thousand feet. Anything higher would not have an adequate amount of oxygen. But because of the low altitude Crash was at when she bailed out, the seat deployed its chute almost immediately after it stabilized. Soon the seat released and fell away, leaving the survival gear hanging below from the harness straps of her parachute.

Crash slowed to a nice, gentle decent. She'd survived the first of what undoubtedly would be an endless stream of tests and challenges. Her breathing became hurried and rushed. She still didn't know what had happened to the aircraft. It was probably not antiaircraft fire. Surface-to-air missiles would have been detected by her early-warning systems, and she would certainly have seen 23mm antiaircraft rounds if an S60 gun had been firing high-explosive rounds at her. Possibly a mechanical problem or maybe hitting a bird in flight caused the jet to become uncontrollable. The Super Hornet was plagued with problems during procurement because of dangerous wing separations at high speeds. If it wasn't from antiaircraft fire, then the demise of the aircraft was probably from the severe flying Sara had to perform to avoid the missiles and gunfire. She'd probably never know the whole truth.

A rush of light emerged as the F/A-18E slammed into the earth, but there was no explosion. Reality hit her. Now was not the time to worry about what caused the jet to crash, but about what happened next. Sara scanned the dark ground below her. She was already low and the treetops were coming fast.

The final seconds of the descent were purely horrifying. Trees rushed up with no sight of a clear opening for landing. Crash's body pierced through the top branches. Snaps and cracks of wood broke the silent air, as did Crash's muffled responses to the many wounds she received from the impacts. The parachute entered the jungle's canopy and became tangled in the treetops, leaving Crash hanging thirty feet from the ground.

Remaining completely motionless, she listened carefully for any sounds. The sound of bombs could be heard far off, resembling a coming thunderstorm. In between the thunder, sounds of jet aircraft filled the sky above. The buzz and hum of the jungle below concealed any sound of men on the ground. Crash could not tell if she was being hunted yet. She strained her eyes, attempting to see into the blackness below her but saw nothing since she did not have night-vision goggles.

Stories of other American POWs filled her brain. Capture meant horrible things. Many of the POWs from both Gulf Wars were sexually assaulted—both the men and the women. She had to evade. Maybe a pickup would happen tonight, or at least tomorrow. But not from here. She needed to get to the ground and find a clearing where a helicopter could land and pick her up. Better yet, getting to the highest branch possible would allow a combat search-and-rescue helicopter to winch her up. The beacon would transmit her position and bring U.S. aircraft to the area. From higher branches it would also be possible to signal rescue aircraft with an infrared strobe, enabling the rescue team to pinpoint her position. The infrared strobe was only visible through night-vision devices, something the San Selvan undoubtedly had in their possession, but the strobe could be made directional, meaning that its light could be projected to the sky without being seen below on the ground.

Crash decided she needed to climb up the tree. The first thing she needed to do was get to the tree's trunk, or at least a solid branch. Grabbing a handful of smaller branches, she pulled her way hand over hand toward the tree trunk. Her stomach jumped as the parachute above ripped, sending her down a few inches in a jarring drop.

The point of no return had already passed. Releasing the grip on the branches would result in a swinging motion that could only create more ripping. Slowly she reached for the next handfull of branches, careful not to rip more of the parachute. Then she reached again. The branches got bigger with each grab, making it more likely that Crash could hold on if the parachute ripped again. Then another jarring drop weakened her grip, causing her hands to painfully slide down the branches. Her hands were cut and the branches were not large enough to hold her.

Crash could feel the parachute giving way little by little. She slid farther down the branches, now nearing the thin ends that would certainly break under her weight. Knowing that she had no other choice, Crash made a daring grab with her left hand while pulling hard with her right, just like climbing a rope. But the motion was too much for the parachute and the thin branches. The inevitable occurred. Crash's right hand slid down the branches as any holding ability of the ripped parachute disappeared. She tumbled in a fast fall to the ground. The branches slapped at her body and one whipped her legs upward. She landed almost flat on her back, but her head hit the hard ground with a *thud,* bouncing her brain off the inside of her skull and knocking her unconscious.

Chapter Eighteen

Norfolk, Virginia

It took three rings before Peter Linsey realized the sound was not part of his dream. Reaching for the phone, he mumbled "hello" into the telephone receiver.

"Yes, good morning, Mr. Linsey?"

"Yes, who is this?" He looked at the clock on his nightstand. "Do you know what time it is?" Next he looked at the window. The damn sun was barely up.

"I'm terribly sorry to bother you at this difficult time, Mr. Linsey, but I just had a few questions—"

"I said, *who* is this?"

"Oh, yes, sir. I'm sorry. This is Fred Turlock from Channel Ten Action News. Again, I'm sorry to bother you, but I had some questions concerning your wife."

"*Sara!* What do you want to know about Sara?"

"I, ahh . . . well. You don't know. Do you?"

"Know? Know what? Who the hell is this, again? What are you talking about?"

"Well . . . I hate to be the one who has to bring this up, but . . . Do you mind if I record this, Mr. Linsey?"

"Tell me, damn it. What are you talking about?"

"One of our reporters say they saw a picture of wreckage in San Selva. It's an F-14 and the name on the fuselage is Lieutenant Commander S.A. 'Crash' Linsey. That's you wife, right? Sara Linsey?"

"That's impossible. I haven't been told anything and . . . and . . . There must be a mistake. Sara flies F/A-18s, not F-14s."

"Maybe it's an F-18 then. I don't know. Can you tell me when the last time was that you heard from your wife."

"*No!* Hell no!" Infuriated, Peter slammed the phone down. He didn't know what to think. Thoughts swirled through his head: *Could it be a mistake or a cruel joke? Who to call? Who would know?*

He needed to see the pictures himself. Jumping out of bed and rushing downstairs to the computer, Peter frantically tried to log on to the Internet to see what he could learn. He didn't know the strikes had started. The television news had said nothing about downed aircraft. It had reported on an American bomb hitting a building with civilians in it. The computer still wouldn't log on. The damn thing wouldn't work right. Who the hell could he call?

Suddenly the television caught Peter's attention and he froze. The tightness in his chest interfered with his breathing. He sat openmouthed and gazed at the screen, eyes fixed on the horrid scene. He leaned forward in his chair until he fell from it and landed on his knees in the middle of the living room. If he could have spoken, Peter would have screamed. But he knelt quietly transfixed on the television. He heard nothing that the commentator said. He only saw the ugly image of a mutilated body. The body of an American dragged through the streets of San Selva's capital city, Macapa. Stripped clean of any uniform or clothing, the corpse appeared badly beaten and already was beginning to stiffen. Both arms were obviously broken. The face and head looked grossly swollen and deformed. Also covered, but rather poorly, was the man's genitalia. Deep abrasions could be seen from time to time on the corpse's penis and buttocks—a result of the body being dragged over the rough roads. *Thank God there's a penis. That can't be Sara. But if they are doing that to him, then what are they doing to her?*

One of the legs was missing, looking as if it had been hacked away with an ax or a machete. The mob raged with a drunk lust for violence. A lust that they had tried to curb by tearing apart the American body, but the act only heightened their desires. A teenager appeared in the television screen and raised an object over his head to strike the body. As it hit the body, Peter could see in horrifying detail that the object was the severed leg from the American body.

The occasional stick struck the corpse, but Peter saw no sign of any other weapons. He didn't see any uniforms either. Those in the mob were civilians. Constant blows from sticks and kicks hit the body. A girl threw a can of liquid on the body and tried unsuccessfully to light it with a match. Others joined her in her efforts, and before long the body exploded in flames. More objects struck the body as it burned, including the severed leg, and someone else threw another can of liquid on the American to create a flash of flames.

Then Peter's head snapped to the right. He stared at the door. Someone was knocking.

Hurlburt, Florida

"This is too much!" shrieked Christine Collins. Knowing she would be late for work but not caring, Christine grabbed the phone book and began to search for the number to the television station. There was no reason for them to be showing this horrible image over and over again. For all she knew this could be a pilot that Randy worked with.

"Come in," she yelled at a knock on the door, not wanting to be distracted from her search for the phone number. Looking up, she was surprised and smiled warmly. "Well, good morning, Chaplain Stevens."

"Chris," he said dryly.

"What are you so dressed up for?" The Air Force chaplain's blue dress uniform looked a little disheveled, like he'd put it on in a hurry. On the epaulets of the uniform were simple crosses, which indicated that he was a man of God, not of the sword. But he was also a man of enormous courage, and the mission he came here for was one that the bravest and toughest warrior would have actively avoided.

Noticing that the chaplain looked in horror at the television screen, Christine said, "Isn't that just horrible? I'm trying to find the phone number of the television station right now so I can complain. These damn people have no decency. They'll show anything that will increase their ratings."

As the chaplain walked to the television to turn it off, the Collins children came into the room and ran about. All of them were getting so big: Randy Jr. was almost ten and Alexis was eight. They were such beautiful children, with blazing red hair that they inherited from their father.

207

"Chris, please, I need you to sit down. I asked to talk to you alone first, before the others come in."

USS Beirut, *North Atlantic Ocean*

"I can't believe these motherfucking sanchos."

Second Lieutenant Bert Dunne looked back at Jake Climer, one of his roommates and fellow platoon commanders in Company C, First Battalion, Eighth Marines. There was a tone of hostility in the other man's voice that couldn't be anything other than ominous. Turning his attention back to the television set, Dunne couldn't help but wonder how the networks could be allowed to show something like this. Bert sat at one of the room's two small desks looking almost straight up. Above him, forced into a cupboard built into the room's bulkhead, was a thirteen-inch television purchased by the lieutenants for watching nightly movies on the ship's internal television network. But right now they watched something worse than the scariest horror movie. The grainy television picture from a satellite feed showed the Marines and sailors on the ship what the world now saw. An American fighting man's body being ravaged in the streets of a city that most Americans couldn't even find on a map. But for these men it was more than just an American body. For each of them there was the knowledge that it could be them or one of their Marines who might experience the same fate.

"Why the hell would they ever even want to show this?" asked Lieutenant Dunne.

"They don't goddamn care about anything other than ratings," snapped Brian Kenny, another second lieutenant and roommate. "When it's another reporter being killed or mutilated, they don't show it out of respect for the family, but when it's one of us it's okay."

"The word is that these guys couldn't get the fire support they were requesting," said Shane Conolly, the final roommate and fellow platoon commander.

The four lieutenants lived together in the stateroom that was about the size of a walk-in closet. Field packs and combat gear hung from the pipes on the ceiling and bulkheads of the room, swinging and swaying with the motion of the ship. The dull yellowish paint on the walls presented a pleasant feeling when compared to the drab gray in most parts of the ship, but the yellow was initially deceiving—the small room quickly became anything but pleasant. There were, of course, no windows; none of the billeting areas had a window because it was too dangerous to have such a thing on a warship.

"We were standing up the TRAP when they lost contact with them. I didn't hear it myself, but in the operations center they said that the last transmission warned that they were running out of ammunition."

"Shit, they're showing it again," said Dunne.

"Good," snapped an even angrier Climer. "Keep showing it. People back home need to know what these fuckers are like. Then maybe they won't whine and wring their hands when we kill hordes of them."

Disturbed as much by his peer's hostility as the ghastly images, Dunne shook his head and turned away from the television screen. "I'm out of here. I've seen enough." He got up and turned for the door. Exiting the room, Lieutenant Dunne immediately felt relieved. He needed to go outside, he decided. Fresh air would be good right now.

Walking quickly through the maze of passageways, he entered the weight room and was shocked by the inactivity. The normally busy weight room seemed frozen as Marines and sailors stood in corners and stared at television screens. The harsh rays of the sun burned Bert's eyes as he stepped out of the hatch and onto the catwalk, turning to crank the door's locking handle downward before continuing to the ladder. The fresh sea air felt good, and Dunne squinted as the powerful light continued to sting his eyes. The ship had been at flight quarters for most daylight hours during the past few days, preventing Bert and most others on board from exiting the steel skin of the USS *Beirut* (LHD-14) to see the outside world.

Moving to the stern of the ship, Bert watched the winding tail of wake created by the forty-thousand-ton ship. Eight hundred feet long and one hundred feet wide, the Navy-gray *Beirut* was one of the largest amphibious ships in the world. Its class was the first to be specifically designed to accommodate the Marine Corps' new MV-22 Osprey tilt-rotor aircraft and LCAC hovercraft, along with the full range of Navy and Marine helicopters, conventional landing craft, and amphibious assault vehicles to support a Marine landing force. The ship also carried some of the most sophisticated communications devices, electronic systems, defensive weaponry, and command-and-control capabilities afloat. It was essentially a floating military base.

The *Beirut* was designed to transport and land ashore not only troops, but also the tanks, trucks, artillery cannons, ammunition, and various supplies necessary to support the amphibious assault mission. The LCACs could "fly" out of the dry well deck; or the well deck could be ballasted down for conventional craft to float out on their way to the assault area. Helicopter flights could also transfer troops and equipment to the beach, while the ship's air-traffic-control capability simultaneously directed close air support provided by embarked jet aircraft and helicopter gunships.

Accompanying the *Beirut* were three smaller ships: the USS *New Orleans* (LPD-18), USS *Carter Hill* (LSD-50), and USS *Zumwalt* (DD-21). The *Beirut* had accommodations for three thousand men and women, with one-third being ship's crew and the remaining two-thirds for embarked Marines. The *New Orleans* and *Carter Hill* carried about one thousand men and women apiece. The *Zumwalt* was a land-attack destroyer with only a few embarked troops. Embarked on all four ships were over two thousand Marines from the Twenty-second Marine Expeditionary Unit (Special Operations Capable).

It was fitting that Dunne's unit was on the USS *Beirut*. First Battalion, Eighth Marines was the unit on the ground in Beirut, Lebanon, when a truck bomb plowed into a Marine barracks the morning of October 23, 1983. In the flash of an eye, two hundred and forty-one Americans were dead: two hundred and twenty Marines, eighteen sailors, and three soldiers. Many now consider the attack as the opening volley in the terrorism war that led to the 2001 World Trade Center and Pentagon attacks. Dunne just hoped the unit was not cursed in some way, because he was certain that the medals earned for the coming action in San Selva would be paid for with more American blood.

Marine Expeditionary Units combined air, ground, information warfare, and combat service-support units into one cohesive organization. With every Marine being a rifleman first, the Twenty-second's Marines were all trained for combat. Forged in the fire of the Crucible—a fifty-four-hour endurance course that served as the culmination of the three-month Marine Corps Boot Camp—the Marines received their initial training at recruit depots in San Diego and Parris Island. After earning the title "Marine," all attended Marine Combat Training at the homes of the First and Second Marine Divisions in Camp Pendleton, California, and Camp Lejeune, North Carolina, respectively.

Then, only after completing the four months of initial training to become a basic Marine rifleman, did the aircraft mechanics, truck drivers, and administrators go to learn their trades.

But at the heart of each Marine Expeditionary Unit was a Battalion Landing Team of eleven hundred men—the professional warriors who lived the life of a rifleman every day. A small headquarters company provided support for three rifle companies that had one hundred and fifty men apiece. The rifle companies were all "light," meaning they were foot mobile, but they could still provide quite a punch. Each company's three rifle platoons were armed with a healthy mix of assault rifles, light machine guns, and grenade launchers; while the weapons platoon provided more firepower with its six medium machine guns, six rocket launchers, and three 60mm mortars.

The fourth company in the Battalion Landing Team was a weapons company armed with 81mm mortars, heavy machine guns, and antitank missile launchers. What made the infantry battalion a battalion-landing team was its many attachments: six-gun artillery battery, M1A3 tank platoon, advanced armored amphibious vehicle platoon, combat engineer platoon, reconnaissance platoon, and light-armor-vehicle platoon. Together, the battalion-landing team created a unit that was light enough to be rapidly landed ashore but heavy enough to fight and win on the modern battlefield.

Working alongside the battalion was a composite squadron with a robust mix of assault-support and fire-support aircraft. Six Joint Strike Fighter jets provided fixed-wing air support to troops on the ground. These jet aircraft use vertical takeoff and landing (VTOL) technology to adjust the jet engines in a manner that allowed the fighter to hover in midair. This capability served the Marines well, making it possible for the jets to use the USS *Beirut* for takeoff and landing. For close air support the squadron was armed with six AH-1Z Cobras, the four-bladed version of the attack helicopter that was born during the Vietnam War. Twelve MV-22 Osprey aircraft could simultaneously lift three hundred Marines from the deck of the *Beirut*, and the four CH-53E Super Stallion helicopters could carry either up to fifty Marines apiece or vehicles and artillery howitzers ashore. The UN-1Y Huey helicopters not only brought back images of the Vietnam movie *Apocalypse Now*, but they also provided an airborne command and control center, additional fire-support platforms, or the ability to extract or insert small groups from tight landing zones.

Supporting the battalion and squadron was a combat service support group and information warfare company. Tasked with providing maintenance and logistical support to the force, the combat service support group had been part of the organization since the MEU's inception in the early 1980s. The information warfare element, however, was a new addition. Its ranks were filled with men and women who specialized in collecting enemy intelligence while at the same time distributing information to intimidate or mislead the enemy and keep civilians informed. Sometimes the information warfare Marines dropped leaflets to motivate enemy soldiers to surrender. Other times they established shipboard radio stations that played local music favorites and pro-American news reports. In just its first few years of existence, the information warfare company proved to be a valuable addition to the MEU.

The Twenty-second was one of three Marine Expeditionary Units that the Department of Defense always had deployed outside the Continental United States, with one in the Mediterranean, one in the Persian Gulf, and one in the Western Pacific. As was usually the case with naval forces, they were often the first to respond to a crisis overseas. Many a president had uttered the question, "Where is the nearest MEU?" when combat power was needed somewhere. Over the past few decades MEUs reinforced embassies, evacuated civilians, destroyed enemy positions, and rescued American and allied pilots from hostile shores.

Thinking that he might be headed for a hostile shore of his own, Dunne was overcome with an enormous sense of dread as he remembered the image of the Air Force PJ or Army pilot, he was not sure which, being dragged through the streets by that mob. Much to Hollywood's chagrin, most military officers did not willingly place their men and women in harm's way because it suited their opportunity for medals or career advancement. A much more dangerous attitude persisted, which advocated that it was better to kill a hundred "enemy" to protect the life of one uniformed American. Dunne took the ROE card out of his pocket and tried to reason how it could apply after such savage brutality. Strict ROE had been blamed as one of the problems leading to the 1983 bombing. Now after what he just saw, Dunne was ready to disregard the idea of ROE, and it seemed from the tone of his fellow lieutenants that they already had.

Operation Greenhouse
Joint Task Force San Selva

Rules of Engagement:
1. The U.S. is not at war.
2. You always have the right to defend yourself and other U.S. forces.
3. You can use force, to include deadly force, in self-defense and the defense of other U.S. forces.
4. You may use force, to include deadly force, in defense of U.S. nationals and designated third country nationals supporting Operation Greenhouse.
5. You may use force, to include deadly force, in defense of designated U.S. installations and mission essential property.
6. You may use force, but not deadly force, in defense of U.S. installations and property.
7. You may use force, but not deadly force, to detain personnel who obstruct U.S. forces.
8. Civilians are to be treated with dignity and respect.

(front)

**Operation Greenhouse
Joint Task Force San Selva**

Use of Force:
—Hostile intent must be observed for use of force.
—Hostile act must be observed for use of deadly force.
—Always use minimum force necessary.
—Stop using force as soon as possible.
—Never retaliate or commit an act of revenge.
—Use non-lethal munitions first if possible.
—Riot control agents may not be used unless authorized by designated commanders.
—If you must open fire:
  —Fire only well aimed shots.
  —Fire no more rounds than is necessary.
  —Stop firing as soon as the situation permits.
—Impacts of indirect fire must be observed.
—Precision munitions are to be used if possible.

**USE OF DEADLY FORCE
SHOULD BE A LAST RESORT**
(back)

The face of war continued to change in the twenty-first century. Fewer countries warred against each other. Identifying friend and foe became more and more difficult. Criminal armies still used violence to achieve an aim. Terrorists killed innocent people. Machete-yielding mobs and gun-toting irregulars who wore no uniforms presented a difficult adversary. Treaties didn't work because no central leadership could control these groups. Western countries, unable or unwilling to understand the hate that motivated the fighting, believed that establishing "legitimate" governments would solve the problem, thus creating an era where the military used a combination of brute force, humanitarian assistance, and peacekeeping operations to build a nation.

Predictably, it didn't work. Nationalists and fundamentalists hardened their positions with Western response. Especially true because both needed an enemy for the leadership to rally against. If not, what would you have then: freedom and peace? All too often the followers of these groups came from a warrior culture and were completely willing to accept casualties. Their purpose or cause was worthy of life because it was their life. There was only one way to deal with such an enemy, and it was usually too bloody for the American public to stomach.

Chapter Nineteen

Outside Macapa, San Selva

It was hard to tell if the knocking sound came from a frog or a bird. Part croak and part cluck, the calming rhythm caught a listener's attention. A combination of birds and animals created the jungle song that filled Crash's ears and began to bring her out of the blackness. Along the way to consciousness she took a quick detour into fantasyland, dreaming that she walked through the zoo with her two babies, Madelyn and Peter. The sounds in her ears fit the images in her brain.

Consciousness came slowly, with Sara trying to remain with the comforting experience of being with her kids on a family outing. Suddenly, she clearly heard the world outside her head. Then came the brightness of the light. Even awake, she still took several seconds to realize she was not with her family. Lying on her back and looking up, she could see a bright collection of green vegetation behind beams of sunlight penetrating through the thick leaves and branches.

Crash's head ached. Slowly moving it to the left and right, she felt pain in her neck too, but she still struggled to sit up and see where she was. The ground seemed to rise in all directions, and she could see very little of the terrain around her. She looked up, and began to remember the previous night. She could remember hanging in the tree from her parachute but little else. *How did I get there? And how the hell did I get here?* She strained to see through the thick vegetation. She saw no wreckage from the aircraft and no remains of her parachute. Worst of all, she heard no sound of jets. She was alone.

Sara finally got to her feet and started moving to the closest piece of high ground. A rather short walk, it only took her a few minutes to break the crest of the small hill. The vantage point was not much better. Vegetation stretched in all directions, and she could see little above the jungle's thick canopy.

Then another sense returned: smell. The odor of woody-smelling smoke filled her nostrils and triggered Sara's brain to remember the San Selvan fires and more of her flight the night prior. She couldn't remember what happened, but she at least could guess that she had bailed out of her F/A-18E Super Hornet for some reason. In a flash, she came to the unwanted realization that she stood somewhere in San Selva.

Thinking for the first time about a rescue team, Sara reached for the survival radio. It should have been in a pocket of her flight vest, but it wasn't there. She was very alone. Retracing her steps from where she had woken, she searched frantically for the radio. That radio provided her only ability to communicate with the aircraft that would come looking for her. Without the radio it might be impossible to get rescued.

Sara tried to remember the circumstances of her ejection. She could remember being up in the tree but nothing else. The radio must have been ripped from her gear when she ejected. Damn last-minute issue of the new radios, she cursed. How the hell would she ever get rescued now? The thought of being captured horrified Sara. The San Selvans didn't have any known rules concerning prisoners, but from what had happened to them in San Selva's war of independence from Brazil, it was not difficult for Sara to imagine the inhumane treatment she would receive.

Never before had she been scared to be a woman, but now, shot down behind enemy lines and faced with the thought of capture, she wished more than anything she were a man. She knew that male prisoners were often raped and sodomized by their captors, but she thought it would probably be much more likely for a female prisoner. And how long could she go without her birth control pills before risking pregnancy?

As a military pilot Crash was always risking death, but this was one of the few times she'd really felt her mortality. The only other incident that had come close was the death of a good friend and fellow pilot a few years before. She was not sure if she was ready or willing to die, regardless of what the first article of the Code of Conduct said: *I am an American, fighting in the forces that guard my country and our way of life. I am prepared to give my life in their defense.* But Sara believed that she was trained to fight, not die; to make the other side die for their cause. She started moving through the jungle. Somehow she'd find a way to signal an aircraft to rescue her. The bottom line was that she had to refuse to accept death without a fight. She had too much to live for.

But she didn't get far. Suddenly, out of the corner of her eye, Crash detected movement. She snapped her head to the right, setting her view on a small dog. It had probably smelt her before it saw her, but now the dog confirmed something foreign in its domain. It came immediately alive with horrendous noise as it began to yelp and bark.

Sara jumped. She panicked for a second, unable to decide her next move. She started to move away from the area, but the dog pursued, barking.

She kicked at the dog and tried to shoo it away. It was domestic, so people must be nearby. Sara thought about the smoke scent in the air. *Could it be from cooking fires?*

Aarf! Aarf!

"No, boy," pleaded Crash. She stopped moving. "Sshhhh! Please, boy." The dog continued barking. Its tail wagged as it came closer to Crash. She needed to quiet the dog. "Come here, boy," said Crash, dropping to one knee. "Come on, boy."

Aarf! Aarf!

The dog drew closer, still waging its tail and now barking less aggressively than before. Getting the dog to close the last few feet was the hardest, and Crash wished she had food to lure it in. It seemed as if it had been barking for hours, and Crash looked around for people. Someone had to have heard the dog. The question now was whether or not anyone would come to investigate.

"Come here, boy." Crash patted the ground in front of her and sweetened her tone to calm the animal. Now just out of her reach, it only needed to move a few steps farther. Right before it came close enough for her to grab, the dog bounced back and began barking again.

"Come on," said Sara.

The dog tilted its head and wagged its tail. It posed no physical threat, but it would draw too much attention to her. It took another step closer. Crash could not risk any more barking. It had already gone on for too long. The dog had to be silenced permanently. Finally it came close enough for Crash to touch. She stuck her hand out for it to sniff her, and then gradually began to pet it on the head. "Good boy." The dog didn't bark, but how long before it started again? It put her life at risk.

In one smooth swoop of her left hand, Crash grabbed the dog by the snout and pulled it close to her body. Her hand fully grasped the dog's long nose, forcing its mouth shut and preventing it from barking again. Almost as if the dog could read Crash's mind, it kicked its legs in a futile panic as Crash's right hand produced her knife. Swinging it high above her head, she drove it into the neck of the animal. The blade penetrated the skin, which *popped* like a plump tomato, and the dog made one final whimper before Crash thrust the knife blade away from her, ripping the animal's throat out.

The dog's body convulsed and violently kicked. *God, what have I done?* Crash thought. She lay down on the carcass to prevent the flopping from making too much noise. Although the body still squirmed, the dog was obviously dead. Crash held it as still as possible. She was still alive. That was the most important thing. But she still could not stop herself from crying. *I think I would rather have killed another person.*

Crash sensed that she was being watched before she actually saw the movement. Jerking her head to the left, she locked eyes with a small boy. His dark brown eyes were penetrating, and the look of terror swept across his chocolate-colored face. Only a few feet away he stood, having witnessed the brutal killing of his pet dog.

In an instinctive survival reaction, Crash reached for her 9-mm pistol. Drawing it from the shoulder holster with her right hand, she flipped off the safety and brought the sights to center on the child. The boy would obviously go tell others what he saw. He had to be stopped. Then she paused, not because of a change in desire to kill the child, but because she realized that firing the weapon would warn others in the area of her presence. That pause triggered a spark in her brain that made her realize that she was seconds away from killing a child not much older than her own daughter. Sara smiled awkwardly and pointed the gun at the ground. The knife dropped from her hand and she motioned for the boy to come closer. He stood solid as a statue, frozen in fear. Sara realized that the boy focused on her outreached hand. She looked down at it and saw that the dog's blood covered her hand. As she stood up and stepped toward the terrified boy, he jumped to life and ran back into the jungle. He disappeared in the blink of an eye, and Sara heard his yelling and yelping as he ran away.

How could I come so close to killing a child? Crash dropped down to her knees and let the pistol fall from her hands. The mix of emotions—the anger and desire to live coupled with the regret of killing the dog and the love of her own children—created an explosion of thoughts in her head. She felt dizzy and thought for a second that she was going crazy. Her brain throbbed from the pressure of the moment. Pulling herself into reality, she was hit with a terrifying thought: they would be coming for her.

She picked up her pistol and knife and ran in the

opposite direction as the boy. Ran faster and harder than she ever had before. She gripped the pistol in her hand, moving as fast as she could through the thick brush. Soon they were coming. She heard them coming. The voices' numbers grew. Sara was hidden in the thick jungle, but the San Selvans were using trails and clearings to move faster and get ahead of her. Soon they were everywhere. Plans and counterplans ran through Crash's head as she moved. She had to get away or find a place to hide before more San Selvans came to join the search. If she could just hide until it got darker. She heard a truck screech to a halt, and then people yelling. More were coming. She hoped her pursuers were just common villagers, not gunmen. They would move cautiously and would most likely not have radios to coordinate the search. Maybe she could try and hijack a vehicle. Then she might be able to get away from the San Selvans chasing her. Maybe she should head east or west. The San Selvans had to expect her to head south toward the border. Could she hijack a vehicle? Sara frantically craned her neck and moved her head to catch a glimpse of her pursuers. She saw nothing and only heard the San Selvans breaking through the brush and calling to each other. They gained on her. Now very close, Crash had little chance of outrunning them. Noise to the front. *Are they up there also? Too many of them.* They knew the terrain. This was their backyard. She had to hide and hope they would overlook her in their haste.

Maybe some danger would slow them. She pointed her pistol back at her pursuers and fired off two rounds. The sound of the weapon discharging exhilarated her. *I can make it.* The gunshots would scare the untrained villagers and make them more cautious.

Make them fear for their lives. All she needed was for them to slow down until it got dark.

Pulling herself into the nearest bush she could use as concealment, Crash rubbed mud on her face. She pulled her knees to her chest to roll into as small a target as possible. The pistol in her right hand, she tried to be quiet but her heart kept pounding on the inside of her chest. The sound of her breathing was loud enough to break records on a decibel scale.

A foot plopped down right next to her and then was suddenly gone. The man had run right past her, missing her by inches. There was the sound of another vehicle stopping. The smell of exhaust filtered by. More sounds of voices yelling in a language she couldn't identify. She heard more dogs. Crash did not attempt to catch a view of her pursuers anymore. She lay still as possible to avoid detection.

She could do nothing but hope and pray. The pistol in her hand provided few options. The M9's magazine carried maybe twelve more bullets; her spare magazine held fifteen rounds. Could she kill all of them and get away? For a mere second Sara considered shooting herself. It would be a way to end everything: the pain, the fear, and the anxiety of the impending torture and rape at the hands of the San Selvans. Suddenly she noticed the quietness.

"Mui! Mui!" someone shouted. She didn't know the language, but it became clear to her that they had found her. More yelling and sounds of the San Selvans moving through the brush and surrounding her. Crash unrolled from her ball and knelt in a firing position. Movement of vegetation seemed endless. She scanned for targets.

"Hands up! Hands up!" yelled an unseen voice in English.

Crash moved her head around looking for any sight

of the San Selvans. What could she do to escape? There was the flash of a young man's face only ten feet away through the leaves. Crash instinctively fired two rounds from the pistol. Her ears rang from the violent blast, but the sound inspired her again. Maybe she could get out of this. Even as a pilot, she was better trained than many of these boys surrounding her. If she could kill one and take his rifle, then she would be able to stand and fight.

"You are circled! Hands up!" In an act rooted with the Second Article of the Code of Conduct—I will never surrender of my own free will—Crash answered the demand with another two rounds.

Bullets zinged overhead as the San Selvans returned fire, sending Crash to her stomach. Crawling out of the line of the fire and into a depression, she hustled away in a bent-over run. A gunman appeared to Crash's left. She saw the terrified eyes of a young gunman, who turned to run away. Crash raised her pistol and fired two rounds into his back. Shooting someone came easier than she thought it would. Just like the pistol range. Crash rushed at the gunman's body to retrieve his weapon. A *thud* impacted her left shoulder. She felt no pain from the wound, but immediately lost control of her arm. Another gunman who stood to her left fired again. Sara fell to the ground as more rounds snapped through the vegetation. Now on her back, she fired again and again with her good arm until the gunman that shot her dropped.

Crawling for a weapon, Crash felt her mind flipping in slow motion. The first man she shot started moving, jerking as his body convulsed. Crash fired more lead into his body, and kept firing until the upper slide of the M9 locked back, indicating the ammunition magazine was empty. There was no time to reload, and with her left arm disabled she wouldn't be able to anyway. Rolling to her feet, she ran for the nearest body. She needed a new weapon—a rifle.

Just before she got to the gunman's weapon, a group of San Selvans broke from the vegetation and rushed at her. She threw her empty pistol at them and dove for a dead man's rifle. Someone jumped on her back, as another gunman stepped on her injured arm. Crash continued to fight and prayed for the San Selvans to kill her. With her right hand she pulled her knife out and flipped the still-bloody blade open. Blood sprayed and splattered after Sara blindly thrust the knife into the mass of flesh on top of her.

For the first time in her life, Sara *really* contemplated her death. The panic of the situation was replaced by sadness as she thought of her family. Her husband Peter was still young. Maybe he would remarry so at least the kids would have a mother. God, she hoped it was someone who would be good to them. Someone that little Madelyn would want with her on her wedding day when she was jittery and getting dressed in her gown. The woman would need to be good with boys too, because Peter Jr., even at his young age, already showed signs of being as rambunctious as any male. *I wonder if he is old enough to even remember me.* A wave of jealousy rushed over Sara as she thought of another woman mothering her children and loving her husband. Then there was guilt that she was thinking of herself when Peter and the kids were in need.

A boot flashed in the corner of her eye just before it connected against the side of her head. Something else slammed into her teeth. *They want me alive. I'm going to be a fucking POW!* It was her last conscious thoughts. Then there was only blackness again.

Maj. James B. Woulfe, USMC

Norfolk, Virginia

Peter Linsey still didn't know what to say to the children. They knew something was terribly wrong, but he still had not found the strength to tell them that their mother was missing in action. He'd been able to mutter that Mommy was alive, leaving out the truth that he *hoped* she was alive, but that didn't end the questions. The kids knew there was more.

"Mommy's plane crashed last night and they haven't found her yet," Peter finally said. "She's okay, though. I'm sure of i . . ." He broke down in tears and turned his face away from the children.

Soon they were all crying. Peter because he couldn't face his children to tell them that their mother might be dead or hurt or a prisoner of war, and the children because their father was so upset. As he sobbed into his hands, Peter's behavior terrified the children. He was so often the pillar of strength; they had never seen their father fall apart like this. He'd been an emotional wreck from the very moment that he'd opened the front door and saw the Navy chaplain and accompanying officers wearing their dress uniforms. Peter immediately called Sara's parents to inform them and they'd be here soon, but neighbors and friends still didn't know about Sara. The Navy officers asked Peter not to talk to anyone. They said that it was for Sara's safety, because the San Selvans were offering a cash reward to anyone who delivered a live American pilot. Peter couldn't help but think it was more that they didn't want to deal with the political embarrassment of the situation. American politicians and generals were terrified that Sara had been captured. Not only would a prisoner of war be a great propaganda victory for the San Selvans, but also the fact that the prisoner was a woman would likely strike deep at the heart of America's support for the operation. The consequences were unclear. Either the American people would scream for an end of hostilities or they would rally for decisive action to punish San Selvans for their sin.

But Peter knew it was only a matter of time before the media would be camped out on the front lawn. He was surprised it had not started already. He had expected the packs of reporters and cameramen in a frenzy like hyenas looking to steal a corpse from another animal in the wild. They knew about Sara's aircraft. Hell, they were the ones who had told him.

The next time Peter looked out the window, a dozen news trucks were parked out front. Then the reporters started knocking on the door: "I'm so sorry to bother you at this difficult time, but can you answer a few questions for me?"

Chapter Twenty

Small City, San Selvan Coast

Exiting from a plain garage in a residential area, the truck drove in the direction of the beach. There was no time to waste. It swerved through the narrow city streets in a rush to get to the coast before American warplanes appeared overhead and ruined everything. Mounted in the cargo area of the truck was a long-range antiship missile. An all-weather day-and-night-capable weapon, the missile was an intelligent munition that used advanced navigation systems for guidance. Its target was already programmed with the latest coordinates, which had been determined after sifting through hundreds of reports from local coast watchers and native boat crews.

The missile's target had made a mistake. Not of its own choosing, but rather of U.S. Navy doctrine. Attempting to deconflict sea space between ships, the Navy had given each vessel an area of ocean to remain in. Unfortunately, or fortunately if you were a San Selvan, the practice created a pattern that could be exploited. Ships avoided the shore and stayed twenty-five miles from the coast because of the coastal radar, seamine, and anti-ship-missile threats. But twenty-five miles was not enough, especially when the Internet worked and the enemy could access satellite pictures from businesses that sold such images on-line. The last time the United States Navy had faced such a threat in combat—long-range, precision munitions in great numbers—was against the kamikazes during the Okinawa campaign in 1945. The impact on the fleet was horrid, with over three hundred and fifty ships damaged and thirty-six sunk. Ominous numbers, especially since the U.S. Navy was now slightly more than three hundred active ships, of which only thirty-six were amphibious ships designed to carry Marines.

As the crew of the truck-mounted antiship missile came to their firing point, they finalized the firing procedure for the "fire and forget" weapon and launched it from the truck's bed. The stream of light rocketed into the sky, as the men jumped from the vehicle and ran in several different directions into the city's streets. The truck sat abandoned and waiting to be destroyed by any American reaction to the missile attack.

USS The Sullivans, *North Atlantic Ocean*

Not knowing that death was closing at over five hundred miles an hour, Seaman First Class Shauna Stout sat in the berthing area on the USS *The Sullivans*. She had experienced a long day and night of preparing for battle with San Selva, and she foolishly thought her war was over for the time being and that she was safe. But her ship was a poignant reminder of the deadly nature of naval warfare. Named for five brothers who lost their lives during World War II, *The Sullivans* was a symbol of the sacrifices families made during war. The five Sullivan boys enlisted in the Navy after a family friend was killed in the attack on Pearl Harbor, and the brothers gained permission for all of them to serve on the light cruiser, USS *Juneau*. In November 1942, the *Juneau* was bringing much-needed supplies and reinforcements to Guadalcanal when it was torpedoed by a Japanese submarine and destroyed. All the Sullivans boys perished, with George Sullivan being the last and possibly most horribly killed—a shark ate him.

Now Stout and her shipmates were minutes away from meeting a similar fate as the Sullivan boys. But fortunately their ship had many protective measures that ships from past generations did not. Hopefully they would work, because they certainly were not foolproof.

RBS-15, Airspace Over the North Atlantic Ocean

Flying at a low, sea-skimming altitude, the antiship missile passed its second waypoint at a speed of over five hundred miles an hour.

USS The Sullivans, *North Atlantic Ocean*

An alarm screamed through horns on the bridge as the on-duty watch realized that there was an incoming missile. Their first reaction was disbelief, followed closely by terror. The realization that the San Selvans had actually fired an advanced missile and that it had gotten this close sent chills up many spines. The first attempt to defeat the missile was by electronic jamming, but the RBS-15 was designed to defeat such attempts. A missile just like this one had killed thirty-seven sailors on board the USS *Stark* in 1987.

RBS-15, Airspace Over the North Atlantic Ocean

Making a hard ninety-degree turn after passing its final waypoint, the RBS-15 antiship missile could "see" its target. Designed to fly low and fast to make detection and counterattack difficult, the Swedish-built missile automatically made erratic movements to defeat the American ship's countermeasure system.

USS The Sullivans, *North Atlantic Ocean*

While still attempting to turn away from the missile to provide a smaller target, *The Sullivans'* fire-control center locked on to the incoming missile six miles away and fired a Sea Sparrow anti-missile missile.

RBS-15, Airspace Over the North Atlantic Ocean

The RBS-15 confirmed the target, using its sophisticated target discrimination system to verify that it was heading toward the right ship.

Sea Sparrow, Airspace Over the North Atlantic Ocean

The Sea Sparrow's Mk 58 solid-propellant rocket motor pushed the two-hundred-thousand-dollar missile to exceed two thousand miles an hour. It was missile versus missile now, with one trying to force a meeting and the other trying to avoid one.

RBS-15, Airspace Over the North Atlantic Ocean

Seeing the Sea Sparrow, the RBS-15 launched countermeasures of its own, causing the Sea Sparrow to fly off course and away from the antiship missile.

USS The Sullivans, *North Atlantic Ocean*

Panic swept through the crew on the bridge of *The Sullivans* as they realized the Sea Sparrow missed. The officer of the deck screamed for the collision alarm to be sounded, which startled Stout and her shipmates down below. Confused, the sailors had no understanding of the danger that honed in on the bulkhead of their berthing area. They complained about the noise, not knowing its purpose.

The sailors on the bridge of the ship who knew what was happening prayed, even those who'd never stepped foot in a church, mosque, or synagogue. Death could be seconds away. Young men and women who'd never felt the realization of their mortality now knew that they were human.

Finally the fate of the ship was announced to all as the loudspeakers shrieked: "Inbound missile. . . . Brace for shock!" If the missile hit the ship its high-explosive warhead would penetrate the ship's hull before detonating. This delay in the explosion was intended only to cause more damage and kill more people.

RBS-15, Airspace Over the North Atlantic Ocean

Now within one mile of the USS *The Sullivans*, the RBS-15 missile came under the umbrella of the Sea

Sparrow's minimum range. Seven seconds until impact.

USS The Sullivans, *North Atlantic Ocean*

Sparks and flares erupted into the air as the ship's AN/SLQ-32 automatically fired chaff and countermeasures to confuse the missile.

RBS-15, Airspace Over the North Atlantic Ocean

The missile gained elevation quickly as it attempted to beat the ship's last means of defense.

USS The Sullivans, *North Atlantic Ocean*

The Phalanx Mk-15 Close In Weapons System (CIWS)—pronounced "see-wiz"—was a 20mm radar-controlled Gatling gun that fired three thousand rounds per minute. Looking like the robot R2D2 from the 1977 movie *Star Wars*, the Phalanx automatically elevated its gun and fired a quick burst. Then, with its radar locked on to the incoming missile, the Mk-15 jerked down and left—firing another short burst. Even with its incredible rate of fire, its magazine could only hold fifteen hundred rounds, so none of the ammunition could be wasted. After another sporadic jerk, the Phalanx fired a third burst, which hit the RBS-15 only two hundred meters from the ship. Fragments from the missile struck the side of the ship, causing minor damage to exposed electrical systems, but the ship was intact and still ready to fulfill its mission.

The crew breathed a sigh of relief. At first, even with its solemn name, the USS *The Sullivans* seemed to be blessed. It had been the original target of the terrorists who blew a huge hole in the side of the USS *Cole* and killed seventeen sailors during October 2000. Months before the attack, in January 2000, the *Cole* attackers tried to bomb *The Sullivans* when it stopped to refuel in Yemen, but the terrorists' explosive-laden small boat sank a few hundred meters from the ship. Now the USS *The Sullivans* and her crew would never view Operation Greenhouse the same way.

But the relief of defeating the missile would only last for a few seconds, maybe one minute, because a second missile closed on the ship. Launched from a small patrol craft operating one hundred miles from the shore, the missile neared the opposite side of the ship. Alarms continued and the sparks and flares erupted as the confused sailors decided it must be a mistake. The ship's electronic systems knew of the coming danger, but the human crew refused to accept it. None acknowledged the presence of the second missile before it was far too late. Much in the same way that the shark mercilessly attacked George Sullivan, the last of the Sullivan boys, the missile showed no mercy as it penetrated the ship's protective plating and exploded within the confines of the female berthing area. The temperature of the fires that followed the blast quickly exceeded three thousand degrees. Shauna only had to suffer for a few horrible seconds before she died.

Chapter Twenty-one

U.S. Embassy, Bogota, Colombia

Exiting the elevator, Major Steve Macomb gave the Marine guard at the front desk a friendly nod. "Bigger protest outside today, huh?" he said. Then he produced his access card.

"Shit, sir," said the Marine as he took the card, "I'd call it more of a fucking riot."

"Probably won't end any day soon, either." Many Colombian civilians supported the San Selvan movement and they despised the United States for insisting on becoming involved in Latin American affairs. Non-essential personnel and State Department employees' families were evacuated from the country right about the time that Macomb and his team arrived.

The Marine checked the access roster, although he knew Macomb had full access to the building, and handed the card back. "You're good to go, sir."

Moving first to the coffeepot, Macomb poured himself a cup before he entered the vault and sat down at his desk to review the latest reports. The Styrofoam cup sat where he placed it for over an hour until he picked it up and took a sip of the now cold liquid. Macomb hadn't been in Colombia long. The Colombian ambassador had served as State Department coordinator for counterterrorism years ago, so he knew all the secret tools in the U.S. arsenal. He knew exactly what he wanted when he put out a special call for Macomb after tensions in the region began to rise.

For the previous three weeks, Macomb had secretly worked from a locked-down section on the windowless fifth floor of the bunkerlike U.S. embassy in Bogota, where few people beyond the ambassador and the CIA station chief knew exactly who he was or what he did. In fact, Steve Macomb wasn't even his real name. It was one of four identities he could assume at any moment, each supported by passports and credit cards. Changing into each one became like slipping on a new pair of shoes.

Macomb ran a covert operation for one of the most classified units in the U.S. Army, a highly specialized cadre of communications experts that had gone by a variety of cover names over the years. It had been called Torn Victory, Cemetery Wind, Capacity Gear, and Robin Court. Today, it went by "Centra Spike."

Macomb was a career soldier and a new kind of spy. Intelligence collection had changed with the profusion of small-scale, specialized American military operations being launched in exotic places by small units of unconventional soldiers dispatched on short notice. America's newest enemies were not only regional powers and dictators and their armies, but now terrorists, crime bosses, and drug traffickers. Military commanders who once focused on enemy troop maneuvers and missile capabilities now needed more timely, localized, and specific information: How many doors and windows did the target building have? What kind of weapons did the bodyguards carry? Where did the target eat dinner? Where did he sleep last night and the night before?

Centra Spike had evolved to provide the kind of precise, real-time intelligence that big spy outfits like the CIA were not designed to collect. Over time, the unit's primary specialty had become finding people, directly contributing to the arrests of terrorists who had bombed the American embassies in Eastern Africa and the USS *Cole*. They came to Colombia because the ambassador thought their services might be helpful in preventing attacks on the embassy, but now Macomb and his team searched not for a foe but for a comrade. Their new mission was to locate the whereabouts of Lieutenant Commander Sara "Crash" Linsey.

After two hours of reviewing the reports, Macomb switched his attention to plotting coordination for a new flight. There were some indications in the reports that might mean something, but he would not know for sure until he confirmed his estimates with precise data. Techniques for eavesdropping on radio and telephone conversations from the air, both traditional and cellular, had been perfected during the Colombian drug wars. There were other military and spy units that could do it too, but what distinguished Centra Spike was its accuracy. It was capable of pinpointing the origin of a call within seconds.

Electronic detection had advanced far beyond the primitive days of World War II, when ground-based antennas could do little more than determine the general vicinity of a radio signal. By the Vietnam War,

Army direction finders had perfected techniques for quickly locating a radio signal to within a half mile of its origin. In the nineties, when Macomb joined a precursor of Centra Spike, that capability had been reduced to a few hundred meters. Now it was even better. Instead of triangulating from three receivers on the ground, the unit did it from one small airplane. Airborne equipment took readings from different points along a plane's flight path. When a signal was intercepted, the pilot would fly an arc around it. With onboard computers providing instantaneous calculations, operators could begin triangulating off points in that arc within seconds. If the plane had time to complete a half circle around the signal, its origin could be narrowed to less than ten meters. While a radio or phone signal could be encrypted, there was no way to disguise its origin without high-tech frequency-hopping equipment. And the system worked in any kind of weather or terrain with a range of up to one thousand miles.

The only problem to starting the Colombian operation was getting Centra Spike's aircraft into the country without arousing suspicion. Anyone looking for America's most sophisticated eavesdropping equipment would be watching for something high-flying and fancy, with great bulbous features and bristling with antennas. They probably wouldn't be looking for two perfectly ordinary Beechcrafts.

Inside and out, the Beechcrafts looked like standard twin-propeller, six-passenger commercial planes common in South America. But these Beechcrafts were multimillion-dollar spy planes crammed with state-of-the-art electronic eavesdropping and direction-finding equipment. A close examination of the planes would have revealed a wingspan about six inches longer than the normal models to accommodate the two main eavesdropping antennas built inside. Five more antennas could be lowered from the plane's belly in flight. In the cockpit was more instrumentation than the original space shuttle. Once the plane had reached its maximum altitude, operators switched on laptop computers plugged into the plane's mainframe and power centers. Wearing headsets, the operators could monitor four frequencies simultaneously. The laptops displayed the planes' positions and the estimated positions of signals being tracked. Because the planes flew so high, no one on the ground could see or hear them. It was an extraordinary capability, particularly useful because it was unknown to even the most sophisticated telecommunications experts—the kind of people San Selvan officials hired to advise them on ways to avoid detection.

But Macomb and Centra Spike were now fully up and running in Colombia, peering over the border with their electronic instruments to gain information about what was happening in San Selva. Macomb was confident that if the San Selvans found Lieutenant Commander Linsey, his team or one in another country would know within hours.

Command Bunker, Macapa, San Selvan

Crash didn't expect the rifle butt that slammed into the back of her head. When you're a kid in a playground fight or participating in rough play, the adrenaline is pumping and your body is braced for any coming blows. Being caught unexpectedly as Crash was now only enhanced the rifle butt's affects, knocking her from the chair to the hard concrete floor. She'd been in and out of consciousness since her capture. It was difficult for her to estimate how much time had passed. She didn't even know the time of day. She remembered being beaten, bound, and blindfolded before she was thrown into the trunk of a car and driven on a bumpy road to a smoother one that brought her to this building. Maybe it took six hours. Occasionally she heard gunfire and explosions during the drive. It could have been only two hours or maybe even one.

She now sensed that she sat in a large, empty room. The acoustics seemed like a locker-room shower. Footsteps of her captors echoed with every step, and the movement of the chair she had been in was magnified by the lack of carpeting or furniture in the room. The odor of the room was dominated by stale cigarette smoke. The air was hot and humid. The mood morbid—at least Crash's mood.

The hands picked her up and threw her back into the chair, but then a moment later an unseen force knocked her to the floor again. Kicks came from all directions. Some were heels of boots, others from the instep portion of the foot, but the worst pain came from the steel-tipped toes that mercilessly beat at her midsection. With the blindfold on she couldn't see the blows coming, and with her hands tied behind her back she couldn't raise them in front of her for protection. Crash lifted her knees to her chest to protect as much of her body as she could.

She lost more and more of her senses with each of these beatings. She couldn't even taste the blood in her mouth anymore. If the pain hadn't been so great she would have screamed out, but she could barely breathe with her nose swelled shut and her mouth a bloody mess. Drowning in her own blood was a possibility. She tried to time her spitting between blows to clear her airway, but there was no rhythm to the attack. No order or reason either. Just pure hate carried out by men who directed all of their revenge for the bombings on the only American they'd ever seen.

Hands grabbed at her armpits before the kicking stopped. She flew back into the seat and suffered several slaps. Then she heard footsteps walk behind her. The pain was overwhelming. Ribs had to be broken. Same with her nose and possibly an eye socket. Her kidneys ached. Joints swelled painfully. Pain overwhelmed every sense. She could not function as before. She had no idea of how many occupied the room or its layout. The pain dominated everything. Childbirth was almost this bad.

"What is your name?" said a voice in perfect English. There was no hint of an accent.

"Linsey," choked Crash.

This had to be a warm-up question. They already knew Crash's name from her dog tags. At SERE school she'd been taught to start with the first name. It made you more human as a prisoner and also started the resistance that would be needed for the torture and questioning that would come. Make the interrogator work. Make him ask for the full name. But Crash didn't want to give her full name because then her secret would be out. Thoughts ran through her head of what she should say when asked. She had not thought to come up with a fake name beforehand. At first she decided on using her husband's name, Peter. But then, fortunately, even through the fog that lingered in her mind, she realized that would be a horrid mistake. Her dog tags that were in San Selvan hands listed her initials S.A. for Sara Ann. Telling them that her name was Peter would not have made her experience any easier. She had to figure out what to say. The questions were going to require answers.

She dreaded their discovering that she was a woman. They had the information from her dog tags now, but fortunately the tags did not mention her sex. Only name, Social Security number, service, religion, and gas mask size, which happened to be medium and was therefore represented with an M that might help Crash by making her captors think it meant "male."

The Third Article of the Code of Conduct—*If I am captured I will continue to resist by all means available*—was at the forefront of her thoughts, but every POW Crash had heard talk during schools and seminars spoke of "breaking down." Anyone who didn't have a breaking point only ended up dead, and survival was the goal—survival with honor. Crash needed to start being a hard case now. She knew that in the end the San Selvans would get more information out of her than she wanted to give, but she couldn't make it easy. She needed to make them work for it. They had to learn that she would not offer information without a fight.

Hollywood movies and bravado military writers warped Americans' understanding of being a prisoner. There is no slap across the face followed by a witty line from a pretty-boy actor. That would at least mean unconsciousness, if not death. The key to survival is to put on an entirely different acting performance. The point to the beatings is to inflict pain—to brutally induce suffering on the prisoner. So the best thing to do is exaggerate the pain. Let the captor think he is achieving his goal. If he didn't want to kill you, then he would stop when he thought you'd had enough. Make him stop as early as possible so you can conserve strength, because it would be needed to survive with honor.

"What is your rank?" said the voice. A great question. They'd moved right past the first question without getting into Crash's full name. Hopefully she would be known only as Linsey to these people. Linsey the poor American pilot who didn't know anything important.

"Lieu . . . ," she gasped. "Lieutenant . . ." Her words came harder now. The pain surprised her. Every syllable created a new hell. "Com . . ." Another painful gasp. ". . . ander."

"Yes, Lieutenant Commander Linsey," mocked the voice. "Navy?"

Crash nodded her head. Not wanting to live through the pain of giving a verbal response, but also trying to control some part of her life. Could she get away with nods and head shakes?

White flashes of light scrambled through her head and it took a second for the pain of the blow to be felt. Lesson one: nods were not a good idea. Thank God it wasn't that rifle butt again, she thought. There must have been a nod from the voice to a goon behind her that authorized the blow. Crash began to regain her awareness. The voice was running things. The others took cues from him.

"Navy?"

"Yes," gasped Crash. Technically, the question was not part of the "big four"—name, rank, serial number, and date of birth—but they knew the answer already. The Air Force, Army, and Marine Corps did not have lieutenant commanders, only the Navy. Besides, her service was printed on the dog tags the San Selvans had taken from her.

"And you are a pilot, yes?"

A different question altogether. Not from the big four, but the answer was probably known by the San Selvans anyway. It should have been clear to the San Selvans that Crash was a pilot. They certainly found the wreckage of her aircraft. She'd been found in her flight suit. She was an officer, not enlisted flight crew. There couldn't be many more, if any, aircraft that had gone down. The San Selvans had to know she was a pilot, but her answer would confirm their suspicion. There would be no outside validation other than her answer to the question.

So the game began. Crash knew that they knew she was a pilot but wanted to force her to say it. It was information they already had, so she would probably answer the question in due time, but for now it came down to a test of wills. How much pain would she be willing to endure to avoid answering a question they knew the answer to?

Shaking her head, Sara knew what was coming. She received the rifle butt again and was unconscious before her body slammed into the hard floor.

Fort Bragg, North Carolina

Several thousand miles away at an isolated area of Fort Bragg, men dressed in black nomex fired .45-caliber submachine guns in an indoor training range. They had to be inside. Anything outside could be seen from the satellites orbiting the heavens. The building was inconspicuous. It looked like many of the other buildings on base. A very well trained and knowledgeable observer might spot the only strange thing about the building. On the roof of the building were two large blowers to force the combustion created by the live-fire rehearsals out of the structure. Inside, the rehearsal range was completely empty, a fresh "block of clay" that would be molded into whatever objective was to be hit. Sometimes it was an aircraft fuselage. Other times it was a building or a small group of several buildings. Right now it was a cell block, and everyone knew they needed to be ready.

Chapter Twenty-two

EC-130E Commando Solo, Brazilian Airspace

Air Force Lieutenant Colonel Alex "Thor" Thompson of the Forty-first Electronic Combat Squadron leveled off his aircraft from its climb. He flew at a high altitude to provide the maximum propaganda pattern when the Command Solo crew began to work its magic. Buzzing around the San Selvan and Brazilian border, Thor piloted one of the Air Force's EC-130 aircraft. The EC-130E did not join the Air Force inventory until 1990, when it was almost immediately thrown into action by broadcasting the "Voice of the Gulf," which encouraged Iraqi soldiers to surrender during Desert Storm. It had been used in every war since, most extensively in the antiterrorism battles across the globe, especially Afghanistan.

Thor's aircraft was armed with a strange kind of

weapon. The EC-130E was a highly sophisticated electronic warfare aircraft, capable of jamming enemy radio and television signals and then replacing them with American propaganda messages. With proper planning, the replacement message could be formatted to resemble a normally scheduled show. The radio listeners or television viewers might not know that they were being fed an American propaganda message.

Tonight the EC-130E broadcast covered both radio and television messages. For hours it transmitted and told the people in San Selva they were "condemned" if they opposed efforts to put out the burning rain forests. The messages also suggested that U.S. troops would eventually be on the ground in that country:

When you decide to surrender, approach United States forces with your hands in the air. Sling your weapon across your back muzzle toward the ground. Remove your magazine and expel any rounds. Doing this is your only chance of survival. The firepower you face is too much to fight off. Our forces are armed with state-of-the-art military equipment. What are you using, obsolete and ineffective weaponry? Our helicopters will rain fire down upon your camps before you detect them on your radar. Our bombs are so accurate we can drop them right through your windows. Our infantry is trained for any climate and terrain on earth. United States soldiers fire with superior marksmanship and are armed with superior weapons. We only want to protect the global environment. You have only one choice. Surrender now and we will give you a second chance. We will let you live. If you surrender, no harm will come to you. When you decide to surrender, approach United States forces with your hands in the air. Sling your weapon across your back muzzle toward the ground. Remove your magazine and expel any rounds. Doing this is your only chance of survival.

The powerful message was merely one weapon in the propaganda war. Across the Amazon Basin, C-17 transports air-dropped humanitarian relief supplies to villages. Many of the supplies fell into the hands of San Selvan gunman who would oppose any American landing force, but the airdrops were a public relations coup with the American public. The C-17s also dropped leaflets, which read "The Organization of American States is here to help." The small bright yellow food boxes demonstrated a willingness to help people even when America opposes them. Bomb them, feed them, and encourage them to surrender. The airdrops would continue, and schoolkids back home even drew pictures in class to be dropped to San Selvan children during a later flight.

Not that all of this made much sense, but neither did much of this war. This war, more than any other, used information and influence as weapons. Well beyond deception and intelligence and deep into the hearts and minds of the global community, especially American citizens, to shore up public opinion.

Preventing the San Selvans from gaining information or gaining influence over people removed two valuable weapons from their arsenal. On the other hand, the San Selvans knew that they controlled an important ecological area, which gave them power over the global community. They focused on attacking the United States by destroying its economic security. Because of the Child Care computer virus, the Internet and the New York Stock Exchange were still closed and would be for some time. This was the longest period of time that the markets were closed, even longer than after the 2001 World Trade Center attacks. And the Internet might be forever destroyed.

Maj. James B. Woulfe, USMC

Somewhere In San Selva

Sitting in a tree on a hilltop overlooking a small urban area, the soldier lined up the vehicle in the sights of the Viper Series IX Targeting System and pushed the FIRE button. There was no visible response by the Viper, but when he looked down to the ground he saw the patrol leader giving him the thumbs-up. The radio operator lay next to the patrol leader, and the long cable from the Viper was plugged into the PSC-7 satellite communication system.

With that push of the FIRE button the soldier sent an instant fire mission. Part binoculars, digital camera, laser range finder, and global-positioning system, the Viper sent a digital message down the long cable and through the PSC-7 satellite-communication set to aircraft in the area and ships at sea, but specifically to an A-10 Thunderbolt that was on its way to the patrol's location. The message not only provided an exact map grid of the target and the soldiers' observation point, but also a photograph of the heavy-caliber weapon mounted to the bed of an old pickup truck.

Antiaircraft weapons had been declared "hostile" by the National Command Authority, which meant they could be attacked on sight. The powerful machine gun was both a ground and antiair weapon. It just depended on how the San Selvans chose to use it, and whether or not the A-10 would destroy the target depended on how the aircraft's pilot classified the picture that he saw displayed in his cockpit.

"He's inbound," whispered the radio operator.

"Good shit," said the patrol leader. "I was worried he'd say he couldn't hit it because of the rules of engagement."

The patrol leader liked working with A-10s. The

pilots were usually like their aircraft: down and dirty. They were "warthogs" and proud of it. The patrol leader looked up at the sky. It would be dark soon. He preferred the safety that came with nighttime. With tonight's darkness they would move to another objective area. The prepositioning of the Special Forces teams proved ingenious. With the smoke reducing visibility and interfering with airborne laser designators, the soldiers on the ground enabled targets to be hit. Some would be destroyed like this truck by an aircraft dropping laser-guided bombs targeted by the ground troops. Other targets needed to be attacked by weapons that used GPS guidance systems. Those targets would be destroyed later tonight by cruise missiles and aircraft dropped JDAMs (Joint Direct Attack Munitions). The target locations came from teams using the Viper to pinpoint coordinates and send back pictures and grids.

The truck presented an opportune target, but the patrol still searched for a specific vehicle: the Rolands. They provided the San Selvans' with their only medium-altitude antiaircraft capability. The soldiers needed to find the Rolands, because they might soon threaten transport aircraft bringing in parachutists.

"He's on the hook," said the radio operator, handing the radio headset to the patrol leader.

"Hog One Two, this is Badger," said the patrol leader. Another patrol member aimed the laser designator at the truck. The single-seat Thunderbolt was specifically designed for close air support below one thousand feet elevation, with a titanium-armor-plated cockpit capable of taking direct hits from a 23-mm antiaircraft gun. The A-10 could loiter over an objective area for long periods of time, and it carried a wide variety of weapon systems on its eleven weapon pylons. Its 30mm GAU-8 Avenger was a seven-barrel

Gatling gun. It fired a variety of rounds, including the highly deadly depleted-uranium round. With a half-life of four and a half billion years, depleted uranium is a powerful substance. So powerful that it was considered by some to be the cause of the mysterious Gulf War syndrome. The rounds literally disintegrated the area around the truck, so the close proximity of the vehicle to a building did not allow for use of the 30-mm. There was too great a chance for collateral damage; the rounds were capable of penetrating the thickest armor on the battlefield.

"Roger, Badger," answered the pilot of the lead A-10. "We're moving from HA Louise to IP Condor."

"Roger," said the patrol leader. "From IP Ford, two two zero degrees magnetic. Offset left. Distance: six point three miles. Target elevation: three hundred and seventy feet. Gun vehicle. Laser code: four two hundred. Laser target line: one seven zero. Friendlies: six hundred meters south. Time on target: five two, over."

"Roger, Badger," said the pilot. "Time on target: five two."

The men near the truck sat lazily around the vehicle, unaware of the danger that bore down on them. The aircraft's twin turbofan engines pushed the A-10 to a speed of over four hundred miles an hour. From the holding area the section of two A-10s moved to Initial Point Ford to start their attack run on the truck. Coming in at treetop level, the aircraft began to search for the patrol's laser mark when they were seven miles from the target.

"Ten seconds," said the pilot.

"Stand by," the patrol leader whispered to the laser operator.

"Hey, boss," said the radio operator. "We got a hot message here."

The patrol leader did not stir. "Gotta wait one."

"Laser on," said the pilot.

"Roger," answered the patrol leader. Turning to the laser operator, he said, "Turn it on."

Remarkably quiet, the Thunderbolt's turbofan engines could barely be heard when the pilot said, "Spot," which meant that the AGM-65E Maverick air-to-surface missile had acquired the target. Designed as a standoff weapon for point targets, the AGM-65E's shape charge produced good penetration of targets like a tank or bunker. The missile could be launched from a distance of seventeen miles, but in terrain like this the A-10 needed to be much closer.

The A-10 never even flew over the truck, pulling away as soon as the pilot released the Maverick missile. The San Selvans barely had time to react. Gunmen near the truck fired wildly at the incoming object, not realizing that the best thing to do would have been to run. The truck and gunmen simply disappeared behind a fireball.

The patrol leader smiled and gave proud nods to the Special Forces soldiers near him. Then he turned to the radio operator and said, "What's the message?"

"You're not going to believe this."

Chapter Twenty-three

USS Zumwalt, *North Atlantic Ocean*

One of the newest ships in the U.S. Navy, a Land Attack Destroyer, the USS *Zumwalt* was designed to replace the World War II–era battleships that were retired after Desert Storm, as well as newer destroyers and frigates. It was named after Admiral Elmo R. Zumwalt Jr., the youngest officer promoted to admiral and the Navy's youngest Chief of Naval Operations. He presided over the Navy's revitalization during the 1970s, a time when many reforms were initiated.

The battleships that the *Zumwalt* replaced had provided fire support to troops ashore for generations, but they became too expensive and vulnerable during the latter part of the twentieth century. The old battleships needed to be within a few miles of a coast to provide fires ashore, making them a prime target for anti-ship-missile systems. They were also vulnerable to sophisticated antiship mines; the battleships were so heavy that most modern mines would cause the ship to break in half if it detonated anywhere in the middle one-third of the ship's frame.

With a crew of less than one hundred sailors operating the stealthy ship, the *Zumwalt* embodied the fighting spirit that was meant to be employed in the Land Attack Destroyer. The *Zumwalt* was designed to provide naval surface fire support to Marines fighting ashore. Along with long-range missiles, two 155mm guns could fire up to twelve rounds per minute at targets one hundred miles away. It was a deadly fire support platform, so it was assigned as the fourth ship to the Amphibious Ready Group supporting the Twenty-second Marine Expeditionary Unit for their deployment.

Sitting precariously on the *Zumwalt*'s dual-rail launching pad, the unmanned aerial vehicle, or UAV, went through its final preflight checks before being launched from the ship's deck. Over fifteen feet long with a wingspan of eighteen feet, the UAV could be flown as far as two hundred miles into hostile territory. Its small size made it difficult to shoot down, and the fact that it did not carry a human life made it more expendable. These two things meant that it was very easy for military leaders to decide to send the UAV into harm's way.

Satellite and aerial photographs had been pouring into the *Zumwalt*'s joint intelligence center, but the ship's captain wanted precise targeting data. Luckily, he had his own organic intelligence-gathering device— the UAV. After military operations during the early 1980s in Lebanon and Grenada, the U.S. Navy identified the need for an on-call reconnaissance capability for local commanders. The Israelis had experienced impressive success with UAVs during the same period, and the Secretary of the Navy ordered an immediate appropriation program.

By late 1986, the first UAV deployed with the battleship USS *Iowa*. It became an immediate favorite of the ship's captain, and more UAVs were acquired. By the time the Gulf War began in 1991, the UAV was a common sight on Navy ships. UAVs flew over three hundred combat missions in Kuwait and Iraq, becoming known as the "vulture" to the Iraqis, who identified that its ugly presence was often followed by incoming naval gunfire.

Up on the *Zumwalt*'s deck, the UAV's rockets ignited and launched the older model Pioneer Short Range UAV off the rails and into the sky. Newer, more sophisticated UAVs—like the RQ-1A Global Hawk and RQ-3A Dark Star—had been developed in recent years for the Defense Airborne Reconnaissance Office by the Advanced Research Projects Agency. With a wingspan of over one hundred feet, the Global Hawk was capable of climbing to sixty thousand feet and traveling over three thousand miles while remaining in the air for twenty-four continuous hours. The Dark Star, on the other hand, was only seventy feet by fifteen feet and capable of staying in the air for eight hours to cover five hundred miles at an altitude of fifty thousand feet, but it also used stealth technology to make it almost invisible to radar. Both of the newer UAVs were operated by the Air Force and they used satellite communication systems to send information collected by electrooptical, infrared, and synthetic-aperture radar. More advances would lie in the future, with varying degrees of success during experiments for in-flight refueling to prolong UAV flight time.

The Pioneer UAV left the ship's airspace and continued along its path toward San Selva. A naval officer sat at the controls of the UAV in a specially designed space tucked away inside the *Zumwalt*. He carefully flew the unmanned aircraft as the UAV's maintenance crew sat behind him and watched the view from the UAV's video camera displayed on a television screen inside the control console.

After more than an hour of flying over the water, the UAV finally neared the San Selvan coast. The pilot, sitting comfortably in an air-conditioned space on the USS *Zumwalt*, sipped at his coffee between manipulations of the control console's stick. The UAV handled nicely, and the pilot enjoyed a little extra latitude with the maneuvers he put the small aircraft through.

"It's handling much better than before," the pilot said to one of the technicians. "Whatever you did fixed the problem with the flaps. Good job."

"The thingamjig was just a little worn out." The young sailor beamed with pride.

At only one thousand feet, the UAV was able to see many things that a normal aircraft would not. It was also able to see these things without placing a pilot in danger of being shot down. A fighter or bomber flying at this altitude over San Selva would have been a literal surface-to-air missile magnet, but the small UAV was hard to see, even when it was so close to the ground. Although not impossible, it was difficult to shoot down a UAV because most of the San Selvans' modern SA-18 missiles were designed to hone in on the heat signature of a jet aircraft.

Through the smoke and haze of San Selva's fires, the UAV's camera caught a glimpse of a San Selvan gun position near the beach. "Bingo," said the pilot. "We got one!" The position was no threat to American aircraft and ships, but it would be a threat to forces going ashore. Besides, the weapons could always be moved to another location. Might as well destroy it now while the opportunity presented itself. The control console displayed the exact location of the UAVs, as well as a distance and magnetic direction to the target. More advanced UAVs were capable of firing their own missiles and guiding smart bombs with a laser designator. "Someone call the fire direction control center and make sure they are up on this."

One of the UAV's maintenance crew grabbed the phone off the wall and quickly tapped in a number. He had a short conversation before turning back to the pilot. "They got it and they're working a mission now."

The UAV crew knew that the fire-direction control center finished calculating the coordinates for the fire mission when they heard the loud *boom* from the ship's main gun. A 155mm improved conventional munition was on the way to the San Selvan coast sixty miles away. It took several minutes for the round to finally impact, falling less than one hundred meters from the targeted gun site. The ground exploded as the 155mm projectile deployed hundreds of baseball-sized submunitions over the area.

"Oouu!" squealed a sailor. "Just a little off. Do you think you'll get a second chance?"

The range of the *Zumwalt*'s guns improved its survivability by allowing it to sit far off a hostile shore, but the time of flight for the rounds could be considered slow and unresponsive. For a Marine or SEAL ashore and in need of fire support, several minutes could be a lifetime—*or the end of a lifetime!* The enemy could move, meaning that the crew members in the fire-direction control center had to move fast. There was an image of the UAV's camera displayed on a television screen in their compartment, and they already worked on an adjustment to the first round.

"It looks like they're hunkering down and taking cover," said the pilot. That would prove to be fatal for the enemy soldiers at the gun position. The 155mm gun did not fare well against a moving target.

Boom! Boom! Boom! Three rounds fired in rapid succession. The first round had been an adjustment round. Now these next three were expected to hit their target and destroy something.

"Time?" asked the pilot.

"Probably four more minutes," said a sailor behind him.

"All right, I got to make a head call and get more coffee. Who wants to fly for a minute?" The question was stupid. All of them wanted to fly the UAV, even if only for a minute. The job description called for commissioned officers who attended several months of flying school and even wore little flight wing devices on their uniforms, but the enlisted sailors flew the UAV almost as well as the officers. All of the men and women of the detachment had a little "stick time" that they'd talked pilots into giving them during training.

The pilot left the compartment but returned from the head just in time to see the three rounds impact within effective range of the target. "Whoaa! Good shot!" He retook his seat at the controls of the UAV. "Let's see if they can get a direct hit this time." The fire-direction computers worked to calculate the data that needed to be put on the 155mm guns in order for them to get even closer to the target. Everything was taken into account: the ship's position, wind speed, target location, rotation of the earth, and so on before the stabilized weapon discharged each deadly load.

Boom! Boom! Boom!

Another wait for the time of flight and another three impacts. This time landing right on the gun position and destroying it. Several secondary explosions amplified the 155mm rounds impacts as the enemy's ammunition stores ignited.

"Okay, one down," said the pilot. "Let's see if we can find some more before we bingo on gas."

Belem, Brazil

First Sergeant Brown sat on top of one of the company's lightly armored vehicles. The plan had hardly begun and things were already running behind schedule. Half the company should already have been loaded by now. There just wasn't enough time to do everything that needed to be done before tonight. Complicating the matter even more was unexpected activity at the air base. Protests outside the gates started early and then grew to a size and level of violence that worried American commanders. Especially if the chaos poured over the gates and into the compound. Even if the mobs were forced back out without creating any damage, they still would see things they should not. Much like what Brown and Summer just saw. They couldn't help but think that they were intruding on a private function.

Brown wiped the sweat off his face with an olive-drab bandanna. "So whada you think about that there, sir?"

Summer paused before responding. Both had just heard of the attack on *The Sullivans* and they were ready to believe just about anything could happen next. He too caught a glimpse of what was in the two C-17 transport aircraft. The bubble-shaped "Little Birds" were flown only by special operations pilots. "I know what we'll be doing tonight. I just wish I knew what they were doing, too."

USS Zumwalt, *North Atlantic Ocean*

There was still enough light to see clearly, but it was always difficult to land the UAV. The pilot really earned his pay now, focusing on the video image of the *Zumwalt* growing larger and larger. Checking the gauges on the control console, the pilot manipulated the UAV's wing flaps to properly position it. He slowed the air speed, careful to aim the UAV dead center of the net. The *Zumwalt* seemed very close now. Close enough for the pilot to make out images of heads looking out the windows of the bridge. The UAV's mission had been very successful, and no one wanted it to end with a crash. Sometimes the pilotless aircraft clipped a side railing and fell into the ocean during landings, and the pilot didn't want to have the UAV's million-dollar price tag tied around his neck. Suddenly only the net could be seen. The pilot cut all power to the aircraft just before impact.

Another pilot sat at another nearby console. A second UAV was already loaded on the launch railings waiting for its rockets to be ignited. This UAV had an IR camera, making it the perfect aerial observation unit for nighttime missions. Outside, the maintenance men and women started to remove the first UAV from the landing net. They carefully checked for damage caused by antiaircraft fire or the landing. They needed to move quickly to clear the ship's deck. It was already getting dark.

Chapter Twenty-four

San Selvan Coast Near the Amazon River

U.S. Navy Lieutenant Jason Barret neared the surface, but he kept his body under the water for as long as possible. His head slowly broke the surface, bringing the lens from the AN/PVS-15 submersible night-vision goggles out of the water to scan the area. He and his men had barely made it ashore in the two minisubs, and Barret didn't want his good luck to be wasted by a San Selvan gunman who happened to be on the beach. A daylight insertion was not the preferred way to land, but there was no other choice. The SEALs needed to be in position shortly after sunset.

This might be the most dangerous mission of his life. If things did not go perfect, then the mission could only end in tragedy. End in the same manner that his mission in the former Yugoslavia had ended several years before. Too much of this reminded him of the Yugoslav mission. Except on this mission it was *his* men who would die if things went wrong. Although it shouldn't have mattered, and he couldn't figure out why it did, losing a man from his platoon troubled him more than losing a buddy. The SEALs in his platoon were not much younger than he, but there was almost a paternal instinct that he had to take care of them.

Barret's group of SEALs numbered twelve, including him. All the men packed more weapons and ammunition than normal. It would be needed. On this mission the SEALs expected contact with the enemy. Not finding it meant mission failure.

Command Bunker, Macapa, San Selva

The ground felt hard. Crash wasn't quite conscious in the small four-by-four-foot concrete cell but she at least knew that. There were no windows and barely a door, making the cell more like a storage space for cleaning supplies than a place to put a human being. Some light shone through the steel door, but for the most part it was dark. The stench of feces and urine was what really brought Crash back to reality. It smelled so bad in the cell that it made it hard to breathe. As she became more awake, Crash began to feel her injuries, especially the pain from the wounds in her mouth. Breathing in the rancid air hurt. She moved her hand around the cell's floor, feeling for the limits of her new world. Even in her clouded state of mind, it did not take long for Crash to realize that she couldn't stand in the small cell. Positioning herself diagonally across the cell, she would barely be able to extend her body.

She could hear sounds of yelling coming from

somewhere else in the building and wondered if maybe other Americans were being held here too. As much as she hated to think of another American going through the same experience as she, Crash admitted to herself that she would find strength in the presence of a comrade. There was just something so terrible about being alone. *Would they let us talk?* Probably not, but even if she knew there was another prisoner, Crash would find a way. POWs in Vietnam had developed secret codes similar to Morse code so they could tap to each other and communicate.

Once again Crash thought of her family. Peter and her parents always worried when she deployed for an operation, but now the children were old enough to understand when something was wrong. By now the Navy had to have told Peter that she was missing, but did they know that she was a prisoner? *What would be worse: thinking I'm dead or knowing I'm held captive in brutal conditions? How long can this war go on for?* Wars in the past few decades had been all quick, lasting only a couple of months. The pilots shot down in the first year of the Vietnam War must have thought that the war would be quick, only to spend up to eight years as a prisoner. So many of them lasted for years without providing information that the enemy wanted. Crash began to feel guilty about telling the San Selvans that she was from the Navy. *I gave in too easily!* Admiral James Stockdale, the senior American held in Vietnam, tried to kill himself once when he was afraid he would break and give information to the enemy that would place other prisoners in peril. His action scared the Vietnamese, and the other prisoners noticed that their captors became more hesitant to torture a man to the breaking point. Stockdale had received the Medal of Honor for his courageous leadership. *Next time they'll have to work harder to get anything out of me.*

The cold cement and slimy mess that she lay in made a chill flow through her body. As Crash began to wonder where these San Selvan barbarians expected her to go to the bathroom, she suddenly realized that she was naked. She closed her eyes and let the reality sink into her head; then she conducted a painful physical check of her vagina with her aching hands. She remembered nothing since the blindfolded interrogation. She wished she had enough light to conduct a more thorough inspection. Her entire body ached, and it was impossible for her to ascertain whether or not she'd been raped. But now they knew she was a woman.

At that same moment, outside the building and unbeknownst to Sara or her San Selvan captors, a plainly clothed Hispanic man walked across the front of the structure and down one side. He never looked at the prison. He already knew it well, having taken hundreds of digital photographs during previous walks through this area. It surprised him how easily he had found it, but there were really only a few buildings like this. It was also one of the few that had not been attacked in air strikes. The San Selvans knew the Americans would not purposely target a building with civilians in it, even if the civilians were criminals. And common sense would also dictate that if it was not being hit in strikes, then the satellites probably would not watch it closely, which was what made it perfect.

Hector Valdez lifted his old, oily Marborlo hat and scratched his head. He'd had the hat for years. It was his favorite fishing hat, and on an operation like this one he felt safe just having it with him. The hat was worn well beyond what most people would consider acceptable. Its bent bill and faded color topped off Hector's "local" appearance. Dressed in old jeans and a brown, striped shirt with ceramic snaps instead of buttons, Valdez blended in well with the rest of the people walking through the streets of the poor South American town.

This section of Macapa was primitive. A few large buildings, like the hospital and church, which were other buildings he had watched because they were not targeted either, dominated the small dwellings that occupied most of the landscape. The small homes in the area had been constructed with a mix of building supplies. Running water in the structures was unlikely, but it looked as if most had wood floors.

Located at the mouth of the Amazon River, Macapa supported itself economically by selling goods to those that transited the river. The town sat right near the border of San Selva and Brazil, making it an easy place for Valdez to infiltrate into. He'd learned much since arriving, especially that the common San Selvan despised America's military action. Invasion was going to be tough. Everyone was armed, and Hector had never seen so many assault rifles and rocket-propelled grenades. So many, in fact, that he had to start carrying an AK-47 so he could remain inconspicuous. Warlords ruled over different towns and parts of large cities, occasionally clashing with each other in what seemed to be practice for the combined fight against the Americans. Most important, the average San Selvan did not understand why a rich country like the United States was so insistent on bullying a poor country like San Selva. Instead of trying to help fix San Selva's internal problems, the United States wanted to create more by refusing to allow the civilians even to clear land so they could feed their families. The San Selvans planned on fighting Americans in the streets of their cities, which should have been a predictable response. What would Americans do if a foreign force rolled into New York, Los Angeles, or Houston and demanded subservience?

Valdez was the closest thing to the 007 James Bond character that the United States could produce. He was a secret agent with the Special Collection Service. A joint CIA/NSA organization, the Maryland-based SCS had agents around the world that specialized in planting eavesdropping devices and collecting other information that satellites or aircraft were incapable of obtaining. Valdez and his buddies were often the most important part of America's information-gathering network. Aerial photographs could tell a military leader a lot about the ground and damage produced by bombs, but only someone like Hector could help predict how the San Selvans would react to foreign intervention. Many lessons had been learned by the United States from occupation duty in Somalia, the former Yugoslavia, and Afghanistan. Even if warlords were defeated, if the citizens of a nation did not want the foreign force involved, then there was friction and turmoil that greatly complicated the situation.

Hector walked into one of the measly little cantinas on the main street and sat down at a back table. He had sat at this same table the past two days, except on those visits when he pulled out a secure satellite phone from his waistband and pressed a button that automatically dialed a number to another phone just across the Amazon in Brazil. The sight was not that far from the ordinary. San Selva had few landline telephones. By the time the country advanced it was cheaper and easier to install cellular telephone and wireless Internet systems. Once connected to the other party, Hector had attached his digital camera to the phone and sent the hundreds of pictures across the Amazon with a single-burst transmission. Then he erased the photographs from the memory bank of his digital camera. Each of those previous missions took less than ten minutes. In ten minutes valuable intelligence photographs were safely sent out of the country and in the hands of agents who would see they'd get to those who needed them. If the decision was made to assault the building, then the photographs would be there and ready for the commandos to review.

Hector signaled for a waitress. He did not have any photographs to send today, so he might as well have a beer. He'd be here for a while, he reasoned, and it helped him blend in with the group. It was hard for him to believe that anything worth reporting would happen anyway.

Dirt Airstrip Near the Brazil and San Selva Border

The Air Force C-17 landed in a plume of dust and dirt, quickly taxiing to one side of the small, unimproved strip so the other C-17 could land too. There were no lights. Everyone wore night-vision devices, and everyone, regardless of rank or seniority, worked hard. There were too few people and too little time for anyone from the raid force to remove himself from the requirement of physical labor.

With the engines still running and the second C-17 not yet at a complete stop, the commandos began to unload the first of eight small helicopters from the large cargo aircraft.

Somewhere in San Selva

The patrol leader scanned the fresh darkness. They had said there was a chance they might come during daylight, but no other word was passed over the radio. It looked like the original L-hour was to be used. It would be dark soon and he still was not sure what to expect. In all of their years as special operators, none of the men had been part of anything like this before.

Chapter Twenty-five

MH-6J Cayuse, San Selvan Airspace Nearing Macapa

Small and black, the MH-6J Cayuse helicopters flew in complete darkness through the tree line and down a riverbed at a speed of one hundred knots. Definitely not the fastest helicopters in the American fleet, the MH-6J, more commonly known as "Little Birds," were loved not for speed but for their small size and agility. Less than ten feet high and with about a twenty-five-foot rotor diameter, the Little Birds normally flew at speeds of over one hundred and fifty knots, but with tonight's heavy loads and the lack of doors creating drag, one hundred knots was fast enough.

At the controls of the special-operations birds were pilots from the "Nightstalkers," the Army's 160th Special Operations Aviation Regiment, called Task

Force 160. The Nightstalkers were undoubtedly the finest group of helicopter pilots in the world. Created in the early 1980s, Task Force 160's first operational experience was flying from U.S. Navy frigates in the Persian Gulf during the "Tanker Wars" between Iraq and Iran. When a Navy P-3 Orion discovered the Iran *Ajr* laying mines in the Straits of Hormuz on September 20, 1987, the Nightstalkers were sent out to destroy the Iranian vessel. The few Iranian survivors of the attack best summarized the deadly ability of the Little Birds; they called them "Sea Bats."

Just a few years later, in 1989, the Nightstalkers flew commandos onto a Panamanian prison to rescue a CIA operative during the opening hours of Operation Just Cause. A relationship between the Nightstalkers and the special-operation community solidified, and they were always the force of choice for a mission like tonight's. Most of Task Force 160's work was done during black operations with the Army's mythical Delta Force. Officials at the Pentagon never commented on Delta, leading to an endless number of rumors spoken by everyone from well-informed military officers to Internet conspiracy theorists: *All Army? Descendants of SEAL Team Six? A joint group of the best from all the military services?* No one was really sure where the Delta commandos came from; and their long hair, sideburns, and facial hair made them hard to identify as military at all.

Special Operations Detachment-Delta was a super-secret counterterrorism unit created in 1977. Its first operation experience ended in failure during the 1980 attempt to rescue the American hostages from Iran. Other operations were more successful: from stealing a Russian-built Mi-24 HIND helicopter from an African country in the 1980s to snatching terrorists from their safe havens in the Middle East during the 2000s.

271

Modeled after the British Special Air Service, Delta Force had three troops of commandos. Each troop specialized in a different means of insertion: Scuba, parachute, and helicopter. Although all Delta commandos were qualified in each of the three skills, the individual troops took their insertion method and turned qualification into obsessive perfection.

Tonight, the MH-6Js each carried four Delta Commandos from C Squadron. The commandos were armed with more than enough firepower and they wore heavy bulletproof vests capable of stopping a high-powered rifle bullet, because they knew the enemy was armed too. The commandos' small, hockey-style helmets held night-vision devices, radio earpieces, and microphones. Black baklavas hid their faces, and laser-safe goggles covered their eyes. The goggles protected the men from inexpensive and easy-to-obtain lasers—like laser pointers—that caused permanent eye damage if aimed directly at a human eye for anything more than a few seconds. Thigh holsters held submachine gun magazines, .45-caliber pistols, and stun grenades—essentially a grenade simulator with enough explosive blast to produce a blinding flash that disoriented and a loud sound that disrupted the inner ear's mechanism for balance. Leather gloves protected hands. Hard plastic pads covered elbows and knees. Boots were steel tipped. Some carried blowtorches and radios on their backs. Everyone was heavily armed. And everything that the men were wearing was basic black, a dark and deadly black that covered the features someone might mistake for human. No insignias were on the black uniforms, with each commando leaving behind anything that would identify the man.

Two motorcycles hung off racks on the sides of each helicopter, and escorting the flight of four MH-6Js were four attack variants of the Little Bird, which were vicious in a fight. Each AH-6J was armed with two M134 electrically driven Gatling guns, two M26 rocket pods, and two AGM-114F Hellfire missiles. The assault force was small enough to get to the target without detection and deadly enough to kill anyone who tried to stop them from accomplishing their mission.

The past twenty-four hours had been busy for the Delta-Nightstalker team. Two special operations Air Force C-17 transports had departed before the sun came up over Fort Bragg. The aircraft carried the commandos, helicopter pilots, a small support team, and an even smaller command element from JSOC (Joint Special Operations Command). They sat staged at the Belem Airport most of the day. Positioning them in South America early was a risk, but the team had to be ready to conduct a daylight assault if something occurred that indicated the target was going to be moved or killed.

The raid force landed at the isolated airfield near the Brazil and San Selva border and the eight helicopters were unloaded and ready to fly in less than fifteen minutes. It was there, on the border, that Delta received its final intelligence dump. The landing zone security force barely got into position after hasty tasking and dangerous daylight movement. A Global Hawk UAV circled high over the objective and beamed live video images to the C-17 at the airfield. Now the mission moved along smoothly, but there was little time to waste. If they were not successful on this first try, there might never be the opportunity for a second.

F-117A Nighthawk, San Selvan Air Space Over Macapa

Air Force Major Ken "Wig" Davelle opened doors to the internal weapon bay on the stealth fighter's fuselage as the target came into view. As he released the special weapons directly over the target, the bombs flew for only a second before exploding in the air and deploying thousands of metal fibers that floated down into the power plant. The metal fibers shorted out the power plant, sending San Selva's capital city of Macapa into complete darkness.

MH-6J Cayuse, San Selvan Airspace Nearing Macapa

Flying into the wind to reduce the likelihood of enemy personnel on the objective hearing the approaching raid force, the men in the MH-6Js saw the lights of the city go dark when the helicopters were still fifteen miles from the target site.

Outside Macapa, San Selva

"Nightstalker Three Two, Nightstalker Three Two, this is Badger." The patrol leader barely saw the helicopters in his thermal viewer. They still weren't close enough to pick up with night-vision goggles.

"Roger, Badger. We're just a couple of minutes out."

"Gotcha. Zone is cold. Wind is out of the west. My team is surrounding the zone. We're ready to mark with IR strobe or smoke."

"Negative, Badger. No mark. I don't want anyone else seeing it. We'll pick your body heat up on our thermals. That'll be our mark."

The patrol leader never used that technique for marking a helicopter landing zone, but he also never worked with warriors like the Nightstalkers and Delta Force. Even though he was a highly trained Special Forces soldier, much of what he saw tonight was new to him. The task to secure and mark this zone had come midday over the satcom. The patrol had rushed here soon after to make sure the zone was suitable for the operation and in case the mission went early.

"I see the zone, Badger. We're landing in one package."

It didn't look like there was enough room to fit all four of the MH-6Js, and the helicopters came dangerously close to each other during the landing. As commandos debarked the helicopters, the AH-6Js circled overhead and searched for targets with their night vision and thermal sights. The motorcycles were unloaded and started before the MH-6Js were back in the air. Two Delta warriors rode on each motorcycle as they exited the makeshift landing zone and traveled cross-country to a hard-surface road that led straight to their objective. The patrol watched in awe at the precision. The bikes sped away without acknowledging the patrol leader and his soldiers.

The motorcycle drivers wore night-vision goggles and drove too fast. Insanely fast! The mission had been rehearsed several times over, with more and more detail added as intelligence reports increased the raid force's knowledge of the objective. The plans for the full-scale rehearsal site were created from satellite imagery and ground-level photographs taken by operatives like Hector Valdez and other Special Collection Service agents. The Delta commandos' high level of training paid big dividends, because information for the assault poured in quickly and gave little time to prepare. Everything was rushed. The commandos had gone straight from the live-fire rehearsal to the aircraft for the flight to Brazil.

EH-60A Eagle Hawk, San Selvan Airspace

Using the AN/ALQ-151 electronic warfare system, the U.S. Army EH-60 helicopter began broadband jamming of San Selvan military communications. The unique helicopter could also use directional-finding equipment to locate the source of radio signals, if it wanted to destroy them with munitions from other aircraft. But for tonight's mission the specially equipped Black Hawk would conduct only electrical attacks on San Selvan targets.

Macapa, San Selva

The men were quickly surrounded by structures as their motorcycles rocketed through squalor and past unsuspecting San Selvans. The four motorcycles with the eight Delta Force commandos charged at the target building. Taking down a building was a Delta Force specialty. Surprise was key. Surprise and speed. When a structure was filled with sudden violence, those inside were disoriented and frozen in fright. Most fell and crawled to a corner, reacting with amazing obedience when told by a commando to do something. At least they had better, because the commandos did not have time to repeat themselves. The momentum of the attack needed to be maintained so that reaction continued. Thirty minutes on the ground was too long. Failure came when the enemy had a chance to think.

San Selvan Coast Near the Amazon River

"Holy shit," whispered one of the SEALs. "They were right. Here it comes."

Barret shook his head in disbelief. The intelligence reports were accurate. The vehicle drove down the road toward the bridge just like they said it would. Now the SEALs just needed to spring the trap and seal the deal.

Macapa, San Selva

The commando driving the lead motorcycle knew that the guard at the front of the building had to hear the approaching motorcycles, but the guard wouldn't be as alarmed as if he heard helicopters. Helicopters could only have come from Americans. Many San Selvans drove wildly through the streets without lights on because they were afraid of the American aircraft overhead.

Coming to within one hundred meters of the target building, the second commando on the lead bike steadied his .45-caliber submachine gun and pointed the laser aimer at the guard's forehead. Squeezing the trigger of the submachine gun, he fired a single round of the silenced weapon that blew the guard's brains out the back of his head. The submachine gun bolt slapped back and then forward to chamber another round, but the sound was much quieter than the typical sound of a gunshot.

The motorcycles stopped in front of the building and the second commando on each vehicle jumped off and attacked the main door. Drivers remained in the street and discriminatorily fired their weapons to cover the assault. Most of the San Selvans remained oblivious of the threat that loomed, literally, at their doorstep. The motorcycle drivers piled their bikes in the middle of the street and yanked the rings on the fuse igniters attached to explosive packs on the gas tank of each bike. They then formed into a trail assault force to follow the lead commandos.

Inside the building a killing spree evolved. The commandos danced with the grace of ballerinas but the deadliness of vampires, scanning for any new targets that they could destroy. The first floor was cleared quickly and the men prepared to move to the second. One at a time, the commandos inserted a full magazine into their weapons. The magazines being removed were not empty, but it was important to ensure that they were ready to kill as many bad guys as possible. At the top of the stairs the killing commenced again. The men consistently blew heads apart and chests wide open as they made their way through the simple, three-story building. Thick chunks of blood-covered brain matter splattered on the walls. The suppressed sound from the silenced weapons still prevented most in the building from knowing something was wrong. At the main door of the cell block on the second floor, the point commando started cutting through the lock with a blowtorch.

The assault leader looked at his watch. Less than thirty seconds before the motorcycles outside blew, probably ten seconds until the door was open. The explosion outside would lift the veil of surprise that the commandos now operated under, but it would also create confusion and help expedite their withdrawal. The rush of adrenaline and ringing in the ears after the explosion would delay the San Selvans from noticing that helicopters were coming. By then it would be too late. The raid would be almost over at that point.

As the door flew open, the first four commandos rushed into the cell block. "Linsey, get down! *Get down, Linsey!*" yelled the lead commando. Hopefully his objective, Lieutenant Commander Sara "Crash" Linsey, if still here, remembered her training as a Navy fighter pilot and would get down on the floor until the rescue force was ready for her.

The Americans scanned and searched for targets to kill. The first few seconds were for killing; then would come the rescue. Most San Selvans tried to run away, which made their death that much easier. The commandos paused for a second and made sure that the laser aimer pointed in the back of each San Selvan head before pulling the trigger.

After killing every living thing in the hallway and adjoining offices, a commando yelled, "Linsey, we're Americans. Where ar—"

"Here!" Sara screamed painfully.

Boom! The motorcycles outside exploded right before the commandos reached Sara's door. Pulling back the horizontal locking bar, the lead commando opened the door. He saw Sara huddled in a corner of the cell.

"Suit her up," yelled the assault leader. One commando guarded down each side of the hallway as the fourth, a medic, dropped to a knee and reached for Sara. The medic started to remove her from the small cell to place a bulletproof vest and helmet on Sara. There was no reason to risk the hostage's life any more than necessary. Because of her injuries, putting the protective gear on her was going to be harder than normal, but the commando was prepared for that. What he wasn't prepared for was her being naked and covered in feces and urine.

"For Christ's sake," gasped the combat-hardened medic. "She doesn't have any clothes." His voice cracked with emotion. He had witnessed and participated in some of the most ghastly brutality man had inflicted on man in the opening years of the twenty-first century, but the commando was the only boy in a family with four children. As he dressed Sara with the gentleness that he would have used with any of his sisters, on the inside the medic boiled with rage.

In less than a minute Sara was dressed in her vest and helmet. "Ma'am, I'm going to pick you up now."

"No," said Sara. "I can . . . walk . . ."

"Sorry, ma'am. Speed takes precedence over ego." Before Sara could respond again, the commando lifted her in his arms and moved toward the door. "And it's much faster if you let my legs do the work for the both of us." Then yelling, "Moving to extract with one hotel."

The trail commando led the way out of the cellblock. Word traveled through the raid force that Sara had been found in her cell naked, and the men's imaginations now filled with the ugliest of images. Conditioned by sociological norms and driven by a natural instinct to protect women, the deadly men seethed as they looked for targets to direct their rage. Their .45-caliber rounds from the submachine guns reaped their revenge.

They all moved to the stairs, which the second team had secured, and leaped up to the roof. The sound of helicopters grew closer as the eight commandos and their objective fell out on the building's roof.

The viciousness of the AH-6J became painfully obvious as the helicopters drew closer. Two of the attack helicopters focused on the outer perimeter, as the other two circled the roof and spat a stream of fire and death that tore the building and surrounding structures apart.

Kill all of them—damn monsters! Killing. Raping. Hacking up those pilots and PJs.

In a parting act of chivalry, one of the commandos magically produced a blanket and wrapped it around Sara to at least give her back part of her dignity. The AH-6Js made another run, this time firing their flechette rockets that hurled thousands of deadly nails around the perimeter.

Toe-curling screams could be heard in the mix of noise. The commandos now fired at targets indiscriminately. One San Selvan was literally nailed to a wall by one of the long flechettes that affixed his leg to a stone fence. From his rooftop perch, a commando took careful aim before firing a series of rounds at the San Selvan: first bullet to the groin; next the gut; finally through the head. Every round had hit exactly where the commando wanted it to hit.

Fucking sancho, the commando thought. Then he regretted his actions. *I should have let the bastard suffer longer!*

San Selvan Coast Near the Amazon River

The flash of light surprised even Barret, who had squeezed the firing device to detonate the mine. The concussion from the explosion swept over the men before they began to fire their weapons. *Pops* quickly joined to create a roar as the ambush started. The vehicle careened away from the SEALs' kill zone, disappearing on the far side of the road. The firing tapered off, seemingly right after it had begun.

"Well . . . what the fuck?"

Barret sat stunned. *This is like a Keystone Cops movie.* He had blown the vehicle right out of the ambush's kill zone. "Mount up! Grab your shit and let's go. Get on line and attack across the road."

He had to get to the vehicle to confirm that the mission was successful.

Macapa, San Selva

As the first MH-6J touched down on the roof, two commandos carried Sara and ran to the helicopter. The other six commandos and the AH-6J covered their movement with a volley of lead and fire. The commandos loaded their precious cargo in the lead Little Bird and it took off quickly. Seconds after the first

MH-6J lifted off the roof, the second one landed and the six commandos jumped onto the benches strapped to the sides of the small helicopter.

The two helicopters lifted from the roof only four minutes after the first commando had entered the building. Dozens of San Selvans lay dead, and most still had no idea what happened. The San Selvans thought the helicopters on the roof were dropping American soldiers off, not extracting them. More gunmen came running to the prison, and the AH-6Js fired again and again.

Flying higher, an AC-130U gunship added additional deadliness to the battlefield. With a crew of fourteen operating a number of deadly weapons, the heavily armed turboprop airplane was designed to provide close air support, air interdiction, and armed reconnaissance. It was the best friend of a lightly armed special ops warrior. The aircraft's crew used the sophisticated sensors, navigation equipment, and fire-control systems to provide surgical firepower with the 105-mm howitzer. Two men worked the weapon like a musical instrument, firing twenty rounds in the first minute. They manhandled the fifty-pound rounds into the howitzer as another airman used the low-light-level television camera and infrared sensors to select targets around the soldiers on the ground.

Buildings below crumbled. Between the howitzer shots, bursts of 25mm rounds from the Gatling gun sent hundreds of rounds per minute through the roofs of buildings. A crew member had to use a snow shovel to throw spent brass from the aircraft. The 40mm Bofors cannon fired occasionally to add additional death and destruction on the ground below.

Down in the middle of the fiery hell, the commandos fired their weapons from the helicopter benches as the aircraft gained altitude, taking every opportunity to kill. Two empty MH-6Js followed as backup birds, a hard lesson that still remained from Desert One in Iran. The AH-6Js surrounded the MH-6Js to provide protection. After the hostage and the assault force extracted from the objective, the two empty MH-6Js would pick up the patrol and they would all soon make the short flight back to the airstrip.

Both commandos with Crash were qualified Special Forces medics. They did their best to treat her wounds and make her as comfortable as possible, but they could do little to relieve the pain. She'd been hurt too severely and needed the doctors at the C-17. The men had come just in time. The injuries she'd sustained would soon have killed her.

San Selvan Coast Near the Amazon River

The ground dropped down from the road to the crash site. The SEALs reached the edge of the road and fired down on the wounded vehicle below. One began throwing M67 fragmentation grenades, as another unloaded with bursts from an M249 Squad Automatic Weapon. Although the M249 was primarily used as an automatic rifle, it was only forty-one inches long and weighed twenty-two pounds when fully loaded, making it light enough for soldiers to take with them in an assault on an enemy position. The M249's standard ammunition feed was by two-hundred-round disintegrating belts, but it was also capable of firing ammunition from standard M16 magazines inserted in a magazine well in the bottom of the SAW. This ability to interchange ammunition made the weapons complementary; therefore, the weapons were perfect for small patrols like this one.

The occupants of the vehicle were completely outmatched, and the small number who survived the initial, limb-ripping destruction of the explosion and crash only fired off a few futile shots before being pounded into a bloody pile of human mush. The fight was not fair, but it wasn't meant to be either. This was an ambush, and ambushes were for killing.

After emptying their magazines, each SEAL reloaded his weapon and waited for the firing to stop. Suddenly it was silent except for the sounds of the SAW gunner lifting the feed-tray cover of his weapon to load another belt of ammunition. A thin cloud of smoke hung over the ambush site. There were no moans from wounded in the kill zone; the savage violence of the men had killed every living thing that was before them. At least that was what they thought. After a slam of the feed-tray cover and the cocking of the SAW, the gunner yelled that he was reloaded.

"Lieutenant Markwell, take a team down there and search the car," ordered Barret. "Chief, set up perimeter security up here."

Markwell led with a hand grenade thrown into an open door of the sedan as the men moved down to the objective and fired at everything that moved. There was no time to ensure that each San Selvan held a weapon. Rifles spat bullets into bodies that flopped around on the ground in dying agony. Someone threw another hand grenade into the car before venturing inside to search for General Moreno.

"One in here is hurt bad but still kicking, boss," yelled one of the SEALs.

"Doc," yelled Barret, "get down there and treat him as best you can." *How the hell did anyone survive that?* It almost seemed more humane just to kill the man. Barret barely had the ability to extract any of his own wounded, so there was no way he could get a flight for an enemy gunman; not that he really wanted to anyway. No, treating him and leaving him on the objective was the only answer, even though the San Selvan would probably suffer alone in the dark until death came.

"Is Moreno in there?" yelled Markwell.

"Hell, I can't tell. There's too much fucking mess. I think there's a woman's body in here, too."

Barret shook his head. *More Keystone Cops.* "I coming down there for a look." He began to climb down the embankment. "Start wrapping your shit up. I want to be out of here in two minutes." He peered into the vehicle. Everything twisted together in a ghastly mess. Four bloody and burnt bodies littered the debris, including the wounded man who was more dead than alive. Barret looked at each face. All were too disfigured to identify. Barret couldn't judge if any was General Moreno. A decision needed to be made quickly. Killing the San Selvan military leader would be an important step toward victory. Was the mission a success or not?

"Doc, forget about him and get over here. I need a blood prick from each one." Mission confirmation just might come down to DNA testing.

Chapter Twenty-six

Norfolk, Virginia

"Madelyn, honey," said Peter Linsey. "Wake up, baby." Sara's mother was already rousting Peter Jr. from his blissful slumber. "We're going to go for a little drive."

"Where are we going?" asked Madelyn.

"Somewhere where people can't bother us."

"Can you turn on the light, Daddy?" said Madelyn.

"No, honey. We need to keep the lights off so no one can see us leave."

With the kids collected up but still rubbing the sleep from their eyes, the three generations that made up Sara Linsey's family slipped into the backyard. Sara's father had removed two boards from the back fence, and the five moved quickly through the hole and into the home of their neighbors, the Amarosas. Waiting for them there were two Navy officers dressed in civilian clothes.

"We have a car in the garage, sir."

"Okay," said Peter. "Let's get going. I want to go right now."

"Please call us if you need anything at all, Peter," said Sally Amarosa.

"I will," answered Peter. "Thank you for helping us get away." Parked in the garage of the Amarosa home was the large, nine-passenger sports utility vehicle that served as the family's freedom bird. Sara's mother strapped the two children into the child seats that the Navy officers had thought to bring with them, and then hugged Sally good-bye.

"I'll be back sometime tomorrow to get more of the kids' stuff," said Sara's father, shaking Mario Amarosa's hand.

"I'll be here all day," said Mario, turning to shake Peter's hand. "And I don't want to see you until all this is over. You don't need to put up with any more of this *crap*."

"Thanks again, Mario."

"Daddy, when will we come home?"

"I don't know, honey," Peter said painfully. "I don't know."

"I want Dolly!"

"I'll get it for you later today when I come back with these great guys," said Madelyn's smiling grandfather, motioning to the Navy officers, "to pick up some more of your stuff."

"I should have thought of the damn doll," whispered Peter.

"I want it now," cried Madelyn. "Please, Papa."

"I'm sorry, honey. We need to go now."

Doors slammed shut and the vehicle exited the garage and drove out of the busy neighborhood, giving

Peter a quick glimpse of the mayhem outside his once quite home. Madelyn was still crying ten minutes later when the vehicle turned off of the main thoroughfare to enter Norfolk Naval Base. Even with the horrible sounds of his daughter weeping, a wave of relief hit Peter as the family entered the main gate of the base. The home had been obtained from the goodwill of another naval officer, who agreed to keep Peter's family in temporary lodging facilities so he and the children could find refuge on the base. Neighbors had collected furniture and basic supplies, as the Navy family did what they could to care for the family of a captured comrade. The media would probably still find ways onto the base, but most of them would have to set up their camps outside the base's gates, leaving the family to suffer in peace.

Television Sets Across America

Action news music again.

"We interrupt our regularly scheduled programming to bring you this breaking story." The still screen of the BREAKING NEWS image switched to a makeup-covered face. "The lights are out in Macapa as American forces invade San Selva. Our forces in Brazil have been seen fueling vehicles in preparation to cross the border into San Selva. We believe Special Forces have gained control of radio and television stations, because they are now broadcasting messages from the American military. Small-arms fire has been heard in and around Macapa. And most telling of all, the Eighty-second Airborne Division is loading into Air Force aircraft. To bring us this developing story, we go right to our field correspondent, Sally Sanders, at Fort Benning, Georgia."

"Good evening, Peter. Behind me Air Force C-17

transports load three thousand soldiers from the elite 'All American' Eighty-second Airborne Division. These men will be parachuting into San Selva in a few short hours, and . . ."

Behind Sally Sanders, maroon-beret-wearing members of First Battalion, 504th Parachute Regiment, First Brigade, Eighty-second Airborne Division rushed about as they prepared for war. Born in 1917, the Eighty-second Division became airborne during World War II, and it had fought in battles from World War I to Afghanistan. The Second and Third Battalions from the 504th were already loaded in aircraft and heading for San Selva. Each battalion included seven hundred men divided into five companies. Headquarters company included two hundred men and provided fire support to the battalion with its four 81 mm mortars. The three rifle companies each had over one hundred men and two of their own 60mm mortars and six medium machine guns. And, the antiarmor company included one hundred men armed with heavy machine guns and antitank missiles mounted on Humvees that would be airdropped.

". . . the United States Army has only executed six combat parachute drops since World War Two. Two took place during Korea, one in Vietnam, and the Rangers jumped into Grenada and Afghanistan, but Panama was the only time that the Eighty-second Airborne Division had executed a combat jump since World War Two. Normally, the division plans on four percent casualties from the parachute drop alone, and in Panama they experienced the ghastly statistic of over sixty percent equipment loss during the drop. Leaders tonight are hoping that things will fare better during the next few hours."

"Thank you, Sally." The anchorman turned to face the camera again. "Meanwhile, in San Selva, there are reports flowing in that Marines are beginning to assault beaches south of Acapa. . . ."

Norfolk Naval Base, Virginia

Peter first thought that the officer's gleeful smile seemed inappropriate. Peter felt grateful to the Navy for rescuing his family from the hell their home in town had become, but the fact remained that his wife and his children's mother was still being tortured as a prisoner of war.

"Mr. Linsey," said the officer, his voice shaking with emotion, "we got her."

Peter didn't understand.

"Your wife just entered into Brazilian airspace a few minutes ago."

Chapter Twenty-seven

Calcoene, San Selvan Coast

Three trucks exited their urban hiding place and sped in separate directions toward the beach. There was no mystery where the Americans would try to land. There were few suitable beaches to support an amphibious landing, and the Marines had been seen clearing lanes in the minefields. The trucks just needed to get into a firing position so they could launch their antiship missiles.

The first sign that something might be wrong came in the form of a *whooping* sound that was carried inland by the ocean breeze.

Maj. James B. Woulfe, USMC

AH-1Z Cobra, San Selvan Airspace Near Calcoene

"They see us," said the pilot, as the AN/AVR-2 Laser Warning System indicated that the San Selvan trucks fired a laser beam at the helicopter.

"Smart move," said the gunner in the front seat of the two-seat aircraft. "They're blocking our optic devices with that damn thing."

"Fine with me," chimed the pilot. "It means I get to do some of the shooting tonight."

The narrow attack helicopter increased speed and moved in for an old-fashioned rocket run against the truck-mounted antiship missile system. Only three feet wide, the Cobra was hard to hit when it was making a frontal gun run. The Americans' ambush might be foiled, but the mission would still be accomplished by the Marine pilots. The Cobra's gunner could fire a number of missiles: Sidewinder air-to-air, Sidearm antiradiation, and Hellfire air-to-ground. But the pilot controlled the less sophisticated weapons systems, the rockets and three-barrel 20mm Gatling gun.

The four-bladed AH-1Z was a noticeable improvement over older two-bladed Cobras. It accelerated to a speed of three hundred knots as the pilot swooped down on the San Selvan truck. These attack helicopters were only one piece of a much larger and deadly team. Attack aircraft from all four of the armed services now joined in tactical attacks to destroy the last of San Selva's coastal and air defenses.

"Deploying chaff and flares," said the gunner, responding to the AN/APR-44 Radar Warning that indicated a surface-to-air missile was aimed at the helicopter. Next, the gunner activated the AN/ALQ-144 Infrared Countermeasure System to further confuse the San Selvans weapons.

Closing to within one mile of the truck, the pilot let lose with the 20mm Gatling gun. The laser warning light went out as the San Selvans ducked to seek cover from the incoming high-explosive rounds, but the Marines didn't care about the men. It was the missile that they wanted. The pilot fired his 2.75-inch rockets and made a sharp turn as the rockets exploded around the truck.

"We're locked on," said the pilot of the second helicopter.

"Roger." The lead bird made a sharp turn. "We're clear."

"On the way" echoed over the radio as the second helicopter fired a Hellfire missile from over three miles away. Following a track of laser energy, the Hellfire plowed into the side of the truck and destroyed the antiship missile system.

Another flight of two Cobras won a second fight with a different truck, leaving the third truck to be chased down and massacred by all four Cobras working together.

USS Beirut, *Near the San Selvan Coast*

Sitting in the uncomfortable jump seat between the cockpit and troop compartment of the CH-53E Super Stallion, Dunne looked over the pilots' shoulders to see the *Beirut* disappear into the darkness. Then he looked back at his reinforced platoon. Over fifty men were packed into the belly of the aircraft, with most sitting on the floor. Safety limitations for the number of passengers allowed in a CH-53E had been waived to allow the large load. A necessary step, since it would be too dangerous for the aircraft to make more than one touchdown at each landing site.

A Marine Corps rifle company was made up of three

rifle platoons and one weapons platoon. The rifle platoons were about thirty-five men split into three squads. The weapons platoon was slightly larger and armed with heavier weapon systems: six M240G machine guns, six Mk153 rocket launchers, and three 60mm mortars. Dunne had three rifle squads of nine or ten Marines. A full squad was thirteen men, but the Corps never had enough Marines to make full squads. Attached to the platoon were two Marines from the Information Warfare Element, a six-man machine gun squad with two machine guns, and a four-man urban mobility team from the Engineer Platoon.

The men wore black and gray urban camouflage utilities, bulletproof vests, and plastic knee and elbow pads. Most of the faces were so young they barely needed to shave in the morning. At twenty-three years old, Dunne was one of the oldest in the platoon. Extra ammunition had been stuffed into every pocket and pouch, along with night-vision goggles and hundreds of other pieces of equipment. They were armed with an even mix of conventional and less lethal munitions for their weapons because the threat ashore was mixed: armed enemy and unarmed but hostile mobs.

It was hard for Dunne to believe that he was leading his Marines into harm's way for an environmental issue. It didn't seem to fit into his oath of service—*to protect and serve the Constitution of the United States against all enemies, both foreign and domestic*. He and his Marines were trained to perform missions that ranged from peacekeeping to war, but he couldn't figure out what might be required on this operation. This week had been a tough one for the country: images of an American body being dragged through the streets, the bruised face of a female pilot, and the burning hull of the USS *The Sullivans*. Nothing back home worked right. The Internet might never be the same. People were afraid to leave their homes. Dunne had received a panic-stricken message from his wife after she had been threatened via e-mails and phone calls, and now, despite the fact that he headed into combat, Bert worried more about Elizabeth's safety than his own. America was forever changed yet again.

Dunne's objective was a four-story building of weathered cinder block and wood with a flat roof. It was a large building considering the blocks and blocks of tin-roofed homes that surrounded it. Dunne's unit would conduct a platoon-size seizure of the building because it overlooked a needed port facility. Other platoons from Dunne's company were to seize buildings to the left of his objective, and a second company would seize a larger high-rise on the right. Marines needed the high buildings, or "key terrain," so the remainder of the landing force could seize the port below.

The entire Twenty-second Marine Expeditionary Unit was needed to support the landing force. The third company from the battalion landing team was already ashore on a small island a few miles off the San Selvan coast. The small chunk of uninhabited dirt and sand provided little tactical value to most forces, but the Marines needed it for a fire-support base. The rifle company landed by small rubber boats to seize a beach-landing site. Several minutes behind the small boats, flying at forty knots, the first LCAC slowed as it came within feet of the San Selvan coast. The LCAC hovercraft was the premier landing craft for getting Marine Corps forces ashore to build up combat power. It could land on over eighty percent of the world's beaches, whereas normal landing craft could barely cross twenty percent. It could also travel on its air cushion over obstacles as high as four feet, allowing it to move over coral reefs and defenses on the landing beach.

The hull of the ninety-by-fifty-feet LCAC flew above the water, with the craftmaster steering cautiously by slightly manipulating the yoke and foot rudder control. Massive gas turbine engines turned four fans and propelled the craft to speeds in excess of forty knots. The four fans swung in different directions as the pilot maneuvered the LCAC to the beach. With six dimensions of motion, the ride was like being in an airplane in rough turbulence. Large doors dropped and 155mm howitzers rolled ashore behind powerful seven-ton trucks. Within minutes the artillery battery was ready to fire. With the artillery unit in place in case firepower was needed to support the landing force, Dunne's CH-53E pushed in toward the insert point. Behind him powering through the choppy North Atlantic Ocean, an armada of military power headed for the coast of San Selva.

Other LCACs neared the waterborne minefields and headed to the beach to use their breaching systems. The minefields still posed a deadly nuisance. With the fields accurately mapped, the LCACs knew the best places to fire their line charges. Riverine assault craft escorted the LCACs to make sure the enemy didn't interfere with the LCACs time-consuming mission. A couple of old PC-1 Cyclone boats patrolled the coast. A newer PC-14 Tornado worked the shoreline too, along with several small Mark V Special Operation Crafts with SEALs and SBU (Special Boat Unit) sailors. The littoral penetration points that the LCACs opened would allow Marines to hit the beach in their amtracks. But before the Marines could enter the port, Dunne and his Marines needed to seize their objective. Even a small enemy force holding a prominent position in one of the buildings would do horrible damage to the Marine landing force.

C-17 Globemaster, San Selvan Airspace

Despite the stress of imminent danger, Specialist Scott Deforeno still had been lulled asleep from the drone of the C-17's four turbofan engines. He could catch a quick nap anywhere and at any time. Even smashed in a one-hundred-and-seventy-foot-long aircraft flying into combat at a speed of four hundred and fifty knots. Capable of flying over five thousand miles without refueling, the C-17 from the Air Force Reserve's 315th Airlift Wing made its final preparations for dispersing its human cargo.

A friendly hand shook Deforeno awake just before it was too late. He looked around at his fellow Rangers. Well armed and hardened by the fire of grueling training, the one hundred Rangers seated in the belly of the C-17 were some of the toughest men in the American military.

At the front of the aircraft near the two side doors, the C-17's loadmaster and the Ranger company's commanding officer unstrapped and stood. Deforeno looked across the crowded aisle and winked at Specialist Mario Jackson. Most men checked their parachute straps, but Deforeno focused on his M240G medium machine gun. Built by Fabrique Nationale to replace the Vietnam era M60 machine gun, the M240 was a ground-mount version of the 7.62mm machine gun used on tanks and armored vehicles for years. It was a big weapon, but Def didn't mind its twenty-four pounds and awkward forty-seven inches, because the nasty, black machine gun could fire seven hundred rounds a minute at targets over one mile away. *Good shit!*

"Outboard, stand," commanded the loadmaster near the door. The men struggled to their feet. As the door opened, the "Hawk" hit Deforeno—that mix of adrenaline and rush of cold air that joined just before a parachute jump. His nipples hardened and goose bumps peppered his body. He swallowed hard, unnerved by the sensation.

"Inboard, stand." The row that had been sitting across from Deforeno stood and joined into the column that his row had formed. Signals came back to hook the static line to the cable overhead, and then each man checked the Ranger to his front and rear. No one wanted to lose a nervous comrade who didn't attach his parachute static line properly. Right after the "all okay" had been sent to the front of the column, one of the scariest yet most motivating things Deforeno ever heard was passed back the line of men: "five hundred feet!"

CH-53E Super Stallion, San Selvan Airspace

The huge helicopter swept just above the wave tops like a seabird. Dunne smelled the woody odor first. Then the city appeared through the haze. After spending endless hours watching video from an unmanned aerial vehicle, déjà vu hit Dunne as the urban skyline rocketed toward him. The city was black, electricity temporarily cut off by another fiber bomb dropped by Air Force aircraft. A monocular covered Dunne's nonshooting eye, leaving his shooting eye ready to use the iron sights of his weapons if necessary. Through his night-vision monocular, Dunne could see the narrow silhouette of an AH-1Z Cobra gunship buzz around a building, scanning rooftops and the ground for potential threats. They were also on the lookout for SAMbushes—volley attacks with rocket-propelled grenades and antiair missiles to down an aircraft. Forward-looking infrared optics worked well for those threats in the open, but the heat that the optics looked for could not penetrate walls or even glass windows. Anyone inside a structure remained hidden.

Huey helicopters with a nonlethal sound weapon mounted inside attempted to force people out of and away from the buildings that the Marines would attack. The sound weapon was ingenious. It created a "soft kill" capability by using acoustic waves to vibrate human organs to debilitate people. A small box held a spark-plug-like device that fired continuously, creating small explosions as fuel was spat into the box. It was similar to the way an internal combustible engine works. The hundreds of explosions each second created concussions that were sent down a long gun-barrel-like tube that then projected the sound waves at a target. When the sound waves hit a human body, they created vibrations of internal organs. Either someone got out of the way of the sound waves or the person dropped into the fetal position in a puddle of his or her own vomit. Walls and windows reduced the effects of the sound weapon, but they didn't render it completely impotent. And, if the Marines were lucky, the vibrations from the sound weapon would break the windows, increasing the effectiveness of both the infrared optics and the sound weapon. The only problem was that the helicopter needed to come dangerously close to its target to use the sound weapon. The "soft kill" capability also provided a "soft target" for the San Selvans to shoot at, and the Huey's crew watched carefully for any sign of a threat. They'd be moving out of the area in a hurry if any gunmen appeared.

The CH-53E came in lower than the buildings as it crossed the beach and then popped up to rooftop level at the last minute. The Marines poured out of the CH-53E and onto the rooftop, just as they had dozens of times during rehearsals in the simulation room and on the flight deck of the *Beirut*. To avoid being hit by San Selvan gunfire, the CH-53E rocketed away from the city right after the last man cleared the ramp of the helicopter.

Combat engineers had been first out the back and they immediately ran to the stairway door and slammed it with a sledgehammer. The door failed to open, so a second Marine fired "lock-buster" rounds from his shotgun into the hinges, but the second swing didn't work either. Two more engineers used a gas-operated concrete circular saw and a chain saw to cut up the door. As it fell apart, the Marines saw that the stairwell had been packed with office furniture.

"Start cutting through the roof," Dunne ordered the engineer squad leader. "First Squad, clear the damn stairs." Whichever breach was completed first would be exploited, but for now his platoon needed to take up defensive positions on the rooftop.

Dunne looked at his wristwatch. There was little time to waste. The building needed to be secured within forty-five minutes. Advanced Armored Amphibious Vehicles (AAAV) had exited the ships a few minutes ago. The AAAVs had probably retracted their suspension systems already and deployed appendages that allowed for high-speed water movement by bringing the thirty-ton armored vehicle up on hydroplane. Once ready, the AAAVs would automatically deploy into formation and increase their speed to twenty-five knots as they crossed the line of departure twenty nautical miles from the coast but closing the distance fast.

C-17 Globemaster, Airspace Over Calcoene Airport, San Selva

Echoes of *Go! Go! Go!* thundered through the aircraft as the drop light turned green. The men ran in mass toward the open doors. Before they knew it, the steel of the C-17 disappeared below their feet and then there was the jerk of the static line going taut, which was quickly followed by the shock of the canopy opening.

With the C-17s coming in low to be a difficult target for antiaircraft missiles, people on the ground barely heard anything before the aircraft came roaring over the drop zone at an altitude of five hundred feet. Almost immediately parachutes became visible in the night sky, and the telltale snap of opening parachutes filled the air. Specialist Deforeno instinctively looked up and grabbed his parachute's risers. Seeing all was in order with his suspension lines, he released his equipment bag and let it fall. It gave him a quick tug when it reached the limit of its line. The ground came fast, with only a minute from aircraft to ground when dropped at this low an altitude. Looking out at the dark horizon and preparing to allow his body to collapse upon impact with the ground, Def was thankful that no one seemed to be shooting at them yet. Hopefully everyone's parachute had opened and deployed properly. At five hundred feet there wouldn't be time to pull the reserve chute before smashing into the ground.

In just a few minutes, five hundred men from the Third Battalion, Seventy-fifth Ranger Regiment, true to their motto that "Rangers lead the way," had landed on the airfield. Divided into three rifle companies of one hundred and fifty men each, the Rangers were armed and organized for light infantry tactics. Tonight the Rangers landed in advance of the elements from the Eighty-second Airborne to secure the drop zone. The next wave of aircraft would bring seven thousand parachutists. Landing in a drop zone by parachute did not allow for a unit to hit the ground as a cohesive fighting force. Units landed intermixed and needed to separate from each other so they could move from the zone to accomplish their missions. And the missions were challenging, because by the time the sun came up this would be the busiest airport in South America.

Calcoene Port, San Selva

A Marine from the Information Warfare Element detachment already had his loudspeaker set up and began broadcasting taped announcements to the San Selvan civilians. Leaflet drops had been frequent and continued so that there would be plenty of pro-American propaganda available when the sun rose. The other Marines from the detachment set up the video-observation unit, which was a standard camcorder with color LCD monitor and garden-hose-like lens that could be pushed around corners and into holes. The observation unit was capable of seeing through the dark with infrared and night-vision devices, even thin walls with the thermal sight.

"Stand clear," yelled the engineer squad leader. "We're ready to blow it."

"Sir." Dunne's radio operator pushed the radio handset at Bert. "It's Six, sir."

"Phoenix Six, this is Phoenix Two, over," said Dunne into the handset.

"Two, this is Six," yelled the company commander.

"We're conducting an emergency extract. Building is on fire. Don't know how. Be watchful for fire attacks."

"Roger." Dunne looked over at the building that the other platoons assaulted and saw the bright glow. It looked bad. Tracers flew from the building and into the surrounding neighborhood as the Marines fired on some unseen target. Dunne wondered if there was any chance they would get all the Marines off the roof before fire consumed it. He became overwhelmed with an urge to get to the bottom floor of his own building before the same fate hit his platoon.

The engineers' explosion from the breaching charges rocked the building and blew a six-by-six-foot hole in the roof. Two stun grenades flew into the hole, followed closely by an entire fire team armed with M16A2s and M203s. They carried their weapons with one hand on the pistol grip and the other on the magazine—both index fingers resting on triggers. Depending on the threat encountered, the Marines were ready to fire either a 5.56mm bullet from the M16A2 or a 40-mm beanbag round from the M203. Thumbs rested on switches for laser spotters and flashlights that could also illuminate shadows where the Marines' night-vision goggles had difficulty seeing. All the maneuvering of the fingers sounded complex, but it was child's play, literally, for a generation that was raised on video games.

There was no gunfire so other Marines jumped into the hole, falling awkwardly amongst the rubble caused by the breach. Their elbow and knee pads knocked into chunks of concrete. They fanned out and searched the floor like a spreading ink blot, with several men carrying fire extinguishers and spraying any sign of smoke or flame. Furniture was strewn about, and the stairs were still blocked, but Marines positioned to cover them anyway.

An industrial drill punched a hole in the floor and more stun grenades fell into it and to the floor below. The small explosive blast produced a blinding flash and loud sound that disoriented anyone occupying the floor below. As engineers started cutting to create a breach to the next floor, an information warfare Marine searched the room below through the hole with the video-observation unit. The old building had no elevator, and sending Marines down the side of the structure was too risky. Using explosives on the wood floor would only increase the likelihood of fire. Cutting down was the only option. Fortunately, the interior floors were thinner and easier to cut through than the roof.

Calcoene Airport, San Selva

"Are you a medic?" shouted a soldier.

"When's the last time you saw a medic humping the hog?" Def said, jerking his head at his M240G, often called the "pig."

"I need a medic, asshole!" snapped the soldier. "This guy is hurt."

"What's wrong with him?" asked Def. The hurt man looked lifeless.

"He must have had a streamer or something. He's all fucked up. Blood is coming from his ears. Go see if you can find a medic."

Deforeno collected his gear quickly and moved out. He had to stop and load his weapon, something that he had forgotten to do in all the excitement of landing. He asked passing men if they knew where he could find a medic. None knew. Everyone seemed to be lost. The drop zone, without a doubt, was the worst he'd seen in his short Ranger career. Around the flat airfield, the urban terrain rolled wildly. Buildings towered everywhere and their different levels and heights made it impossible to determine what the ground below was like. The only thing that appeared flat was the airfield itself. LGOPs—little groups of paratroopers—ran all over the airfield. A Ranger Special Operations Vehicle with a heavy machine gun and two motorcycles went sailing down the runway. The vehicles had been parachuted in with the Ranger battalion.

Def quickly moved through the drop zone to the company's rally point. He couldn't spend any more time looking for a medic. On the way he passed an Air Force Combat Controller Team that had already worked hard to set up the runway to accept aircraft with heavier reinforcements on board. Part air-traffic controllers and part commandos, the CCT airmen are experts in clearing and marking runways.

Well-organized chaos swept across the airfield. It was a miracle that the Rangers could land without being ripped apart from enemy gunmen in the windows of the buildings. A miracle that follow-on waves might not experience. The *pops* of small-arms firing became more frequent until a constant roar of rifle and machine-gun fire echoed throughout the area. Caught in the middle of a growing inferno, Deforeno stopped when he saw a group of Rangers taking refuge behind a car. Gunmen in the windows above fired down on the Americans. The Rangers were pinned down and barely able to return fire. Deforeno threw the bipod legs of his M240G onto the hood of a car and let loose with a long burst from the weapon. A stream of red poured into the second story of the building. One in four of the 7.62mm bullets were tracer rounds, burning red as they traveled toward the target. Def thought of the old Ranger saying that *when the going gets tough, the tough goes cyclic.*

He shortened his pulls of the trigger to six-to-eight-round bursts. Tracers slapped against the building and ricocheted into surrounding buildings. Many rounds penetrated the building's thin walls and some even entered through the windows unimpeded. The Rangers behind the vehicle cheered at Deforeno. One of the Rangers fired two M203 rounds, dropping them right into a second-story window. The blasts rippled through the building and smoke poured from the window. The group of Rangers used the machine-gun fire and explosions as an opportunity to break across the open ground from the vehicle to the gunmen's building. Only when they began to enter the first floor of the building did Deforeno stop firing and continue to his company's rally point, yelling a motivated Ranger *Hoooaahh!* back to the men. Sweat-drenched and high on adrenaline, he didn't know that he had just killed another human being.

Calcoene Port, San Selva

Dunne's platoon progressed quickly at first, but then gunfire erupted as men jumped from the third floor to the second. The men on the second floor were immediately pinned down and unable to move forward. The M240G squad positioned on the third floor in a covering role started firing through the floor at the enemy. One Marine panicked and scampered back up to the third floor and left his weapon on the floor below. The rest of the Marines fought for their lives, and the firefight raged with no visibility between the combatants—the two sides firing through floors and walls at each other. The deafening noise forced Dunne to send a Marine down to the second floor to stop the Marines from moving too far forward.

Dunne's action was a common requirement in dimensional warfare. This fight didn't just involve two units maneuvering around each other. The units were above and below each other, often with the enemy between two units that could rip each other apart as they both tried to kill the enemy. The fight was brutal. The violence was devastating, with bullets ripping chunks out of the thin walls, creating gaps that M203 gunners fired through with high-explosive grenades. Some did not detonate because they didn't travel the minimum arming distance. Most exploded and sent violent concussions rippling through the building. An engineer on the third floor drilled another hole and explosives were thrown down on the enemy. The crossfire created by the machine guns and the rifle squad gained the desired result: the enemy stopped firing.

After the Marines on the third floor ceased fire, those on the second prepared to make a final assault on the room.

"Bayonets!" yelled the Squad Leader. "Fix bayonets!"

Water sprayed from holes, reducing visibility. Dunne worried there also might be ruptured gas lines. "Tell me if you smell gas down there!" Gas would be bad with all of the small fires burning.

"Anyone smell gas?"

The men below saw the lead Marine lift his foot to kick in the door, then *boom*! Everything disappeared. A flash rocketed from the room, driving heat that singed Dunne's eyebrows up through the hole in the floor. The booby trap was well placed and showed no mercy. None of the Marines below escaped the bloodshed: two killed and three wounded. And the enemy was not even in the room; they had been firing from another building.

Dunne's platoon corpsman jumped over everyone and down into the dark abyss of the smoke-filled hole.

"Doc!" yelled a Marine. "Stay down, Doc. They might not be done."

Dunne jumped down the hole to the second floor. Small fires burned. Dust and smoke made it impossible to see. Dunne choked as he crawled on his hands and knees in search of his wounded Marines. Through the deadly fog he quickly found the corpsman working feverishly on a bloody and burnt Marine. The wounded man's legs convulsed violently as the doc tried to stop the blood that spouted from the Marine's neck. Only twenty-three years old, Dunne now found himself in the horrid position of knowing that at least some of the fifty Marines he led into combat were now dead. The thought caused him to gasp for air, and then the smell hit him. First it seemed like the pungent odor came from burnt hair, but then it took on the fragrance of roasting pork as the Marines' bodies smoked and sizzled. He'd been well prepared for the mechanics of war, but the horror of it overwhelmed him. The sights of the wounds were ghastly. Not only did bullets and shrapnel from the enemy weapons rip through the Marines, but so did jewelry, pieces of equipment, and even bone fragments and body parts from fellow Americans. One man had the severed arm of another Marine protruding from his back. A gut had been ripped wide open. The stench. The blood. The heart-wrenching screams of pain. Everything spun out of control. There was no preparation for that. It looked like pure hell. Hell that the San Selvans were accustomed to, for they had been fighting in these very streets for years already.

More Marines began to join Dunne and the corpsman on the second floor. Squad radios chattered as the Marines all tried to talk at the same time. The San Selvans' position sat in a place where it could not be fired at from the Marines on the roof. The machine-gun squad leader on the third floor directed his Marines to a window where they could fire on the enemy. Exposing his machine gun squad to the danger of the window was the last decision the young Marine ever made. *Crack!* A sniper fired one shot and then disappeared into the urban maze.

"Fuck! Washington is hit. Doc!"

Doc was too busy with the carnage on the second floor to help Washington, but it didn't matter anyway. Washington was dead the moment the sniper's round split through the Marine's head.

Dunne grabbed the radio handset and called to the roof. Staff Sergeant Lee, the platoon sergeant, held the roof with the extra supplies and a dozen Marines. "Staff Sergeant, I've got wounded down here. Call for a medevac. And I'm going to need help," said Dunne. Not only did the wounded and dead reduce the platoon's combat power, but moving them back through the breaches to the roof for evacuation was going to be a laborious, timely evolution.

Dunne looked around fearfully. There was no enemy in the building. It was all a carefully laid trap. The platoon attacked an unoccupied building, yet three Marines lay dead and four more screamed from their wounds, including two key leaders. Worst of all, he had to get to the ground floor and extinguish the fires before the building erupted in flames, trapping and killing the rest of his platoon. Fighting back feelings of nausea, he signaled for the engineers to start cutting another hole so they could get to the first floor. Dunne couldn't even pause to evacuate his wounded.

Calcoene Airport, San Selva

The gunfire from surrounding streets and buildings grew. An occasional explosion from a grenade or rocket shook the ground angrily. If the Rangers didn't begin to gain control of the situation on the ground, the gunmen with antiaircraft missiles would soon threaten the next wave of transports.

As Deforeno reached the company rally point on the north end of the north-south-running airfield, he was relieved to finally join soldiers from his platoon. The platoon consisted of thirty-two Rangers split into three squads. The first two squads were nine-man rifle squads and the third was a ten-man machine-gun squad. The platoon headquarters accounted for the remaining men: platoon commander, platoon sergeant, radio operator, and medic. The Ranger company had three rifle platoons that were supported by a weapons platoon consisting of twenty men armed with two 60mm mortars and three rocket launchers.

"Get the hell over here with that gun, Deforeno," yelled Def's machine-gun squad leader, Staff Sergeant Misha. "The lieutenant has been all over my ass about where you've been with that machine gun."

"Hell, Staff Sergeant," said Deforeno, "I was helping some other company win the war."

"I'll bet you were. Are you set to go?"

"Yes, Staff Sergeant."

"We'll be moving out in a heartbeat or two. Be ready."

Chapter Twenty-eight

Calcoene Port, San Selva

O'Brien screamed again. A tough kid from south Boston, he was one of Dunne's favorites and the funniest Marine in the platoon, always telling jokes and stories with his thick Massachusetts accent. He never seemed to be without a smile or a motivating hand if someone needed help. His mother had raised him, and he always said that he joined only for the GI Bill money so he could go to college. But that wasn't really true. He could have joined another service and sat in a comfortable chair for four years and received the same benefits. No, he signed up to be a Marine and take on the challenge of harsh training and exposure to the elements. That gung ho attitude might mean his death.

Wounded by a booby trap, O'Brien was only trying to help other Marines when he was hit. His wounded buddies needed to get to the roof, and O'Brien rallied Marines around him to move the furniture from the stairs to clear a route. After a few minutes of working, *boom!* Then the screams started. Now O'Brien lay in a pool of his own blood and screamed again as the platoon corpsman worked an IV into his arm.

"Hold on, O'Brien," yelled Doc. "We're working on getting you out of here."

"Sergeant Moore, get your people over here," ordered Dunne, pointing to a network of rooms on the ground floor of his objective building. "Watch the perimeter. Nobody gets in."

"Sir!" screamed Doc. "He's lost a lot of blood. We gotta get him out of here!"

"I'm doing everything I can, Doc, but there's nowhere to put a bird down outside. Is he stable enough to move to the roof?"

The corpsman looked back down at O'Brien. He'd been hit in the stomach. A gut wound—one of the most painful kinds of wounds there was. With the stairs blocked, O'Brien would need to be awkwardly lifted through the holes in the ceiling of each floor. "I don't think we should. I don't know if he'll make the climb. I'm worried it'll put him into shock."

Dunne looked up helplessly at the hole in the ceiling. Dragging O'Brien up that would probably kill him. There was no place a helicopter could land outside until the amtracks landed. The engineers would never get through the booby-trapped stairs in there. O'Brien was going to die and there was nothing Dunne could do to stop it.

Calcoene Airport, San Selva

"Gun one!," yelled Staff Sergeant Misha. "Cover the left side of the objective. Gun two! Cover the right side. Watch for bad guys now, Rangers."

"Down here, Def," ordered Corporal Patrick Hernandez, Def's machine-gun team leader. Deforeno dropped his body down to the hard ground and threw the butt stock of his M240G machine gun into his shoulder. Specialist Mario Jackson connected the short belt of linked ammunition already loaded in the machine gun to a larger belt that he pulled from ammunition cans. At the same time, the team leader attached the thermal sight to the top of the weapon.

"Gun two up!" yelled Corporal Hernandez when the well-rehearsed gun drill was complete.

Deforeno pressed his eye to the rubber cup on the PAS-13 thermal sight. The six-pound PAS-13 was a forward-looking infrared scope capable of seeing two thousand meters through the dark night. Through the device Deforeno couldn't see any movement, but he knew that the Rangers from the rifle squads were somewhere in the periphery moving against the flank of the platoon's objective. A small concrete wall surrounded the single-story building, and the flat roof extended beyond the walls of the structure.

"There's movement on the rooftop," yelled a Ranger.

"See anything, Def?" asked Hernandez, as he looked through his night-vision device.

"Negative, man. I can't see any damn movement."

"Movement on the roof!" screamed a Ranger. "Watch the damn roof!"

"Where?" yelled Hernandez.

"Settle down, people," ordered Staff Sergeant Misha. "Watch your sectors. Remember, when I give the order, I want the rapid for one and then the sustained. Don't be going wild on me either. Change barrels just like the range. Got it?"

"Roger that, Sarge," answered Corporal Hernandez.

Deforeno and his team were responsible for covering the right side of the one-story building. The building looked solidly constructed of cinder block and cement. It had one main entrance that opened to a hallway and eight or nine different offices. Normally the building served as an administrative office for the airport's maintenance facility, but its prominent location near the airport fence line made it an important piece of terrain for the Ranger invasion force.

Deforeno jumped as the machine gun to his left began to fire at the objective. He must have seen something, thought Deforeno. He began to fire also, throwing two hundred rounds at the target in the first minute. Hernandez became caught up in the moment, and although he didn't know why the other machine gun had begun firing, he began yelling instructions to Deforeno.

"Bring it down some, Def. Good, good. Work the whole sector." The tracer rounds burned brightly in the night-vision devices. Machine gun rounds poured across the one-hundred-foot open area between the support by fire position and the target. It disintegrated as chips of concrete and chunks of cinder block fell to the ground.

"Sustained," yelled Misha. He had not seen a target either, but he wasn't going to tell his Rangers to cease fire until he knew that the attacking rifle squads did not walk into an ambush. "Sustained!"

Deforeno decreased his rate of fire to one hundred rounds per minute. His eruptions of gunfire came in short but brutal bursts timed with the gunfire of the other machine gun. "Talking guns," it was called—each weapon taking turns firing its deadly bursts. With each pull of the trigger Deforeno coolly moved the rounds across the side of the building. Once he reached one side of his sector, he began to work the impacts of his bullets back toward the other side.

"Gun one changing barrels," yelled a Ranger to Deforeno's left.

"Gun two, pick it up! *Pick it up!*" yelled Staff Sergeant Misha, ordering Hernandez's machine-gun team to increase their rate of fire to compensate for the lapse as the other team switched machine-gun barrels. Because of the high rate of fire and heat created by so many rounds firing down the barrel of the M240G, it was necessary to change barrels every four or five hundred rounds. Def pulled back on the trigger and quickened his firing.

"Gun one up," yelled the first team leader to signal that his machine-gun team had completed their barrel change. Deforeno brought his rate of fire back down to the sustained rate as the other machine gun started firing again.

"Changing barrels!" yelled Hernandez when Deferano's belt of ammunition ran out.

"Pick it up, gun one!"

As the team leader reached forward and pressed the latch that released the barrel from the machine gun, Deforeno grabbed the last box of ammunition. "Ammo!"

Jackson quickly ran to Deforeno and placed more ammunition next to the machine gun. The team leader grabbed the hot barrel by the carrying handle and carefully laid it down before picking up the spare barrel and connecting it to the machine gun. He gave the barrel a knock with the palm of his hand to ensure that the latch had secured it properly. By the time the team leader finished, Deforeno had already placed a belt of ammunition across the feed tray and slammed the cover closed.

"Gun two up!" yelled Hernandez, just a millisecond before Deforeno started firing again.

Deforeno heard the familiar *whoosh* of a Ranger antiarmor and antipersonnel weapon system to his left as the rocket-launcher team attached to the platoon fired a high-explosive projectile at the target. There was a thunderous *boom* as the rocket crashed into the building. Through the thermal sight, Def clearly saw the ghostly image of a figure moving in a window. He instinctively fired and the image disappeared. Pausing openmouthed for a second, he considered asking one of the others if they had seen it too, but another rocket slammed into the building. The two rockets were supposed to create a breach for the rifle squads to enter the objective. There wasn't any time for Def or the others to talk. He placed his cheek back on the machine gun and pulled the trigger again. Shortly after the second rocket shook the building, the platoon commander fired a flare into the objective area, signaling the machine gun squad to cease fire so the Rangers in the rifle squads could enter the hole that the rockets created and attack the building.

"Cease fire," ordered Staff Sergeant Misha. "Gun one, shift to cover the left flank. Now that they're in the building we don't have anyone coming up on our flank over there. Gun two, keep an eye on the objective."

"Roger."

"How we looking, people?"

As the team leaders made their reports to Staff Sergeant Misha, Deforeno carefully scanned the objective area. He was careful to keep his weapon pointed above the building. The last thing he wanted to do was accidentally shoot a fellow Ranger. Deforeno's ears rang because of the loud explosions from hundreds of machine-gun rounds being fired, but he could still hear the firing and yelling of the rifle squads as they moved through the objective. He heard an occasional explosion, which Deforeno guessed to be hand grenades thrown by the Rangers as they progressed in their assault. At least he hoped that it was the Rangers, because the enemy held an advantage over the Americans. The close confines bunched people up, lending the possibility that one hand grenade from the enemy could wound many. Gunmen could hide behind every corner and shoot several soldiers before being taken out. Urban combat was costly, both physically and psychologically, on soldiers and civilians.

Calcoene Port, San Selva

"Pull, Devil Dogs—*pull!*" shouted Staff Sergeant Lee on the floor above. Dunne watched as the feet of one of his dead Marines disappeared though the hole in the ceiling. A Marine specially trained for rope operations at the Corps' Mountain Training Center in Bridgeport, California, was on the roof constructing another apparatus to move the dead and injured up. Dunne now had eight men down. Three dead and O'Brien dying; four others wounded.

Thankfully, a helicopter was inbound to medevac most of the casualties. But O'Brien still lay on the floor below writhing in pain. He wouldn't be able to survive the move to the roof. Until the landing force secured the area outside so a helicopter could land on the ground, there was nothing that could be done except make O'Brien as comfortable as possible.

O'Brien's painful gasps sounded far too loud, especially since there had been little gunfire in Dunne's area since the firefight. The only other bullets impacting the building came from other Marines' weapons as they cleared the buildings around Dunne's. He had to make sure everyone stayed away from the windows. Not only would they be vulnerable to more snipers, but Dunne also didn't want any Marines wounded by friendly fire. There was little to see from the windows anyway. The San Selvans started fires in the middle of the streets to reduce the effectiveness of night-vision devices and thermal sights. The glaring flame and heat from the fires washed out the Marines' expensive devices, preventing the men from seeing what the San Selvans did behind the fires. It was a maddening experience to deal with.

Climbing to the roof, Dunne saw the medevac helicopter come into view. It drifted slowly to the building and lightly touched the roof. Staff Sergeant Lee had the men well prepared to quickly load the wounded Marines onto the medevac bird. Cobra gunships swooped around the building to prevent gunmen from getting clean shots at the helicopter on the roof. The dead bodies ended up being the hardest to move, and a scuffle broke out amongst the Marines as one became enraged when a dead buddy was being partially dragged across the building's roof. Anger consumed the Marines. Their blood boiled. They wanted to fight with someone, but they hadn't seen one San Selvan yet—*none!* Not even any civilians.

Loaded up and ready to go, the medevac helicopter lurched from the building's rooftop as one of the Cobras came around. Everyone gasped as the two birds violently jerked in different directions to avoid hitting each other. Dunne looked at the medevac helicopter, praying that it stayed airborne with his wounded Marines. It continued to rise and the Cobra followed. Dunne shook his head and wondered how many more would die before he even saw his first enemy gunman. *This isn't the way to do it,* he thought. *We should have been shooting the hell out of the place when we came in*. He'd have at least six of his Marines back if they'd done the attack differently.

Explosions and rifle fire could be heard at other units' objectives, as could the horrifying *krumpt* sound made by San Selvan mortar rounds impacting in the port below. The damn port they fought so hard for. It was a small affair, barely worthy of being called a port. From his position, Dunne saw a few office buildings and a small, broken-down warehouse, all of which had no roof. He didn't see a serviceable pier either. The goods coming to the beach would need to be unloaded by manual labor, as in the nineteenth century, which was the period that the city of Calcoene seemed stuck in. Notorious for harboring robbers and pirates, Calcoene also had gunmen that used an armada of converted craft to wreak havoc on the surrounding seas.

Thinking again about O'Brien, Dunne wondered what the chances were that he could get a Huey to land outside on the ground. O'Brien was not going to last until the port was secured by the landing force. If the AAAVs now entered the minefields—right on time—it would be several minutes before the surface force crossed the beach and drove to the port. About one mile from the shoreline, the AAAVs would begin their transition from high-speed water to ground movement.

The amtracks had to transition before entering the minefields for a number of reasons. First, the process took forty-five seconds to complete. That forty-five seconds left the AAAVs extremely vulnerable to fire from enemy on the shore, so it couldn't be conducted too close to the beach. The shallow beach gradient also interfered because the transition from high-speed water to ground movement had to be done in at least fifteen feet of water. There was also a danger that the system would jam before retracting the water plane appendages and deploying the suspension systems for ground movement. The Marines didn't want to be adrift with reduced maneuverability in a minefield and close to shore.

In ground-movement mode and not able to hydroplane, the last mile of water movement would be covered at a maximum speed of ten knots, which meant it took a long seven or eight minutes before the AAAVs neared the high-water mark. On the small island-turned-firebase, the artillery battery would fire a smoke screen to obscure the amtracks during their movement, but the last part of the swim would be the most dangerous. There was always the threat of antipersonnel and antitank mines buried on the beach in the sand. Exiting the water, the amtracks would be in a vulnerable single-file formation. They'd quickly spin across the beach and up into the port. Even with fellow Marines in the surrounding buildings, there would still be a fight for the port. As Dunne was learning, the San Selvans didn't let anything come easy.

Calcoene Airport, San Selva

The hundred-round box of ammunition bounced against his M240G as Deforeno ran from his position to the objective. "In here. In here," yelled a Ranger, waving the machine-gun squad into a doorway. Other members of the Ranger platoon fanned out and searched nearby structures for enemy. Rangers bounced from position to position, covering each other's movement. Weapons pointed in every direction and the occasional sound from a round being fired blasted through the air. The huge transport airplanes would be landing soon. The airfield had to be secured. Flying over a city to drop parachutists had been dangerous, but landing transports would be a different story. The aircraft would be completely vulnerable when on the ground, and it took at least a few minutes to unload the aircraft and get them back in the sky.

"Where do you want us to consolidate?" Staff Sergeant Misha asked the lieutenant. He squatted down to get his head below the windows. Rangers scampered around the structure, yelling instructions and reports to each other.

"What the hell were you guys shooting at?" snapped the lieutenant.

"Well . . . hell, the sanchos that were in here."

"No gunmen are in here. Did you take fire?"

"Sir?" Staff Sergeant Misha looked to one of the other machine gunners for answers. "Everything just exploded and we started shooting."

"Shit," griped the lieutenant. "What's your ammunition status?"

"Down to about five hundred per gun."

"Well, let's break out ammo from the rifle squads' packs then. But watch what the hell you're shooting at. We wasted two rockets and a bunch of grenades too." The lieutenant couldn't be too pissed at his men. At least they erred on the side of violence. "Take your squad over to that side of the building and set up a blocking position covering down the street."

"Check, sir."

"Oh, hey, but watch out, Staff Sergeant. There's a dead civ in there."

"What? I thought you said no one was in here."

"I said no gunmen, but I don't know what in the hell she was doing in here."

Misha's soldiers were wondering the same thing as they stared at the corpse. Most gagged shortly after entering the room. Guts and flesh splattered the floor and walls. Gone was the sweet smell of gunpowder, replaced now by the horrid smell of blood. Def entered and first saw twisted legs. Then he identified that they belonged to an old woman lying in the corner, obviously dead. He saw no weapon or gunman. He looked at the window, then back to the carnage. *Did I do this?*

Chapter Twenty-nine

C-5B Galaxy, San Selvan Airspace

U.S. Army Captain Ray Summer watched his radio operator look down at his wristwatch for the tenth time in the last ten minutes. It was fascinating how time passed. You sat around for days that dragged into weeks, waiting. Then the word to go came and time rushed in front of your eyes; there was always more that needed to be done and nothing could be done quick enough. But now, sitting in the aircraft and waiting to land in a combat zone, time practically stood still.

All the soldiers wanted to get on the ground safely. They flew too low and fast for surface-to-air missiles and too high for rocket-propelled grenades to be much of a threat, but there was always the old-fashioned antiaircraft guns that could easily rip through the thin metal skin of the Galaxy. Hopefully the attack aircraft escorting the flights would continue to be successful in destroying the antiaircraft gun positions quickly.

Sitting in the upper deck of the huge transport plane, Summer admitted to himself that he felt anxious too. He wanted to get to San Selva before the fight ended and he missed another opportunity for action. Over fifty of his soldiers sat in the troop compartment with him. They wore modern gladiator uniforms, dressed for war in their gray neoprene tanker suits. The men had little of their gear with them in the troop compartment. Weapons, radios, and all other mission-essential gear was staged downstairs in the Stryker vehicles parked in the aircraft's huge cargo hold.

Summer's Company, fourteen vehicles total, flew in four C-5Bs. Ray's unit led his battalion's landing in San Selva. Two other companies would follow, and a battery of rocket launchers from the artillery battalion. Sixty vehicles in all would land at the airfield tonight; that is, if everything went well. It remained unclear to Summer if the rest of the Arrowhead Brigade would join him and his men in Calcoene. It all mattered how Operation Greenhouse progressed.

The airborne troops who landed in the first waves reported that they had established a perimeter around the Calcoene Airport. Resistance had been light. The shock of having thousands of soldiers jump onto the airport unexpectedly had surprised the San Selvans. Positions were secured quickly, and now it was important to build up combat power before the sun's rays shone on the besieged city of Calcoene. The lightly armed airborne troops were well prepared to seize the airport, but securing a route through the city to the Marine-held port would take a heavier and much more mobile force like the Arrowhead Brigade.

Summer looked at his wristwatch. The Marines should be landing in force about now. They also made initial landings with lightning-fast infantry attacks but the tanklike AAAVs would soon rumble ashore to reinforce the port. The San Selvans had expected the Americans to land farther down the coast. When the sun dropped, the last view that the San Selvans had of the American fleet was near the mouth of the Amazon. But when the daylight came they would be surprised to see that the ships had moved almost two hundred miles to draw close enough to Calcoene to deploy their amphibious warriors.

"This is it," yelled an Air Force crewman. "Be sure you're buckled in. It's going to be a rough fucking landing. And thank you for flying San Selva Airlines."

As high as a six-story building and as big as a football field, the Galaxy dropped out of the dark sky and approached the blacked-out runway. The Air Force Combat Controller Team had the runway marked with infrared lights, and the pilots wore night-vision goggles. The pilots of the 436th Airlift Wing from Dover Air Force Base were the only ones in the Air Force who trained to land the massive C-5Bs in total darkness. After the pilot announced that he had started on his approach, a controller on the ground sent a radio signal to the infrared lights' receiver to turn them all on remotely. The runway's limits became clear to the pilots through their night-vision goggles. They slowed the C-5B from its cruising speed of five hundred knots. The city shook as the plane came screaming in. People on the ground barely had time to hear the squeal of the Galaxy's engines before its twenty-eight landing wheels screeched on the asphalt runway.

Summer and his soldiers jumped out of their seats and ran downstairs to their vehicles before the aircraft finished its move down to the end of the runway.

Crews checked the Stryker vehicles and the infantry-men checked their weapons. Vehicle drivers brought the turbocharged V-8 diesel engines to life as the massive aircraft reached the end of the runway and spun around in a quick U-turn. The Air Force loadmasters started removing the chains that held the fifteen-ton vehicles in place during flight. The huge cargo door in back of the C-5B opened. Summer's six-wheeled, all-terrain, light-armored vehicle exited the belly of the massive aircraft and turned to drive off the runway. The gunner checked sensors and fire-control equipment for the Cockrill Mk-3 90mm gun.

Once clear of the aircraft, Summer's driver parked the vehicle off to one side of the runway. A number of other lightly armored vehicles stopped on the left and right, getting out of the way so the transport plane could get in the air and clear the runway for more aircraft.

Dunne may have been disappointed with the port facility, but Summer liked the airport. The largest building looked to be a U-shaped, three-story structure. The control tower sat on top of the building and offered a commanding view of the entire area. The single airstrip stretched out over several thousand feet. One of the setbacks to having an aircraft as large as the C-5B was that it was difficult to find facilities that allowed several to land and taxi at the same time. Until the Galaxy that brought in Summer returned to the air, another C-5B could not land.

Summer stood in the vehicle-commander couplet and looked back as the C-5B's engine whined and the aircraft rumbled down the runway to take off. Soon another landed with more of Summer's soldiers, and then a third with the final elements of his company. A carefully coordinated dance occurred when each aircraft landed, taxied to the edge of the runway, dropped off its troops and cargo, and then rumbled down the runway until it disappeared into the darkness. Most Stryker vehicles carried a squad of nine soldiers in its troop compartment. Protected by ballistic steel plates that could stop 7.62mm rounds, the vehicles provide much better protection to occupants than the other vehicles that had been parachuted onto the airfield. Since the Eighty-second Airborne Division no longer had the light Sheridan tanks, the airborne soldiers only had Hummers that they used during the airdrops. Now, with Summer and his soldiers on the ground, the soldiers had more shock power. Before long another company was on the ground.

With the initial positions that the airborne troops seized and the reinforcements flown in, the U.S. Army soon had the airport secure. A few sniper shots could be heard from time to time, but most fighting had ceased well before the sun came up. Summer's company didn't have a position to occupy in the defense. They stayed back from the lines as a reaction force for any unexpected situations that arose. All nodded confidently when the six-wheeled High Mobility Artillery Rocket Systems (HIMARS) vehicles finally rolled off a Galaxy aircraft. Each vehicle carried six rockets that each held six hundred and fifty grenadelike bomblets that covered a football-field-size area with deadly munitions twenty miles away.

Let the sanchos try something now. Hopefully they will, Summer wished to himself. He and his men wanted to get into the action. Ray didn't want to miss another opportunity to participate in combat. But the soldiers in the Stryker vehicles didn't know that their shock power was not needed to protect the airfield. The San Selvans would pick another battlefield for their counterattack.

327

Chapter Thirty

Alexandria, Virginia

Her sweet innocence never seemed to fade. It was probably the reason he still loved her so much. Most couples went through their seven-year itch right about now. Those others became bored with each other and might even start to wander from their vows. Not them, however. Every day each loved the other more than the day previous. And soon there would be a child—a product of their love, as they liked to joke.

"Did you order anything through the mail?" she asked. Her hands were full with a box she had found on the front stoop. Placing the box on the kitchen table, she began to open it.

"No," he answered, shutting the refrigerator door. "It's probably something else for the baby." He smiled and looked back in her direction just in time to see her disappear. At one moment she was grinning with anticipation, and in the next blink there was a violent flash, a belch of blood and goo that sprayed him along with the rest of the kitchen. She fell back against the wall, decapitated and scorched.

The Mall, Washington, D.C.

The area was just starting to become congested. A few early morning joggers filled the sidewalks and bike lanes. Workers drove or walked from any of the many government buildings surrounding the Mall. Only a few early birds visited the monuments at this hour. Most people were in their cars headed to work. One unnoticeable man exited a vehicle in the parking lot near the Franklin D. Roosevelt Memorial and calmly walked away. The Dodge Minivan blended in with the other cars, but the vehicle was not at all like the others. If there had been time, a closer inspection would have revealed slight discoloration of the car's roof, a result of the metal being replaced with a thin layer of paper and repainted. The trick was not new. The same technique had been used during an Irish Republican Army attack on British Prime Minister Margaret Thatcher's home in the 1980s. This morning's target would be much more valuable, however.

When the timers detonated the explosive charge at the bottom of the 4.2-inch pipes, a projectile in each pipe flew upward and out of the makeshift mortar tube. The homemade weapons blew their deadly munitions through the paper roof of the van and toward the target. The mortar, being an area-fire weapon, didn't need to have a direct hit to be effective. Careful calculations with computers and a global-positioning system increased the likelihood that the mortar rounds would hit their target, but even if they didn't the mission was already a success. With the propaganda that would be gained by the attack it didn't really matter if the mortar rounds hit the target or not. They didn't even need to hurt anyone.

Saint Paul, Minnesota

"Pete's Place, Cathy speaking."

"Is Pete there?"

"Well . . . no, sir. I don't think there really is a Pete."

"Oh. Okay. There's a bomb in your building. You have fifteen minutes." *Click.*

The White House, D.C.

The uniformed Secret Service officer's head snapped in the direction of the audible alarm. The AN/TPQ-47 Firefinder radar had never before activated outside of a test. Its thirty-five-mile range provided continuous counterbattery-target acquisition, meaning it detected incoming indirect fire. The military used the Firefinder to warn of incoming artillery and mortar rounds, and also to determine the location where the rounds were fired from so, if possible, fire could be returned at the enemy.

Computer screens blurred and radios buzzed when the Secret Service officer activated the AN/VLQ-11 Shortstop. The Shortstop caused interference with electronic devices for miles around as the multidirectional antenna put a force field around the White House's airspace. Hastily created during Desert Storm, the Shortstop was an electronic protection system that caused premature detonation of fuses on mortar and artillery rounds. Secret Service agents' earpieces chattered with radio calls, as the incoming mortar rounds met the electronic shock wave and detonated one hundred feet above the South Lawn. The confused president was physically manhandled by his protection team through a stairway and down into an underground escape tunnel.

At first, it seemed as if the attack had been thwarted—that the rounds had detonated too high to be harmful. But standing guard at White House post number three, Marine Lance Corporal Bradley noticed a *puff* when the round detonated, not an explosion. A recent graduate of Marine Corps basic training, Bradley realized that the detonation seemed more like chemical munitions than a high-explosive round. The next indication that something was wrong came when his throat began to burn.

Golden Gate Park, San Francisco, California

It erupted just behind him. He was so totally shocked by being blasted forward that it didn't register what happen. He wouldn't have comprehended it anyway. It was just too out of the question to be true. That type of thing could never happen here and especially to him. More rounds from the assault rifle passed over him with violent *pops*. Still no idea. When he looked up a woman stood near him yanking items of clothing off her body. She rolled a scarf and then pressed it against his shoulder. *What the hell are you doing— Ahhh!* The pain hit him. Then he noticed the ooze covering his torso. Someone screamed. He went to sit up and blood streamed down his arm and pooled in the palm of his hand until it spilled to the ground.

The attacks preyed on the freedom embodied in the word *American*. No need for large car bombs or flying commercial planes into high-rise buildings. A mail bomb here; a drive-by shooting there. No weapon was even needed. Leave a mysterious package on the subway ramp. Phone in a threat to a place of business. Rush through an airport security checkpoint and then blend in with the crowd. The act itself would shut the place down for hours. But sometimes a weapon was needed, and, fortunately for the terrorists, they were easy to find in the United States. The attacks, threats, and bluffs were easy to pull off, and the media would sensationalize all of it until the American public crumbled in panic.

Back in Washington, D.C., it didn't matter if Lance Corporal Bradley died from the VX nerve agent dispensed from the mortar rounds. The purpose behind the attack was to strike fear into the souls of the American public. Panic could be a weapon. The San Selvans learned that during their war for independence. The nerve gas attack on the subway in Brazil worked. The deaths the attack caused meant little. The fact that the Brazilian population and economy shuddered was the real victory. It would work even better in a society like the United States. The San Selvans had successfully launched an attack against the most secure building in the country. Pandemonium would rein. Now with everyone feeling vulnerable, threats would prove to be just as effective as actual attacks. Hundreds of warnings called into schools, business, and other public places would paralyze the country. Everyone would be afraid to leave his or her home. The panic would be worse than during the bioterrorism attacks in 2001, because the threat was greater. Anthrax and smallpox could be treated with proper medical care. The only response appropriate after a nerve-gas attack was a coroner.

The news media would remind Americans that anyone with a lab could create chemical or biological weapons. All they needed is some off-the-shelf materials and information that could be downloaded off the Internet (that is, before the Child Care virus crashed the Internet). There were also plenty of opportunities to buy already processed weapons from arms dealers. The Soviets and the United States both had had secret chemical and biological weapons programs during the Cold War. The public only heard about them when there were tragic accidents. The early 1990s saw attempts to destroy stockpiles of these weapons of mass destruction, but it was too late. The Soviet Union was in chaos after the fall of communism and had lost control of much of its chemical and biological weapons.

The economy would take further hits. The stock markets wouldn't open for who knew how long. As the rain forests continued to burn and damage the global environment, the U.S. economy would collapse and the American way of life would change forever. With the combined affects of the Child Care virus, the worldwide terrorist attacks on mostly civilian targets, and now the nerve-gas attack on the White House, the San Selvans were winning the war. Sitting in an armored sport utility vehicle, the president looked at the faces of the heavily armed Secret Service agents surrounding him. He wondered if he too looked as scared as they did, and also asked himself how this "war" could be "won" quickly.

Chapter Thirty-one

The White House, Washington, D.C.

"My fellow Americans, this afternoon for the first time in several days, the skies over San Selva are free of bombs and missiles. A peace deal has been signed. The San Selvan rebels are standing down their forces. The demands of an outraged and united international community have been met. I can report to the American people that we have achieved our objectives for a safer world, for our democratic values, and for a stronger America. Our goals have been achieved. This conflict has been brought to a just and honorable conclusion.

"I want to express my profound gratitude to the men and women of our armed forces and those of our allies. Day after day, night after night they risked their lives to accomplish their missions and to avoid civilian casualties when they were fired upon from populated areas. I ask every American to join me in saying to them, thank you, you've made us very proud. I'm also proud of the American people for standing with our men and women in uniform against this awful environmental atrocity.

"When our diplomatic efforts to avert this horror were rebuffed and the damage to the environment mounted, we and our allies chose to act decisively. This triumph makes it all the more likely that we will turn the tide of global warming. Now we're entering a new phase: building of global harmony. And there are formidable challenges. First, we must be sure the San Selvan authorities meet their commitments. We are prepared to resume our military campaign should they fail to do so. Next, we must get the international fire-fighting force into San Selva safely. More minefields will have to be cleared and protection needs to be provided for the fire-fighting forces that will soon land. To that end, some twenty thousand troops from almost a dozen countries are deploying to San Selva.

"This next phase also will be dangerous. Bitter memories will still be fresh. There may well be some that will continue to oppose us. So we have made sure that the force going into San Selva will be strong and will operate by guidelines set by the United Nations. It will have the means and the mandate to protect itself while doing its job.

"I also want to say a few words to the San Selvan people this morning. I know that you too have suffered because of your government's actions. You endured our bombing, but we are ready to provide more humanitarian aid and to help to build a better future for San Selva, too.

"My fellow Americans, all these challenges are substantial, but they are far preferable to the challenges of continued damage to our global environment. We have sent a message of determination and hope to the entire world. Think of all the millions of innocent people whose lives will be better in the future. Tonight, I ask you to be proud of your country and very proud of the men and women who serve it in uniform—for in South America, we did the right thing. We did it the right way. And now we will finish the job. Thank you for your support, and may God bless our wonderful United States of America."

Calcoene Airport, San Selva

"That's it," Summer said to his lieutenants and senior enlisted soldiers. He rubbed his head and gazed at the horizon. A depressing mist of gray gloom hung over the city. Smoke from the night's battle and burning rain forest hid any trace of blue in the sky. He'd missed another fight. "There's a peace deal now, which means we went from combat to peacekeeping duty in the bat of an eye. People back home are already screaming for us to put out the damn fires.

"Delta grabbed that female POW last night. She was beat up pretty bad, and over at the headquarters they're saying she was practically raped to death." Faces grimaced. "I haven't heard anything about those PJs' bodies yet. I assume we will in the coming days, but I doubt there is much left to recover after what the sanchos did. The Marines hold the port and the Army holds the airport. Now we need to establish a ground route from here to there. That's the main purpose behind this patrol. Fire-fighting personnel and equipment will be flown and shipped in and then moved out the fire lines."

"Any change in the ROE, sir?"

Summer knelt on a knee and picked up a few pebbles. What was the best way to say this without being openly treasonous? He flicked a pebble across the hard ground. So much had changed so quickly. It seemed as if the president and his administration were now open to the possibility of an independent or at least autonomous San Selva. The rules of engagement, much like the current shift in the mission, made no sense. He flicked another pebble. "There's talk about that up at the CP. Something about the CTF producing a revised ROE, but until we see anything I don't want the men confused. Just stick with what we have now for this *presence* patrol."

Doctrinal publications spoke of three patrols for a unit like the Arrowhead Brigade: reconnaissance, security, and ambush. A "presence" patrol was something new. Someone somewhere thought such patrols would help reassure the San Selvan people and maintain order within the city, even though the people didn't want the help of the soldiers in the first place. Two platoons from Summer's company, nine vehicles in all, were to conduct a security patrol from the airfield to the port. Aggressive patrolling was to become the main activity. Marines and soldiers would conduct foot patrols in the neighborhoods outside their perimeters at the airport and port, while light-armored vehicles and amtracks conducted mounted patrols of the route that the fire-fighting force would rely on. "We'll have some public-affairs bubbas tagging along too."

"Sir?" asked First Sergeant Brown. "Isn't that jumping the gun just a wee bit? We don't even know if it's safe out there."

"I hear ya," said Summer, "but as I've been told, they *are* soldiers. Besides, we need to get them to the port to link up with the civilian media before the Marines steal all the headlines. It's not that far to the port, anyway. The Marines drove the route earlier in their amtracks. If the jar heads could do it, we shouldn't have any problem at all."

The men mounted their vehicles and made last-minute checks to their systems. Summer's First and Third Platoons would be going on the patrol, along with Summer's command vehicle. The nine vehicles formed up at the front gate of the airfield waiting for the public-affairs soldiers to join them. Hummers from the Eighty-second Airborne guarded the gate. Soldiers in the Hummers' weapon turrets manned M2 .50-caliber machine guns. Steel plates protected the gunners from small-arms fire. The plates were the result of a lesson that had to be learned not once but *twice*: once in Somalia and then again in the Balkans. In those contingencies, gunmen easily picked off the exposed gunners. Now the steel plates that surrounded the gunners provided some protection.

Summer's temper brewed about being stuck in the middle of a public relations game, but seeing the soldiers that would accompany his patrol nearly sent him into a full-blown rage. Exiting the back of a cargo Hummer, the two soldiers wore the standard, bulky flak jackets and load-bearing vest. But plopping out from under one of the Kevlar helmets appeared to be long strands of dark brown hair. Soldiers' heads turned as the soft skin and blazing blue eyes of Sergeant Arial Ross came into view. Endless hours of equal opportunity training just couldn't compete with pop culture. The soldiers were mostly eighteen- and nineteen-year-old men that had been inundated with MTV and *Maxim* magazine their entire lives. There were no hoots or catcalls, but Summer could feel the column of men stir. *What else would anyone expect?*

A public-affairs specialist with the Eighty-second Airborne Division, Sergeant Ross had parachuted into San Selva the night before—a combat jump! She'd almost finished up her four-year enlistment and looked forward to leaving the Army to start college, even though she'd seriously considered going to work for the United Nations as a public affairs representative. With starting pay of over ninety thousand dollars a year, Arial had come close to dropping her plans for college to work for the U.N. She was surprised that they could pay so much money. *That's a ridiculous sum to pay someone for taking pictures of hungry and homeless refugees.* She passed on the offer because the U.N. job seemed too much like her current Army job. She had no complaints about her four years as a soldier journalist. She just wanted to do something new. Her time with Army public affairs had been rewarding, with Arial making many friends of civilian reporters traveling with the Pentagon Press Pool. Friends that she hoped might give her the connections to find a job in broadcasting after she graduated from college.

Since hitting the ground Arial Ross was busy with one fight after another. First there was the task of documenting the fight for the airfield; then another battle she had with her boyfriend after the sun came up. Ross's boyfriend, another public-affairs soldier, was mad that she would be on the first Stryker patrol to leave the airfield. At least that was what he'd said bothered him. Arial thought it was more likely that he was mad that she went with Sergeant Rick Kapenski, a good-looking Army photographer. Now another fight loomed ahead: getting to the port to wrestle some of the civilian journalists away from the Marines.

"Good morning, sir," said Sergeant Ross, saluting Captain Summer. "I'm Sergeant Ross and this is Sergeant Kapenski."

"Good morning," answered Captain Summer, not

returning the soldiers' salutes. "If you could cut that salute now, I'd appreciate it. I'd like to avoid being a target for any sancho snipers who didn't get the word that we're at *peace* now."

"Oh . . . I'm sorry, sir." Arial dropped her hand. "Sorry about being late, too."

"Great. You'll be riding in my vehicle, and we're in a hurry, so load up."

"Yes, sir," barked Arial. She and Kapenski moved to the back of the light-armored vehicle and entered through the troop hatch. Summer already felt annoyed at the way his soldiers reacted to the female soldier. One man grabbed her M16A2 to help her get in the vehicle, ignoring Sergeant Kapenski, who carried an even heavier load. Another became more boisterous as he postured and strutted like a rooster near a new hen in the farmyard.

"What's that for?" Arial asked one of the soldiers in back, pointing at an ax handle.

"It's my *sancho* stick," answered the smiling soldier, his tone ringing with adolescent machismo. "Give 'em a little wood shampoo, you know what I mean?"

"No," answered Sergeant Kapenski, "I have no idea what you're talking about."

"Well, I don't think I was even talking to you. *Was* I?" Turning back to Arial, he said, "This"—he held up the long piece of wood—"is for beating the sanchos off the vehicle."

"What's the nail for?" asked Sergeant Kapenski, gesturing to the four-inch nail that had been hammered through the top of the ax handle.

"Just a little bite." The soldier smiled. "In case it's needed."

"What the fuck are you talking about?" snapped Arial. "You're going to maim people with a spiked stick? Are you some serial killer in training?"

"Sir," Sergeant Kapenski said to Captain Summer. "Sir, this isn't right. You can't let him do that."

"Sergeant," sighed Summer impatiently. He stood in the vehicle couplet, holding his helmet in his hands. "If someone jumps on this vehicle to steal . . . say, that chow," pointing at a brown cardboard box, "what are we supposed to do? Shoot 'em? I don't think that's *right*. Nonlethal munitions won't work either because they'll be so close we'll tear limbs off if we hit them with a beanbag or rubber bullet. You want to wrestle with them and take the chance of being pulled from the vehicle? Have you seen what these people did to those PJs? Did you hear what they did to that female Navy pilot? The most human thing to do—the *right* thing to do—is knock the people off the vehicle before we have to kill them. And if the blow from the ax handle doesn't work, then Smity there," gesturing to the soldier who had been talking before, "can flip it around and give a quick shot with the nail. Somalia, Haiti, Bosnia, Yugoslavia, Afghanistan—these lessons have been written in the blood of other soldiers. So sit down, take your pictures, and shut up! I don't need you showing up late and interfering with our work. Understand?"

Captain Summer didn't hear Ross's and Kapenski's response because the roar of the light-armored vehicles' 270-horsepower engine shuttered through the air. The four vehicles from Third Platoon exited the airfield's main gate and entered the abyss of Calcoene. The port was only a few miles away, but the Arrowhead Brigade didn't want to take too many chances. The top hatches on the troop compartment of the light-armored vehicle remained open so the soldiers could stand and provide local security around the vehicles. This would make it harder for a gunman to get a clean shot at the vehicle because eyes and weapons aimed in every direction. Layers of sandbags covered the floor to absorb the shock of a land mine.

The command vehicle followed the last one in the column from Third Platoon, and First Platoon followed it. All the soldiers were drenched in sweat before the last vehicle passed the airport's main gate. The canyons of buildings prevented any sea breezes from penetrating the town and also helped trap the humidity.

Summer's first glimpse of Calcoene shocked him. The road exiting the airport turned to a traffic circle with a magnificent stone fountain in the middle of it. It seemed so out of place. The fountain looked as if it had not held water for some time, but it presented the impression that at some point in history someone had tried to make the nasty little city into a jewel. Confusing clutter lay everywhere. Several goats roamed freely in the tall vegetation around the fountain.

Moving past the circle, Summer saw little that looked like battle damage, but the place was a disaster. Primitive structures mixed with neglected buildings and twisted into an urban mess. Businesses and homes pushed together in no apparent order. There were few trees or other vegetation. Garbage and debris had been thrown everywhere. Boxes here. Baskets there. Mounds of partially burnt and smoldering garbage appeared every so often. Piles of plastic bits and pieces that had presumably been sifted out of garbage dumps sat bundled as if readied for sale to someone. *Who would buy something like that?* Disintegrating automobiles cluttered every block. A rare car or truck wheezed by the formation and the troops watched it pass, the vehicle's black smoke adding to the claustrophobic atmosphere. Also contributing to the soot were countless cooking fires coming from homes. It was hard to comprehend how the mass of people managed to fuel open-flame fires day and night, especially without burning down the squalor. The fire risk probably explained the construction: corrugated steel and cinder block, with little wood visible other than a rickety door or dilapidated window frame.

Roads bent off in all directions, many too narrow for the light-armored vehicles to move through. The main road was paved, but all of the side streets were only oil-stained dirt. Little vegetation grew on the outlying hills, and every piece of space in the valley seemed occupied by primitive structures. BAR DOS BOIS said one freshly painted sign. The old paint and rusted tin roof of the building appeared to be fifty years old, but it almost looked as if the San Selvans' business was readied to open for the newly arriving Americans. There was no telling how long American forces would be here. If past operations were any indication, it would likely be years. Where the deployment of military forces used to indicate a failure in American foreign policy, nowadays it was used as a substitution for having a policy.

A few of the buildings looked to be of more sturdy construction than others. VIVA SAN SELVA LAUROSA! was printed on one in faded blue paint. Summer did not know what the words meant. It was the first three-story building he saw. Then he saw more like it. Surrounded by small walls, these buildings were two to four stories high and constructed of cement or cinder block. The combination of the severely impoverished and moderately wealthy in such close confines was something Summer had seen many times in other Third World countries, but it never ceased to amaze him how most people lived. Although Western countries basked in metropolis, the majority of people on the earth wallowed under conditions reminiscent of the nineteenth century.

A group of young men or old boys—too hard to tell the difference—sat together on a corner wall. No guns, but they eyed the Americans menacingly. Plenty of little girls and weathered old women, but few young females. Childbirth must age them rapidly. The San Selvan people affected Summer's psyche. A level of savagery was present in their glares that couldn't be anything other than intimidating. First of all, the San Selvans sought eye contact. In much the same way that an animal in the wild or a prisoner in a jail will lock eyes with a newcomer to establish dominance. Summer found it best to give hard, eye-to-eye looks before deliberately looking for another San Selvan to lock eyes with. His men seemed to do one of the opposite extremes, which was something he'd need to correct during debriefing with his lieutenants after the patrol. Avoiding eye contact presented a sign of weakness. Getting caught in a staring contest reduced situational awareness. Neither of the two things is good for a soldier on patrol in a potentially hostile city.

"Apache Six, Apache Six, this is Apache Three Actual."

"Go Three," answered Captain Summer. His Third Platoon commander, Lieutenant Randy Chin, was for the most part a good officer. Technically proficient but a little reckless. Summer tried to temper the lieutenant's aggressiveness until he gained experience to balance it himself.

"Bridge! We have a bridge to our front. Request permission to dismount and take the bridge so follow-on forces can cross, over."

"Three Six. Is there something on the bridge that blocks your progress?" Summer looked at his map.

The patrol had already driven halfway to the port, but no bridge appeared on the map.

"Negative, sir. The bridge is clear, over."

"Roger, remain mounted, push forward, and establish security on the far side. One, conduct passage of lines with Three on far side and take lead."

"Apache Six, this is Apache Three—roger!"

"One copies, moving to lead." Lieutenant Phil Clark, the always calm and professional leader of Summer's First Platoon. If Third Platoon could just get across the bridge without Chin starting World War III, Ray would feel more confident with his First Platoon in the lead. He'd initially put Third Platoon in the lead because he thought that the simple road march would be too easy to screw up, but it'd take forever if Lieutenant Chin wanted to take every opportunity he could find to put his platoon into a deliberate attack.

"We'll stop behind Third Platoon and then follow First's last vehicle," Summer said to the driver, Private First Class Garcia. Nine soldiers rode in Summer's command vehicle. Garcia drove and Corporal Zeberman sat behind the 90mm cannon. The two sat in the forward compartment of the vehicle. In the troop compartment behind Ray, his radio operator, Specialist "Smitty" Smith, tightly held his M16A2 with the "sancho stick" sitting close by. Corporal Harp, a second radio operator, stood on the other side with his weapon ready. Specialist Gadden was the company medic. First Sergeant Brown stood back there too, as did the two public-affairs sergeants.

As Summer's Stryker stopped behind one of Third Platoon's, Summer could see the "bridge" that Chin was concerned about. It was nothing. The roadway simply passed over a wide culvert. The water passing underneath the road looked filthy and not worthy of flushing toilets. San Selvan homes opened right onto the canal that ran perpendicular to the road. Naked kids swam in the water yelling. A few of the soldiers threw coins and food to them. One or two of the children squealed for more before First Sergeant Brown bellowed a "Knock it off!" that cowered the soldiers back into their vehicles. Some San Selvans dipped buckets into the water, presumably for drinking or cooking water.

First Platoon's vehicles roared by as they crossed the culvert to take the company's lead. Summer's vehicle followed behind the platoon's last light-armored vehicle. They moved at a speed of fifteen miles an hour before the patrol skidded to a sudden stop. Vehicles braked unexpectedly, compacting the convoy so the vehicles ended up only a few meters away from each other.

"Apache Six . . . we have . . . There's a situation," Lieutenant Clark babbled. "We've . . ." There was a long pause.

"One, this is Six," said Summer. "What the hell is going on?" He strained to see down the street.

"Apache One One hit someone."

"I'm coming forward," said Summer, then switching to his internal frequency. "Move forward, Garcia. *Move up!*"

Chapter Thirty-two

Streets of Calcoene, San Selva

As Summer pulled forward to First Platoon's position he could see that a woman had been hit by the lead vehicle. Lieutenant Clark stood in the street talking to an angry group of San Selvans, but no one helped the lady. Clark's four vehicles sat single file and only a few meters apart.

"Pull next to the lead vehicle and stop," Summer ordered his driver. "Doc, get out and check the injured lady," he yelled back to the troop compartment. "First Sergeant, get One to pull their heads out of their asses. Have them circle the wagons and establish security. Smitty, call Third and tell them to hold where they're at."

"What do you want us to do, sir?" asked Sergeant

Ross. Her piercing blue eyes didn't look as pretty now that they showed her fright.

"Stay in the damn vehicle," snapped Captain Summer.

Summer jumped off his armored vehicle and moved to where Lieutenant Clark tried to talk to someone from the group of civilians. Specialist Gadden ran to the lady and started to assess her condition. Vehicles started to move as First Sergeant Brown got a hold of the platoon sergeant from First Platoon.

"Phil," yelled Summer, "what the hell are you doing?" He swung his arm around. "Don't forget that you have a platoon to lead."

"Sir," stammered Clark, "she just came out of nowhere. We couldn't stop."

"I'm talking about everything else, damn it. You've got to remember that we're in a potentially dangerous situation. You left your platoon just hanging—" Summer stopped talking midsentence. He noticed the growing crowd. People collected into the streets. The group was no longer just angry; now they were *pissed*. The San Selvans screamed in a language he couldn't understand. Someone threw something, and Summer immediately became concerned that things were about to turn very ugly.

"Mount up!" yelled Summer. "Get on the vehicles and let's go." People began to get closer and closer to the soldiers. A few more started throwing things. Summer jumped up on his light-armored vehicle and became terrified by the scene he saw as he climbed into the troop commander's couplet. Dozens of people milled right in front of them and even more were down the streets. More and more rocks and debris began to be thrown at the Americans. All of the San Selvans seemed to start screaming at once. "Let's get moving!"

"Doc is not back, sir," yelled Brown.

Looking to where the injured woman lay, Summer saw Gadden pushed by an angry San Selvan. Gadden continued to try and render medical attention to the woman. A man grabbed Gadden's arm and pushed him away from the woman.

"Get him in here, First Sergeant," Summer yelled, then turned to Smitty. "Tell One to move back behind Three's position."

Smitty echoed his commanding officer's instructions over the radio as First Sergeant Brown and Corporal Harp jumped from the light-armored vehicle. First Platoon moved fast, too fast in fact, because the command vehicle was soon alone. An angry San Selvan man grabbed Doc, and then another one appeared with a machete in his belt. Harp immediately raised his M16A2 to the ready position and pointed it at the man with the machete. Most San Selvans backed away from the American's show of force, but a few became more enraged. San Selvans yelled and waved their arms about. The crowd grew more hostile. First Sergeant Brown had his hand extended with the palm facing the man with the machete, trying to visually communicate to the man that he needed to back up.

"Sshhiit!" exclaimed Summer as one of the San Selvans grabbed for Brown's arm. A woman hit herself in the chest and yelled at Harp like she challenged him to shoot her. The crowd pressed. Summer jumped, and just as his boots hit the ground, another Stryker vehicle screeched to a stop next to him.

"Let's go," yelled Lieutenant Chin to his men. "Push them back! Push them back!" A squad of soldiers poured from the rear door of the light-armored vehicle and deployed to physically separate Doc, Brown, and Harp from the clutches of the angry mob.

One of the men shot a wood baton round from the

40mm grenade launcher. He fired the round so it impacted a few feet in front of the San Selvans, causing
three wood dowels to skip off the ground and fly a
foot high until they smashed into the shins of two San
Selvans. The two fell in the street as the squad of soldiers surged forward. The crowd surrendered ground.

Summer had never been so happy to see Lieutenant
Chin. A few minutes ago he had cursed the young
lieutenant's aggressiveness, but he now welcomed it.
The crowd backed away from the attacking Americans. Ray noticed that Sergeants Kapenski and Ross
had exited the vehicle to help the soldiers from Third
Platoon. Another soldier fired a nonlethal round as
others swung the butt stocks of their rifles to hit San
Selvans who came too close. A tall man stepped forward and struck a soldier with a large stick. The blow
hit the soldier's body armor, so it didn't cause any
physical damage, but the young man's blood boiled.
He swiftly butt-stroked the man, who, because he was
leaning forward to deliver another blow with the stick,
took the brunt of the impact in the mouth. The San
Selvan man's head snapped back with teeth flying in
a spray of blood. Summer felt oddly guilty that the
man had been hurt.

Specialist Gadden ran up to Summer. "Sir, the lady
needs to get to a doctor."

"Doc," exclaimed a surprised Summer, "we need to
get the hell out of here. Get your ass in the vehicle!"

The squad fought with the mob. Hundreds of people filled the street now. Rocks and bottles fell around
the Americans.

"She's going to die," Doc pleaded. "We have to help
her."

"Go, Doc!" Brown shoved Gadden toward the vehicle.

Suddenly the area jumped as the *crack* of a rifle

being fired blasted over the roar of the crowd. Soldiers scampered for cover. The San Selvans backed away. A clearing opened in the middle of the street. Summer turned to see the squad from Third Platoon running for cover behind a nearby wall. Brown, Doc, and Harp pressed up against the front of the command vehicle. Only the two public-affairs soldiers remained in the middle of the street, with Kapenski lying facedown.

Another round from the sniper impacted at Ross's feet. Standing defiantly in place, she fired several rounds from her rifle before quickly slinging it and grabbing Kapenski at the shoulders. Ross tried to pull the man out of the line of fire, but her feet slipped out from under her. Again she tried, but Kapenski proved to be too heavy. She didn't have the strength to move him. Now kneeling, Ross threw the butt stock of her weapon back into her shoulder and fired again. Other soldiers joined in, and soon gunfire echoed throughout the area.

"Other side of the street," yelled Chin, pointing to a new sniper on a rooftop. The soldier next to him doubled over as a large red *splat* hit the wall. "Medic!"

Brown moved into the open ground to drag Kapenski out of the street. Ross continued firing her rifle at the original sniper. The soldiers tried to select targets from the area where the snipers fired. Too many civilians were in the way. Hundreds more flooded into the area from adjoining streets like streams coming together to create a flash flood. The stick stirred the hornet's nest. Volleys of rocks bombarded the soldiers. Hundreds of articles were thrown by the growing mob. The gunmen were even worse. Passing bullets made a loud *crack,* and the baptism of fire seemed remarkably familiar. Just like a live-fire attack range, thought Summer. But there was the new sensation that these bullets came from people aiming at him. *Son of a bitch! He could have hurt me,* raced through heads as innocence washed away, leaving overwhelming rage in its wake.

Summer scanned the scene. The confusion made it hard for him to orient himself. There were still lots of unarmed people in the streets. One of his soldiers hit a San Selvan with a gun in a window of a building. Another threw flash bangs at the San Selvans in the street. Someone from the crowd opened fire with a pistol or rifle. Then more shots started to come from the San Selvans on the ground. At first the soldiers fired well-aimed shots only at the San Selvans who fired at them, but as the firefight became more intense they began firing at everyone with a weapon. Third Platoon remained in a good position but the headquarters group needed to move. Brown stood near the command vehicle protecting Doc, who treated Kapenski's wounds. Harp swung the butt stock of his rifle at someone. *Where the hell is Smith?* Ross fired her rifle. Chin yelled instructions to soldiers. Summer spotted Smith in the command vehicle and started to move toward him when the tide of the battle turned. *Crack!* A rifle bullet tore through Ross's upper torso and sent her tumbling. As she hit the ground, Summer could feel the discipline of his unit sucked away as everything seemed to freeze. All the soldiers stopped firing at once, leaving no one to shoot at the San Selvan gunmen. There was a short period of near silence when most of the men ran into the street to help the female soldier. The crowd pushed forward. Gunfire erupted from every direction and half a dozen Americans fell. Summer ran into the street and grabbed one of the wounded soldier's M16A2. He fired at the crowd. "Goddamn fire!" he yelled at his soldiers.

To everyone's surprise, Ross was the first to respond to the order. She rolled over and fired her weapon despite her wound. A soldier with an M249 joined her by firing a burst of SAW rounds into the crowd. The bullets cut through the mass like a sickle through wheat, leaving a pile of bleeding and screaming people. If the damage had been done by a jet whose bomb dropped in the wrong place because the pilot tried to escape antiaircraft fire, there would be no thought of the term "war criminal." But up close like this there was always that potential. The soldier holding the machine gun had no hateful intent in his actions. He was too terrified to be mean spirited. Scared into action by the situation that unfolded around him. The sights. The sounds. The blood spraying everywhere. It horrified him. Whether there ever was a war crimes trial or not, the young man with the M249 SAW was still sentenced to a lifetime of nightmares.

Behind Summer, two blocks away, he could see the other Stryker vehicles across a sea of San Selvans. *Why doesn't Clark come to help?* "Smitty!" screamed Summer. "Tell them to come up here!" But Smith continued to point his weapon at the crowd from the troop compartment of the command vehicle. The noise of the battle was too loud. He couldn't hear Summer's command.

"Smitty!" Summer yelled again, running to the command vehicle. Someone else screamed in pain. Debris crashed into the street. Corporal Zeberman spun the gun turret of the light-armored vehicle to face the two-story building that held some San Selvan gunmen and opened fire. *Boom!* The huge 90mm round tore a hole in the side of the concrete building. Smoke poured from the windows. Summer fired the rifle again and continued to move to Smitty. Chin and those who could still fight now fired indiscriminately in all directions as others tried to drag the wounded to the vehicles. Doc Gadden courageously performed his duties but the stress was overwhelming. He argued with First Sergeant Brown for a few seconds about how to place a tourniquet on a wound, only to realize that Brown was right. Gadden tried to tie the tourniquet *below* the wound where it would have done nothing to help the wounded man. There was just so much happening that it became hard to think. Grenades exploded. Guns fired. The noise was relentless.

"Handset," yelled Summer, pumping his hand to communicate visually with the radio operator. "Give me the fucking handset!" He snatched it from the dazzled Smith's hands. Putting the radio's handset to his head, Summer said, "Apache One, this is Six. Move up! I want you to move up here!"

"We've got people all around us," yelled an obviously stressed-out Clark. "I can't move without running over people. I need to fall back."

"*Fall Back?*" screamed Summer. "I've got *several* wounded. Get your ass up here! Run over them if you have to, damn it!"

"I can't, sir. They're rocking our vehicles. We can't move up. I've got to head back to the airfield."

The sight of a new horror rolling in to join the battle ended the discussion. A pickup truck with a 12.7mm antiaircraft machine gun mounted in the bed stopped at an intersection down the street. Zeberman rotated the vehicle's turret to bring the 90mm main gun's sights on the new threat, as the deep recourse of the San Selvan heavy machine gun echoed. *Dud-dud-dud.* Flaming golf balls whipped over the heads of the crowd and plowed into the side of Chin's vehicle. *Boom!* Zeberman fired back.

At first confused by the rapid increase in violence and lethality, the men hesitated. Swish*Boom*. The scream of an incoming rocket-propelled grenade quickly ended the hesitation. The soldiers threw themselves to the ground as the high-explosive warhead detonated into the side of Third Platoon's light-armored vehicle. A fireball swept over the men as the vehicle burst into flames. Another grenade came streaking across the street and impacted against the corner of a building near Summer's command vehicle. He felt himself fall from the blast, so totally shocked by the unexpected force that he at first didn't notice he had hit the ground. A wallop of pressure filled chests and ears. Chunks of concrete fell from the building. Swish*Boom.*

Chin knelt over Summer. He cringed as bullets from the 12.7-mm slammed into his Stryker and it started smoking. "Get out!" yelled Chin, waving at the others. "Get out of the vehicle!" Swish*Boom!*

Nothing registered right in Summer's head.

"You all right, sir?"

Summer opened his mouth and tried to talk but couldn't. The wind had been knocked out of him. Painful puncture wounds riddled his legs. He shook his head and looked around. They were all going to die in this street.

"In that building." Chin pointed. "Move!" As Chin helped Summer to his feet, he threw the injured captain's arm over his shoulder. "Go!" he yelled at Zeberman and Garcia. Summer could see that the lieutenant directed all of the soldiers into a building. "We gotta get the fuck out of the street, sir."

"Who was in your vehicle?" asked Summer after he caught his breath. His inaction embarrassed him. He needed to say something.

"Sanders and Rios," answered Chin. His voice was dry and amazingly calm. "We won't be able to get to their bodies until the fire stops and the vehicle cools."

Soldiers dragged the dead and wounded into the

building. Smitty led the group, helping no one and running wildly with the radio strapped to his back and the handset bouncing off the ground as the radio cord dragged it. Brown carried Kapenski. Ross pushed Doc Gadden toward the building, turning to fire her weapon before following him. Everyone was already covered in blood. For most it was their own and for a few it came from their buddies. Those not moving people out of the street fired their weapons at everything that moved. A grenade from someone's M203 hit the crowd and blew a man's leg off. Another rocket-propelled grenade crashed into the command vehicle and destroyed it as Chin and Summer reached the building with the last of the wounded from the street. It was chaos. Uncontrollable and frenzied chaos.

More explosions ripped through the street as ammunition in the vehicles began to detonate. Chin dragged Summer through the wrought-iron gate at the entrance of the small L-shaped building. Past the gate was a small stone wall, and behind that an open courtyard where Chin finally dropped Summer. It looked like the structure had three rooms adjoined to the courtyard. The Americans forcibly expelled the occupants from their homes. The soldiers acted as if they owned the world. Whatever they needed they took. Anyone in the way had half a heartbeat to run or be killed. No time for arguments. Everything was linked to survival now. One soldier wisely climbed onto the roof and started shooting to drive San Selvans back from behind the building.

Flames and smoke poured from both vehicles in the street. The seriously wounded ended up piled near the apex of the L-shaped building, as everyone else frantically worked to create barriers. All furniture was thrown against exterior walls, including the stone wall at the entrance, and firing positions were created to cover windows and doors, but gaps in the perimeter that the San Selvans could exploit were plentiful. Rocket-propelled grenades shook the building. Several more soldiers climbed to the roof to occupy firing positions. One of them fired a burst from an M249 SAW. More screams. The rocket-propelled grenade gunners ran. *We can defend from here,* thought Summer. All they needed to do was get everyone behind the safe protection of the walls to wait until a relief force arrived.

Ross had to be told by Brown to stop working and get medical attention. Doc Gadden began treating her right after he stabilized Kapenski. Using a pair of heavy-duty scissors, he cut away her T-shirt and bra. The sniper's round had hit her high in the upper chest and exited right below her breast. The men had all seen hideous wounds at this point in the fight, but the sight of Ross made all of them cringe. There was something so terrible about seeing a bloody boob. Chunks of white cottage-cheese-looking fat dripped from the exit wound. One of the men gagged.

Summer couldn't help but wonder why her nipple was hard. It created such a weird sight. Maybe shock to the body or something, he thought. But the sight of her nipple suddenly turned his thoughts to his wife. He wondered if he was ever going to be able to see her naked body again without picturing this horrible image in his head.

A small explosion brought Summer's attention back to the battle. The rocket-propelled grenade gunners had not returned but several women had thrown Molotov cocktails that hit the wrought-iron fences and sprayed flames across the stone wall. The gasoline-filled bottles would be trouble. The flames stayed far enough away that they didn't harm any of the Americans, but the experience disturbed them all. Burning them out of their hiding place like rats might be the San Selvans' plan. It would work. They could not stay if the building became engulfed in flames. They were already in enough trouble. Summer didn't know how many wounded he had with him. He didn't even know how many soldiers he should have, and he also had to worry about establishing the best defense possible.

"Smitty," yelled Summer. "Smitty, radio!" *Where the hell could he be?* Summer found Specialist Smith huddled in a corner wearing his radio pack. "Are you hit, Smitty?"

"I don't think so, sir."

"Well, what are you doing hiding over here?"

"There was too much fire, sir. I couldn't move anywhere without risking being hit," whined Smith.

Summer looked at Smith suspiciously. The soldier was cracking up. "I just walked over here, Specialist Smith. *Didn't I?*" Summer took the radio handset. "Tomahawk, this is Apache Six."

"Where the hell have you been, Apache?" answered a radio operator from the battalion command post. "We've been trying to reach you."

Summer frowned at Smith. "We've been hit hard. I need air support and a relief force. I've got many wounded and two vehicles down. Currently surrounded. In the vicinity of checkpoint forty-two. Unsure actually where. I'm cut off from most of my force."

"Huh . . . Wait one, Apache Six."

"Sir," said First Sergeant Brown. The massive soldier looked like a mess, with his uniform covered in dirt, sweat, and blood. Summer had seen him several times during the fight in the street carrying a wounded soldier or attacking a group of San Selvans. "Lieutenant Chin is checking the lines. We're hurt pretty bad. There were eleven from the platoon's vehicle and nine from ours. Two got killed in the vehicles. I think everyone is wounded, but—"

"What about the girl?" asked Summer, surprising himself. He didn't know why he worried most about her. He didn't mean to but subconsciously he saw her first as a woman and then as a soldier. Even after all of the equal opportunity training he'd had drilled into his head, it still came down to the fact that when he saw the female soldier, Summer thought of his mother or wife. He couldn't help but be protective of her.

"She's good to go, sir. Doc's getting her patched up and as soon as he's done I'm going to give her a rifle and have her man one of the positions."

"No!" said Summer. "Pull her off the line. Put her with the wounded. The men just lost it when she was hit earlier. Our worst enemy right now is if she gets hit again."

"Okay, sir." Brown paused. "The other PR sergeant is hit the worst. Anderson and Baxter from Third are also both down hard. And we're missing Harp."

"What the hell do you mean *missing* Harp?" Summer thought of his inaction in the street.

"Lieutenant Chin is double-checking, but I think he's still out in the street, sir."

"Goddamn it, where? How the hell could I have left him out there?"

"Apache Six, this is Tomahawk Three," came over the radio handset. Tomahawk Three was the call sign for Major Jose Martinez, the battalion operations officer. "Apache One just rolled in here with seven of your vehicles. What the hell is going on?"

"Clark is back there?" asked Summer. *That fucking coward! He actually pulled back to the airfield and left us here.* Clark had run!

"Affirm. He says both of your vehicles were destroyed."

"Shit," said Summer, then keying the handset microphone, "I've got two KIA and one MIA. Everyone is wounded. We need help."

"Roger," answered Martinez. "Stand by."

"*Stand by?* For Christ's sake, you gotta get us out of here. The sanchos are everywhere."

Rising to walk away from the radio, Summer thought that everything was only a nightmare. *This can't be happening,* he thought. Not only the fight, but now it was raining outside. The presence of the rain only added to the surreal experience. All of this was just so outrageous. Summer's head was swimming. The thoughts that passed through his mind were a mix of images that could not be compared to anything rational. Trying to control the spinning to restore logical thinking, Ray instead stumbled across horrid shame of his earlier performance. It was Chin who had saved the men, while Summer lay in the street dazed and confused. He gave no thought to the fact that the concussion of the rocket-propelled grenade had numbed his senses. To do so would be logical, which was something Summer still had not been able to produce in his head. The dread felt after dropping the ball in a playground game or the embarrassment of making a mistake at work was as close as most people would ever feel to Summer's pain. This was so much worse. He did not perform as he should have, and now soldiers lay dead in the street. It was his fault.

Calcoene Airport, San Selva

Deforeno's eyes snapped open and he sat up. He shook his head. The image would not leave. He still saw the woman's mouth twisted in a scream but producing no sound. A greasy layer of sweat covered his body and his mouth felt painfully dry. The vision of the woman had been a nightmare, but Deforeno wondered if he'd ever learn the truth about what killed her. Should he even risk trying to find out?

Suddenly, Deforeno's lower intestines rumbled violently. He leaned forward and held his head in his hands, but it didn't help. He knew what came next. It had happened all night. Deforeno rolled forward to his knees and wretched in painful dry heaves but produced only bile from his empty stomach. Everything had been puked from his system hours ago.

"You all right, Def?"

Silence.

"Def?"

"Just leave me the fuck alone."

Def removed the top from his canteen and took a swig, swishing the water around in his mouth and spitting it out next to his vomit. He was afraid to swallow anything. It all just came back up. Deforeno's ears still rang from the sounds of combat the night prior, so he didn't hear the distant thunder of Summer's battle. He sat up and looked around at the soldiers around him. A few others slept too, as the rest of the platoon did work or stood security watch. Even now, hours after the last shot had been fired, Def still assessed the true consequences of the fight. These feelings surpassed anything he had ever imagined before. Little of it involved the threat of physical injury or death. The loss of innocence was the most painful consequence. Even worse was the glee in which he had fired his weapon. His conduct had been at least careless, but Def's guilt-ridden mind-set pushed his thoughts to new depths. He thought of himself as evil.

Standing and walking over to the window, Def

leaned out of the opening and scanned the horizon. His platoon occupied a defensive position along the airfield's perimeter. Everything in the neighborhood appeared quiet, but snipers were still a threat. No one else would expose himself like this, but Def didn't really care anymore. He looked out at the haze over the city and noted the column of thick black smoke that rose from the north. There was no telling what was going on. Could just be a San Selvan fire or another result of a clash between Americans and San Selvans. Hopefully the Americans would be careful, he prayed. Def didn't want anyone to accidentally hurt someone like that poor woman he had shot last night.

Chapter Thirty-three

Port Calcoene, San Selva

The *squeak* of the tracks was the first warning to Dunne that the situation below might soon change. The streets below Dunne had been blocked by debris that Marine bulldozers moved to create barriers around the port. Marines occupied the high buildings now. The port was sealed like a walled fortress, yet a reinforced company of Marines prepared to exit the protection of the walls to help Summer's trapped unit.

Weighing thirty-three tons, the Advanced Armored Amphibious Vehicle was an impressive combat machine. Its 30mm cannon fired several types of sophisticated rounds at a rate of five hundred per minute at targets as far as three miles across the battlefield. Even more impressive than the amtracks, two M1A3 main battle tanks led the column exiting the port's defenses.

With turrets swinging, the 120mm smoothbore main guns threatened the street. Cobra attack helicopters buzzed overhead, with ferocious-looking missiles and rockets hanging off of weapon pylons.

But as impressive as the sight of the air-ground force seemed, Dunne knew before the action even started that it meant little to the San Selvan warriors. Had the force driven through Iraq or Afghanistan, the combat power would be well designed to counter the enemy threat. Here in San Selva the vehicles were instead at risk.

What was not evident to most of the Americans was the simple fact that computer-driven fire-control systems would not provide the lethality needed to defeat the San Selvan spirit. Such spirit could only be defeated with the ferociousness of hand-to-hand combat. The concept proved incomprehensible to most Americans, merely one indication of how civilized the United States had become—in some ways too civilized to contend with the savagery of their newest enemy. A society like San Selva had little to do other than fight. America relied on anger management and conflict-resolution seminars instead. Negotiations with the San Selvan president accomplished little; the peace plan he signed meant even less.

Looking back to the puddles, Dunne saw that the kids who had been playing in them had disappeared. "Pull them back, goddamn it!" ordered Dunne. "Get your Marines away from the windows." All hell was about to break loose. He needed to keep his Marines safe. If they moved too close to the windows, they'd probably just add to the list of casualties. The Marines were discovering that peace could be as painful as war. Now these Marines experienced the same frustrations their predecessors had in Beirut and Mogadishu.

Streets of Calcoene, San Selva

The rain lessened, but the surreal experience did not. Now a mist, the sun began to poke though the thunderstorm's clouds as it dissipated and moved on. Could have been ten minutes or two hours, Summer did not know how long the rain had lasted. He had lost his ability to gauge time and didn't think enough to look at his wristwatch. Now every thought was linked to the fight for survival. San Selvan gunman fired from all directions and the Americans fired at everything perceived as a threat. Bodies littered the streets and blood stained the walls. Civilians still ran through in the street despite all the firing. Some even participated in the mayhem. Several San Selvan children came into the street and began pointing to the soldiers' positions for the hidden gunmen. A soldier hurled a flash bang at one group.

"Sir," said Lieutenant Chin, "I found Harp."

"Is he okay?" asked Summer.

"He's wounded but alive in the street. We're putting together a rescue force now."

"Can we see him from here?" Summer rose and limped back to the doorway that exited to the street.

"Yes, sir, but you have to go outside to see him. It looks like he's hurt bad but we can get to him if we provide enough cover fire."

Two of Chin's soldiers used the stone wall for cover and fired in both directions down the street. Summer couldn't see their targets, but he hoped they were hitting. The ammunition wouldn't last forever. Summer made a quick leap to the wrought-iron fence and peeked out into the street. He could see Harp lying amongst San Selvan bodies across the street. Harp's right leg had been blown off above the knee and he had tied a tourniquet around his thigh to stop the bleeding. He fired at San Selvans that came close to him.

"First Sergeant and I will go get him," said Chin. He motioned to the two soldiers covering down the street. "They're going to provide cover fire."

"No, I need to go," responded Summer.

"There's no way, sir. You're hurt too bad."

"We can't just leave him out there, Chin," snapped Summer. "What the fuck are you thinking?"

"Sir, if you go out there you're just going to make the situation worse," Chin snapped back. "I'll go with the First Sergeant."

"Damn it," swore Summer in reluctant agreement. There had to be something he could do to help. He loaded a fresh magazine into the M16A2 he'd picked up. If he couldn't go into the street he could at least keep the sanchos back.

"Captain, it's bullshit that you're putting me with the wounded," yelled Ross, obviously livid that Summer didn't want her manning a position on the perimeter. "I can still fucking fight."

"Get your ass back there, Sergeant, and shut up," said Summer, pointing to the courtyard. He couldn't have the men react again like they did before when she was wounded. Summer caught a glimpse of Smith cowering in the corner. "Get over here now, Smith!"

The kids in the street started pointing at Harp's position. Soldiers yelled and tried to use 40mm riot-control munitions from the M203, but they were too far and out of range. Summer fired a burst from his M16A2 over the kids' heads to scare them away. Few moved. His second burst impacted near their feet and most ran away. As the dust cleared Summer could see little feet lying in the street. Everything stopped.

"You got one, sir!" hooted a soldier.

"Shut the fuck up!" screamed another.

The child was motionless. Summer could not determine if he or she was dead or injured. He had only wanted to scare them. Was it a justified shooting? Although the kid was unarmed, his actions were still deadly. He or she pointed out Harp's position for the San Selvans who shot at his men. Summer looked to check Harp.

"He's moving, sir," yelled someone. "Should I shoot him?"

"Fuck no!" yelled Brown.

Summer watched as the child rolled over onto one side. He saw a little girl, not the deadly threat that had pointed at Harp's position a minute earlier. Her face looked pale and her eyes empty. She was dying. Her mouth opened to release an inhuman wail, producing the kind of animal-like sound that a person can make only when so badly hurt that he or she completely loses control. The sound filled the quiet created by the lapse in the firefight. No one fired. An uneasy ceasefire had settled over the area. *This could be our chance to get Harp.* Summer was desperate to get all of his soldiers into the building without more bloodshed. He tried to look around to get a fix on the situation. The two destroyed vehicles burned out in the street. He could talk on the radios to the battalion at the airfield. Help had to be on the way. If he could get everyone in here, then maybe they could hold out.

"A lady is going after the kid," someone yelled. "A lady is going after the kid."

Immediately Summer knew what the lady wanted. He snapped his head back to the direction of the wounded girl and saw a San Selvan woman run to the child he had shot moments before. "Hold your fire," yelled Summer. "Let her be." Turning to Chin he said, "You need to go now."

"We're all set," yelled Chin.

"Then go!" ordered Summer. "Move fucking fast."

As First Sergeant Brown and Lieutenant Chin ran into the street, San Selvans started firing again. A gunman about one hundred meters down the street stuck his head out and fired a burst with an AK-47. Smitty, who sat in the best position to return fire, panicked and looked for a place to hide. One of Chin's soldiers fired a burst of automatic fire from the M249. Ross jumped to the wall and started firing her weapon. Before Summer could yell at her, a second burst of San Selvan fire bounced around him and kicked up dirt and rocks. It felt as if someone hit him with a baseball bat in the hand, and he screamed as blood sprayed on Ross's face. Summer looked down at his wound. His hand was twisted into a bloody mess.

"Shoot the fuck back!" Summer shouted at Smith. He felt more anger than anything else. Ross and the two soldiers fired, but Smith remained on the ground and cried. His rifle sat in the dirt and his hands held his head. Doc Gadden ran over and immediately started trying to treat Summer's mangled hand. "It's all right, Doc." Summer looked back to the street. Brown picked up Harp, and Chin fired his rifle to cover them. An ugly *slap* echoed through the street as Chin fell over.

"Medic," yelled Brown instinctively. "Medic up!" He kept running with Harp over his shoulder.

Doc Gadden bolted from the building to Chin, passing Brown with Harp as they entered the wrought-iron fence. Brown, huffing and puffing from the sprint, passed Summer and ran into the courtyard. At this point in the fight hundreds of rounds had been fired. With each round a brass shell casing had ejected from the weapons, so the floor of the courtyard was cluttered with the debris of battle. Brown stepped on one of these cylindrical objects as he entered the building. Like someone trying to run on ice, Brown's feet shot up into the air as his legs slipped out from under his body. The force of both his and Harp's weight drove Brown into the hard ground. He landed square on his ass, producing an audible *crack* when his back fractured.

"I got a bleeder here," shouted Doc from the middle of the street. He ripped Chin's trousers and tried to place a pressure dressing on to the wound but blood spurted out. A San Selvan fired a burst of machine gun fire, and Doc covered Lieutenant Chin with his body as San Selvans began to throw grenades into the street.

"Doc! Get behind some fucking cover!" yelled a soldier.

Gadden took out his scissors and started to cut off Chin's trousers. He needed to remove the material out of the way so he could properly place the pressure dressing. Chin squirmed and wrenched in pain.

"*Doc!*" screamed someone else. There was another burst of gunfire. The soldier with the SAW cut another San Selvan down, sending fresh blood and flesh into the air.

"I can't move him." The medic's hands were covered in blood. "I need to stop the bleeding first."

"She's got a gun," yelled someone.

"*Kill her!*" Summer screamed back, assuming it was the woman who had been working on the wounded child but he didn't really know.

The sounds of firing and explosions increased. Summer's eyes focused on the scene just as the woman and girl were disemboweled in a hail of American firepower. He saw the woman's gun in her waistband. Summer thought that she had had it in her hand when the soldier yelled. He wouldn't have given the order to fire if he knew that it was in her waistband, but he had more important things to worry about at the moment. Could he risk putting more men into the street to get Chin and Gadden? Everything was going crazy. He had to get everyone in the building and hold out long enough for the relief force to fight their way in to rescue them.

"Cover me," yelled Ross. "I'll go help Doc."

"Bullshit!" Summer grabbed the back of Ross's gear with his unwounded hand and flung her back to the wall. "Goddamn shoot. You're not going anywhere."

The soldiers fired wildly from the wall and the roof. Smith was still on the ground crying. Brown moaned painfully. No one could help him yet. Soldiers yelled for Doc to hurry. Gadden started dragging Chin to safety. Bullets kicked up dirt around the two soldiers in the street, and Gadden flinched in pain. He had been wounded now, too.

Another soldier ran toward the street. Summer didn't try to stop him, but the man retreated back to the wall when a burst of gunfire impacted in front of him. The soldiers on the wall all gasped as a hand grenade landed right on top of Chin. American style, noted Summer. Just like a baseball. Gadden grabbed the grenade with both hands and twisted his torso to fling it away.

Boom! Gadden and Chin disappeared behind smoke and dirt from the grenade explosion.

"Fire, fire, fire!" yelled Arial. *"Kill the fuckers!"*

Steams of deadly lead flew through the city block and explosions rumbled. Bullets chipped away at building walls. High-explosive rounds *zinged* shrapnel. Smoke drifted everywhere from the numerous small fires that had sparked to life. Everyone yelled. Few people listened. And the violence peaked after a couple of minutes and began to wane.

"Oh, Jesus Christ," exclaimed one of the soldiers when the smoke began to clear.

The grenade blast had blown off most of both Doc's hands. The red and black remnants looked so horrid that they appeared fake, but that didn't stop the medic. There was only a brief pause before Gadden snapped again into action. He hardly seemed fazed. Doc jammed the bloody stumps that remained of his arms and hands into Chin's cartridge belt and continued to try and pull the lieutenant to a covered position.

"Cover me!" yelled Summer. He had to go help the two. Someone had to and there was no way he could send another man into the street to almost certain death. He dropped his rifle and bounded from the stone wall. His leg wounds sent stabs of pain through his body. He couldn't fully control his bloody hand.

Just when Summer reached the wrought-iron gate another flash and explosion sent him tumbling backward and to the ground. He looked into the street to see what had happened but only saw smoke and dust. *"What the fuck happened?"* he yelled.

"Get back here, sir." Ross reached around the wall and grabbed Summer's collar.

"They blew up?" One of the soldiers screamed hysterically. "They fucking blew up!"

"Let go of me," shouted Summer.

"They're gone!"

"What the fuck . . ." Summer's head snapped back toward the street.

". . . they goddamn blew up—they're fucking gone!"

There appeared to be little left in the area where the medic had dragged Chin across the street. A rocket-propelled grenade had had a direct hit. Only burnt and bloody chunks of human meat could be seen.

Both were gone. Chin and Gadden were dead.

"Inside! Everyone get the fuck back inside!"

Someone yelled that the First Sergeant was down hard. So many people had been hit. Summer didn't know how many were dead and wounded now. He could see very little of his force. He knew about at least four dead. Everyone seemed to be hit somewhere, but only five were too hurt to fight. Smith still hadn't fired his weapon, and the way he babbled he probably wouldn't be able to talk on the radio either. Could the ten be still able to hold back the masses?

A *swishing* sound signaled the approach of another rocket-propelled grenade as everyone tried to enter the building's door at the same time. Smith actually acted violently, pushing the others out of the way so he could get to safety. The grenade went off with a brilliant flash and tore out a chunk of the wall. The building shook violently, stopping for a mere second of calmness before the second rocket-propelled grenade impacted. Then a third . . . and a fourth . . . and a fifth . . . The soldiers all crawled away from the walls as the force of the explosions drove them in search of more cover.

The rocket-propelled grenades only stopped when a Marine Corps Cobra slipped overhead and opened fire with its 20-mm cannon aiming straight down. The powerful weapon, which could punch holes in an armored vehicle, ripped San Selvans apart. Parts of flesh flew around the street as the large high-explosive rounds scored direct hits on people. The scene looked horrific, but Summer became reassured with the gunship overhead. The shrapnel from the Cobra's rounds ricocheted all over the street and began to hit the building that Summer's soldiers took cover in.

"Cease fire!" Smith screamed into the radio handset. *"Cease fucking fire!* You're hitting us."

"No!" yelled Summer. "What the fuck are you doing, Smitty?"

Ceasing fire, the helicopter slid back behind the buildings. Without the helicopters firing there was no way that they could survive. San Selvans again began to mass on them in all directions. One gunman got close enough to fire through a back window and one of the wounded men fired a burst of gunfire into the sancho's chest. The rounds that didn't exit through the window hit the wall and ricocheted in the room, hitting one of the soldiers. Hundreds of San Selvans circled the building and pressed.

Summer grabbed the handset. "Keep firing! This is Apache Six," he yelled. "Everyone down here is wounded. I need fire support."

"Roger, Apache. This is Cutter One One." Additional explosions from the gunships could be heard outside. The scream of an incoming Joint Strike Fighter thundered through the air. The aircraft dropped several tear gas canisters before disappearing into the distance. Then Summer could hear the radio again. "Apache, I say again. Can you get to an LZ?"

"Understand," Summer said angrily, "I'm in the middle of the *goddamn* city. *There are no fucking LZs!* I can't move from my current position without help. Everyone is wounded."

Thoughts of the disaster with the Army and Air Force helicopters in Macapa ran through Summer's mind. *How can they get us out of here?* He started to think to himself that they might never escape. They would fight until they ran out of ammunition and then the San Selvans would brutally attack. Summer considered saving a few rounds so he could shoot the soldiers that remained still alive when the San Selvans came. It would be the most humane thing to do for his soldiers. Wouldn't it? He couldn't allow them to be tortured and ripped apart by the savage mob. And what would they do to Ross?

Thank God Clark had moved the rest of the company back to the airfield or there would be over a hundred men stuck out here, and Summer originally had considered Clark a coward. What decision had been more courageous? The one for Clark to pull back or the one that Chin made when he ran into the street? Both decisions were so different yet so brave. Which one would the history books pick as best? Ten years from now one man would be an idiotic failure and the other would be a brilliant hero.

"Apache, how many do you have down there?" asked the pilot.

"I've got twenty. Four are KIA and I can't get to their bodies." Summer looked back toward the street. He realized that he might have to extract without the bodies of his dead. Not that there was much to collect, but there was still no way he could pull the two soldiers from the still-smoldering light-armored vehicle or go out in the street to pick up the pieces of Doc and Chin. The living needed to be saved, but how did you rip sixteen souls from the clutches of a bloodthirsty enemy? "I have sixteen that need extract. About half are litter cases. We'll need a relief force or we're not going to make it out of here."

"Sorry, Apache, there's no additional troops coming in to your position. The Marines already tried to send a force in amtracks but they got the shit shot out of them. A lot of casualties. San Selvans are setting up roadblocks and ambushes everywhere. The only way we're going to be able to get you out of there is by air. Helicopters from the ships. The roof of your building is going to have to serve as your LZ."

So they were going to the roof. Summer looked up and wondered how they would get everyone up there.

It would be a bitch. "Sergeant Ross, I need you to get furniture piled so we can climb onto the roof."

Ross looked up and nodded. The soldier next to her was collecting ammunition from the wounded and dead so he'd be ready for the coming onslaught of San Selvans, which soon came. A soldier with a SAW fired into a crowd and knocked a dozen San Selvans down into a pile in the street. He continued to pull the trigger and send 5.56mm bullets and tracers ripping into the squirming mass. Anarchy ruled. The San Selvans traveled around the area in small groups hunting Americans. One group would press the American position from one direction and get ripped apart by the American firepower. Then another group of San Selvans, oblivious of the massacre that had just happened, would see the Americans and begin attacking from another direction. Another small massacre would occur. The soldiers dropped San Selvans with every pull of the trigger. One would expose to shoot at the Americans and a soldier would fire two rounds into the San Selvan's chest or head. A woman carrying ammunition tried to run across the street only to be cut down by a well-aimed burst from an M16A2 or M249. The trick to hitting a moving target like that was just to lead them a little. It was just like shooting on the moving-target range.

Even with all of the killing, the San Selvans still succeeded in getting within the perimeter. At one point slight movement came from behind one of the room doors and created a flurry of excitement. A soldier kicked the door and slammed a San Selvan against the wall inside. The San Selvan man threw a pistol out into the open and came out of the doorway with his hands above his head. He knelt down in front of the door. Confusion overwhelmed the moment. Most yelled at the man while a few soldiers continued to fire their weapons out windows and doors. More fire from outside impacted the structure. One American told the prisoner to stand up and another soldier said to lie down. Someone opened fire. The San Selvan man fell to the ground and writhed in pain. Even the men involved didn't know which one fired. It all happened so fast.

"Fucking leave him and get moving," ordered Ross. The soldiers could do little for the sancho and the Americans ran too low on medical supplies even to try. Besides, they didn't really care. "Help the others get up on the roof."

A few miles away, an MV-22 Osprey lumbered in behind the Cobras' fire toward the besieged soldiers. The pilot knew that his large tilt-rotor was going to be a tight fit in the urban mess, and he needed to conduct at least one fly-over before attempting to land and rescue the soldiers. But the San Selvans had expected an aircraft. A volley of rocket-propelled grenades streaked for the MV-22 when it neared Summer's position, sending the pilot into frenzied evasive maneuvering. The Osprey swung violently as one high-explosive warhead detonated in the bird's belly, and then another clipped a wing. Fighting for control, the pilot swung the nose of the aircraft in the direction of the port and said a prayer that they would make it to friendly lines before crashing.

Calcoene Port, San Selva

Dunne spat a stream of brown tobacco juice onto the floor. As the wounded Osprey came into view, he thought that an extract from the air looked hopeless too. *Amtracks failed. Now helos failed. Those guys are fucked.* The bird fought for altitude, with a trail of smoke following. The right wing lifted higher than the

Against All Enemies

left, making it look like a wounded prehistoric beast. The entire Marine line seemed to gasp as the aircraft fell in a stomach-turning drop, but it hung in flight just above the rooftops, straining for one last burst of energy as it limped over a Marine-held building and crashed into the port. The beast then died, falling over and bursting into flames. Marines from nearby positions jumped into the wreckage to pry the crew from the deadly grip of the flames. How many more were going to die?

Krumpt! A mortar round impacted in the port.

Streets of Calcoene, San Selva

The air was filled with small, tumbling objects as more Joint Strike Fighters from the USS *Beirut* screamed overhead and dropped another tear gas bomb. The sizzling and smoking bomblets formed a cloud of white smoke. The sounds of San Selvans gasping and retching from the painful vapor filled the air as the jets and their noise flew away. Then Ray's head snapped to the right after he faintly heard what Smith said into the radio. "What did you say?" asked Summer, looking at Smith in disbelief. "Did you say that or did they?"

"The pilot just said 'Bloody Spear,'" answered Smith.

"There's got to be mistake," replied a shocked Summer. But Summer did not understand how badly the attempts to rescue him and his men had failed. Other elements of the Arrowhead Brigade had been stopped in their light-armored vehicles before they even exited the gates of the airfield, and now both air and ground attempts from the Marines had only produced more casualties. Attacks to hold back the mob with tear gas and other nonlethal weapons had failed miserably.

Thousands of armed and unarmed San Selvan civilians patrolled the streets looking for their opportunity to attack the Americans. It also started to get dark. The noose around Summer and his men continued to grow tighter. Ammunition was running low. Soon the San Selvans would have all of them if something drastic didn't occur.

But Bloody Spear, for Christ's sake! This had to be the first time since the Vietnam War that "Bloody Spear" had blared over the radios of U.S. military forces. Bloody Spear meant that an American unit was in danger of being decimated, and the commanding general of Operation Greenhouse now authorized for all available fire support to be used to extract Summer and his soldiers. The only way to free the Americans from the grip of thousands of San Selvans was to create a box of fire around the soldiers so a helicopter could drop down and extract them.

As two more Marine Corps Cobras arrived from the deck of the *Beirut* to the battle site, the four attack helicopters began the onslaught of destruction. They fired rockets and missiles into the few buildings in surrounding neighborhoods that stood two or three stories high before working down to street level. The AH-1Zs moved continuously, refusing to let gunmen with rocket-propelled grenades and surface-to-air missiles get a clean shot.

Soldiers at the airfield prepared the High Mobility Artillery Rocket Systems (HIMARS) mounted on twelve-ton vehicles with six wheels. The Marine pilots sent back exact coordinates of the soldiers' position, and HIMARSs' three-man gun crews fired the 274mm rockets into the city. The M26A1 warheads streaked to their targets and deployed over five hundred baseball-sized submunitions onto the rooftops and into the streets and alleys. Small explosions rained down and bounced around the buildings on the San Selvans.

But most deadly of all, on the USS *Ronald Reagan* crews from Crash's old squadron loaded a specific type of bomb on their aircraft. They looked forward to using it.

Chapter Thirty-four

USS Beirut, *North Atlantic Ocean*

On the flight deck of the helicopter carrier, Marines and sailors watched one of the Navy SH-60S Sea Hawks being stripped of all nonessential gear so it could carry the weight of the sixteen soldiers. Even the door guns were being removed, which would make it totally reliant on accompanying gunships for protection. Marine MV-22s and CH-53E were too large for the stunt. The Hueys too small. No Air Force or Army helicopters were in position to get to the site in time. Part Army Black Hawk and part Navy Sea Knight, the SH-60S had become the Navy's work-horse early in the twenty-first century when they replaced the Navy's Vietnam-era SH-46. Now the SH-60S was the only aircraft small enough to get into the landing zone and powerful enough to lift out all of the survivors. Summer didn't know it yet but the Sea Hawk would be his last chance for rescue.

Smirks and expressions of disgust swept across the observers' faces as men from the SEAL platoon were denied seats on the flight. After refusing to listen to the orders of the officer running the flight deck, a group of Marines and sailors was formed to forcibly remove the SEALs. Naively, the SEALs wanted to go on the helicopter. Although they argued that they needed to go on the rescue mission, there was just no room for them and they were delaying the SH-60's departure. The SEALs also did not understand that they were woefully unprepared for what was ashore.

AC-130U Spooky Gunship, San Selvan Airspace

As the Cobras returned to the USS *Beirut* to rearm and refit, an Air Force AC-130U Spooky gunship positioned itself ten thousand feet over Summer's head and rained down a storm of destruction.

"SAM," said one airman calmly, telling the rest of the crew that a surface-to-air missile had been fired at the aircraft. The AAR-44 sensor system automatically dispersed flares, and as the airman activated the ALQ-172 electronic jammer and deployed chaff from the AN/ALE-47 and QRC-84 countermeasure systems, another airman checked the multimode strike radar. The radar provided long-range target identification capable of tracking a projectile as small as forty millimeters, so it easily detected the source of the surface-to-air missile. Spooky's weapon systems momentarily turned their attention to the SAM's source before returning to the task of pounding everything around Summer into rubble.

The pilot also lifted the aircraft higher so it would be beyond the maximum range of SA-18 surface-to-air missiles. An SA-7 or SA-14 was easily defeated by the Spooky's countermeasure system. Only the SA-18 could break through, and even then it was rare, but the pilot didn't need to take any extra chances. Besides, the AC-130U could easily operate from as high as fifteen thousand feet. Flying in slow circles over a target might make the gunship vulnerable, but it also provided opportunity that aircraft like fixed-wing fighters and bombers didn't possess. An Advanced Synthetic Aperture Radar System (ASARS) cut through the smoke and presented a detailed digital image of the battle area. The ASARS detected and located stationary and moving ground targets and represented them on a computer screen. The high-resolution images were precise enough to identify individual people on the ground, so as long as the gunship's crew knew the soldiers' perimeter, the airmen and women could lay down a circle of lead.

F/A-18E Super Hornet, San Selvan Airspace

Some probably thought the sudden silence signaled a letup in the intensity of the bombing, not the coming of an increase. The roar of an incoming jet caught many off guard. The flight of four Navy F/A-18Es from the USS *Ronald Reagan* came screaming in at a speed of over four hundred knots above the city at rooftop level. The pilots welcomed the flight into danger. Although they knew Sara had been rescued, a rumor floated through the U.S. military about her being nearly raped to death. Misunderstood reports of Arial's fate on the ground added to their rage. The fact that she'd been shot in the chest area became exaggerated and now many believed that the San Selvans had somehow cut off her breast during a sexual attack. The soldiers, sailors, airmen, and Marines seethed. The stories conjured up a red-hot anger and desire for revenge.

The jets hit their mark and gained altitude so they could release the CBU-72B FAE bombs. The bombs were some of the most powerful in the American arsenal, generating enough heat to rival the sun. FAE—fuel air explosive—was the modern version of the napalm dropped on enemies during the Korea and Vietnam Wars. The Marine Corps had dropped over two hundred and fifty CBU-72s on Iraqi troops during the Gulf War, burning the enemy soldiers to death in their trenches. The press harshly criticized them. God only knows what they'd say after today.

Falling from the jets the FAE bombs deployed their three submunitions one hundred feet from the ground. Each submunition contained seventy-five pounds of ethylene oxide, which created a cloud that grew to eighty feet in diameter and eight feet thick. The embedded detonator ignited the cloud when it came within thirty feet of the ground, sending a fiery rain down on the neighborhood around Summer.

Streets of Calcoene, San Selva

First came the concussion, then the blast. Summer had just climbed onto the roof when the FAE bombs started to ignite. The massive amount of fire support provided by the aircraft had created the opportunity for his thrashed force to get on the roof. Getting the seriously wounded up to the roof, especially Brown with his broken back, had taken every able-bodied soldier. Ross and the others too hurt to help lift the wounded stood guard on the roof, selecting their shots carefully to preserve their dwindling ammunition supplies. But they fired few rounds from their weapons. So much shrapnel and fire flew through the air that the San Selvans did not have an opportunity to do anything other than seek cover.

Summer had just recovered from the concussion of the FAE when a sharp piece of shrapnel cut into the meaty side of his torso, right below his flak jacket. The hot steel had come from "friendly fire," but he wouldn't take a risk and call for a cease-fire. The aircraft had to drop their bombs and fire their rounds this close to the Americans because that was where the sanchos were too. More jets rolled in and dropped their FAE bombs.

After the last jet streaked out of sight, the gunships returned. Now with four of the Marine Corps Cobras and the AC-130U firing one last volley, the rescue helicopter made a dangerous approach. The sleek Sea Hawk came in at nearly one hundred knots before flaring upward to force a stop over the building. Within a second it landed on the roof.

"Get on!" yelled Summer. He knelt on the roof firing a wounded man's M249. He spewed a deadly stream from the automatic weapon, but it seemed like a BB gun compared to the death and destruction being caused by the aircraft overhead. "Get the fuck on!"

No one could hear Summer but the soldiers didn't need to be told that the helicopter provided their only ride to survival. Looking back, Summer noted that Smith jumped on the Sea Hawk first. Others wrestled the wounded on to the helicopter. Wind from the powerful rotors kicked up junk on the roof. Ross and another soldier stood on the other side of the helicopter firing their weapons. A wounded soldier grabbed Summer and began dragging the immobile captain toward the helicopter. Another man fired down into the courtyard. Arial Ross came around the helicopter and dropped a grenade to the ground.

"Go! Let's fucking go!" Smith hysterically

screamed, even though more still needed to load the SH-60S.

Summer looked around and tried to count his soldiers, but with everyone piled on top of one another he only saw a confusing mess. The last three soldiers jumped onto the edge of the Sea Hawk's troop compartment. They were forced to hang their legs over the helicopter's sides. Summer instinctively grabbed Ross's gear to make sure she didn't fall out. Again disgusted with himself for treating her differently, he tried to grab the soldier sitting next to her, but his wounded hand prevented him from doing so. He yelled for others to hold on to those near the open doors, not releasing his grip on Ross. Summer tried to count the soldiers again as the overloaded helicopter fought to lift off from the building's roof. Everyone bled, he noticed. Sergeant Kapenski was pale, obviously in shock if not already dead. Well, at least his body wouldn't be left on the ground for the San Selvans to mutilate, reasoned Summer. Hopefully there was not enough left of the other dead men for the sanchos to cut up.

Ross and the others fired wildly as the helicopter cleared the roof and lifted into the sky. Below him, Summer couldn't believe the death and destruction that he saw. Everything appeared smeared with a deadly layer of black. All the buildings had been pounded into rubble, and he couldn't even make out the usually easily identifiable features of the Strykers in the wreckage that remained in the area. Hundreds of bodies littered the streets. They were all different shapes, sexes, and sizes. All with horrible wounds: missing limbs, headless bodies, upper torsos separated from legs. Some of the bodies and body parts still jerked about as the muscles twitched and spasmed.

As the Sea Hawk gained altitude, a missile from one of the Cobra's impacted in the side of a building and collapsed part of the structure. The large 105mm rounds from the AC-130U blew more gaping holes into roofs. The soldiers at the helicopter's doors kept firing their weapons. When ammunition magazines emptied, the soldiers replaced them with new ones. They fired until they ran completely out of ammunition. Another flight of Super Hornets came in behind the Sea Hawk and dropped even more FAE on the city.

The view of the Marine-held port facility came faster than Captain Summer had expected. Before he knew it the coastline was behind them and the Navy Sea Hawk was approaching the huge flight deck of the USS *Beirut*. As the helicopter landed right in front of the ship's center island, the wounded soldiers literally fell out onto the hard deck. Doctors and corpsmen shouted instructions. Deck hands grabbed at the wounded and threw them into stretchers, quickly rushing them into the mass casualty triage center where more medical personnel waited to help. Everyone was wounded. Summer looked around still trying to triple-check that he had everyone.

"This one is urgent!" shouted a doctor who was kneeling over Harp. "Get him down to OR ASAP!"

"Can you feel your feet?" someone else was asking First Sergeant Brown.

"They were everywhere, man. It was hand-to-hand all the way," bragged Smith. He was the only soldier standing. "You would have been shaking like a dog shitting razor blades. We fought like hell though. I wacked one closer to me than you are right now. Then . . ."

Arial Ross asked someone about Sergeant Kapenski, and after being told that he was dead she began to cry.

The medical personnel divided up groups of wounded based on the seriousness of their injuries. The most serious cases immediately went to the elevator and moved down one deck to the *Beirut*'s medical facility. All six of the operating rooms would be used to save the soldiers. And if there were many more days like today, all six hundred beds might be filled soon.

"You've got to lie back down," a corpsman said to Summer. Lying back down on his stretcher, he stared at the steel I-beams overhead. He continued to stare at the ceiling until he was finally placed on the elevator and moved below decks. His wounds were not nearly as serious as many of the others, but he still needed surgery. Summer welcomed unconsciousness when the anesthesiologist started working on him.

Epilogue:
The Agony of Victory

Arlington National Cemetery, Washington, D.C.

The morning chill still hung in the air, leaving an indication that a light rain or mist might begin. Mandy held little Molly's hand as the military honor guard folded the American flag over the black coffin. Gordo's girls both wore simple black dresses. A crowd behind them numbered only a few dozen, mostly men in uniform and a few others dressed in black dresses or suits. Shrines and headstones sat in perfect military alignment. Men and women from America's earliest conflicts had been buried centuries ago in nearby plots. Now more graves would be dug in the coming days for other men and women killed in San Selva.

Molly watched the soldiers intently, wondering why they moved in such a robotic manner. She didn't like it. "What's wrong with them, Mommy?" she asked.

The chaplain turned and smiled. She was only four years old and she didn't understand the significance of the event. She even enjoyed the day. Enjoyed all of the attention she received from her mother and all of the other grown-ups. For Molly this presented an opportunity to put on a pretty dress, even though it was black and not her favorite color. She just wished her daddy could be here too.

"Ssshhh, sweetie." Mandy bent over to get closer to Molly. "Cover your ears, honey. The soldiers are going to make loud noises now."

Mandy placed her left hand on her swollen stomach as she stood back up. Being almost five months pregnant, she was just beginning to show. Gordon had been so excited when Mandy told him that she was expecting again, especially since it looked like he would be home for the baby's birth. Gordon had missed Molly's birth. Now the thought of bringing a new baby into the world without her partner and best friend horrified Mandy. She closed her eyes and prayed that when she opened them she would wake up from this nightmare. Crying had been continuous for the past few days; her eyes barely teared anymore. She opened her eyes and the funeral continued.

The honor guard raised their weapons to a forty-five-degree angle to fire a salute to their fallen comrade. Her husband: Technical Sergeant Gordon Harris, USAF. Pararescue jumper. Killed in action. Remains unrecovered because there was nothing left to recover. Recommended for the Medal of Honor.

Mandy had originally asked for the firing of the weapons to be removed from the ceremony, but then she recanted on her request. As a PJ, Gordon had been both a medic and a warrior, and he would have wanted the funeral service to be carried out with all the proud traditions of the military that he loved. She thought it was ironic that Americans celebrated the end of the conflict and the beginning of the fire-fighting effort, while she mourned. The United States had *won* the war. But what the hell did it win? Another opportunity to get caught in a quagmire? Occupation seemed necessary. More young men would probably die before America quietly pulled out of San Selva.

The first indication that something was wrong had come to Mandy with a visit from an Air Force officer and chaplain. Mandy had warmly greeted them at the door, failing to recognize the grim looks on their faces. Only when they asked her to sit down did she realize. "There must be some mistake," Mandy said over and over again. *Who identified the body? Did they do DNA testing? There must be a mistake! He said it would be a short deployment. How can this be true?* But it was true. And there was no body to recover. The San Selvans had destroyed it. Nothing remained to bury, so Mandy demanded the fastest funeral the Air Force could produce. She thought it would give closure and end to the pain. It didn't work. Standing here now she couldn't help but wonder what, if anything, was in the coffin.

Although the funeral represented a significant event for all involved, there would be little notice of it beyond the small group formed at the cemetery, except maybe a short news video or article. Newspaper editors and television show producers already thought other things were more important now.

But of those involved, only Molly was spared the pain caused by Gordon's death. She could see that her mother and others were upset, but she didn't understand why. The grown-ups were not too sure themselves.

"*We* need to do something" turned into "Look what *they* did" after images of Calcoene were broadcasted. Pretty faces and talking heads made comparisons between Summer's fight and Calley's My Lai, although if they understood anything about either incident, they'd know that the two had more differences than commonalities. The "Carnage in Calcoene" became the catchy phrase and headline. Many called for a United Nations' fact-finding team to investigate, and some even discussed the possibility of war crime charges being levied against Americans. Pundits debated the success of the war as bases planned celebrations for returning service men and women. There might even be a parade or two, but soon Americans would forget and go back to their normal lives.

Mandy and Molly would never forget, and the newborn baby would never really know. The casualty count so far was low enough to be tolerated. Much higher than Haiti or Bosnia, but around the same as Grenada, Panama, Somalia, or Afghanistan. Thankfully, nowhere near the numbers of Lebanon or either Gulf War. Hopefully it would stay that way.

Mandy couldn't help but wonder what had really been accomplished. Like most wars of the modern era, there was no decisive victory. Very different from the days of the Mongols and the Spartans, when an enemy nation ended up dead or imprisoned. Even different than the unconditional surrender demanded from Japan and Germany during World War II. That was the last war we really won, wasn't it? Way back when we had a Department of War, not a Department of Defense. It was the last time we declared *war*, too. Regardless of the reason for fighting, was it really fair to send Gordon to risk, and in this case *lose*, his life when Americans were not even willing to officially call it a war?

The ceremony ended and Mandy walked with Molly to the black sedan. Molly shocked all that were within earshot when she made a statement that ripped the hearts out of chests: "Daddy is going to teach me to play soccer when he gets home."

Mandy stood frozen in shocked silence by her daughter's comment, not knowing at first if she could respond. Then she smiled. "No, honey. Mommy is going to have to teach you, but your daddy will be watching from heaven."

✂

☐ **YES!**

Sign me up for the Leisure Thriller Book Club and send
my FREE BOOKS! If I choose to stay in the club, I will
pay only $4.25* each month, a savings of $3.74!

NAME: _____

ADDRESS: _____

TELEPHONE: _____

EMAIL: _____

☐ I want to pay by credit card.

☐ **VISA**   ☐ **MasterCard.**   ☐ **DISCOVER**

ACCOUNT #: _____

EXPIRATION DATE: _____

SIGNATURE: _____

Mail this page along with $2.00 shipping and handling to:
Leisure Thriller Book Club
PO Box 6640
Wayne, PA 19087
Or fax (must include credit card information) to:
610-995-9274

You can also sign up online at **www.dorchesterpub.com**.
*Plus $2.00 for shipping. Offer open to residents of the U.S. and Canada only.
Canadian residents please call 1-800-481-9191 for pricing information.
If under 18, a parent or guardian must sign. Terms, prices and conditions subject to
change. Subscription subject to acceptance. Dorchester Publishing reserves the right
to reject any order or cancel any subscription.